THE POSING PLAYWRIGHT

Esther & Jack Enright Mystery
Book Five

David Field

THE POSING
PLAYWRIGHT

Published by Sapere Books.

11 Bank Chambers, Hornsey, London, N8 7NN,
United Kingdom

saperebooks.com

ISBN: 978-1-912786-27-5

ACKNOWLEDGEMENTS

I take this opportunity to acknowledge the invaluable contribution of my lifelong friend, former co-author, career railwayman and keen historian, Alan Dance towards the technical aspects of the plot of *The Posing Playwright* that involve the disappearance of an entire railway carriage during its journey from London to Holyhead.

Chapter One

The front doors of the Albemarle Club burst open following a determined boot thrust from John Sholto Douglas, 9th Marquess of Queensberry, allowing a few snow flurries to blow in behind him from the February pavement outside. The hall porter rushed to intercept him and enquire whether or not he was a member.

'Why would I wish to associate my good name with this coven of perverts and deviants?' Queensberry demanded. 'I'm seeking the alleged playwright Wilde, in order to give him a thorough thrashing in front of his fellow members!'

'If you are referring to Mr Oscar Wilde, sir, then he is indeed a member here, but I can advise you that he's currently at the theatre, rehearsing his latest play. The St James Theatre, if I recall correctly, and I don't know whether or not we expect him for dinner.'

'No matter,' Queensberry replied gruffly. 'Just give him this calling card and direct his attention to the inscription on the reverse side.'

'Yes, certainly, sir,' the hall porter assured him reverentially. 'I'll see that he gets it immediately upon his return.'

It was late afternoon before the man who delighted in the name of Oscar Fingal O'Flahertie Wills Wilde wafted into his club on a wave of second-hand champagne fumes. He enquired as to whether or not he had any messages and the hall porter reached down under his counter and produced the calling card.

'Only this, sir, if you could call it a message.'

Wilde looked first at the name on the card and his face set in a snarl of disapproval. Then he turned it over and read the message on its reverse and tutted.

'Just goes to prove what I've always maintained regarding the English aristocracy. They're born with a silver spoon in their mouths and at some stage it penetrates their brains, leaving them with lifelong afflictions. In the case of Queensberry, that affliction is a terminal conflict with the English language. What would you say this word is?'

The porter perched his glasses onto the end of his nose and squinted.

'Shocking handwriting, I agree. But he seems to be applying some sort of description to you. This word looks like "Somdomite", sir.'

'Ever heard of one of those?'

'No, sir.'

'Well, assuming for the moment that it's not a reference to a species of fossil, or a South Sea Island chieftain, what's the nearest word you could take it for in the English language that those of us with an education beyond a grouse moor have learned to cherish?'

'I don't like to say, sir.'

'It would be "sodomite", would it not?'

'Most likely, sir.'

'And do you know what one of those is?'

'Again, I don't like to say, sir.'

'But nevertheless, you would conclude, would you not, that the so-called "gentleman" who gave you that calling card was accusing a member of this club of being a "Mary-Anne" or whatever you care to call it?'

'Yes, sir,' the porter conceded with a blush.

'And you would not resile from that opinion, even if required to repeat it in a court of law?'

'No, sir.'

'Good man. A true descendent of those who made this nation great, unlike those who cling to titles in the vain hope of somehow seeming important. And he calls *me* a poser! Nothing could be worse than posing as part of the fabric of our great Empire, when the only Empire to which the Marquess of Queensberry might feasibly lay claim would be one of the many music halls that bear the name.'

A small brass band stood to attention on the quayside at Kingston, instruments poised and eyes fixed on the raised baton in their conductor's hand, as the gangplank was lowered on board the *Wicklow Lady*. The passengers began to disembark with their travelling bags, porters, ladies' maids and assorted attendants, as the Chairman of the Welcoming Committee, Patrick Delaney, sidled up to the band conductor and whispered, 'I'll give ye the word as soon as his Lordship begins to walk the plank.'

They were gathered — a respectable number of party members, considering the early morning arrival of the overnight steamer from Holyhead — to welcome home the local hero of the Loyal and Patriotic Union movement, Lord Stranmillis. He belonged to the group of Tories in the House of Lords who were implacably opposed to any form of Irish self-government and who had, almost two years previously, thrown out Gladstone's second attempt at an Irish Home Rule Bill by a staggering ten to one majority. He had not been back to the land of his birth since then, given his several English estates, and this was the first opportunity that his enthusiastic and largely sycophantic Dublin supporters had been afforded to doff their caps in gratitude for his resolute courage in the face of all the Fenian threats to which he'd been subjected in the months leading up to the vote.

As the last of the passengers descended to quay level and walked to the railway platform for the train that would convey them on the final short leg of their journey to Dublin, Patrick Delaney made his anxious way across the cobbles to where a deckhand was untying the ropes that had held the gangplank in place.

'Where's Lord Stranmillis?' he demanded. 'We've been waiting since your boat landed, but no sign of him.'

'Them's all ashore what was on board,' the deckhand replied.

'Did he take a later boat?'

The deckhand shrugged and nodded towards the railhead a few yards down the quay. 'They can tell you in the office over that way. They've got the passenger manifests for all the vessels, or so I'm told.'

Delaney bustled off to the railhead office of the shipping line, where a florid-faced clerk searched the list that had just been handed in off the incoming *Wicklow Lady*.

'Youse must have missed your man,' Delaney was advised, 'for sure and wasn't he on the vessel, accordin' to what's in me hand here?'

'That can't be right,' Delaney protested. 'I've met the man several times, and his portrait hangs in the party office in Dorset Street, so there's no way I could have missed him. Are you sure that he was on that vessel?'

'How would I be after knowin' that, when I never met the man?' the clerk demanded with a disdainful sneer.

With a dismissive snort, Delaney turned his back and walked disconsolately back onto the quay. His Lordship had clearly changed his travel plans without advising his supporters in Dublin.

Back in his party office, Delaney sent his clerk to the Post Office with instructions to cable Lord Stranmillis at his London home, enquiring as to when it was intended that he would make the long-anticipated journey. The return cable sent him scurrying in person to the nearest DMP office.

Chapter Two

'At least you had the decency to hold this christening in the local church,' Constance Enright announced as she turned to smile at Esther. 'I don't blame you for the last debacle, my dear, since I know how stubborn Jackson can be in these matters. But since he deprived us of a local christening for Bertie, the least he could do to make amends was to have the lovely Miriam baptised where she belongs, here in Barking, and not in some heathen edifice in Clerkenwell.'

Esther smiled back dutifully and looked for someone to rescue her from the corner of the marquee on the lawn in which she'd been ambushed by her mother-in-law while trying to persuade the star of the show to take some bottled milk, in the hope that she'd stop whimpering. Then again, Esther reasoned, being held in the arms of that drip-faced misery of a local vicar, then tipped almost upside down backwards and having cold water dripped onto one's head, was hardly a comforting experience for a three-week-old infant.

She caught Jack's glance as he looked across from where he was talking to Uncle Percy and Aunt Beattie and signalled with her eyes that she needed to be rescued. He nodded and said something to Percy. As all three of them wandered over and Constance caught sight of them she expanded on her earlier observation.

'There you are. I was just saying to Esther how nice it was to be able to christen dear little Miriam in the place where hopefully she'll be living soon. Surely by now, Jackson's got that police nonsense out of his head — no thanks to you,

Percy — and will come home with his family and begin a worthwhile and more respectable career.'

It was a well-worn theme. When Jack was aged only fourteen, his father had died, and Jack had gone to live with his late father's brother Percy and his wife in London, since they had no children of their own. Percy was a career police officer, and from him Jack had caught the bug for police work that — to his mother's horror — had led him into the Metropolitan Police, where he'd been stoned, attacked with a knife, shot at, and trampled under a horse, resulting in a broken leg that had never fully healed even after the intervening year. Somehow the bravery medal that had gone with saving two unsuspecting children from its hooves had never quite compensated for the persistent dull ache on frosty mornings.

His mother Constance was forever campaigning for Jack to pursue a more commercial career, such as the insurance business in which his father had made a modest fortune before moving his family to Barking. It didn't help that Jack's younger sister Lucy had 'married well' to a successful architect, and even though she'd also moved into London, it was the more respectable and fashionable Holborn, rather than the second-floor set of rooms in Clerkenwell in which Jack and Esther had set up home after their marriage.

However, the birth of their third child had supplied Constance Enright with another battle banner that she waved on all family occasions. According to Constance, it was high time that Jack and Esther sought another place to live, and given the lower house prices in outer suburbs such as Barking, on the north bank of the Thames in Essex, there was only one obvious place.

'The old Bentley house is still on the market,' she announced as she turned and waved for more champagne from the formally clad waitress employed by the private caterers who had also supplied the marquee and buffet luncheon. 'They could probably be persuaded to lower their asking price, and it's got four bedrooms, as you know, and is handy for the station.'

'It's so handy that the trains clatter past the bottom of the garden at all hours,' Jack reminded her, 'and we have enough problems getting Bertie to sleep as it is. But apart from that — and for the umpteenth time, Mother — I'm required to live within the boundaries of the Met as a condition of my employment.'

'That just confirms what a poor choice of employment you made,' Constance snorted. 'When your dear father made his money, he was able to choose wherever he wanted to live. And now that you're in a promoted rank, surely you should be allowed to raise the tone of the locality in which you bring up your family?'

'I'm only a sergeant,' Jack reminded her.

'But you're earning more money than previously, and from what I can gather from the little that I can get out of either you or your uncle, you're no longer required to plod the streets swinging your truncheon. You're more confined to the office these days, isn't that right, Percy?'

Percy frowned and cleared his mouth of the remainder of his seventh chicken vol-a-vent before replying. 'The nature of the work on which Jack and I are currently engaged is confidential, Constance. In fact, so confidential that even half of our colleagues at the Yard don't know what we do.'

'Jackson?' Constance enquired with eyebrows raised in disbelief.

Jack smiled. 'I can hardly override my Inspector's authority, now can I?'

Constance tutted, but appeared to be partly mollified. 'At least you're no longer under threat on those dreadful East End streets, so I suppose I should be grateful. I just hope it's not something *really* dangerous, like taking on those murderous "Athenians", or whatever they're called.'

'Fenians,' Percy corrected her with amusement written all over his face. 'But rest assured, we have an Irish Branch dealing with those. What we do has more to do with English politics, the royal family and so on.'

'Like standing in front of her Majesty while someone takes aim at her, you mean?' Constance shot back, and this time even Esther looked concerned.

Percy shook his head with a condescending smile. 'We have an Armed Protection Group for that, as well. Nothing to do with us.'

'You wouldn't admit it anyway,' Constance replied dismissively. 'And until you choose to be completely honest about the nature of your work, I'll think the worst.'

'So will I,' Esther added with a glare at Percy. 'You have Jack well trained, because he won't even tell me what you two are up to these days. At least you won't be able to wheedle me into any of your devious schemes in future.'

The following day, Percy and Jack received a summons from their senior officer, Chief Superintendent Bray, and they were met by the man himself in his outer office, where he briefed them quickly. 'We have two important visitors in there, one of them being the Home Secretary. The man with him is a Queen's Counsel who's got some very disturbing news to impart. Let them do the talking, only ask questions that you regard as relevant, and — above all — no smart comments from either of you. Understood?'

Percy nodded, and Jack remained silent as usual, as they were led into the inner room. Seated at the large table that seemed to occupy most of the room space were two distinguished looking men deep in conversation, who stopped and looked up as soon as Superintendent Bray entered and began the introductions.

'Gentlemen, may I introduce Inspector Enright and Sergeant Enright, from our Political Branch? Take a seat, both of you, while I introduce our visitors.'

Percy and Jack slipped silently into the seats on the far side of the over-long and highly polished mahogany table, and adopted suitable facial expressions of polite interest, as Bray completed the introductions.

'You have probably not had occasion to meet our current Home Secretary, Mr Asquith, although you no doubt know him by sight. He's taking a personal interest in a delicate matter that's been brought to our attention by the gentleman to his left, who's Mr Edward Carson, QC. He's currently engaged in preparing for a case that will hit the front page of every newspaper in the country and has uncovered some very alarming information which he has very properly referred to the Home Secretary, who in turn has handed us the task of investigating the matter further and minimising the potential political damage. I'll let Mr Carson himself take over at this point.'

Although he remained seated, it was obvious that this already famous barrister was over six feet in height, with a leonine head in which were set the most disturbingly piercing eyes that seemed to bore into the face of everyone on whom they were focused. His voice, when he began to speak, was more than capable of penetrating the background noise in any courtroom, so as to boom out at any jury he might be addressing, or any unfortunate witness that he might be cross-examining. There could be no suggestion of anyone interrupting as he began his explanation in stentorian tones, flavoured with a rich Irish brogue, that seemed capable of rattling the water carafe and accompanying glasses in the centre of the table.

'I've been retained by the Marquess of Queensberry to defend him against an allegation of criminal libel instigated by a well-known playwright called Oscar Wilde. Because of his notoriety in certain West End circles, the very name of Mr Wilde is likely to generate a good deal of popular interest, fanned by the more sensationalist and prurient of our national newspapers. The action arises from an implied allegation by his Lordship that Mr Wilde is a practising sodomite. Under the law as it sits at present, that is of course a criminal offence, which is why my client is charged with libel.'

Home Secretary Asquith gave a polite cough by way of a warning that he was about to add something to the explanation, and Carson paused briefly in order to pour himself a glass of water.

'I should perhaps answer a question that may already have presented itself to you, gentlemen,' Asquith explained. 'A "criminal libel", as you will no doubt be aware, is normally a matter for prosecution by the authorities, but in view of the subject matter of this particular one — and certain other matters that Mr Carson will reveal in a moment — the Solicitor General declined to approve the matter for a public prosecution. Mr Wilde therefore opted to prosecute the matter privately. Pray continue, Mr Carson.'

'Thank you, Home Secretary. At the risk of boring you all with points of law, it is necessary, for my client's defence, to prove two things. The first is that Mr Wilde has indeed posed as a sodomite in the past, and the second is that it was in the "public interest" that Queensberry reveal that fact. But in proving the first of those, my instructing solicitors have uncovered information that I felt compelled to bring to the attention of the Home Secretary, hence our presence here today. Even though he and I are on opposite sides of the political divide, these matters are too important to ignore.'

'What Mr Carson means,' Home Secretary Asquith added, 'is that the poison that he has been handed in order to defend his client — and which he is professionally obliged to disclose, if he is to perform his professional duties in accordance with his ethical code — may extend beyond the Mary-Annes, male prostitutes and other assorted riff-raff who may be expected to give evidence.'

'You've secured their attendance as witnesses?' Chief Superintendent Bray enquired sceptically.

Carson nodded. 'In some cases we have been obliged to defray what we shall choose to call their "legitimate expenses" in attending court, and in other cases it was seen by them as a preferable alternative to being prosecuted themselves. But yes, they will be testifying, should Mr Wilde not choose to concede the truth of the allegation against him — an unlikely prospect, you would agree — but our concern lies in what was revealed regarding the extent of the depraved circles in which he was engaging in such activities.'

'Members of the Government?' Percy enquired, despite the earlier instruction to remain silent.

Chief Superintendent Bray frowned disapprovingly, but the Home Secretary nodded sadly. 'Regrettably, we believe so. But also other areas of public life in which revelations could be embarrassing, with the potential to make British society a laughing stock throughout Europe and the rest of the world. Matters are particularly fraught with Prussia and Austria at the moment and, through them, with the Balkans. The last thing we need is for Britain to be portrayed as a haven for this sort of depraved activity.'

'Please forgive me, but I have to ask,' Bray interjected. 'Could it extend as far as — the royal family?'

'Please God, no,' Asquith replied, ashen faced, 'but that's one of the reasons why we wish your people to begin a very thorough investigation, using the initial "leads" that Mr Carson's instructing solicitors can supply.'

Percy looked at the Superintendent with raised eyebrows and received a confirming nod.

'I believe that Inspector Enright has further questions,' Bray announced, 'if you'd be so good as to supply whatever additional information he feels that he requires.'

'First of all,' Percy asked Carson, 'do you already have enough to defend your client with, without digging any deeper, and are any of your potential witnesses appropriately placed to be able to make, shall we say, "inconvenient" revelations?'

'We clearly have more than enough,' Carson replied, 'and from what I've read in their depositions — that's "witness statements" in your language — they won't be revealing more than the usual sorry tale of houses of convenience where like-minded deviants could meet and carry on their practices. However, it has been hinted that among those frequenting these dens of depravity are to be found prominent members of society and the professions. Regrettably including my own, but also several religious denominations.'

'But if you are to serve your client fully,' Percy continued with a puzzled frown, 'it will be necessary for all this to come out into the open, will it not?'

'In terms of accusation and innuendo, certainly,' Carson conceded, 'but I was led to believe that it might be possible for

Scotland Yard to, as it were, dispose of the evidence, so that if any unfortunate allegations *are* made, our friends in the popular press won't be able to confirm the shocking details, and the Home Secretary here can issue a denial.'

'And of course,' Asquith added hastily, 'we would expect anyone in a position to embarrass the Government by virtue of their — "predilections", shall we call them? — to be referred to my Office, rather than prosecuted.'

'May I ask a question?' Jack spoke up.

Bray nodded.

'Why — and for that matter, how — did your client Queensberry come to be motivated to make these allegations? Presumably he's not "one of those" himself?'

'Indeed not,' Carson confirmed, 'but his son is, it would seem. I don't believe I'm breaching any client confidentiality when I advise you that my client's motivation for making the allegation — which he did by way of a calling card left at Wilde's club — is the belief that his third oldest son, christened "Alfred", but known affectionately within family circles as "Bosie", has formed a homosexual relationship with Wilde. This is doubly unfortunate, given the tragedy that surrounded the death of the oldest son, Francis. It's an open secret that Francis, "Viscount Drumlanrig" to give him his title, blew his brains out late last year, after the gutter press threatened to reveal his homosexual relationship with our current Prime Minister — the Liberal leader, Rosebery.'

'That's quite enough, Carson,' Asquith growled, before Jack pursued the line his mind was taking.

'So Queensberry was concerned that his other son might be going the same way, sexually I mean?'

'Precisely,' Asquith confirmed. 'In fact, since Carson's finally let the cat out of the bag, I can further reveal that when

Queensberry was leaning on us to prosecute Wilde, he threatened to expose the Prime Minister's alleged bisexuality. Had it not been for the active interest of certain journalists of the lower sort, dissatisfied with the official verdict that Drumlanrig died accidentally during a shooting accident, we would have reported the blackmail attempt to the Yard.'

'With instructions to bury the accusation — or perhaps Queensberry himself — under the carpet?' Percy said with a cynical smile.

Carson replied with a smirk of his own. 'Apart from the loss of my considerable fee for appearing for him in this matter, even I would not mourn the passing of Queensberry. He's a most unpleasant Atheist bigot who lists pugilism as his main interest in life, along with horse racing. He's been married twice, both wives accusing him of brutish behaviour before ending their relationship. There are now suggestions of insanity arising from syphilis, and he's prone to bouts of wild temper. All in all, I've had easier clients to get along with, but his money's still good.'

'So if we manage to uncover evidence of *his* misbehaviour, you wouldn't complain?' Percy asked.

'Not once he's paid my fees, no. But there is another matter that I'd be grateful if you'd investigate for me. It may be related to the Wilde matter, but somehow I doubt it.'

'I *did* tell Mr Carson that we'd at least look into it, given his public spiritedness in bringing the possible ramifications of the Wilde matter to our attention,' Bray confirmed, and Carson continued as if the involvement of the Yard was beyond further argument.

'There is a spurious connection with Wilde, in the sense that he and I were students at the same time at Trinity College Dublin. A fellow student of ours, reading Natural Sciences, and also a former school friend of mine, was Lord Stranmillis, who recently went missing.'

'Before Inspector Enright advises you that the Yard doesn't conduct missing persons enquiries,' Bray intervened hastily, 'perhaps the Home Secretary could give us the broader picture.'

'Certainly,' Asquith agreed. 'As you cannot fail to be aware, if only from the newspapers, we are currently pursuing negotiations with certain "organisations", shall we call them, regarding the future governance of Ireland.'

'Home Rule?' Percy enquired.

Asquith nodded. 'Clearly, Mr Carson and I occupy different positions across the fence on this one, since he is a diehard Unionist, and one of those with Tory leanings who are opposed to any form of independent Ireland. My Government, on the other hand, has now promoted two Bills in Parliament, with the intention of granting limited independence to the Irish, the second of which was blocked by the Tories a little under two years ago now. It is likely to be the main issue on the hustings in the General Election which is imminent.'

'Please get to the point, Bertie, and leave your Liberal propaganda in your valise,' Carson muttered. Asquith glared at him and made a theatrical wave of the hand for Carson to take over the briefing.

'My lifelong friend Lord Stranmillis is in many ways a duplicate of myself, in the sense that our lives have been curiously parallel to this point. We are both men who grew up as Protestants in an aggressively Catholic Dublin, and we both acquired property to the north, in Belfast, although his is a rural estate to the south of the town, from which his title is derived by descent from his uncle. Like myself, he is a supporter of the Tory Party, and also like myself, he is what has become known as a "Unionist", by which is meant a fervent opponent of Irish Home Rule. He was, in fact, one of those in the House of Lords who overwhelmingly threw out Gladstone's second attempt at legislating for the unthinkable and unworkable. I believe that this has made him a target for Fenian thugs.'

'In what way?' Percy asked. 'How, where, and when did he go missing?'

'Two weeks ago, he was expected on the overnight vessel from Holyhead at a place called Kingston, which is a few miles south of Dublin, and one of its main ports of entry. He's something of a local hero in Dublin among those who oppose any form of Home Rule, and the members of the local branch of the Loyal and Patriotic Union that he helped to found had prepared a very warm welcome for him on the quayside, complete with a brass band. He failed to disembark from the vessel, and there's no trace of the railway carriage in which he'd travelled from Euston the previous day.'

'It definitely left Euston?' Percy enquired.

Carson nodded. 'According to the station staff there, and we have no reason to doubt them. It was also noted in Crewe, where the train halted briefly to change engines, but no-one can be found who saw it at the railhead at Holyhead. It's certainly not there now, nor is there any trace of it in the carriage sidings at Kings Cross, where it's normally kept.'

'Why King's Cross? The train left Euston, didn't you say?'

'That train, certainly,' Carson confirmed, 'but it was the first time for several years that his Lordship had returned to Ireland, and his carriage was normally employed on the GNR route to Edinburgh, where it could be detached at the private halt that his Lordship maintains at a place called Cockburnspath, in the Scottish Borders. That's his country seat, where he spends most of his time when not in the House of Lords.'

'And the carriage isn't there either, I take it?'

Carson shook his head. 'Enquiries have been made there, obviously, but to no avail.'

'And this was two weeks ago?' Percy persevered.

'Correct.'

'And his Lordship's body hasn't been found, obviously.'

'Of course not.'

'What makes you suspect the Fenians in his disappearance?'

'The obvious reason — he'd stood in the way of Home Rule being voted in.'

'But he wasn't the only one, from what you told us earlier.'

'Indeed not — there were over four hundred opposed to it, in total.'

'And as I understand the methods of these murderous bastards,' Percy added, to the visible discomfort of the Home Secretary, 'they'd have made a big display of his body, would they not?'

'Most likely,' Carson conceded.

'And if the motive was financial or political, in the sense that your friend was kidnapped for money, or as a hostage to Home Rule, then in my experience there would have been a demand of some sort by now,' Percy added. 'I think that the reason for the disappearance may be more personal than you at first thought, Mr Carson.'

'I'm not sure what you mean,' Carson replied with a frown.

'Neither am I,' Percy smiled back reassuringly, 'but in the absence of either a demand or a body after two weeks, I think you may reasonably relax in the knowledge that your friend is still alive somewhere. My task — and that of my colleague here

— is to find out where, and why. To succeed in that we must first work out "how", must we not?'

'So you'll conduct the necessary enquiries?'

Percy gave Carson a sarcastically exaggerated smile. 'I wasn't aware that we had a choice.'

Chapter Three

'Uncle Percy!' Esther exclaimed in surprise as she opened the front door in response to his knock, a sleepy looking Miriam perched face down on the towel that was draped across her shoulder. 'It's not like you to call in the middle of a working morning — I hope you're not here with bad news about Jack?'

'No, far from it — may I come in?'

Esther stood back in the hallway to allow him to stride towards the kitchen as he asked whether or not there was tea on the boil.

'I've just fed Miriam,' Esther explained as she placed the biscuit tin on the table between them, 'and for once she didn't spew it all back all over me, so hopefully she'll settle when I put her in the cot. Alice is keeping Lily and Bertie amused as usual, so once I come back we can talk. I assume that you don't want Jack to hear whatever's on your mind.'

She returned five minutes later and Percy smiled.

'You never cease to amaze me with your perceptive powers, young lady.'

'Please dispense with the oil, Percy, and get to the point. What can you possibly have to say that Jack can't overhear?'

'He *will* get to learn of this conversation, if you agree to what I have to ask. But I must also alert you to the fact that he'll be exposed to some particularly stressful experiences during the next few weeks, so you'll need to go easy on him.'

'Now you *are* scaring me.'

'Well, first of all, I wonder if you'd be prepared to get involved in some more police work — but this time from the safety of your own home?'

'You mean you don't want me to act as a sitting duck for another homicidal maniac?'

'No, nothing like that. I wasn't just flattering you a moment ago — I really *do* have a high opinion of the way your brain works. Jack and I have taken on a very complex case that has two distinct lines of enquiry to be pursued. I personally believe that the two may be connected, although Jack's less convinced. The part that I'm going to be investigating for myself is a real puzzle, and I'll need an independent person with a clear and logical head to double-think me through the conclusions to be drawn from each fact as I unearth it. I haven't started yet, but I can give you the background for as long as these biscuits last.'

'You mentioned that Jack will be under extra stress when investigating his part of this double puzzle,' Esther reminded him. 'Have you left him the dangerous bits?'

'No,' Percy smiled reassuringly. 'It's not physically dangerous in any way, but he may be in severe moral danger.'

'Please don't talk in riddles, Uncle — what do you mean?'

'He's going to be conducting detailed investigations inside a series of local "Molly Houses". Ever heard of those?'

'Can't say I have,' Esther admitted.

Percy coughed with slight embarrassment, but pushed on.

'A "Molly House" is a meeting place for homosexual men. Not just "Mary-Annes" of the traditional sort, but any man in a relationship with another man that verges on the sexual. They're obviously very discreet, and some of them cater only for the wealthy and privileged, although at the lower end they're little different from traditional brothels, except that those employed there are men, and usually boys.'

'And these places really exist, here in modern London?' Esther tried not to giggle. If it was important enough for the

Yard to be investigating these things, then it behoved her to keep a straight face.

'Indeed they do, and both Jack and I have had occasion to visit them from time to time. Normally the Met tends to turn a blind eye, just as they do to normal brothels if they're properly run, but if someone is knifed, or money gets stolen, or some other crime's committed, we have to go in and do our duty.'

'Why would Jack find that stressful, exactly?'

'He's a good-looking boy, and he's not exactly going to be kicking doors down while dressed in a police uniform, assuming that he still fits into his. He'll be going in sneakily, perhaps even having to pose as a Mary-Anne.'

Esther burst out laughing at the mere thought but quickly overcame her mirth when she saw the look on Percy's face.

'This is serious stuff, my dear,' he reminded her.

'Please do not call me "my dear", in that patronising manner, if you want to enlist my services as a spare brain,' Esther replied starchily. 'But remind me — wasn't there some scandal a few years ago, involving telegraph boys and a high-class brothel somewhere — Camden, as I recall? And weren't there rumours that Scotland Yard had stepped in to hush up who was involved?'

'Nothing wrong with your memory,' Percy grinned. 'It was the so-called "Cleveland Street Affair", and it was investigated by a man you met during that Ripper business — Fred Abberline. We learned that some telegraph boys employed by the Post Office were delivering more than telegraphs to certain wealthy houses in the West End, and from them we learned of a very high-class male bordello operating in Cleveland Street. Its clientele included some very high-ranking politicians, but the biggest catch was Lord Somerset, an equerry of the Prince of Wales, and there was serious talk of prosecuting the Prince's son, Prince Albert Victor, who is, of course, the Queen's grandson. It was then that somebody high up in Government circles, and probably the Lord Chancellor, ordered Abberline to close down his investigations, and the Political Branch that Jack and I work in was first proposed.'

'What I believe is known as a "cover up",' Esther tutted. 'So they made a big noise about prosecuting the telegraph boys, and hoped that would be enough to satisfy the public and the newspapers?'

'Actually, the telegraph boys received such light sentences that one or two bolder journalists began asking questions, and one of them unearthed a male prostitute called John Saul, who revealed a frightening connection with guardsmen at Dublin Castle a few years before that. But despite allegations of a cover-up at high levels, most of the high-ranking Mary-Annes suspected of using the Cleveland Street "facilities", shall we call them, had managed to slip away abroad. But what makes me suspicious of this current pretence at a prosecution is that the Home Secretary who's called in the Political Branch was, while a practising barrister, one of the counsel who defended the boldest of the journalists, a man named Ernest Parke, when he was accused of libelling the Earl of Euston by claiming that he was implicated in the Cleveland Street scandal.'

'Surely, that means that he was determined to get to the truth?' Esther suggested.

Percy shook his head. 'It's also rumoured that the defence team went soft in order to ensure that Parke was found to have libelled Euston, who walked out of court with his reputation intact. Asquith is now our Home Secretary, and the senior barrister for the defence, Frank Lockwood, became Solicitor General. In both cases, I suspect, those were their rewards for their assistance in a cover-up.'

'I gather that you and Jack have now been brought in to investigate another similar scandal, and from what you were saying just then, you suspect another cover-up. Am I right?'

Percy beamed his appreciation. 'You *really* should join the Yard when they decide to employ females. You're one hundred per cent correct, I'm afraid. The Political Branch are known informally within Met circles as "The Whitewash Boys", and I for one deeply resent having my talents wasted in complex investigations which by some mysterious process never make it to court. Nor am I even allowed to exact any justice of my own devising. I don't want Jack disillusioned in his first promoted position.'

'You haven't yet mentioned why Jack will be required to visit male brothels. What's this latest scandal?'

'Possibly a storm in a teacup, or just a bad-tempered display of pique by two people who don't like each other. Ever heard of a playwright called Oscar Wilde?'

'Can't say I have, but what's he done?'

'Nothing, according to him. But a prominent peer of the realm called the Marquess of Queensberry has accused him of sodomy, and Wilde's decided to prosecute him for criminal libel.'

'Did I just mishear you? Don't the authorities prosecute?'

'Normally, yes, but they ducked this one and refused to proceed, which makes me even more suspicious of a cover-up. Undaunted, Mr Wilde has brought a private prosecution, which he's entitled to do, and Queensberry's defence counsel, Edward Carson, has employed private detectives by the coach-load to investigate Wilde's private life. That's why we were called in.'

'I'll take a guess that Mr Wilde can be proved to have been associating with some very prominent people, and it's time for more whitewash.'

'Precisely. That will be Jack's main task — asking awkward questions in dens of depraved iniquity in which silence and diplomacy are combined with dubious practices, and whose no doubt substantial income depends on their managers' abilities to suppress individual identity and wipe away any stains on the reputations of those able to pay for the service.'

'I can now appreciate why you're concerned that Jack will be even more grumpy than usual when he comes home at night. I don't think you need worry about any attacks on his morals, but he'll most certainly get moody if he thinks he's getting nowhere. He's very stubborn, as you no doubt had occasion to note when he was growing up. But if he's going to be doing all the legwork on the investigation that your department's been handed, what are you going to be doing, and what part in it do you think I can play?'

'Simply being a sounding board for my ideas and giving me a fresh pair of suspicious eyes when I'm in danger of missing something.'

'Something to do with *what*, exactly?'

'Do you have a pencil and notepad handy? You might be as well writing down the bare facts that I'm going to give you, then we can add to them as I winkle out more, except that I suspect that I'll be out of London for long periods of time.'

After being reassured by Alice that playing at "baddies and goodies" with Lily and Bertie in the front living room was what she had been born to do with her life, Esther retreated back into the kitchen armed with a drawing pad and pencils of various hues and sat down with an expectant look on her face.

'Very well. The facts, please.'

'In return for tipping us off regarding what his bloodhounds had discovered, Edward Carson — you remember, Queensberry's barrister? — asked us to conduct a missing person enquiry.'

'Which the Yard doesn't do, or so you told us when Alice asked you to look for her missing niece Emily that time. Or are you compromised already?'

'Probably, but leaving aside the politics of the matter, this man might be connected with the enquiries that Jack's going to be conducting. That's another reason why I want you on the case — making sure that nothing slips between the floorboards as our two separate enquiries proceed.'

'So who's your missing man? Someone connected with this Wilde person?'

'Could be, which is what makes the hairs on the back of my neck stand on end, never a good sign. How coincidental is it that a prominent playwright moving in the best of social circles is accused of sodomy, while a prominent member of society disappears? The missing man is called "Lord Stranmillis". He's a peer of the realm, in other words a member of the House of Lords, and he was recently one of those who voted against Irish Home Rule, which has given Mr Carson reason to believe that he may have abducted by Fenians — you've heard of those, I take it?'

'Irish independence rebels?'

'"Terrorists", to give them their more accurate label. What they can't achieve politically they hope to bring about with murder, arson, explosives and fear.'

'So this man may have been abducted for what reason? To kill him and leave his body somewhere prominent and embarrassing, or to pressure the Government into casting Ireland off into the western ocean?'

'That's what Carson thinks. But Stranmillis has been missing for over two weeks, and in my experience, if he'd been abducted, those responsible would have advised us by now.'

'If not abducted, then what?' Esther asked, pencil poised.

'I have a feeling that he's made it look as if he's been abducted and has simply made off into the sunset for reasons of his own.'

'Connected with Mr Wilde?'

'Perhaps. Certainly, at present, I'm working on the theory that the two matters are connected.'

'So how and when did he disappear?'

'He was booked on the boat train from Euston to Holyhead, from where he was due to board an overnight ferry to one of Dublin's ports of entry — a place called Kingston. So far as we know, he disappeared somewhere en route. We certainly know he never stepped off the boat in Kingston.'

'How do we know he even boarded the train at Euston?'

'Good thinking. But he made the journey in his own private Pullman carriage — that's a posh passenger wagon to you — and I'm advised that he was seen getting into it by platform staff at Euston. I'll obviously be checking on that point as one of my first actions, but no doubt he was well known for the size of his tips to luggage porters.'

'He was wealthy?'

'Was he ever! They don't come much richer than Lord Stranmillis, again so I've been informed, and again so I'll be investigating.'

'Silly question, perhaps, but has the Pullman carriage been examined for signs of violence?'

'That's the first thing I'll be ordering when we find it.'

'It's gone missing?'

'Why else would we be looking for it?'

'Do we know approximately where it went missing?'

'No idea yet. I've contacted the London and North Western Railway, who advise me that the train had two scheduled stops, at Rugby and Crewe, both in order to change engines.'

'Time enough for his Lordship to make himself scarce?'

'Obviously, but before I can confirm that promising theory I'll need to speak to the station staff on duty at both stations.'

'How can the Pullman carriage have disappeared *during* the journey?' Esther said as she looked up from the notepad, which now had its front page decorated with her scribbles.

'It was at the back of the train, even behind the guard's van, so it could have easily been detached.'

Esther stared at the far wall before voicing what was on her mind. 'If Lord Stranmillis simply wanted to disappear, he could just have stepped out of his carriage during one of the engine stops. Why make the carriage disappear as well?'

'I'm not sure. But if I'm correct in my theory that his Lordship wanted to fake his own disappearance and make it look like an abduction, then one way of making it seem more credible would be to arrange for the carriage to go missing as well. We're meant to think that it was driven off at gunpoint with his Lordship inside and taken to wherever the Fenians, or whoever, are holding him.'

'That would require the active collusion of railway staff, would it not?'

'Unless the Fenians have locomotive engineers among their ranks, yes. Or — another possibility — they forced real railway operatives to drive the Pullman off somewhere, either at gunpoint or under threat to their nearest and dearest. Either way, the railway staff aren't likely to be over-co-operative, even if I can identify them.'

'Tell me more about his Lordship.'

'If I could, I would. Jack's due to meet with Carson again this afternoon, when he gets out of court, in order to collect copies of the evidence against Mr Wilde and also as much information as we can on Lord Stranmillis, who's a personal friend of Mr Carson.'

'How personal?'

'Again, good thinking, and I haven't ruled out that possibility either. One thing's for certain — I'm only going to be told what I need to know, and I'll need to question every single fact I'm given, so that I'm not the one left covered in whitewash. Now I need to leave — may I do so with the happy thought that Mrs Enright will be part of the investigation?'

'Did you ever seriously doubt it? There's a limit to the mental exercise involved in the boiling of nappies.'

Chapter Four

'Thank you for taking the time to wait for me, Sergeant,' Edward Carson boomed as he strode back into his chambers at the Middle Temple, followed by a flurry of clerks carrying bundles of papers. 'One can never predict when a trial judge will hear the call of his bladder or call a halt to proceedings for the day rather than nod off in full view on the Bench, and the commercial matter that I'm currently engaged in seems destined to drone on for another week or so. Come inside and I'll call for some tea. Maurice, could you organise that, please?'

'Now then,' Carson beamed as he perched his legal wig on the top of a hat stand, slipped off his court robe and came back to the large table overflowing with paper, still dressed in his bar jacket with its fancy 'tabs' down the front. 'This pile is a copy of all the statements I've so far been given in connection with the Wilde case. It doesn't make pleasant reading, and you might need a cab in order to get it all back to your office in Whitehall. I'd certainly appreciate it if you wouldn't risk lumbering it all onto a bus.'

'Who are all these witnesses?' Jack enquired.

'A few male prostitutes, a handful of Molly House proprietors, and a selection of domestics who can place Mr Wilde and "Bosie" Douglas in each other's company at various private hotels on the south coast and elsewhere. But perhaps most tellingly, the sad recollections of various young men of lowly origin who were solicited, flattered, entertained and ultimately deflowered by Mr Wilde. They are the ones we've been obliged to remunerate.'

'Won't that open them to cross-examination regarding their motives?' Jack asked, then wished he hadn't as a flash of irritation crossed Carson's face.

'You do your job, and leave me to worry about mine, although since you ask I'm hoping that the mere threat of these young men taking to the witness box will be enough to force Wilde's hand into a retraction.'

'When is the trial expected to begin?'

'A week on Wednesday — the third of April — so far as can be calculated at this stage. It's second on the Old Bailey list of trials for that week before Mr Justice Collins, and the first trial's reckoned to be likely to run no longer than two days.'

'Is there anything in these witness statements that might lead to speculation regarding the extent of Wilde's depraved relationships?'

'Not directly, no. But Wilde's counsel, Sir Edward Clarke is a very adept cross-examiner and he might try pushing some of the less sophisticated witnesses into exaggerating their role in what is likely to be a very highly publicised case. Put another way, these simple young men will become famous overnight and might be tempted to gild the lily in order to make themselves look more important, and perhaps even earn money from the less responsible newspapers in return for their exclusive stories.'

'Would they sink so low?' Jack queried.

Carson treated him to a look of scorn. 'These are young men of the lowest order, prepared to open their arses for a pound a time — sometimes less. What do you think they'd be prepared to do for a hundred pounds?'

'I take your point,' Jack replied, duly chastened. 'But insofar as Mr Wilde's transgressions may extend up the social ladder,

I'll need to make my own enquiries, is that what you're telling me?'

'Isn't that why you're a police officer? As far as that's concerned, I'd recommend that you start here in London, with particular reference to the house in Tite Street, Chelsea, occupied by Wilde, his wife and his two sons. Douglas was a frequent guest there, since he and Wilde struck up a friendship during Douglas's impoverished student days at Oxford. They were introduced in London by a Canadian journalist called Robert Ross. He makes no secret of his homosexuality and we believe that he was the one who effected introductions between Wilde and some of the young boys on our witness list. If he procured for Wilde, he may have done it for others, and the boys may drop their names out at an inconvenient moment.'

'I'll follow up on all those,' Jack promised as he extracted his notebook and pencil. 'Now, the Inspector has asked me to get more information on the missing man, Lord Stranmillis, preferably including a photograph.'

Carson smiled and reached out towards a large silver framed photograph on his desk, which he turned to face Jack.

'The one in the middle,' he said.

Jack found himself looking at a photograph taken during some sort of formal occasion inside a richly equipped hall. There were three men dressed in dinner jackets and white ties, smiling at the camera, and the one on the left was unmistakeably Edward Carson himself.

'Reunion dinner at Trinity last year. "Shorty" Stranmillis is the chappie in the middle, I'm on the left as you look at the photograph, and the one on the right is Phadrig Ryan, the owner of Ryan Industries.'

'Lord Stranmillis's nickname is "Shorty"?'

Carson nodded. 'For obvious reasons, although he did himself no favours standing between myself and Ryan, since we're both over six feet. Poor old Shorty's a mere five foot four or thereabouts.'

'May I keep this?' Jack asked. 'We may need it for identification purposes.'

'If you find his body, you mean?'

'Certainly then, but also when we make enquiries among those who are likely to have seen him last.'

'It's not actually mine to loan out,' Carson advised him with a frown. 'I was sent this by Ryan, who was the one who paid the photographer, then sent copies to Shorty and myself, asking that we keep them safe, in case he was successful in getting his copy of it into the Trinity Old Boys' magazine. But if you promise to look after it very carefully, I can loan it to you for as long as you need it.'

Jack agreed and Carson carefully extracted the cardboard from the rear of the frame, then slid the photograph out and slipped it into a large folded sheet of what looked like title deed paper.

'Thank you for that,' Jack said. 'Now, what else can you tell me about "Shorty" Stranmillis?'

'His real name was Dermot O'Brien and like me he was born in Dublin, of Protestant parents, but in his case with family links to a peerage in the north of the country — the one he inherited from his uncle. He obtained a good honours degree in Natural Sciences, as did Paddy Ryan, who was more his friend than mine during our student days, although Paddy was a good Catholic boy. Shorty lost no time in heading east and set up a business with a steel plant near Sheffield, supplying rail lines just ahead of the massive competition between the rail companies to supply faster and more comfortable services.

Then he transferred his interest to somewhere in the Manchester area, manufacturing pipes for underground cables. Finally, so far as I know, he branched out into quarrying and was supplying building materials under Government contract, just as they were expanding and improving our road networks.'

'It sounds as if your friend Stranmillis had the gift of foresight as to which business to invest in next,' Jack observed suspiciously. 'In fact, some might say that he had inside knowledge.'

'You wouldn't be the first to suggest that,' Carson replied, 'but not a single act of corruption was ever proved against Shorty. When he inherited the peerage, there were of course accusations of nest-feathering and the predictable allegations that he'd bought his seat in the House of Lords, but these came in the main from frustrated business rivals. Shorty seemed to sail through them all unscathed.'

'When did you last see him?'

Carson knitted his brows in thought before replying. 'It must have been when that photograph was taken. That was over a year ago now, so at least it has the virtue of being recent, but it's another reason why I'd like you to treat it with care and give it back when you've finished with it.'

'So you and he didn't mix socially on a regular basis?'

'No, not at all. We exchanged Christmas cards and the occasional letter, the way that former close friends have a habit of doing, but our paths barely crossed. I have a busy practice here in London, whereas Shorty was forever travelling from one business venture to another. Unlike many modern entrepreneurs, Shorty hadn't amalgamated all his companies into one huge "holding" conglomerate, but ran his various enterprises as individual entities, each one with a general manager. I know that because I was once called in to advise him regarding the possible benefits of establishing a holding group.'

'What about his personal life?'

'I'm not sure that he had one, quite frankly. He certainly never married, so far as I'm aware, and he was an only child, so once his own parents died he was alone in this world. He'd occasionally be photographed by the newspapers at some important function like the opening of a new steel plant, or when he was giving a massive donation to some charity or other, and on such occasions there was usually a woman on his arm. But it was a different woman on each occasion, and — well, to be perfectly frank with you — I often suspected that they were hired for the occasion. He was never much of a success with the ladies when we were students together.'

'Where did he normally live?'

'I believe he had a splendid apartment overlooking Regent's Park — Cambridge Terrace, as I recall — where he'd stay whenever his attendance was required in the Lords. He took that aspect of his life very seriously, but for the rest of the time he seemed to stay in local hotels in Manchester, Sheffield or wherever, when his business commitments took him there.'

'His estate in Ireland?'

Carson laughed hollowly. 'I doubt if the retainers on the Stranmillis estate would even recognise him, since he was never there. He had a lodge of some sort in the Borders south of Edinburgh and a house somewhere in Cheshire. I remember the Cheshire house because there was some legal dispute over quarrying rights on the land that went with it, and we were all set to do battle in the local County Court when the opposing party threw in the towel. But other than that I couldn't tell you anything about his life. Sad, really, all that money and no-one to share it with, so far as I'm aware. I should perhaps mention that I'm one of the executors named in his will; myself and Paddy Ryan, funnily enough. So if he turns out to be — you know — deceased, then whoever inherits will need to consult me.'

'Do you happen to recall who inherits?' Jack asked.

Carson smiled back enigmatically. 'Even if I did, professional privilege would prevent me from telling you. But if it helps, my memory tells me that the main beneficiaries will be various charities that he favoured. No one individual that sticks out in my memory, but as I said, professional privilege and all that...'

'Yes, quite,' Jack replied as he rose to leave. 'Thank you, Mr Carson, that gives us something to start with, anyway.'

'I really do hope that nothing awful has happened to him,' Carson observed as he rose out of politeness to show Jack to the door. 'Shorty was a likeable old buffer, at the end of the day.'

'Except, perhaps, to someone who removed him from the boat train,' Jack reminded him in the doorway, wondering whether or not it was just coincidence that Carson had spent the past half hour or so referring to the missing man in the past tense.

Chapter Five

'I suppose I don't mind,' Jack conceded grudgingly, 'provided that there's no danger to Esther, and provided that you bring in fish and fried potatoes for tea every time we get together to exchange notes on the cases.'

Percy grinned at Esther as he cut into his second piece of fried plaice. 'It just goes to prove the old saying that the way to a man's heart is through his stomach.'

'That's for wives, not uncles,' Esther advised him, before turning to Jack. 'You're easily bought, but please don't patronise me with any more nonsense about preserving me from danger. I've probably come closer to death on several occasions than you ever will, and in any case, Uncle Percy only needs my brain.'

'Confirms my suspicion that his own is going as grey as his hair,' Jack quipped. 'Why do we need Esther anyway?'

Percy cleared his mouth and explained. 'You'll be following up those leads on Mr Wilde's lifestyle, while I'll be touring the country like a music hall act, looking for the vanished Lord Stranmillis. We'll be working independently of each other, on two separate lines of enquiry and I've enlisted Esther's support because I believe that the two matters are linked by way of the Irish connection. We need a third brain looking for those links.'

'Even if Stranmillis *was* spirited away by Fenians,' Jack pointed out, 'they've waited long enough to announce the fact and claim either the ransom money or some political favour.'

'Which is why I don't believe that Fenians had anything to do with it,' Percy replied with a smile. 'I favour, instead, the theory that his Lordship chose to disappear for reasons of his own and from what we know of Mr Wilde and his deviant brotherhood I have a feeling in my innards that Lord Stranmillis was otherwise inclined.'

'You mean he was a homosexual?' Jack enquired.

'Yes,' Percy replied. 'Did Carson say when the trial would be starting?'

'A week on Wednesday was the best estimate he could give me,' Jack reported, 'although even that's a guess on his part.'

'Even so, we don't have long,' Percy reminded them, 'and the important first part will be to establish the extent of his little club of deviants, and whether or not they included peers of the realm. It seems that it's become quite the fashion for the high-born and privileged to go slumming in Molly Houses, and that's why we think that the Home Secretary's a bit nervous about what may be revealed during the forthcoming trial.'

'No wonder,' Esther murmured. 'And I assume that's why you think that Lord Stranmillis may have a reason for staging his own disappearance?'

Percy nodded. 'Precisely. According to what Carson told Jack, the man never married, despite his wealth, and hired women to hang on his arm for appearances' sake on public occasions.'

'Perhaps he just never met the right woman? Are you condemning every unmarried man as a …?'

'Sodomite, Mary-Anne, shirt-lifter,' Percy began and Esther raised her hand.

'Yes, thank you, I think "sodomite" will do. But something bothers me already about all this and it may suggest the possible link between the two cases.'

'Yes?' Percy asked with a look of hopeful expectation.

'How did this Carson person know that Stranmillis was missing in the first place?'

'No idea,' Percy replied, 'but it's a very good question. Jack?'

Jack shook his head. 'I never asked him,' he admitted.

'No wonder Uncle Percy wanted me in on this case,' Esther smiled triumphantly back at Jack. 'Now get your elbows off the table, while I clear away and make another pot of tea.'

Jack and his colleague, Detective Constable Will Booth, approached the closed door of the terraced premises in Cavendish Square. There was a light above the ground floor entrance door that might once have been red, but was now a pale pink, and the sign on the door read 'Salvation Club — Members Only'.

'I feel slightly ridiculous in all this finery,' Booth complained as he looked down at the formal evening attire he'd borrowed for the occasion.

Jack smiled sarcastically. 'You might feel more at ease if it fitted you, but the Yard doesn't come equipped with a wardrobe department, like the West End theatres that Mr Wilde patronises. If it's any consolation, mine used to be my father's and he was an inch or so taller than me. My mother thinks I'm visiting the theatre, which is where you and I are to pretend we came from, remember?'

'I suppose so,' Booth grumbled, 'but if we have to go in there holding hands I can't be sure I can keep a straight face.'

'Trust me,' Jack hissed, 'if you so much as even *attempt* to hold my hand, your face will be permanently bent for a week. Now, where's the knocker for this place?'

Eventually he located a button low down on the door, which he pressed, and was gratified to hear the distant tinkle of some sort of bell. A few moments later they were rewarded with the sound of approaching feet, followed by a faint rasping sound as a flap opened in the centre of the door, and a lugubrious face peered out at them.

'Yes?' the face demanded.

'We'd like to be granted admission, if we may,' Jack replied in what he hoped was a bored upper-class drawl. The face studied him more closely.

'It's members' only, like it says on the door. I don't seem to recall having seen you before, so I take it that you're not members?'

'Not yet, no,' Jack admitted, then turned to Booth with a look of frustration. 'How damnably boring! My friend Rupert here and I were advised that we'd be able to find friends here who march to the same regimental drum as we do, if you get my meaning. And there must have been a time when each one of those now inside stood out here on the pavement, after a night at the theatre like us, hoping to become members, so how does one go about it?'

'Which theatre?' the doorman demanded.

Jack mentally congratulated himself on having read some of the background notes he'd been given by Carson. 'The "St James", of course. My friend Oscar's new play is enjoying full houses every night.'

'Oscar Wilde?'

'Who else?'

'Come in.'

They were led down a dimly lit passageway until they reached a door, on the other side of which it sounded as if a large party of drunken females had opened a champagne hamper on the race track. The doorman reached forward and pushed the door open, inviting Jack and Will Booth to step inside.

They were met by a gale of high pitched laughter and the smell of expensive perfume. As their eyes adjusted to the bright light, the scene that confronted them tested every ounce of their credulity, as well as their capacity for maintaining a straight face. Everywhere they looked were men dressed as women, some of them with heavy make-up contrasting incongruously with moustaches and side whiskers. The costumes were expensive and formal, with ball gowns seemingly the preference, although the occasional giggling freak sitting on the knee of another was dressed in the manner of a milkmaid or a serving wench in a low alehouse. They were kissing, holdings hands, running hands underneath gowns to reveal frilly petticoats and even frillier underdrawers, and conducting lewd conversations in high pitched voices that would have been comical and false-sounding were it not for the actions that accompanied their squeals of delight.

Jack took a deep breath and smiled at Will Booth.

'Try not to laugh,' he ordered.

Will smiled back palely. 'A drink might help — chuckie.'

'Don't push your luck,' Jack hissed as he turned to the doorman.

'Where can a girl get a drink in here?' he enquired, and the doorman nodded towards a counter in the corner, behind which stood a man well approaching six feet in height, with a full ginger beard, dressed as a nun. Jack took Will by the elbow and steered him over to the counter.

'My friend and I would like a drink, if you'd be so good.'

'Do you have an account?' the nun enquired.

'With my bookmaker certainly,' Jack replied in his fake bored drawl, 'not to mention my dressmaker, my hairdresser and my favoured ponce. But not here, clearly, since we're not members. Although looking around, this seems to suit us nicely, so perhaps we might join.'

'The first drink's on the house,' the nun advised them, 'so what'll it be?'

Jack pretended to think. 'I could probably manage a teensie weensie gin and lime. What about you, Rupert?'

'A pint of beer,' Will replied without thinking.

Jack leaned forward and smacked his wrist gently. 'Naughty boy! You're among friends here, so have your usual, why don't you?' He turned to the nun and instructed him to 'make his a large port with a slice of lemon.'

'I'll get the Members' Register and sign you up,' the nun replied. 'I'm the Mother Superior in here and it'll cost you each thirty pounds to join.'

Five minutes later, as Jack was pretending to enjoy his gin and lime without actually swallowing any, while Will was fighting a psychological battle with his glass of port, the Mother Superior placed the Members' Register face up on the counter and handed Jack a pen.

'I'll need some sort of identification from each of you,' he advised them.

Jack reached into the pocket of his dinner jacket, removed his police badge, held it up and smiled. 'This will have to do for mine. And she's got one as well,' he indicated with a sideways smirk at Will Booth. 'Outside are a couple of paddy wagons full of nice hairy police constables who'll be taking your ladies for an evening's entertainment in Vine Street police cells. As for the members on this register that you kindly donated, each of them may expect a visit from my colleagues in the course of the next few days.'

'Good luck with that,' the nun replied with a smirk. 'If I had a quid for every time your people have taken that away, I wouldn't need to work here every evening, serving fairy drinks to a bunch of screaming Nancies. Take a quick look and you'll see what I mean — if you can match those names to real people, you might be in business. If not, bugger off back outside and send in your bullies.'

Jack looked down at the open Member's Register with a sinking feeling that sank even lower when he took in names such as 'Pretty Polly', 'Molly the Stroker', 'Sucky Susan' and 'Bendy Wendy'. He glared back up at the smug face under the wimple.

'You must have their real names, surely? How do you manage your membership accounts?'

'What do you think this is — Marshall and bloody Snelgrove's? They all pay cash –in large quantities, usually — and once they come through the front door they leave their real identities behind them. You can throw this lot in your cells, bring them up in front of the beak in the morning, and all you can get them for is behaviour likely to cause a breach of the peace or crimes against fashion. Most of them will be back in here tomorrow evening, believe me.'

'I can get this establishment closed down,' Jack insisted, but the head inside the cowl shook slowly and confidently.

'They managed that — once. We re-opened the following week, and for some inexplicable reason we didn't see a police raid for the best part of another year. You can always try again, for the fifth time since we re-opened, but somehow the matter never gets to court.'

'Police corruption?' Jack suggested helplessly.

The nun smiled. 'You'd know more about that than me, wouldn't you? Now, would you and your boyfriend please finish your drinks, so that I can have the place nice and tidy for tomorrow night? I have a feeling that most of tomorrow is already accounted for.'

'He as good as told me that someone in the Met's being bribed to keep the place open!' Jack complained. 'We made complete idiots of ourselves, exposed ourselves to God knows what foul diseases and didn't even get the real names of their members.'

'Don't be too despondent,' Percy replied consolingly as he gazed out into a busy Whitehall thoroughfare from the cafe in which he was eating a plate of bacon and eggs while Jack was attacking a ham sandwich. 'They'll need to give their real names when they come up in front of the beak and I'll send someone round to collect the list from the Magistrates' Clerk at dinner time. Then you can call on them at inconvenient times — like when their wives are at home — and lean on them hard to peach on their friends in high places.'

'But this could go on for ever,' Jack complained. 'We can raid one Molly House after another, fill our paddy wagons with queers dressed like milkmaids, run them through the courts, ruin their no doubt shaky marriages, and *still* be no nearer flushing out the ones whose existence could be an embarrassment to the authorities.'

'I suggest you speak to the rent boys and assorted perverts on the list Carson gave you,' Percy replied. 'Those who are really highly placed, such as aristocrats, judges, bishops and relatives of our dear sovereign lady the Queen are not likely to be found playing with each other's squidgy bits in posing parlours such as the one in Cavendish Square, which was operating even when I was a beat constable in that area, although it catered for both tastes back then.'

'I really feel like a simpering virgin in this world that we've been asked to enter,' Jack complained. 'If you could have seen what we saw in that place yesterday!'

'All the more reason to avoid calling in on any more of them,' Percy advised him. 'If I were you, I'd be asking some of Carson's star witnesses who their more exclusive clients were. Even if they didn't know their names, the size of the fees they handed over should give us a clue to their social status. Then we can start sticking newspaper clippings under their noses — "You've seen this man announcing the opening of the new Parliamentary sittings; have you ever seen him wearing petticoats and lacy drawers?" That sort of thing.'

'I don't think I want the rest of this sandwich,' Jack complained as he threw it back down on the plate and reached for his tea mug. 'Trust you to allocate yourself the easy job.'

Chapter Six

It was far from obvious to Percy that he'd undertaken the easier part of their conjoined operation as he stood shouting into the face of the dim looking porter on Platform Four of Euston Station in order to be heard above the noise of rumbling luggage trollies, parents shouting to children to keep up as they hurried for departing trains, and steam being periodically expelled from the boilers of locomotives whose drivers were anxious to release the brake and roll north.

The platforms looked like evacuation stations as smartly dressed clerks, office assistants, shop workers and the like alighted from northern dormitory suburbs such as Berkhamsted, Hemel Hempstead, Watford and Harrow, heading for another working day by way of the rapidly expanding Underground Railway. In the end Percy gave up the unequal struggle and indicated for the porter to join him in the waiting room to the side. He'd been pointed out to Percy after a painstakingly thorough search through records had identified him as the lead porter on duty on the day that the Holyhead Boat Train had left Platform Two with Lord Stranmillis installed in his personal Pullman carriage at the rear of the twelve carriage train. The porter's name was Ted Bloxthorpe, and he was far from happy at being taken out of circulation while three northbound expresses were loading, and generous tips were there for the asking from wealthy travellers with excess baggage.

'I told that uvver copper all I knew,' Ted complained, 'an' I really should be out there, seein' ter the passengers what needs their bags carried ter their compartments.'

Percy extracted a pound note and handed it across with a smile.

'That should cover your loss of tips. Now then — the Holyhead Express on the afternoon of Friday 22nd February. Do you remember it?'

'That were the day what 'is posh Lordship 'ad 'is own carriage fixed ter the back o' the normal train, were it?'

'Yes, so I'm told,' Percy confirmed. 'I'm also told that you were the head porter on duty on Platform Two that day — that right?'

'Yeah, that were me. Late turn, two till ten, the 'ole week.'

'And did you assist his Lordship into his private carriage?'

'Yeah. 'E didn't seem to 'ave no-one with 'im, like most o' the posh coves do. Yer know, like carryin' their bags an' suchlike? 'E seemed ter be on 'is own, an' 'e were most grateful when I offered 'im a trolley.'

'He had a lot of luggage, is that what you're telling me?'

'Not 'alf! There musta bin eight or nine bags in all — all them big 'eavy portmanteau things what posh folks carry their clothes in. They was soft, though, like they was full o' clothes, an' they all went onter the one trolley what I pulled ter 'is carriage, then loaded 'em in. 'E give me three quid fer that — biggest tip I've ever 'ad at Euston. Mind you, when I were in Victoria one time…'

'And that was all that was carried on board for him?' Percy interrupted him. 'No food and drink?'

'None what I saw.'

'Did that particular train have a restaurant car attached?'

'Yeah, the 'Olyhead Express always does, but there weren't no corridor link between the Pullman an' the rest o' the train — it were just coupled ter the back o' the luggage van.'

'So if his Lordship had wanted a meal during the journey, could he get one?'

'Only if 'e 'opped off the train at Rugby or Crewe, where it'd stop for a few minutes while they changed engines. But 'e'd only've 'ad time ter grab a sandwich at the buffet, even assumin' it were open. The Pullman carriage 'e 'ad were one o' the early ones, an' while it 'ad a lavatory, it didn't 'ave no galley fer cookin' meals.'

'And how long does it take for the train to get to Holyhead?'

'Nine hours or so, normally.'

'A long time to go without food and drink, wouldn't you say?'

'I couldn'ta done it, let's put it that way.'

'Nor me, I imagine. Just one final question, then I can let you get back to your work. Do you remember how his Lordship was dressed that afternoon?'

'Yeah, like 'e were plannin' on leanin' out the winder an' shootin' at birds an' suchlike. 'E 'ad on this big 'eavy shootin' jacket, an' boots covered wi' them puttee things what keeps mud outa yer socks. An' 'e 'ad one o' they stupid 'ats what makes it difficult ter see whether yer comin' or goin', know what I mean?'

'A deerstalker, you mean?'

'Don't know what yer calls 'em, but yer often sees 'em around the marshes where I used ter live out Essex way. Folks what's shootin' the ducks an' geese out there tends ter wear 'em'

'That's just about all I need trouble you with for the time being,' Percy advised Ted with a broad smile of thanks. 'I'm heading back up to your head office back there near the entrance, and I'll be sure to advise them how helpful you were.'

Back in the office of Herbert Wainwright, Superintendent (Southern Division) of the London and North Western Railway, Percy was offered coffee and biscuits, which he accepted with grateful thanks, and enquired as to where he could obtain details of the journey that would have been completed from Euston to Holyhead on 22nd February. Wainwright leaned forward to extract a document from a pile on his office desk, which he then handed to Percy.

'Those are the scheduled times, and so far as I know there were no major incidents that day, so the train should have reached Holyhead within thirty minutes of its scheduled arrival time. But you'll find detailed records with my two counterparts at Rugby and Crewe. The Superintendent for the Midland Division is Charles Paterson, and you'll find him in the General Office at Rugby Station. At Crewe, you need to speak to Solomon Johnson, since he covers the Northern Division.'

'In each case, how would those in the office get to know of any delays or other incidents?' Percy asked.

'If it involved the train itself, then it would be from one of the guards,' he was advised. 'As well as changing engines, driver and fireman at Rugby and Crewe, they change guards as well. The guard from here to Rugby would be one of our own, based here at Euston, and if anything out of the ordinary had occurred between here and Rugby, he'd be your man. He would have reported it to us, and I can consult our records, if you wish, and see if our guard reported anything that day. It may take me an hour or two, but if it's easier for you I can have it sent up to Scotland Yard on one of our mail coaches.'

'Yes, that might be better,' Percy agreed. 'But I suspect that what I'm really more interested in is what may have happened well north of here. From what I've been told, the Pullman carriage that was attached to the train down here wasn't attached to the train when it reached Holyhead, but the person who'd been travelling in it used his boat ticket in order to travel across the water to Dublin. Rather odd, you'd have to agree.'

'Most intriguing,' Wainwright nodded, 'but once the ticket has been purchased the passenger can travel wherever they wish on the train, consistent with the class of their ticket obviously. But if your missing person had made arrangements to attach the Pullman to the train, then this would entitle them to travel first class on the train and a first-class cabin on the boat. He'd need to show his ticket as he walked through the embarkation point at Holyhead, and then again as he left the gangplank and walked on deck.'

'But anyone in possession of that ticket could have done that?' Percy said. 'I take it that no-one would ever ask for identification documents, or anything like that?'

'Definitely not. All that the Purser would need to see would be the class of ticket. Assuming that he was in possession of a First-Class ticket for that crossing, and gave his name, then your man would have been shown to the cabin allocated to him. Those allocations are managed by the Ship's Purser, and since it was an overnight crossing, it would be a First Class sleeping cabin.'

'So the man who boarded the train here at Euston need not necessarily have been the man who boarded the vessel at Holyhead?'

'Of course not, as I just explained.'

'And if I need to enquire as to anything unusual occurring between the two points, I need to travel to Rugby and Crewe?'

'Again, yes, as I explained.'

'Thank you, Mr Wainwright, I think that's all for now. And thank you also for the delicious coffee and biscuits. If you could send me a copy of any report handed in by your guard on the Euston to Rugby portion of the journey, I'd be most obliged.'

'Delighted to be of assistance,' Wainwright replied, 'and if you do decide to make the journey, let me know and I can organise an "All Stations First Class Pass" for you, which will entitle you to travel anywhere on our network during the duration of the pass. In exchange, please let me know of any irregularities you discover regarding our service that day.'

'My pleasure,' Percy smiled as he rose to leave.

'Make the most of these,' Percy announced as he handed over the large warm parcel to Esther for her to unwrap ahead of placing its contents into the pre-heated gas oven, 'since they may be the last for a while. I have to head north, as I always suspected I'd need to, since the first stage of Stranmillis's journey back to the land of his birth seems to have been almost unremarkable.'

'In what way was it remarkable?' Jack asked.

'He was travelling alone, with a great deal of luggage that one man on his own could not have been expected to handle. The porter at Euston earned himself an extra week's wages by way of a tip in assisting his Lordship aboard the private Pullman, but why was he travelling alone, when he was so dependent on other people to carry his luggage?'

'It makes sense that if he was planning to disappear, he didn't want any witnesses who knew him,' Esther observed as she spread the table cloth and handed Jack the cutlery to put out. 'Do we know what kind of luggage? The family silver, perhaps?'

'Clothing, according to the porter's best guess, so that's at least consistent with a man quietly moving on, like a snail carrying its home on its back. But he was strangely dressed.'

'Strange in what way?' Esther asked as she reached across to the draining board to where she'd transferred her notepad and pencils while laying the table.

'Dressed as if he was going grouse shooting or something,' Percy replied with a frown. 'And yet, officially, when he got to the end of his journey he was heading into Dublin for a political meeting. He wasn't to know about the brass band and all that, but one hardly attends a political meeting dressed like that. And if he *was* planning on stopping off for a day potting ducks or whatever, where was his gun? And why was he booked direct onto the night boat?'

'He really had no intention of completing the journey, had he?' Esther concluded out loud. 'And would I be correct in speculating that his Lordship was dressed inappropriately for someone boarding a train at Euston solely in order that his departure would be easily remembered?'

'Good point,' Percy conceded.

'I take it that the porter who assisted him knew him by sight?' Esther asked.

'Ah! I forgot to ask the porter that very obvious question.'

'But,' Esther persisted, 'if Stranmillis was lumbered with all that luggage, and needed a porter to help him load it on board his carriage, he was clearly expecting some willing hands wherever he got off, and it would have taken a few moments. That suggests that the bags weren't supposed to be heaved out of the train while it was still moving, but were intended to be unloaded when the train stopped at a station. Or somewhere else along the route.'

'Another intelligent deduction, but unfortunately there are only two stations at which that could have happened,' Percy advised her. 'The Holyhead Express only makes two scheduled stops, at Rugby and Crewe. I'll obviously ask when I travel up there, but if the man was intending to slip away quietly he wouldn't risk such a public display of leaving his carriage — one that would probably delay the train and would therefore be reported by the guard.'

'When are you leaving?' Esther asked as she placed the sauce bottles in the centre of the table, along with a large plate of bread and butter, adding, 'Let's get this tea while it's still hot,' before lowering the oven door carefully with her hand wrapped in a tea towel.

'I can leave whenever I like, but the sooner the better, I suppose. The manager at Euston can fix me up with some sort of pass that will entitle me to roam up and down the London and North Western rail lines as if I were one of its directors, and I'll probably do it in two halves. Rugby first, then back here to exchange notes, then up to Crewe. Which reminds me, Jack — what have *you* got to report?'

'Well, there's no way I'm raiding any more Molly Houses, after that last farce. I spent the whole of this morning in court, telling it the way it was, and all afternoon licking my wounds and answering impertinent questions from those with nothing better to do about how a good looking young male colleague and myself happened to be in a Molly House when the police raided it. Tell you what, though — the name of Oscar Wilde did the trick when we were trying to talk our way past the doorman. But despite what the magistrate was told about the disgraceful scenes we witnessed, the place will be open for business as usual this evening, and as far as I'm concerned it can *stay* open. Just don't expect me to go back there, that's all.'

'That's a bit of a shame,' Percy grinned, 'since I want you to sit in the public gallery during the Wilde trial when it starts next week. We may learn of some other good leads — and what do you propose to do with the ones I've already suggested?'

'I've lined that Ross chappie up for tomorrow morning, although I haven't told him yet. Then I'll no doubt need to come home for a good bath.'

Chapter Seven

'I'm told that you wish to see me in connection with some important matter?' Robert Ross smiled at Jack as he waved him into the vacant seat in front of a desk loaded with paper. The room was some sort of garret on the fourth floor of a somewhat faded building in Piccadilly that housed an insurance office on the ground floor and various professional offices on the floors between that seemed to share a reception desk whose guardian had announced Jack's wish to speak with Ross. Ross himself beamed back at Jack with a rosy round face that reminded Jack of an eager schoolboy.

'So what can I do for you?' Ross enquired. 'Are you by any chance an author — perhaps a playwright — or even a publisher? Although you look a bit young for the latter.'

'I'm a police officer,' Jack advised him as he held up his badge. 'Detective Sergeant Enright, Scotland Yard.'

'Will you blood-suckers *never* give up?' Ross's beaming smile was replaced by a crimson snarl, and he sat down heavily in the chair behind his desk. 'Isn't it enough that I'm being forced to give up my closest, dearest friend? Isn't it enough that I'll be ruined professionally — yet again — when the trial's reported? What do you leeching parasites want *this* time — or are you here to tell me that I've been double-crossed, and that I *will* be prosecuted, along with Oscar?'

Jack took a deep breath. 'I was informed that in exchange for testifying against Mr Wilde you won't be prosecuted personally for anything you may reveal, and so far as I'm aware that position has not changed in any way. I'm simply here for more information.'

Ross expelled a large breath of air, like an inflated balloon being released before its end could be appropriately tied. His face resumed its normal hue, and he attempted another smile. 'Forgive that outburst, but you've no idea of the strain I'm under these days. No-one can, unless they suffer from the same — "disease", shall we call it? I've heard it said that we homosexuals can be cured, and if so, believe me, I'll be the first in the queue, but until that happy day I have to live with what I am — what I've been for as long as I can remember. The constant yearning, the constant fear of betrayal and prosecution. The attempts at blackmail. The gnawing fear that the beautiful creature that you've just met, and whose body you've just explored, may prove to be another *agent provocateur* sent by you people, or a blackmailer seeking to suck your last penny out of you. You've no idea.'

'Of course I haven't,' Jack agreed, 'and I'm sorry if my presence here has somehow caused you anxiety. It's just that I need some information from you — information that perhaps only you can supply.'

'Are you about to ask me what it's like to be one of us?' Ross demanded defensively. 'You wouldn't be the first in your line of work to ask me that, usually with an accompanying snigger. Well, let me save you the effort of asking. Assuming that you don't share my affliction, imagine for a moment that you meet the most beautiful woman your mind could ever conjure up. She's your every dream, your every fantasy, and your entire body aches to know every inch of hers, to blend with her in an act of love bordering upon worship. Then you're told that you can't even hold her hand because the law forbids it. Perhaps she turns out to be your sister or something, but whatever the reason, society will condemn you to a lengthy prison sentence if you know her in the only way that every taut fibre in your body demands. *That's* what I live with every day of my life, Mr Policeman, so go ahead and laugh, then get out of here!'

'I *have* experienced something along the lines that you just described,' Jack replied in a voice that shook slightly with emotion. 'But in my case it was in connection with a woman, and I was most fortunate that she consented to be my wife. If she hadn't, I don't know what I'd've done.'

It fell silent for a moment as their eyes met, and Ross seemed to crumple to half his size. Given that he had been somewhat diminutive to start with, he looked even more like a chastened schoolboy as he said quietly, 'Let's start again, shall we? And would you like some tea?'

While he fussed about with the tea things at the small gas stove and table in the corner of the room, Ross was obviously still anxious and suspicious.

'Did Carson send you?'

'Not directly, no,' Jack replied. 'Since we're being honest with each other, I'm prepared to admit that I've been sent to ensure that the — the "group" that you and Mr Wilde were both members of didn't include anyone so highly placed that the revelation could prove to be an embarrassment to the Government.'

Ross managed a chuckle. 'You have no idea, officer ... Sergeant Entwhistle, wasn't it?'

'Enright. But call me Jack, if it's easier to remember.'

'Very kind of you. I'm Robbie. And as I said, you have no idea how many of those responsible for the welfare of this nation share the same affliction as myself and Oscar.'

'I heard a rumour about the Prime Minister,' Jack admitted.

Ross nodded. 'He's not fully committed, of course, since he was married to that Rothschild heiress, and for a while there we half expected him to marry the Duchess of Albany once she was widowed. But then he fell in with Francis Douglas, and the two of them had a high old time until his father threatened to expose their relationship, Archie gave Francis the old heave-ho in order to add the Prime Ministership to his financial fortune, and poor old Francis died of grief.'

'At the end of his own shotgun,' Jack added.

Ross nodded. 'I blame myself for ever introducing them, shortly before I introduced Oscar to Bosie. And that was the biggest mistake of my entire life, since Oscar fell for Bosie like a cartload of bricks, and I never got another look in.'

'So you and Oscar were…'

'Of *course* we were. It was impossible to be the way I am and not find Oscar irresistible. He's so entrancing and mysterious, so gentle and caring, so — well, just so *alluring*. He's like the flame that attracts the moth, and believe me he's known many moths. But once Bosie came along, well, it was like I'd never existed.'

'You're testifying, as I understand it, to the relationship between Mr Wilde and Bosie Douglas. Are you doing so as a sort of jilted lover?'

'How *dare* you! I love Oscar dearly, and always will. I've agreed to tell the court the truth about Oscar and Bosie because of the guilt I feel about Francis's death — it's the very least that I owe to his father. When Queensberry chose to expose what Oscar was up to with Bosie, he only did so because he dreaded another son finishing up like the previous one, in a spiral of despair and self-destruction because of the way Nature had dealt him out. The least I can do is to prevent the poor man going to prison for speaking the truth. And, of course, as I have no doubt you were about to cruelly remind me, by doing this I save myself from prosecution.'

'I gather from what you've been telling me,' Jack ventured as he sipped his tea, 'that there was quite a group of you similarly inclined who formed a sort of social group. Would I be correct in thinking that?'

'Yes indeed,' Ross confirmed as he closed his eyes in reminiscence. 'It began between Oscar and myself, then Bosie came on the scene, then there was a succession of pliant young men, some of whom I have to shamefully admit were not above seeking money. We would meet up for weekends, and sometimes longer, at Bosie's country place in Surrey. He was already in a relationship with the writer George Ives, a hangover from his university days, and a man dedicated to bringing about changes in the law that persecutes those of our "persuasion", shall we call it? Then there's Reggie Turner, another of Oscar's "Aesthete" friends, who also hangs around out of sheer adoration of the man.'

'What was that group you just mentioned?' Jack asked as he prepared to jot down another entry in his notebook, 'And could you spell it please?'

Ross did as requested, before explaining further: 'Aesthetes concentrate on beauty rather than functionality, artistic appeal rather than symbolic meaning. For example, our museums are full of Greek statues depicting nude male forms. You can either consider them, in a functional sense, as representing the Classical depiction of athletic prowess, or simply as depraved images of men's private parts. An aesthete such as Oscar would value them simply as something beautiful in themselves, but you can easily see how such an approach might be misinterpreted as indicative of a perverted sexuality.'

'As it is, in Mr Wilde's case,' Jack pointed out.

Ross treated him to a frown. 'You just don't understand, do you? If the statue in question were of a nude female child, would you not be offended if you admired it for its beauty, and were then denigrated as a pervert with a sexual preference for children?'

'I take your point,' Jack conceded, 'but we're drifting away from why I'm here. I need to know if any others in Mr Wilde's circle of acquaintances, apart from those you've named, and whose names might come out during the trial, may prove to be inconveniently positioned in society.'

'Are there any other screaming Mary-Annes in the Cabinet, you mean?'

'Yes, if you care to put it that way.'

'I can only speak from my own experience,' Ross advised him, 'and Roseberry would be the only one I could point a finger at. However, from time to time there were whispers of highly placed members of our straight-laced and pinch-mouthed Establishment being caught in police raids on "Molly Houses". Presumably you're familiar with those?'

'Only *too* familiar,' Jack confirmed with a grimace. 'I was inside one only a few evenings ago — in the course of my duties, I hasten to add — and it turned my stomach.'

'You have to believe me when I tell you that twittering mincers such as those are not representative of true homosexuals. It's become quite the fashion to frequent these horrible places, in the same way that it was once the done thing to pay money to view the criminally insane inside Bedlam, and the freaks you are likely to encounter in Molly Houses are simply playing out their deranged fantasies. But those of us who have the misfortune to love another man truly and genuinely do not see them primarily as an object of lust. The physical aspect of their relationship flows from the genuine love that they cannot hold back — much like I imagine you feel for your wife.'

'I understand what you're telling me,' Jack persisted, 'but I'm told that many of the witnesses in Wilde's trial against Queensberry will be male prostitutes, so one is bound to observe that perhaps the man upon who you lavish so much affection may have, at least on some occasions, resorted to less justifiable reasons for sexual activity. The concern of the authorities is that these "rent boys", as I believe they have become known, may have sold their "services', we may call them, to persons of high status, such as politicians, clergymen, lawyers — even senior police officers. How may I best go about discovering if that was the case?'

'You might want to speak to a man called Alfred Taylor,' Ross advised him. 'He was another associate of Oscar's, and Alfie's particular interest was in dressing up as a woman and being brutally sodomised in a make-believe fantasy in which he was a woman alone in a room who was raped by an intruder. In order to be able to live out that fantasy, Alfie was obliged to resort to rent boys, and over the course of time he introduced some of them to Oscar, whose particular fantasy was seducing young boys of little to no education. Alfie would arrange for him to accost them in the street, then play the part that Oscar had allocated to them.'

'And you believe that some of these young sexual actors may have been hired for other fantasies by people in high positions in society?'

'I only say that it's possible — you must make your own enquiries.'

'Where will I find this Mr Taylor?'

'He used to reside in Chelsea somewhere, but he was recently arrested, so he may have moved address.'

'If he was recently arrested, I can easily obtain his address,' Jack replied as he rose to his feet. 'Thank you for the tea, and

I'm sorry that I had to deal with matters that must be very distressing for you.'

'Only to be expected,' Ross assured him, 'and my thanks for not being as brutally judgmental as most police officers I've encountered in the past. Not to mention that dreadful man Carson — you'd think I was a witness for the other side, the way he pitched into me.'

'Unfortunate, I agree,' Jack commiserated, 'since I assume that you were the one who started this whole business off by alerting Queensberry to what was going on?'

'No, that wasn't me.' Ross smiled. 'I shouldn't gloat over something so grave, but I still resent Bosie for having stolen Oscar from me. And it was his own stupid patronising arrogance that led to the whole business being revealed.'

'What happened?' Jack enquired as he sat down again.

'Bosie was playing the "Lord Bountiful" — one of his favourite poses — one day with a particularly odious male prostitute called West. In addition to paying his fee, Bosie gave him one of his old suits, without first checking the pockets. When West examined the pockets, he found some old love letters from Oscar to Bosie and set about blackmailing the two of them. He squeezed all he could out of them, then when they refused to pay anything for the final one, West passed it to another rent boy of his acquaintance, a disgusting, snivelling little Scot called Campbell. Campbell tried to get a twenty from the pair of them, and when Oscar sent a bully boy to rearrange his face, Campbell retaliated by giving the letter to an obnoxious blackmailer called Allen, who decided to send the letter to Queensberry, with a request for fifty pounds in exchange for keeping his mouth shut. I believe that Queensberry gave it to his counsel Carson when Wilde had him charged with criminal libel, and I imagine that it will feature in the forthcoming trial.'

Jack put his notebook back in his jacket pocket and stood up. 'I think I'll pay a call on a couple of rent boys.'

Chapter Eight

'They told me you were coming, so I was able to get the information you need ahead of your arrival.' Charlie Paterson smiled at Percy as he beckoned him into the office in which he sat behind a huge desk covered in charts, timetables, staff rosters and company circulars. On one wall of his office was a large, detailed map of the entire LNWR network, while the other wall consisted largely of windows that gave a commanding view of the island platforms below, with their 'scissors crossings' that had been such an inspired piece of engineering innovation when the new Rugby Station opened ten years previously. 'I trust that your journey up here was comfortable?'

Percy nodded. 'I'm not a great fan of rail travel, but at least we were on time. I'm advised by those in the know that this isn't necessarily a feature of all train journeys.'

'It is most of the time on the London and North Western,' Paterson replied proudly, 'although not on the journey you were enquiring about. We experienced a ten minute delay that day.'

'From what I was informed at Euston,' Percy replied, 'the train is scheduled for a ten minute delay anyway, while they change engine, footplate men and guard.'

'Ah yes, but that's allowed for in the schedules. This was an extra ten minutes,' Paterson explained. 'It's all here in the guard's report, although I'm not sure that it will assist in your search for an entire Pullman carriage.'

He handed over the handwritten document and Percy squinted at it, held it out at arm's length, then pulled it closer, and finally gave up the unequal struggle. 'My eyesight isn't what it used to be, and your guard's handwriting leaves a lot to be desired.'

'They aren't employed for their copperplate script,' Paterson explained, 'but the gist of it is that the train was held up for an additional ten minutes because of a minor contretemps at the Telegraph Office. The guard would have been anxious to hand this in, then cross to another platform in order to take an "up" train back to Euston in order to end his shift. And this may be of interest to you, since it concerned the arrogant occupant of the Pullman carriage that went missing.'

'Go on,' Percy replied encouragingly.

Paterson's face assumed a more concentrated expression as he replayed the incident from his memory. 'I was called in to referee, as it happens. The man who was occupying the Pullman apparently alighted from the train as soon as it pulled up on the platform and headed for the Telegraph Office, which is down there on Platform One, and is provided for the convenience of the travelling public. Unfortunately for him it was the day before scheduled horse racing at Wolverhampton, and there was a long queue of customers who'd come in off the street to use the facility in order to contact their bookmakers once the early evening papers published the 'form' guide. When the man hadn't returned to his carriage by its departure time, the guard went looking for him and there was something of a verbal conflict between the two of them. Your man was refusing to re-board his carriage until he managed to send his telegram and was threatening to sue the company if the train left without him.'

'So how was the dilemma resolved?' Percy asked with a smile.

'When the matter was reported to me, I allowed him to use our telegraph facility here in the General Office.'

'Do you by any chance keep a copy of the telegrams you send?'

'Of course, it's company regulations.'

'Do you still have it?'

'Probably, since it was only last month. If you'd like to wait down in the Buffet Restaurant, I'll have it sent down to you. I assume that you haven't had dinner yet, given the hour that you'd have left Euston, so take my pass, and it'll entitle you to anything you like from the extensive list, free of charge and with the compliments of the company.'

'I wish we had these at the Yard.' Percy grinned as he accepted the card that was handed to him and headed off downstairs for a massive feed at someone else's expense.

Twenty minutes later, halfway through the greatest amalgamation of sausages, mashed potato and carrots that he'd ever assembled, Percy heard his name being called and when he raised his hand in acknowledgement a uniformed porter scuttled over with a piece of paper in his hand. Percy thanked him and propped the copy of Stranmillis's telegraph up against a sauce bottle as he continued eating while reading. He was highly skilled in this by dint of experience and if his wife Beattie ever sued for divorce on the ground of mental cruelty, this would be one of the irritating habits that she would cite.

His eyebrows rose as he read the cryptic communication.

Phadrig Ryan,
Ryan Industries,
37 Tavistock Street,
Covent Garden, London
All good. Bunbury goes on stage at Crewe as planned.
Dermy

After taking his time over his first free dinner for as long as he could remember, Percy strolled back upstairs to thank Charlie Paterson for his hospitality and to access the railway's own telegraph office in order to send an instruction to Jack back in London. Before he descended the stairs one final time to await his return train, Percy had one remaining question.

'From what you told me earlier, the train would have been ten minutes late leaving here on its way to Crewe. Would it have been possible for the locomotive driver to regain that lost time?'

'Of course.' Paterson smiled reassuringly. 'Our timetables are as accurate and realistic as possible, but one of our continual failings — which we're constantly seeking to redress — is the late running of some services. The standing instruction to all our drivers is therefore to make an effort to get ahead of time when they can, in order to counteract unforeseen delays.'

'Such as important but belligerent customers refusing to re-board?' Percy grinned.

'That, certainly. But also hazards on the track, such as stray animals or broken down locomotives. And, regrettably, we get our fair share of suicides from people diving off the many road bridges that cross the line. Or simply walking out in front of a speeding express.'

'If there *is* a hazard of some sort ahead of a train that's in motion,' Percy enquired, 'how would you alert the driver to it?'

'That's what signals are for,' he was advised. 'The driver must obey all signals, and either slow down, or stop altogether, and the train won't be driven into the hazard area until the signal's changed.'

'The driver will have no idea of what lies ahead?'

'Not unless it's obvious from his footplate, no.'

'But he'll obey the signal nevertheless?'

'Of course. That's what he's trained to do, and any driver ignoring a signal does so at his own peril, and that of his passengers. You only get to do that once on the LNW, trust me, and if you're caught at it, it's instant dismissal.'

'Thank you again,' Percy smiled appreciatively. 'Both for the information and the best sausages I've tasted in years.'

Jack cursed quietly when Percy's telegraph message was delivered to him, but since he was sitting in Records anyway, he may as well deal with it now, rather than have to return later. Percy wanted him get the full background on 'Ryan Industries'.

The Yard didn't just keep criminal records, it also kept copies of documents filed for company registration purposes, and within minutes of requesting the bulky file Jack was whistling quietly to himself and beginning to appreciate why his mother would have preferred him to pursue a career in commerce.

Ryan Industries had its fingers into everything, it seemed. It had recorded a very acceptable profit for the past few years and its Annual Report to Shareholders spoke of its plans to make even more as it bid for Government contracts for steel, iron ore, coal, road construction and bridge building, not to mention competitive applications to subcontract to the railways and shipyards. And now it seemed that they were planning to venture into something completely new for them — salt mining. Jack wasn't interested in salt, except when it was sprinkled into the saucepan in which potatoes were being boiled, and so he put the company documents to one side with the intention of leaving them for Uncle Percy in his office upstairs and went back to the search for an address for Alfred Taylor.

He wasn't hard to locate, given his undistinguished criminal history. Undistinguished, that is, in terms of the types of offence he committed. Here was no mass murderer, no highly skilled 'peterman' and no armed robber of banks. Just a rather grubby man in his late thirties who had a bad habit of being in the company when a Molly House was raided, or being named as the director of their operations whenever rent boys were intercepted as the result of previous clandestine observations of 'known' houses whose existence had been revealed to police by trade rivals.

Not really expecting to meet with any early success, Jack knocked heavily on the outside door of the house in Cadogan Street, conveniently located for the local lunatic asylum. The man who came to the door reeked of cheap rum and stale sweat and glared at Jack through eyes bleary with recently disturbed sleep. Jack raised his police badge high in the air as he stepped back to avoid the nauseating combination of odours.

'Mr Taylor?'

'Who wants him?'

'Nobody, I'd hazard a guess,' Jack replied sarcastically, 'but I'm really looking for two young men you used to rent out at one time — names of "West" and "Campbell".'

'Yer want 'em both at the same time?' Taylor leered back at him.

'I don't want them for the purpose you normally hire them out for,' Jack persisted. 'I want to speak to them in connection with an enquiry I'm conducting.'

'This got owt ter do wi' Oscar?'

Jack nodded. 'Do you know him?'

'Used ter. 'E were me best customer at one time, 'til 'e started growin' 'is own. But I'm s'posed ter be goin' ter court next week sometime, ter tell the nice man all about it.'

'Along with West and Campbell?'

Taylor shook his head. 'Not Westy. 'E left town on account've 'is 'ealth when 'e 'eard that lawyers was lookin' for 'im. The same ones as found me an' offered me a twenny ter tell 'em 'ow I used ter set Oscar up wi' boys what would pretend ter be chatted up afore 'e got their trousers down.'

'And what about Campbell?'

'Step inside, my friend,' Taylor said invitingly as he moved to one side of the dingy hallway with its peeling wallpaper, and with considerable reluctance Jack followed him until they reached a door that was partially open and opened further when Taylor kicked it with his boot.

There was urgent movement from inside a dirty mass of bed linen and soiled covers, and a dishevelled unshaven face peered out at Jack, then broke into a forced smile that was sickening in its intensity and its exposure of rotten gums.

'Customer?' the gums asked.

Jack involuntarily shook his head in revulsion. 'Some other time, perhaps,' his warped sense of humour obliged him to reply.

'Sae whit youse wantin' wi' me?' the youth enquired in a voice that had never left Glasgow, even though its owner had, ten years previously.

'Some information,' Jack replied as he tried to limit his intake of breath to the minimum consistent with continued life.

The youth rolled out of the bedding onto the floor, completely naked, and Taylor grinned back at Jack sheepishly as his eyebrows shot up in silent enquiry.

'Well, 'e needs ter practice,' was Taylor's justification, as the youth in question farted loudly, then began urinating into a bucket in the corner before unstoppering a bottle of beer that lay on the table and sliding into one of its accompanying chairs.

'Why shid ah tell youse anythin'?' the youth demanded.

Jack slid his police badge carefully onto the table top, keeping as far from Campbell as he could. In its inner fold was a pound note and the youth thanked him before taking a long slug from the beer bottle, and following it up with an explosive belch.

'You *are* named Campbell?' Jack asked.

'Aye, Jamie Campbell, frae Cambuslang if ye've ever heard o' it. Is that all youse is wantin'?'

'Not quite, but almost,' Jack replied. 'Did you ever get the real names of any of your male customers?'

'Whit dae *ye* think?' Campbell chortled.

'So you've no idea if they were members of the aristocracy, or royal family, or anything like that?'

'A couple o' them was proper queens, right enough,' Campbell chuckled, and Taylor joined in the joke. Jack decided that both his health and his temper demanded an early departure, so he extracted the photograph of the three men at the university reunion dinner that he'd received from Carson and laid it carefully on the table in front of Campbell.

'Recognise anyone here?'

Campbell nodded. 'Two o' them anyway,' Campbell confirmed.

'An' the one on the left's there's that Carson bloke,' Taylor added as he peered over Jack's shoulder.

'Which two do you recognise, Jamie?' Jack enquired gently, as a light appeared to be dawning in this shadowy world that he'd recently been occupying.

'The short one in the middle. 'E liked ter dress up as a Mary-Anne while I did the business wi' 'im.'

'And the other one?' Jack held his breath for a different reason than previously.

'That yin on the right,' Jamie confirmed. 'The tall yin — 'e always liked tae be facin' me when we wiz dein' it. Not like maest o' 'em, that prefers it frae behind.'

'There's no doubt in your mind that the one on the right was a customer of yours?' Jack demanded excitedly.

'Dae *ye* ever forget someyin ye've done that to?' Campbell demanded.

Jack decided to leave while he still retained his dinner. Outside, he took in a few deep breaths, and somehow even the faint smell of horse dung seemed fresh and clean. Then he smiled as he began to walk back in the direction of the bus stop in Sloane Street. No wonder Uncle Percy was enquiring about Ryan Industries.

Chapter Nine

'So what have we learned?' Percy asked as Esther placed the bowl of boiled potatoes in the centre of the kitchen table, next to the steaming steak and kidney pie that had gone into the oven as soon as Percy had appeared with it.

'I've learned that I vomit easily if you ask me to interview rent boys, ponces and associated riff-raff. I absolutely refuse to expose myself to any more of them,' Jack insisted.

'I hope you didn't,' Esther quipped. 'It certainly sounds as if you were right, Uncle Percy, and that Stranmillis was planning to disappear quietly. That telegram he sent seemed to be confirming that someone else called "Bunbury" would be taking his place at Crewe. Did you find any evidence that this had happened?'

'I haven't got as far as Crewe yet,' Percy replied, 'but it will be interesting to learn whether or not the Pullman was still attached to the train when it pulled out of there and headed for Holyhead.'

'From what you learned at Euston,' Jack added, not wishing to be left out, 'it sounds as if Stranmillis was taking most of his clothes with him. That tends to confirm a plan to fade from sight for a lengthy period of time.'

'But why employ a substitute?' Esther queried. 'Stranmillis quite obviously had no intention of appearing in Dublin, where he was presumably well known, and yet he went to the trouble of arranging for this "Bunbury" chap to replace him on the train, if we're right about that. Why not simply walk off the train at some point?'

'Weighed down with all that luggage?' Jack offered. 'Sounds to me more as if he was planning on switching to another means of transport somewhere during the journey — maybe another carriage at Crewe, or another train at a later stop.'

'According to the train timetable,' Percy objected, 'there *was* no other stop. Once the train pulled out of Crewe Station, it was non-stop to Holyhead.'

'But the Pullman wasn't on the end of the train at Holyhead?' Esther asked by way of confirmation.

Percy shook his head. 'No. So, somehow or other, it was "disappeared" between Crewe and Holyhead.'

'But why?' Jack objected. 'Why not just let it go through to Holyhead without him in it?'

'Two reasons,' Percy pointed out. 'First of all, the luggage. Why take it with you in the first place, if you intend to abandon it? And if you don't intend to abandon it, you need to get it off the Pullman before it reaches Holyhead, where a substitute — who presumably joined the train at Crewe, according to Stranmillis's telegraph to Patrick Ryan — will use your ticket. The second reason proceeds from the first — you need the Pullman to transport the luggage to somewhere other than Dublin.'

'That's something else that doesn't really make sense,' Esther objected. 'Why go to the trouble of sending a substitute to use your boat ticket, when you intend to disappear somewhere in England, and never set foot in Dublin?'

'To throw us off the scent,' Percy explained. 'If I hadn't come across that telegram alerting us to some sort of substitution at Crewe, we'd still be investigating the possibility that Stranmillis somehow vanished during the boat crossing — by being pushed overboard, or perhaps committing suicide.'

'At least, as the result of my enquiries, we know that Ryan and Stranmillis were both Mary-Annes,' Jack reminded them proudly.

'I'd already deduced that,' Percy replied, as Jack's proud smile evaporated.

'How?' he challenged him.

'He used the name "Dermy" in his telegram,' Percy pointed out. 'Obviously a diminution of his real name — "Dermot" — but also a sort of sweetheart name by which you're known to someone emotionally close to you.'

'A boyfriend, you mean?' Esther said.

Jack snorted. 'You make it sound so "twee". Believe me, what they get up to in these depraved circles is far more sickening.'

'Be that as it may,' Esther insisted, 'they clearly had a relationship that they might wish to keep hidden from public knowledge. So if we're right about Stranmillis disappearing in order to preserve his reputation, he was also doing a favour for Ryan, and this was why Ryan was helping him.'

'Well deduced,' Percy replied, 'and we clearly need to look more closely at Mr Ryan, and his many business concerns. We also need to do the same with Stranmillis — in fact we should probably have done that already. Jack, that's your next job.'

'I thought you wanted me to attend the trial?' Jack objected.

'You've got two more working days before that begins, even if it starts on time,' Percy reminded him, 'and in the meantime I intend to try my hand at being a theatre critic.'

'You're going to watch Wilde's latest play?' Esther asked.

Percy nodded. 'For the reason to which you alluded a moment ago.'

'I did?'

'In a sense, yes. If we assume that it was Stranmillis who had to make himself scarce, then this suggests he had a closer relationship with Wilde than Ryan. I'm hoping to hear something dropped out casually in conversation that suggests what that link may be.'

'But you won't hear anything other than the play itself at the theatre,' Jack protested, 'and didn't I read in the paper that the performances are all sold out?'

'Who says I'm going in the evening?' Percy smiled as he claimed the last of the pie.

Jack muttered obscene things about his Inspector uncle as he stared at the pile of paper that had just been delivered to the room in Records in which he was conducting the latest investigation. Stranmillis was obviously going to pose a huge challenge. It had been easy with Ryan, since all his commercial activities were conveniently housed within the one 'holding' group, "Ryan Industries". Stranmillis, on the other hand, had opted to keep his many enterprises separate, and in consequence it was necessary to wade through a dozen or so sets of records filed by companies of which Stranmillis was listed as Chairman of the Board, or Managing Director, or both. Jack wondered idly how all these organisations, with their hundreds, if not thousands, of employees, would react to the news that 'the boss' had gone missing. On the other hand, Jack mentally filed as a possible additional line of enquiry, it might be possible to deduce where the man had gone if there was future evidence of ongoing prosperity inside one of his many concerns.

It was possible to track Stranmillis's trail of inspired genius since he graduated with his B.Sc from university at approximately the same time as Carson and Ryan. First a modest steelworks in a place called Rotherham, a few miles north of Sheffield, then expansion into a quarrying concern in Nottinghamshire that supplied gravel and road "infill" on Government contracts. He'd followed that up with concrete pipe manufacture and laying operations based in Manchester, and designed to service a massive extension in sewer installation by various local authorities in the region that was still ongoing. Every aspect of his entrepreneurship seemed to have benefitted from Government contracts, which meant that he was well connected.

Jack was beginning to expand, in his mind, an initial theory that Stranmillis had been ordered to disappear by someone highly placed in Government circles whom he'd been bribing when his eye lit upon the latest file, and a loud bell rang in his head. In fact, two bells.

The first was the name of the latest business venture — 'Beeston Salt Pans Ltd'. Jack reminded himself that Ryan Industries had also been recently expanding into salt mining and that it must therefore be not only a profitable line, but also one in which Ryan and Stranmillis might be combining their commercial ambitions. Alternatively, of course, they could be fierce rivals, and this might suggest an alternative explanation for Stranmillis's disappearance. Then, as he began to read the company prospectus in which his Lordships' latest enterprise had been touting for investors, it was as if Jack had been hit between the eyes with something heavy and blunt.

It was not so much what the new venture was being formed to exploit, but *where*. There was, apparently, an existing, but now abandoned, salt extraction site adjacent to an estate in Cheshire that Stranmillis had recently purchased — perhaps the very one that Carson had mentioned that had been the subject of some sort of boundary dispute. It was the intention of this new company to take over an old salt mining complex that had been abandoned ten years previously because of some flooding problem or other, and install new pumping and extraction equipment, in order to exploit what potential shareholders were being assured was still a massive remaining lode of rock salt for which there was a limitless demand worldwide.

Jack's mouth opened in surprised disbelief as he read a paragraph that described how the site was already well served by a railway branch line that exists between the old mine area and the London and North Western Line between Crewe and Chester, to which the extracted salt product could be hauled ready for onward dispatch to the recently opened Lion Salt Works in Northwich.

This was almost too good to be believable. Stranmillis had access to a railway siding that was linked to the main line between Crewe and Chester. It would be stretching coincidence to breaking point if this was not the place in which he'd arranged to hide his Pullman carriage. It could then be emptied of all the bags that the runaway had brought with him, and either he could be hiding on his Cheshire estate, or he could have travelled anywhere, either by coach or by train. While Uncle Percy was wasting his time being bored to death in the St James Theatre, he — Sergeant Jack Enright — had solved the mystery without assistance.

Particularly not any assistance from a wife who would never have let him forget it if she had been the one to uncover this vital information.

Chapter Ten

'Very well, sweethearts, let's do the bit in the first scene where Algie's telling Jack all about the joys of bunburying,' instructed the man in the shirtsleeves, sporting a gaudy multi-coloured waistcoat that looked as if someone had just vomited all down the front of it. 'We've got to get the blocking right, since we've had complaints from the paying guests that they can't see Gwendolen's ankles when she swans in with Lady Bracknell in tow. And Gwenny dear, when you *do* come in stage left, please arrange to be dressed in your stage costume, and not those ridiculous bloomer things that you've got on *ce matin.*'

The man jumped daintily from the stage like a Spring lamb frolicking in the morning dew, waving what was presumably the script. He turned petulantly when he heard a female voice muttering from behind an aspidistra pot, and yelled back up, 'Gwenny, either talk directly to me, or keep your delicate little lipsies sealed until it's your turn. And what exactly is your problem?'

'My costume,' replied the actress who was presumably cast as Gwendolen. 'It's hanging like a beggar's rags after a month on stage, and the boys in the peanut gallery will be seeing a lot more than my ankles if it gets any more threadbare. So why do I need to wear it just for a lighting rehearsal?'

'Because we need to get the tracker spot reorganised,' the man explained. 'At present when you make your grand first entrance it's still focused on Jack's arse. Did your Mummy not teach you what a needle and thread's for?'

'I'm an actress, not a seamstress,' the young lady complained. 'And it's not my fault that you sacked the Wardrobe Mistress.'

'She was already squiffy at eight every morning,' the man reminded her, 'and dear old Chasuble's dog collar was all but strangling him after she took it in at dress rehearsals. Not to mention the gaping hole in the back of Algie's frock coat. Very convenient for his boyfriend, no doubt, but not what the customers are paying to see. Now, can we get on?'

'Not until you tell us where Giles has got to,' replied the man at centre stage who appeared to be playing one of the leading parts that they were about to rehearse. 'He should be standing here wasting *his* time instead of mine — that's what understudies are for, after all, and it's only a lighting rehearsal. He's been gone damned near a month now, and I have a medical appointment.'

'Sorry, sweetie, but we have higher priorities than your piles.'

Without further ado the man in charge raised his hand to gain everyone's attention. 'And *go*!' he commanded, and the scene began to play out from what was obviously the agreed starting line. Percy, sitting several rows back in the dimly lit stalls, settled down to be bored to distraction, until something in the dialogue between the two leading male characters brought him back to attention with a snap.

The character called 'Algernon' was explaining to his friend 'Jack' that whenever he wished to avoid an unwanted social engagement, he invented an invalid friend elsewhere in the country whom he had to visit as a matter of urgency. That make-believe friend was called 'Bunbury', and suddenly Percy was all ears, since this was the man mentioned in Stranmillis's telegram to Ryan — the man who was schedule to go 'on stage' at Crewe.

Not only did this tie in with the suggestion that a fictitious character was somehow being deployed in the Stranmillis disappearance, but it further confirmed some sort of link between Stranmillis and the play currently being rehearsed, which had been playing to capacity houses ever since it opened several weeks ago. Had Stranmillis seen the play, and adapted one of its plot lines to suit his own purpose, or was he familiar with the play anyway because of a deeper relationship with its author Wilde?

'Who are you, and why didn't you come on the same evening as the other theatre critics?' the man in charge demanded as he glared down at Percy, having only just become aware of his presence in the stalls while the cast had been sent grumbling away for a short break. 'This is only a lighting rehearsal, and half the cast are still in mufti, so you won't get the proper effect.'

Mentally thanking the man for accepting his assumed persona, Percy launched into the rest of his prepared explanation. 'I'm from out of town, and I normally cover trials, executions and other delights. But my niece thought I might like to do a piece on this excellent new play that's taken the West End by storm, and I'm so impressed by what I'm experiencing this morning that I'd be delighted to take up her suggestion. I don't suppose Mr Wilde's here this morning? I'd rather like a quote from him.'

'He's otherwise occupied, with his lawyers,' the man explained. 'He normally directs, but on this happy occasion he's left that bed of nails to me. As you will have seen for yourself, if you've been here since we started, when teacher's away the children have a habit of playing awkward. I'm Vernon Treston, Stage Manager. And who, pray tell, is your theatre critic niece with such excellent taste?'

'She's no theatre critic,' Percy replied artlessly, 'just a wardrobe mistress for one of London's most highly regarded amateur groups.'

'Is she by any chance looking for a job?'

'Not so far as I'm aware, given the extent of her other engagements. But I'll enquire, if you wish.'

'Please do — particularly if she can sew as well,' Treston replied. 'Now please feel free to watch the rest of the rehearsal, if I can drag the children back from whichever coffee house they're currently posing in.'

Two hours later Percy was enjoying a free midday meal of chicken salad in the upstairs rooms above the architectural practice in Holborn that was home to Jack's sister Lucy. Lucy smiled as she poured the wine.

'You're famous for never dropping in unless you want something, Uncle, so let's get that over with, shall we, then I can enjoy my dinner? And before you ask, I'm not posing as another corpse for you.'

'Far from it,' Percy assured her with one of his winning smiles. 'But you are still interested in the theatre, are you not?'

'What mother of three wouldn't welcome the chance to pretend that she's the Queen of Egypt, or Joan of Arc, or Lady Macbeth? We employ a nanny, obviously, but even so …'

'I presume you've heard of Oscar Wilde?'

'Of *course* I've heard of Oscar Wilde — he's the talk of the entire West End at present, and not just among theatrical types. Isn't he up on charges of buggery or something? Is that why you're here? If so, I can't imagine how a mother of three with wrinkles to match might interest him sufficiently to let drop some important piece of information on an adjacent pillow. Is he really what they say he is?'

'That will fall to be determined in a trial that starts on Wednesday. In the meantime the company that's putting on this play which is all the rage is short of a wardrobe mistress, it seems. Might you be interested?'

'Who do I have to kill? Are you *really* able to offer me such an important role backstage in the biggest runaway success that the St James Theatre has ever known?'

'Not me, but the Stage Manager who's currently running the show while Mr Wilde is otherwise engaged in what promises to be the legal sensation of the decade. All you have to do is go up there and sound as if it's all a bit of a bore between more exciting engagements. You also have to claim needlework skills that you don't possess.'

'You're about to drag Esther into another of your investigations as well, aren't you?' Lucy said accusingly. 'I'm not sure that she'd be willing, after every other time you've nearly got her killed. And what does Jack have to say about it?'

'I haven't told him that bit yet, but it wouldn't be the first time that four members of the Enright family worked on the same case. You *did* say you'd be prepared to kill in order to get backstage on this runaway success story at the St James Theatre.'

'When would I need to start, and how long will it take? And have you no concept of how difficult it is for a mother of three to have any life of her own?'

'You have a nanny, do you not? And a fulltime, live-in one, what's more. Esther has to rely on her upstairs neighbour.'

'Even if I agree, I'll need a lot more background information. How will I acquire that?'

'Here, tomorrow afternoon at three, at a family tea party.'

Lucy treated him to a look of veiled suspicion. 'Why don't you get Mother to do the catering? Then you'll have the *entire* family involved.'

Percy smiled. 'In my time I've done some dangerous things. I've come face to face with mass murderers, faced a screaming mob in the street, and dived into the Thames to rescue a suicide. But even I'm not brave enough to involve your mother in something that might require her to descend off her high pedestal and wallow in the real world. Tomorrow at three, then.'

'I've spent half the day looking for you!' Jack complained as he finally cornered Percy in the communal tea room on the third floor of the Yard's extensive Whitehall premises. 'Where have you been this time?'

'Having dinner with Lucy.'

'I think I've solved the case.'

'Which case would that be?' Percy said dismissively. 'We're working on two at once, remember.'

'Yours, being the generous person that I am. I think I know where to look for the Stranmillis railway coach.'

'In a sidings near Holyhead?'

'No, in a salt mine in Cheshire. With a branch line from the main railway just west of Crewe.'

'Too good to be true,' Percy muttered.

'That's what I thought,' Jack grinned, 'but here's my evidence.'

He handed Percy the company prospectus for Stranmillis's latest business venture, and Percy whistled softly as he skimmed it.

'Well done, Jack. When I go back up there I'll take a close look at this salt mine at Beeston. But in the meantime I have to arrange a tea party for your sister.'

Jack burst out laughing, then stopped when he realised that Percy wasn't. 'You're serious, aren't you?'

'Have you ever known me refuse free food? Esther's also invited, so I suppose you'd better come along too.'

'Shouldn't we be working? Tomorrow's my last free day before the trial that you want me to attend.'

'We will be working, trust me. All of us. Tell Esther that Alice Bridges may be required to babysit until well into the evening. And for the foreseeable future, during whatever hours the St James Theatre keeps.'

'You're planning on having her conduct discreet enquiries among Wilde's theatrical company?'

'Indeed. You're not the only one who's making progress, and I believe I may have identified the person who helped Stranmillis disappear.'

'One of Wilde's cast?'

'Quite possibly, if we can find him. That'll be Lucy and Esther's job.'

'You've got Lucy involved as well?' Jack enquired with raised eyebrows. 'She swore "never again" after that dreadful business in Wiltshire.'

'That was then, and she's just as bored sitting at home as Esther no doubt is. So this time we employ them both.'

'By "we", you mean that I'll get the blame if either of them finds themselves in danger?'

'Trust me, Jack my boy, I've met this lot they'll be mixing with, and the only danger they'll be courting will be that of dying of laughter. Now go home. In fact, take tomorrow morning off as well — just make sure that you and Esther are at Lucy's by three tomorrow afternoon.'

'So what's the big secret you're about to reveal to us, Uncle?' Lucy asked as the maid backed out through the sitting room door, having laid out the sandwiches, cakes and tea on the table around which the four of them sat.

Percy helped himself to several salmon sandwiches, as he kept it brief.

'Jack and I are working on two separate enquiries, which I am more convinced by the day are linked in some way. The first concerns the trial that begins at the Old Bailey tomorrow, which Jack will be observing on our behalf, in case something comes out in evidence linking Oscar Wilde with some leading figures in this model of Christian propriety that we call English society. I, at the same time, will be sampling the delights of the London and North Western Railway network in the search for a missing peer of the realm called Lord Stranmillis. Esther knows all about these investigations, so she can fill you in on the details.'

'So why are we needed at the theatre?' Esther asked as she selected an 'angel on horseback' cream cake and bit into it with happy memories.

'Because,' Percy explained, 'I believe that his Lordship's disappearance was made possible only with the assistance of a member of Wilde's cast. We need to identify him, find him, bring him in and question him severely.'

'You mean he's missing?' Lucy said.

Percy sighed. 'Why else would we be looking for him? He may be using the name "Bunbury", by the way.'

'How can he be missing halfway through the play's run?' Lucy asked suspiciously, 'or is his part currently being taken by an understudy?'

'He *is* the understudy,' Percy explained, 'or at least he was. May I take it that the role consists of what it sounds like? That he's not actually required during a performance?'

'That's right,' Lucy confirmed with a smile, glad to be making a contribution. 'The role of a male understudy is to learn all the male parts in a play and be prepared to step on stage if a principal actor falls ill or something. It's a most demanding job, but is regarded as the lowest of the low by the cast members. However, it's how many actors who're famous today first made their way in the profession. But what makes you think that this understudy was in some way involved in this disappearance you're investigating?'

'Because,' Percy replied with a self-satisfied smirk, 'his missing Lordship seems to have employed someone to pretend to be him when stepping on board an overnight boat to Dublin. This suggests that he had connections with an actor — in fact, given Mr Wilde's alleged sexual tastes, that connection may have been more than theatrical.'

Lucy grimaced. 'But you want us to learn all we can about this missing understudy? What's his name, by the way?'

'That's your first task,' Percy explained. 'But when the train from which Lord Stranmillis made his escape stopped at Rugby, he sent a telegram back to an associate in London confirming, in so many words, that his substitute would be "going on stage", as he put it, at Crewe. He also called him "Bunbury", which is probably not his real name.'

'Why am I required?' Esther asked.

Percy nodded towards Lucy as he cleared the latest sandwich from his mouth, having transferred his preference to roast beef and pickle.

'Your sister-in-law can't sew, and from what I overheard during the rehearsal that I dropped in on, the stage costumes are getting a bit ragged. Lucy, I'll need you to find out if "Bunbury", as I suggest we call him, took any costumes with him. Male *or* female.'

'Why female?'

Percy smiled condescendingly. 'Best if I don't answer that question. But there's no better disguise for a man than women's clothing, is there?'

'Depends on the man,' Esther observed with a chuckle. 'In some cases the beard might be a bit of a giveaway.'

Jack decided that it was time he spoke. 'In the meantime, I'll have a front row seat at the trial that starts tomorrow.'

'Something else we must prepare ourselves for,' Percy advised them, 'is that if Mr Oscar Wilde's leisure activities are fully revealed for what we know them to have been, then his play may not be running for much longer, so please don't lose any time in getting the information we need.'

'What's this trial all about anyway?' Lucy asked.

'A man called the Marquess of Queensberry allegedly libelled Wilde by calling him a sodomite. That's...'

'Yes, thank you, Jack, I know what one of those is,' Lucy interjected.

Jack continued unabashed, 'Well, Wilde claims that he isn't, and has brought this action against Queensberry. The lawyer for Queensberry who first got us involved in this business has lined up a whole platoon of Mary-Annes to prove that Queensberry was right. It promises to be quite a show.'

'Which reminds me, Jack,' Percy interjected. 'Best get an early night and be first in the queue for the public gallery in the Bailey. Otherwise you won't get a seat, since half the nation's newspaper vultures will be there.'

'Don't I get a reserved seat?'

Percy shook his head. 'The Old Bailey isn't a restaurant. Mind you, it's about to become a theatre.'

Chapter Eleven

Jack yawned for the tenth time and ruefully recalled having slipped from Esther's comforting warmth before the sun had even threatened to rise over the rooftops of Shoreditch to their east. At least the early morning bus had been half empty as it rattled southwards down Farringdon Street and deposited him where it met Newgate Street, leaving him with a stiff walk through the mist of an April early morning to the Old Bailey, in order to join the already lengthening queue for a seat in the public gallery. Squeezed between a fat lady who smelled of cooking fat and an intense looking old man who reeked of pipe smoke far worse than Uncle Percy's, Jack was wondering whether it had all been worth it. Nevertheless, he extracted his notebook and pencil and tried to look the part as the lawyers began to drift in down below him and take their places at the bar table.

Queensberry looked to be the last word in outraged dignity as he squeezed into the dock of the old courtroom and waved his hand for Edward Carson to leave his seat in order to take last-minute instructions. They were engaged in an animated conversation that was almost audible above the murmurs of anticipation and the general clatter of latecomers taking their seats. Then the door behind the bench opened and out walked a pompous looking individual who demanded that everyone rise, which they did to the best of their ability, given the cramped confinement into which they had been squeezed by the ushers who had done their best to accommodate everyone in the queue that began outside and stretched in a long line up the flimsy internal staircase to the public gallery.

Mr Justice Collins took his seat on the bench in a flurry of red robes, the matter of 'Wilde v Queensberry' was called, the charge was read out, and Edward Carson, on behalf of Queensberry, asked that a plea of 'Not Guilty' be entered and announced that his client's defence would be that of justification in the public interest. The judge nodded.

'Very well. Sir Edward?'

Sir Edward Clarke rose to his ponderous feet to outline the case for Wilde. He was an elderly gentleman who seemed to carry all the cares and tribulations of his long professional life on his gowned shoulders and whose lengthy greying side-whiskers trembled with the vibration created by the tremulous voice that intoned the opening address for Wilde.

'May it please you, my Lord, gentlemen of the jury. You have heard the charge against the defendant, which is that he published a false and malicious libel in regard to Mr. Oscar Wilde. That libel was published in the form of a card left by Lord Queensberry at a club to which Mr. Oscar Wilde belonged. It was a visiting card of Lord Queensberry's, with his name printed upon it, and it had written upon it certain words which formed the libel complained of. On that card his lordship wrote: "Oscar Wilde posing as a sodomite."

'Of course, it is a matter of serious moment that such a libel as that which Lord Queensberry wrote upon that card should in any way be connected with a gentleman who has borne a high reputation in this country. You will appreciate that the leaving of such a card openly with the porter of a club is a matter likely to gravely affect the position of the person as to whom that injurious suggestion was made.

'The defendant has said that the statement is true and that it is for the public benefit that the statement was made, and he has given particulars in the plea of matters which he has alleged, to show that the statement is true in regard to Mr. Oscar Wilde. The plea has not been read to you, gentlemen. There is no allegation in the plea that Mr. Oscar Wilde has been guilty of the offence of which I have spoken, but there is a series of accusations in it mentioning the names of persons, and it is said with regard to those persons that Mr. Wilde solicited them to commit with him the grave offence, and that he has been guilty with each and all of them of indecent practices.

'Mr. Oscar Wilde is a gentleman, thirty-nine years of age, the son of Sir William Wilde, a very distinguished Irish surgeon and oculist, who did great public service as chairman of the Census Committee in Ireland. Mr. Oscar Wilde went in the first instance to Trinity College, Dublin, where he greatly distinguished himself for classical knowledge, earning some of the conspicuous rewards which are given to its students by that distinguished University. In 1884 he had the good fortune to marry a daughter of the late Mr. Horace Lloyd, Q.C., and from that day to the present he has lived with his wife, who has borne him two children, at Tite Street, Chelsea. He is a member of the Albemarle Club.

'Among the friends who went to his house in Tite Street was Lord Alfred Douglas, a younger son of Lord Queensberry. In 1891 Lord Alfred Douglas went to Tite Street, being introduced by a friend of Mr. Wilde's. From that time Mr. Wilde has been a friend of Lord Alfred Douglas and also of his mother, Lady Queensberry, from whom, on her petition, the Marquess has been divorced. He has again and again been a guest at Lady Queensberry's houses at Wokingham and Salisbury, being invited to family parties there. Lord Alfred Douglas has been a welcome guest at Mr. Wilde's house, and at Cromer, Goring, Torquay, and Worthing, when Mr. and Mrs.

Wilde were staying there. Until 1893 Mr. Wilde did not know the defendant with the exception that he met him once about 1881.

'Between that time and 1894, Mr. Wilde became aware that certain statements were being made against his character. There was a man named Alfred Wood whom Mr. Wilde had seen once or twice, but knew very little indeed about. Wood had been given some clothes by Lord Alfred Douglas and he stated that in the pocket of a coat so given to him he had found four letters which had been written by Mr. Wilde to Lord Alfred. Whether he did find them in the pocket, or whether he stole them, is a matter on which we can only speculate. But, at all events, Wood went to Mr. Wilde early in 1893 and wanted Mr. Wilde to give him something for the letters, representing that he was in great distress and trouble and wanted to get off to America. Mr. Wilde gave him fifteen or twenty pounds wherewith to pay his passage. Wood then handed over three very ordinary letters which Mr. Wilde had written to Lord Alfred Douglas.

'But, as generally happens when people think they have got hold of letters of some importance, the letters of no importance were given up, and that which was supposed to be of some importance was retained. That was the case in this instance. The people taking part in these transactions were men named Wood, Allen and Cliburn, and something has been found out about this set of people.

'In 1893, Mr. Wilde wrote a play, which afterwards proved a great success at the Haymarket Theatre, "A Woman of No Importance", and while this play was being prepared for production, there came into the hands of Mr. Beerbohm Tree, the manager of that theatre, a piece of paper which purported to be, and to some extent was, a copy of a letter which had been retained by the persons I have named when the other letters were handed over. On this paper was written: "Kindly give this to Mr. Oscar Wilde and oblige yours" and then there followed some initials. Shortly afterwards Allen called on Mr. Wilde, and said he had the original letter. He asked Mr. Wilde to give him something for it. Mr. Wilde absolutely and peremptorily refused, saying: "I have a copy of that letter and the original is no use to me. I look upon it as a work of art. I should have desired to possess it; but, now that you have been good enough to send me a copy, I do not want the original." He then sent Allen away, giving him ten shillings for himself. Almost immediately afterwards Cliburn came to Mr. Wilde and said that Allen had appreciated Mr. Wilde's kindness so much that he sent back the letter. The man then handed over the letter, and Mr. Wilde gave him half-a-sovereign for his trouble. Having once got the original letter into his possession, Mr. Wilde kept it. Now, I will read the letter itself:

'*My Own Boy, Your sonnet is quite lovely, and it is a marvel that those red rose-leaf lips of yours should have been made no less for music of song than for madness of kisses. Your slim gilt soul walks between passion and poetry. I know Hyacinthus, whom Apollo loved so madly, was you in Greek days. Why are you alone in London, and when do you go to Salisbury? Do go there to cool your hands in the grey twilight of Gothic things, and come here whenever you like. It is a lovely place — it only lacks you; but go to Salisbury first. Always, with undying love, Yours, OSCAR.*

'The words of that letter, gentlemen, may appear extravagant to those in the habit of writing commercial correspondence, or those ordinary letters which the necessities of life force upon one every day; but Mr. Wilde is a poet, and the letter is considered by him as a prose sonnet, and one of which he is in no way ashamed and is prepared to produce anywhere as the expression of true poetic feeling, and with no relation whatever to the hateful and repulsive suggestions put to it in the plea in this case.

'In the early part of 1894 Lord Queensberry met Mr. Wilde and Lord Alfred Douglas again at the Cafe Royal. Shortly after that Mr. Wilde became aware that the defendant was writing letters that affected his character and contained suggestions injurious to him. Though he might reasonably — and would probably if his own interests alone were concerned — have brought this to some public notice, he abstained from doing so for reasons which I am not entitled to state, but which I am sure will be obvious before this case has gone very far. And so the latter part of 1894 passed. At an interview in that year, Mr. Wilde gave instructions, in Lord Queensberry's hearing, that the defendant should not be admitted into his house.

'On 28th February Mr. Wilde went to the Albemarle Club, and there received from the porter the card left by Lord Queensberry. On 1st March a warrant was applied for, and on the following day Lord Queensberry was arrested. Hence these criminal proceedings.

'It is said that in the month of July, 1890, Mr. Wilde published, or caused to be published, with his name on the title page, a certain immoral and indecent work with the title of "The Picture of Dorian Gray", which book was intended to be understood by the readers to describe the relations, intimacies, and passions of certain persons guilty of unnatural practices. This is a very gross allegation, and I defy my learned friend to suggest from it anything hostile to the character of Mr. Wilde.

'The volume called "The Picture of Dorian Gray" is one which can be bought at any bookstall in London. It has Mr. Wilde's name on the title page and has been published five years. The story of the book is that of a young man of good birth, great wealth and great personal beauty, whose friend paints a picture of him. Dorian Gray expresses the wish that he could remain as in the picture, while the picture aged with the years. His wish is granted, and he soon knows that upon the picture, and not upon his own face, the scars of trouble and bad conduct are falling. In the end he stabs the picture and falls dead, and the picture is restored to its pristine beauty, while his friends find on the floor the body of a hideous old man. I shall be surprised if my learned friend can pitch upon any passage in that book which does more than describe as novelists and dramatists may, nay must, describe the passions and fashions of life.

'Witnesses will be called who will prove the publication of the libel, and my learned friend has the task of satisfying you that the excuses made are true. Thank you, gentlemen.'

At this point, after a brief consultation with counsel, his Lordship announced a brief adjournment and there was a general rush for the exits by newspaper columnists who wished to begin sending 'copy' by wire at the nearest telegraph office, and by those who were in search of a cup of tea or a lavatory. Jack remained where he was, relieved to have room in which to spread himself, if only for a brief while, and he occupied the five minutes or so copying, in a fair hand, the names he had jotted down during Clarke's opening address. Alfred Wood Jack already knew about, but he had not previously heard the names "Allen" and "Cliburn", and he was hoping upon hope that Carson could supply addresses for them, since he dreaded having to revisit the Taylor house in Chelsea.

Jack was still contemplating that awful possibility when the judge's return was announced and Clarke called his first witness, Sidney Wright, the hall porter at the Albemarle Club. His evidence was largely formal and was not challenged in cross-examination, its sole purpose seemingly that of proving that the allegation that Wilde was 'posing' as a 'sodomite' had been 'published' in written form, and therefore constituted a libel. Since the allegation was that Wilde was posturing as someone who would consent to homosexual activity, it amounted to an accusation of criminal behaviour on Wilde's part, and this made the charge against Queensberry one of 'criminal libel'.

There was an audible shuffle of expectation when Clarke announced that his next witness would be his client, Oscar Wilde. From one of the seats to the side of the court walked a tall, foppishly dressed, effeminate looking individual in a morning suit of deep purple and with a cravat dripping down the front of it that was a garish yellow in hue. He took the witness stand and swept the courtroom with an arrogant but watery gaze that strongly suggested that his precious time might be better employed elsewhere.

Clarke smiled reassuringly at him and invited him to introduce himself to the court.

'My full name is Oscar Fingal O'Flahertie Wills Wilde and I am the prosecutor in this case,' Wilde announced in a languid voice. 'I am thirty-nine years of age. My father was Sir William Wilde, surgeon, of Dublin, and chairman of the Census Commission. He died when I was at Oxford in 1876. I was a student at Trinity College, where I took a classical scholarship and the gold medal for Greek. I then went to Magdalen College, Oxford, where I took a classical scholarship. I took my degree in 1878 and came down at once. From that time I have devoted myself to art and literature. In 1881 I published a volume of poems, and afterwards lectured in England and America. In 1884 I married Miss Lloyd, and from that date till now have lived with her in Tite Street, Chelsea. I have two sons, the elder of whom will be ten in June and the second nine in November.'

'In 1891 did you make the acquaintance of Lord Alfred Douglas?' Clarke enquired, and Wilde nodded.

'Yes; he was brought to my house by a friend. Before then I had been acquainted with Lady Queensberry, but since then I have been a guest in her house many times. I also knew Lord Douglas of Hawick and the late Lord Drumlanrig. Lord Alfred has dined with me from time to time at my house and at the Albemarle Club, of which my wife is a member, and has stayed with us at Cromer, Goring, Worthing and Torquay. In November, 1892, I was lunching with him at the Cafe Royal, where we met Lord Queensberry, and on my suggestion Lord Alfred went up to him and shook hands. I was aware that there had been some estrangement between the two. Lord Queensberry joined us. Lord Alfred had to go away early and Lord Queensberry remained and chatted with me. Afterwards something was said about Torquay and it was arranged that Lord Queensberry should call upon me there, but he did not come. From 3rd November, 1892, till March, 1894, I did not see the defendant, but in 1893 I heard that some letters which I had addressed to Lord Alfred Douglas had come into the hands of certain persons.'

'Did anyone say that he had found letters of yours?'

'Yes. A man named Wood saw me at the rooms of Mr. Alfred Taylor and told me that he had found some letters in a suit of clothes which Lord Alfred Douglas had been good enough to give him.

'Did he ask for anything?'

'I don't think he made a direct demand.'

'What happened next?'

'When he entered the room he said: "I suppose you will think very badly of me." I replied, "I hear that you have letters of mine to Lord Alfred Douglas which you certainly ought to have given back." He handed me three or four letters and said they had been stolen from him "the day before yesterday" by a man named Allen and that he (Wood) had had to employ a detective to get them back. I read the letters and said that I did not think them of any importance. He said, "I am very much afraid of staying in London, as this man and other men are threatening me. I want money to go away to America." I asked what better opening as a clerk he could have in America than in England and he replied that he was anxious to get out of London in order to escape from the man who had taken the letters from him. He made a very strong appeal to me. He said that he could find nothing to do in London. I paid him fifteen pounds. The letters remained in my hand all the time.'

'Did some man shortly afterwards come with another letter?'

'A man called and told me that the letter, a copy of which had been sent to Mr. Beerbohm Tree, was not in his possession. His name was Allen.'

'What happened at that interview?'

'I felt that this was the man who wanted money from me. I said, "I suppose you have come about my beautiful letter to Lord Alfred Douglas. If you had not been so foolish as to send a copy of it to Mr. Beerbohm Tree, I would gladly have paid you a very large sum of money for the letter, as I consider it to be a work of art." He said, "A very curious construction can be put on that letter." I said in reply, "Art is rarely intelligible to the criminal classes." He said, "A man offered me £60 for it." I said to him, "If you take my advice you will go to that man and sell my letter to him for £60. I myself have never received so large a sum for any prose work of that length; but I am glad to find that there is someone in England who considers a letter of mine worth £60." He was somewhat taken aback by my manner, perhaps, and said, "The man is out of town." I replied, "He is sure to come back," and I advised him to get the £60. He then changed his manner a little, saying that he had not a single penny, and that he had been on many occasions trying to find me. I said that I could not guarantee his cab expenses, but that I would gladly give him half-a-sovereign. He took the money and went away.'

'Was anything said about a sonnet?'

'Yes. I said, "The letter, which is a prose poem, will shortly be published in sonnet form in a delightful magazine and I will send you a copy of it".'

'Did Allen then go away?'

'Yes, and in about five minutes Cliburn came to the house. I went out to him and said, "I cannot bother any more about this matter." He produced the letter out of his pocket, saying, "Allen has asked me to give it back to you." I did not take it immediately, but asked: "Why does Allen give me back this letter?" He said, "Well, he says that you were kind to him, and that there is no use trying to rent you as you only laugh at us." I took the letter and said, "I will accept it back, and you can thank Allen from me for all the anxiety he has shown about it." I looked at the letter and saw that it was extremely soiled. I said to him, "I think it is quite unpardonable that better care was not taken of this original manuscript of mine".'

At this point, Wilde was rewarded with general laughter around the courtroom and he paused for a moment to acknowledge it with the smile of a theatrical star being handed a bouquet, before continuing, 'He said he was very sorry, but it had been in so many hands. I gave him half-a-sovereign for his trouble, and then said, "I am afraid you are leading a wonderfully wicked life." He said, "There is good and bad in every one of us." I told him he was a born philosopher, and he then left.'

'Has the letter remained in your possession ever since?'

'Yes. I produce it here today.'

'I pass to the end of 1893. Did Lord Alfred Douglas go to Cairo then?'

'Yes; in December, 1893.'

'On his return were you lunching together in the Cafe Royal when Lord Queensberry came in?'

'Yes. He shook hands and joined us, and we chatted on perfectly friendly terms about Egypt and various other subjects.'

'Shortly after that meeting did you become aware that he was making suggestions with regard to your character and behaviour?'

'Yes. Those suggestions were not contained in letters to me. At the end of June, 1894, there was an interview between Lord Queensberry and myself in my house. He called upon me, not by appointment, about four o'clock in the afternoon, accompanied by a gentleman with whom I was not acquainted. The interview took place in my library. Lord Queensberry was standing by the window. I walked over to the fireplace and he said to me, "Sit down." I said to him, "I do not allow anyone to talk like that to me in my house or anywhere else. I suppose you have come to apologise for the statement you made about my wife and myself in letters you wrote to your son. I should have the right any day I chose to prosecute you for writing such a letter." He said, "The letter was privileged, as it was written to my son." I said, "How dare you say such things to me about your son and me?" He said, "You were both kicked out of the Savoy Hotel at a moment's notice for your disgusting conduct." I said, "That is a lie." He said, "You have taken furnished rooms for him in Piccadilly." I said, "Somebody has been telling you an absurd set of lies about your son and me. I have not done anything of the kind." He said, "I hear you were thoroughly well blackmailed for a disgusting letter you wrote to my son." I said, "The letter was a beautiful letter, and I never write except for publication." Then I asked: "Lord Queensberry, do you seriously accuse your son and me of improper conduct?" He said, "I do not say that you are it, but you look it.'"

The laughter was genuine and louder than before, prompting the judge to bring down his gavel on the wooden pad, announcing, 'I shall have the court cleared if I hear the slightest disturbance again.' The courtroom fell unnaturally quiet and Wilde continued where he had left off.

'Queensbury said, "But you look it and you pose as it, which is just as bad. If I catch you and my son together again in any public restaurant I will thrash you." I said, "I do not know what the Queensberry Rules are, but the Oscar Wilde rule is to shoot at sight." I then told Lord Queensberry to leave my house. He said he would not do so. I told him that I would have him put out by the police. He said, "It is a disgusting scandal." I said, "If it be so, you are the author of the scandal, and no one else." I then went into the hall and pointed him out to my servant. I said, "This is the Marquess of Queensberry, the most infamous brute in London. You are never to allow him to enter my house again." It is not true that I was expelled from the Savoy Hotel at any time. Neither is it true that I took rooms in Piccadilly for Lord Queensberry's son.'

'When was it you heard the first statement affecting your character?'

'I had seen communications from Lord Queensberry, not to his son, but to a third party — members of his own and of his wife's families. I went to the Albemarle Club on the 28th of February and received from the porter the card which has been produced. A warrant was issued on the 1st of March.'

'It is suggested that you are responsible for the publication of the book "Dorian Gray". Was that first published in serial form?'

'It was first published in Lippincott's and afterwards in book form with some additional chapters. It was much reviewed.'

'Your attention has been called to the statements which are made in the pleadings referring to different persons and impugning your conduct with them?'

'Yes.'

'Is there any truth in any of these accusations?'

'There is no truth whatever in any one of them.'

'Thank you, Mr Wilde. Please remain where you are, unless... Your Lordship, I am mindful of the hour...'

'Yes, indeed,' his Lordship agreed. 'Mr Bailiff, please adjourn the court until two in the afternoon.'

As the general stampede for the exits began, Jack decided to hang back, rather than get knocked down the narrow staircase. He was gazing down at the rapidly emptying 'bar' area below when he became aware of a middle-aged man in a frock coat and silver cravat waving uncertainly at him. When Jack returned the wave, the man ventured a tentative question.

'Are you by any chance with Scotland Yard?'

'I am.'

'Ah, good. Mr Carson was hoping someone would be here from the Yard. He wants to see you in the robing chambers during the dinner break.'

'Where will I find them?'

'Ground floor, past the Bailiffs' Lodge, then the last door down on the left. Just head for all the noise.'

The man had certainly not been exaggerating about the wall of animated male bonhomie and cross chatter that assailed Jack's ears as the door was opened to his knock, and when he announced his business he was invited to enter. Seemingly this was the room in which all the barristers congregated when they were not in court and he found Carson in the corner by a huge table on which were several gorgonzola cheeses, a selection of spoons, several large carafes of wine and at least a dozen glasses. Carson was spooning into one of the cheeses as he spotted Jack walking hesitantly towards him. He smiled. 'Ah. Sergeant...?'

'Enright.'

'Yes, quite. I was wondering how the search for Lord Stranmillis was going.'

'Very well,' Jack assured him. 'Inspector Enright's dealing with that aspect of our joint investigation, but it looks increasingly as if your friend staged his own disappearance somewhere near that estate of his in Cheshire. In the meantime, the Inspector's left me to enquire into possible connections that Wilde might have among the wealthy and well-placed members of our society. I watched this morning's proceedings from the public gallery.'

'What did you make of Wilde himself?'

'An arrogant sod, in my opinion. He seemed more interested in his public image than in prosecuting the alleged libel against him.'

'An astute assessment. And Queensberry?'

'He gave me the impression that he was genuine, and I know how I'd feel if it were my son in Wilde's greasy clutches.'

'Quite. Well, I think that you may look forward to an interesting afternoon's entertainment. I get to begin cross-examining Wilde this afternoon, and when I've finished with him the world will see what a pompous, self-satisfied, lying balloon the man really is — and how badly he's corrupting the youth of this country.'

'Actually, I was hoping you could give me addresses for some of the witnesses you have lined up. I'm particularly interested in talking to the man Allen who was mentioned this morning, and who seemed to be behind the attempt to blackmail Wilde over those letters. He may be able to point me towards higher placed individuals.'

'What makes you think that?'

'Well, from what I could gather from what Wilde told his barrister, Allen seemed to quickly lose interest in the final letter — almost as if that wasn't what he was about. I'm speculating that he may have been sent by someone high up to warn Wilde to keep his mouth shut and moderate his behaviour in certain quarters. Wilde's story didn't quite ring true and I think that their real conversation may have been in connection with something else. Or somebody else.'

'Yes, I got that feeling too. I'll get my clerk to give you those addresses. But my main task this afternoon is to convince the jury that Wilde is a posing defiler of young men.'

Chapter Twelve

While Jack had been following the first morning of Wilde's attempt to retrieve his good name, Lucy and Esther had been insinuating their way backstage at the St James Theatre. At first Stage Manager Vernon Treston had looked askance at the two women who had been conducted to his office by the stage doorman and who claimed to have answered his request for a Wardrobe Mistress for the latest production.

'Why are there two of you?' Treston asked suspiciously as he eyed Esther up and down, to her mounting discomfort.

'I was advised that some of your costumes need running repairs,' Lucy replied in the same haughty tone. 'My sister-in-law Esther here has years of experience with needle and thread, and we're a partnership. She sews, while I organise Wardrobe.'

'I can only afford to pay one of you, and it's only five pounds a week.'

'You can give that to Esther,' Lucy replied with a queenly air, 'and she'll be doing us both a favour working for such a pittance, given her normal run of clients. As for me, I'm here to add this prestigious run to my credentials before I apply for a more permanent position in Drury Lane. But if you're not interested, just say so now, and while you're saving yourself some time, you won't be wasting any more of ours.'

That seemed to do the trick, and a few moments later Lucy was organising a provisional stock-take of costumes against an inventory that revealed the absence of a complete set of 'gentleman's morning attire, male understudy.' Several of the cast were watching her indolently as they sat around backstage on chairs that were dotted between the various racks of clothing, and Lucy looked up with a tut.

'Which of you is the male understudy, and why isn't your stage costume back on the rack with the others?'

'It disappeared when he did,' was the tired response of the tall debonair man who was examining his fingernails with disdain.

'Name?' Lucy enquired in the manner of a schoolteacher checking off a class roll.

'Mine or his?'

'Yours, then his.'

'I'm Allan Aynsworth, male lead, playing the part of Algernon Moncrieff. You may have heard of me, if you're "theatre". But I'll almost guarantee that you've never heard of Giles Holloway, the male understudy. He must have got bored waiting for me to die, or to finally succumb to the dreadful slop they serve in my digs, because he took off almost a month or so ago now, complete with the costume that he never got to wear.'

'So you have no male understudy?'

Aynsworth shook his head. 'No, and I urgently need some surgical intervention in a very delicate part of my anatomy, so it's damned annoying. And if one of us goes down with dose of something disagreeable, then Vermin Vernon will have to walk on stage and read the part from the script, which will hardly please the paying guests. So, all in all, it's a bit of a bugger.'

While Lucy was engaging the self-described leading man in conversation, Esther was examining each garment as she took it off the rack and making a mental list of those in most urgent need of some hasty repair work. She gasped in amazement at the hanging portion of a summer dress that had begun to part at the waistband and that with a decent tug would descend to the stage, revealing the rear end of whichever actress was unfortunate enough to be wearing it at the time. Knowing nothing about the play itself, but concluding from the general state of the garment that it normally spent a considerable amount of time on stage, she lifted it down and carried it to a table to the side. She brought over a chair and opened the travelling needlework case that she'd brought with her and began to repair the section of waistband that had come adrift through constant wear.

As she bent over the garment, hard at work with a preliminary running stitch, she was half aware of a young girl — little more than a teenager — lifting down another of the costumes, examining the label on the hanger, then holding it up against herself. There was a small cry of disappointment, then a hesitant silence, before the girl plucked up the courage to speak to Esther.

'Are you the new Wardrobe Mistress?'

'No, that's my sister-in-law Lucy. I just do the repairs for her.'

'How long will you be with Gwendolen's costume for Act One?'

'Is that what this is? Only a few minutes, why?'

'Well, it's just that I need you to make this costume shorter, ready for this evening's performance. Evelyn's got one of her sick headaches, and it's my big chance! But I'm going to be nervous enough as it is, and the last thing I'll need is the worry that I'll trip over the hem at some vital point in the scene.'

She saw the uncomprehending look on Esther's face and grinned self-consciously.

'Sorry. Let me start again. I'm Emily Baxter, female understudy, and my role here is to learn all the female parts in case any of the actresses goes off sick. That's what's happened to Evelyn Millard, who's cast as Cecily Cardew, one of the leading female parts. If Evelyn runs true to form, or so I'm told, she'll be out until next Monday, which gives me several evening performances and a matinee, and if I can pull it off there'll probably be more parts for me in the future, to judge by the critical acclaim for this run. It's just a pity that Giles won't be here to hold my hand in the wings before I go on.'

'Giles?'

'Giles Holloway, my fiancé, and the male understudy. At least, he was, until he took off over three weeks ago. But he's apparently undertaking an acting role for my uncle, who's financing another production in the West Country or somewhere. He's very keen on the theatre, is my uncle, and he put a lot of money into this production, along with his good friend Dermot O'Brien. They're both very good friends of Mr. Wilde's.'

'Give that costume to me,' Esther instructed Emily encouragingly, 'and let me hold it up against you and see how much the hem needs to be raised for it to fit you. I take it that Miss Millard is taller than you?'

'By two inches at least,' Emily admitted ruefully. 'They say I'm really a bit on the short side for an actress, but my uncle's very encouraging towards me in my theatrical ambitions. I think I'm his favourite niece, although he's got heaps, because he has three sisters, and they all had girls. Sorry, I'm prattling on bit, aren't I, when I really should be letting you get on?'

'Not at all. Would you be offended if I asked if your uncle insisted that you be employed as the female understudy in return for his investment in the production?'

'Not at all, and you're absolutely correct. But I intend to make it on my own ability, and Uncle Patrick was only a minor backer compared with his friend Lord Stranmillis.'

Esther's ears pricked up and she beckoned Emily to step forward while she lifted part of the hem and pinned it up as a marker for the amount of shortening required. Then she gestured for the girl to take a seat beside her as she placed the garment she'd been working on down on the side table and began to take up the hem on Emily's costume, while engaging her in seemingly casual conversation.

'I can have this ready for you in ten minutes,' she assured Emily, 'but you'll have to stay here while I do, so that I can check it against you when I've finished. Am I keeping you from anything important?'

'Believe me, nothing's as important to me right now as that dress, so I'll just sit here quietly and let you get on with it.'

'I actually prefer to natter while I work,' Esther assured her, 'so tell me more about your wonderful uncle, Patrick something or other, wasn't it?'

'Patrick Ryan, but most people who know him well call him "Paddy", on account of the fact that he's Irish. He's made an absolute fortune in various engineering enterprises, and he has this big estate in Sussex, where all we girls used to spend every summer. There were always heaps of other people around and we got into the habit of putting on a play every August — that's how I got the acting bug, and Dermot O'Brien was always there. Sometimes Oscar Wilde and one of his friends as well, and when Dermot became Lord Stranmillis and made even more money than Uncle Paddy, they decided to put money into Oscar's plays.'

'And it was your uncle — Patrick Ryan — who found some acting work for your fiancé? What was his name again?' Esther asked as casually as she was able.

'Giles. Giles Holloway. We're planning on getting married next year sometime, but Uncle Paddy wanted Giles to become more established before that happened, so he fixed up for him to go bunburying somewhere out west.'

'What on earth is "bunburying"? Is it something like blackberrying?'

'No,' Emily giggled. 'It's actually something that comes up in the play we're putting on at the moment. The main character — "Algie" — pretends to have a friend called Bunbury who urgently requires his attendance whenever he's trying to avoid some social engagement that he finds tiresome. And the other main character, Jack Worthing, pretends to be two different people in two different places. So "bunburying" has become a popular expression around here for pretending to be somebody else, although the actual "Bunbury" character is fictitious and never appears on stage or anything.'

'So your fiancé's off somewhere pretending to be someone else?'

'I think so. To be perfectly honest, Giles and Uncle Paddy were pretty secretive about the entire business, but Giles was assured that he'd be well paid and that he'd be offered lots more theatrical roles in future. So I assume that he's gone on stage in some production or other that Uncle Paddy's financing. My only concern is that he hasn't been in touch to tell me how it's all going. No letters, or anything. That's not like Giles.'

'Never mind,' Esther replied reassuringly, 'I have a husband who's guilty of not telling me what he's up to and we actually live in the same house.'

Esther had a great deal to tell Uncle Percy when — and always assuming if — he got back from his explorations along the railway line to Holyhead.

Percy had in fact got no further than Crewe at that point. He'd wired ahead regarding the nature of his enquiries and when he was ushered with due ceremony into the office of Solomon Johnson, Northern Regional Superintendent of the LNWR, there was another nervous looking man seated in the other visitor's chair.

'Do come in, Inspector,' Johnson said invitingly. 'I was able to arrange for the attendance of Harry Prentice here, who was the duty guard between Rugby and Crewe on the train in question. A strange business altogether, you'd agree, but all seemed to be in order when the express left Crewe on its final leg.'

Percy shook hands with Harry Prentice and made a mental note of the clammy coolness, usually a sign of apprehension. Apprehension over *what* precisely would remain to be seen.

'Mr Prentice is based here in Crewe,' Johnson explained, 'and will normally work the route from here back to Rugby, and vice versa. He was the guard when the Holyhead express pulled into Crewe that night and would have gone off duty immediately after handing the train over to the Holyhead guard, a Mr Joe Hughes.'

Wondering whether or not Mr Prentice would be allowed to speak for himself, Percy turned to him and smiled. 'Which of you would have waved the train off after the engine had been changed?'

'That were me,' Prentice replied.

'And what was the rearmost carriage on the train when it pulled away from the platform that evening?'

'That there Pullman what went missin' somewhere down the line,' Prentice recalled.

'No doubt in your mind about that?' Percy prompted him.

Prentice shook his head. 'None whatsoever.'

'How was it attached to the rest of the train, exactly?'

'Just the normal hook and chain coupling, along with the screw coupling to tighten the buffers.'

'So if the Pullman were to be removed from the rear of the train, it was just a simple matter of unhooking a chain?'

Prentice shrugged. 'Yer make it sound easy, but there's a special long pole what yer needs ter use ter unhook the chain. There's always one in the guard's van, but otherwise yer'd need ter bring yer own. Yer'd also need to disconnect the brake pipe to the luggage van, along with the steam-heating pipe what's in use this time o' the year, but it's not difficult for someone who knows what they're doing. But the train'd be travellin' at over fifty miles an hour once it got movin', and there's no stops between 'ere an' 'Olyhead, not fer that train anyroad.'

'Presumably the train could be halted by a signal?' Percy probed. 'The train I came up from Euston on this morning stopped several times for unfavourable signals.'

'Oh yeah, o'course,' Prentice confirmed. 'If there's some sorta blockage on the line, like a dead cow or summat, then the signalman responsible fer that section'd drop the signal, an' the driver'd be obliged ter stop the train.'

'At which time the Pullman could simply be unhooked and left standing when the signal was raised for the train to move on?'

'Yeah, s'pose, but they'd 'ave ter take the rear lamp off it an' put it on the back o' the luggage van, otherwise the bloke in the next signal box they went past'd stop the train again. Regulations, them is.'

Percy turned to address Johnson. 'Do you happen to know of any unscheduled stoppages of that particular train that evening?'

Johnson thought for a moment. 'Any unscheduled stop would have to be noted by the guard in his log. The location, and the time taken. From memory the train reached Holyhead about fifteen minutes late, although it was ten minutes late leaving here that evening, due to delays in Rugby.'

'Yes, I know about those,' Percy confirmed, 'but even if we assume that the train was halted for long enough for the Pullman to be removed and left on the line, that wouldn't have taken more than another ten minutes, surely? And a conscientious driver could make up the time on the long haul to Holyhead, could he not, if there were no more delays?'

'Yes, of course. If you wait for just a moment, I'll get the guard's report for the Holyhead leg brought up here.'

As he walked to his office door and shouted an instruction down the stairs, Percy wondered why the man hadn't taken the trouble to have it available for his arrival. Suppressing his annoyance, he turned back to Prentice.

'Do you recall anyone leaving the Pullman during the time that the train was standing at the platform?'

'Just a woman — a low sort, at a guess.'

'Why do you say that?'

'Well, the way she were dressed, for one thing. Kinda rough lookin', wi' a bonnet an' shawl. An' she were carryin' a bag, like she were a traveller o' some sort. Fair enough, it were a cold night, but even so — only *them* sort dresses like that fer a train journey. An' I knew there were a man in the carriage, 'cos I saw 'im go scuttlin' back ter the carriage at Rugby, after 'e 'eld the train back fer some reason. That's why we was late gerrin' in 'ere that evenin'.'

'Did you see the man leave the Pullman carriage again?'

'No, but I coulda missed 'im, on account o' the fact that I were 'andin' the train over ter Joe Hughes. There's a bit o' paperwork involved, an' I were in the guards van wi' 'im while the train were stationary at the platform.'

'So the man could have got out of the Pullman — let's say to use the Buffet — and got back in again without you noticing?'

'Yeah, o'course, but I didn't see owt like that.'

Johnson was back in the chair behind his desk, and Percy's next question was directed to him. 'You presumably have a "Ladies Waiting Room" on the platform that the Holyhead train was stationary at?'

'We have them on both main line platforms,' Johnson assured him, 'plus the General Waiting Room, that women of the lower sort often use, if I may anticipate your next question.'

'So it would be nothing unusual were a woman to enter the General Waiting Room?'

'Not at all.'

'And it has lavatories?'

'Indeed — that's in the main what people use it for.'

'So follow me through this possibility. A man enters the General Waiting Room, disguised as a woman, changes into men's clothing that he's carried in with him, transfers the woman's clothing into the bag, then walks out again dressed as a man and takes a seat in one of the main carriages, probably a First Class one.'

'It's possible,' Johnson conceded, 'although a bit far-fetched, if you don't mind me saying so. Excuse me a moment.'

That last remark had been prompted by a knock on the office door. Johnson went to the door, took the paper he was handed, read it briefly, and walked back to his desk with raised eyebrows.

'It seems that you were right, Inspector,' he smiled. 'The train arrived at Holyhead twelve minutes late and the guard — Joseph Hughes — reported a signal delay not far west of here.'

'Beeston?' Percy said with a smirk.

'How did you guess?'

'I didn't — I was relying on previous enquiries I've been making. Now tell me — where exactly was the train halted, and how close was it to the old branch line to the salt workings?'

'Come and look at this large scale map on the wall,' Johnson invited him.

Percy stood up and walked to the wall, where Johnson pointed with a ruler.

'See there?' he indicated. 'East of Beeston, in the Crewe direction, there's a signal box. The reason for its existence, historically, is the adjacent level crossing, with the gates controlled from the signal box, and the nearby salt workings to which you referred. There's a branch line down to the old workings off the down line — that's the line going west towards Holyhead — and the signal box — "Beeston Main", we call it — controls the signals and points where the old salt sidings join the main line. In the old days they'd be hauling salt out of there to their sidings, just off the main line, but to the side of it. Then the salt wagons could be hauled from the sidings onto the main line during quiet periods and pulled into Chester by one of our goods engines. That was in the old days, of course, but the signal box is still there, since it commands a five mile stretch of line.'

'Is the junction of the main line with the branch line still in working order, and do trains still occasionally use it?' Percy asked.

Johnson thought for a moment. 'Yes. It was closed for a while but has recently come back into use. The signalman at

Beeston Main could give you more details. That box is manned twenty-four hours a day, so whatever time you go there'd be someone there to advise you.'

'Again, thinking out loud,' Percy said, 'if the train were halted at the signal, it might be possible to unhitch the Pullman car and tow it onto the branch line?'

'In theory, yes,' Johnson admitted. 'Provided the man doing so was an experienced shunter, as Harry Prentice has already explained. And as regards the unscheduled stop at Beeston, I suggest you talk to the duty signalman there, since he'll have all the details recorded in his Train Register Book.'

'That's precisely what I intend to do,' Percy announced, 'and thank you for your invaluable assistance this morning. Since I believe I'll be occupied this afternoon, and will require overnight accommodation, may I take it that you have a suitable hotel near to the station?'

'Indeed we do,' Johnson replied with a smile, 'The Crewe Arms, just across the road, and it offers the last word in comfort. I'll arrange a room for you, and please accept our hospitality free of charge. We're only too happy to accommodate an officer from Scotland Yard.'

'Let's hope you still are when you learn of my capacity for food and drink,' Percy replied, grinning.

Chapter Thirteen

Jack made sure that he was back in the public gallery early enough after the dinner break to get a seat near the front, and far away from his malodorous companions of the morning session. He was hoping that he wouldn't nod off from sheer boredom as he recalled what Carson had advised him regarding his tactics for cross-examining Wilde. As far as Jack remembered what he had been told, Carson would begin by attacking Wilde's pretence at being an artistic man of culture — an 'aesthete', as Robbie Ross had termed it.

The judge was escorted back onto the bench and Wilde resumed his position in the witness box, a look of arrogant defiance fixed on the counsel ranged down the bar table. Carson rose to his full six feet two in height, squared his jaw and began.

'You stated that your age was thirty-nine. But I believe you are over forty. You were born on 16th October 1854, were you not?'

'I have no wish to pose as being young.' Wilde smiled back confidently. 'I am thirty-nine. You have my certificate and that settles the matter.'

'But being born in 1854 makes you more than forty?'

'Very well.'

'What age is Lord Alfred Douglas?'

'Lord Alfred Douglas is about twenty-four, and was between twenty and twenty-one years of age when I first knew him.'

'You have stayed with him at many places?'

'Yes.'

'At Oxford? Brighton on several occasions? Worthing?'

'Yes.'

'And in various hotels in London?'

'Yes; at one in Albemarle Street, and in Dover Street, and at the Savoy.'

'Did you ever take rooms yourself in addition to your house in Tite Street?'

'Yes; at 10 and 11 St. James's Place. I kept the rooms from the month of October, 1893, to the end of March, 1894. Lord Alfred Douglas has stayed in those chambers, which are not far from Piccadilly. I have been abroad with him several times and even lately to Monte Carlo.'

'This is in your introduction to Dorian Gray,' Carson announced in a sudden change of tack, as he began to quote from it: '"There is no such thing as a moral or an immoral book. Books are well written, or badly written." That expresses your view?'

'My view on art, yes.'

'Then, I take it, that no matter how immoral a book may be, if it is well written, it is, in your opinion, a good book?'

'Yes, if it were well written so as to produce a sense of beauty, which is the highest sense of which a human being can be capable. If it were badly written, it would produce a sense of disgust.'

'Then a well-written book putting forward perverted moral views may be a good book?'

'No work of art ever puts forward views. Views belong to people who are not artists.'

'A perverted novel might be a good book?'

'I don't know what you mean by a "perverted" novel.'

'Then I will suggest Dorian Gray as open to the interpretation of being such a novel?'

'That could only be to brutes and illiterates. The views of Philistines on art are incalculably stupid.'

'An illiterate person reading Dorian Gray might consider it such a novel?'

'The views of illiterates on art are unaccountable. I am concerned only with my view of art. I don't care two-pence what other people think of it.'

'The majority of persons would come under your definition of Philistines and illiterates?'

'I have found wonderful exceptions.'

'Do you think that the majority of people live up to the position you are giving us?'

'I am afraid they are not cultivated enough.'

'Not cultivated enough to draw the distinction between a good book and a bad book?'

'Certainly not.'

'The affection and love of the artist of Dorian Gray might lead an ordinary individual to believe that it might have a certain tendency?'

'I have no knowledge of the views of ordinary individuals.'

'You did not prevent the ordinary individual from buying your book?'

'I have never discouraged him.'

'Allow me to share a passage with you,' Carson said with heavy sarcasm as he opened his copy of it at a marked page, and for the benefit of the jury announced that it was the scene in which the painter Basil Hallward describes to Lord Henry Wooton his first meeting with Dorian Gray. '"…after I had been in the room about ten minutes, talking to huge overdressed dowagers and tedious Academicians, I suddenly became conscious that someone was looking at me. I turned half-way round, and saw Dorian Gray for the first time. When our eyes met, I felt that I was growing pale. A curious instinct of terror came over me. I knew that I had come face to face with someone whose mere personality was so fascinating that, if I allowed it to do so, it would absorb my whole nature, my whole soul, my very art itself. I did not want any external influence in my life... Something seemed to tell me that I was on the verge of a terrible crisis in my life. I had a strange feeling that Fate had in store for me exquisite joys and exquisite sorrows. I knew that if I spoke to Dorian I would become absolutely devoted to him, and that I ought not to speak to him. I grew afraid, and turned to quit the room... Suddenly I found myself face to face with the young man whose personality had so strangely stirred me. We were quite close, almost touching. Our eyes met again. It was mad of me, but I asked Lady Brandon to introduce me to him. Perhaps it was not so mad, after all. It was simply inevitable. We would have spoken to each other without introduction. I am sure of that. Dorian told me so afterwards. He, too, felt that we were destined to know each other... The merely visible presence of this lad — for he seems to me little more than a lad, though he is really over twenty — his merely visible presence — ah! I wonder can you realize all that that means? Unconsciously he defines for me the lines of a fresh school, a school that is to have in itself all the passion of the romantic spirit, all the perfection of the spirit that is Greek. The harmony of soul and body — how much that is! We in our madness have separated the two, and have invented a realism that is bestial, an ideality that is void. Harry! Harry! if you only knew what Dorian Gray is to me! You remember that landscape of mine, for which Agnew offered me such a huge price, but which I would not part with? It is one of the best things I have ever done. And why is it so? Because, while I was painting it, Dorian Gray sat beside me".

'Now I ask you, Mr. Wilde,' Carson demanded in a stern voice, 'do you consider that that description of the feeling of one man towards a youth just grown up was a proper or an improper feeling?'

'I think it is the most perfect description of what an artist would feel on meeting a beautiful personality that was in some way necessary to his art and life.'

'You think that is a feeling a young man should have towards another?'

'Yes, as an artist.'

Carson glared at him disbelievingly, then stuck out his chin aggressively as he enquired, 'How about this extract, then, Mr Wilde?' and continued reading from the book: '"It is quite true that I have worshipped you with far more romance of feeling than a man usually gives to a friend. Somehow, I have never loved a woman. I suppose I never had time. Perhaps, as Harry says, a really 'grande passion' is the privilege of those who have nothing to do, and that is the use of the idle classes in a country. Well, from the moment I met you, your personality had the most extraordinary influence over me. I quite admit that I adored you madly, extravagantly, absurdly. I was jealous of every one to whom you spoke. I wanted to have you all to myself. I was only happy when I was with you. When I was away from you, you were still present in my art. It was all wrong and foolish. It is all wrong and foolish still. Of course, I never let you know anything about this. It would have been impossible. You would not have understood it; I did not understand it myself. One day I determined to paint a wonderful portrait of you. It was to have been my masterpiece. It is my masterpiece. But, as I worked at it, every flake and film of colour seemed to me to reveal my secret. I grew afraid that the world would know of my idolatry. I felt, Dorian, that I had told too much... You must not be angry with me, Dorian, for what I have told you. As I said to Harry, once, you are made to be worshipped".

'Do you mean to say that that passage describes the natural feeling of one man towards another?' Carson demanded.

'It would be the influence produced by a beautiful personality.'

'A beautiful person?'

'I said a "beautiful personality." You can describe it as you like. Dorian Gray's was a most remarkable personality.'

'May I take it that you, as an artist, have never known the feeling described here?'

'I have never allowed any personality to dominate my art.'

'Then you have never known the feeling you described?'

'No. It is a work of fiction.'

'So far as you are concerned you have no experience as to its being a natural feeling?'

'I think it is perfectly natural for any artist to admire intensely and love a young man. It is an incident in the life of almost every artist.'

'But let us go over it phrase by phrase. "I quite admit that I adored you madly." What do you say to that? Have you ever adored a young man madly?'

'No, not madly; I prefer love — that is a higher form.'

'Never mind about that. Let us keep down to the level we are at now?'

'I have never given adoration to anybody except myself.'

The loud laughter that followed this outrageous posture resulted in the swift application of the judicial gavel. Carson allowed himself a wry smile as he continued the interrogation. 'I suppose you think that a very smart thing?'

'Not at all.'

'Then you have never had that feeling?'

'No. The whole idea was borrowed from Shakespeare, I regret to say.'

'"I have adored you extravagantly"? — Do you mean financially?'

'Oh, yes, financially!' Wilde retorted sarcastically.

Carson frowned. 'Do you think we are talking about finance?'

'I don't know *what* you are talking about.'

'Don't you? Well, I hope I shall make myself very plain before I have done. "I was jealous of every one to whom you spoke." Have you ever been jealous of a young man?'

'Never in my life.'

'"I wanted to have you all to myself." Did you ever have that feeling?'

'No; I should consider it an intense nuisance, an intense bore.'

'"I grew afraid that the world would know of my idolatry." Why should he grow afraid that the world should know of it?'

'Because there are people in the world who cannot understand the intense devotion, affection, and admiration that an artist can feel for a wonderful and beautiful personality. These are the conditions under which we live. I regret them.'

'These unfortunate people, that have not the high understanding that you have, might put it down to something wrong?'

'Undoubtedly; to any point they chose. I am not concerned with the ignorance of others...'

Carson continued reading from *The Picture of Dorian Gray*: "'Sin is a thing that writes itself across a man's face. It cannot be concealed. People talk of secret vices. There are no such things as secret vices. If a wretched man has a vice, it shows itself in the lines of his mouth, the droop of his eyelids, the moulding of his hands even... But you, Dorian, with your pure, bright, innocent face, and your marvellous untroubled youth — I can't believe anything against you. And yet I see you very seldom, and you never come down to the studio now, and when I am away from you, and I hear all these hideous things that people are whispering about you, I don't know what to say. Why is it, Dorian, that a man like the Duke of Berwick leaves the room of a club when you enter it? Why is it that so many gentlemen in London will neither go to your house nor invite you to theirs? Why is your friendship so fateful to young men? There was that wretched boy in the Guards who committed suicide. You were his great friend. There was Sir Henry Ashton, who had to leave England with a tarnished name. You and he were inseparable. What about Adrian Singleton, and his dreadful end? What about Lord Kent's only son, and his career? I met his father yesterday in St. James Street. He seemed broken with shame and sorrow. What about the young Duke of Perth? What sort of life has he got now? What gentleman would associate with him? Dorian, Dorian, your reputation is infamous...'" Does not this passage suggest a charge of unnatural vice?' Carson demanded.

Wilde shook his head. 'It describes Dorian Gray as a man of very corrupt influence, though there is no statement as to the nature of the influence. But as a matter of fact I do not think that one person influences another, nor do I think there is any bad influence in the world.'

'A man never corrupts a youth?'

'I think not.'

'Nothing could corrupt him?'

'If you are talking of separate ages.'

'No, sir,' Carson bellowed, 'I am talking common sense!'

'I do not think one person influences another.'

'You don't think that flattering a young man, making love to him, in fact, would be likely to corrupt him?'

'No.'

Carson allowed a look of sheer disbelief to cross his face, which he shared with the jury as he paused for dramatic effect, then continued, 'Where was Lord Alfred Douglas staying when you wrote that letter to him?'

'At the Savoy; and I was at Babbacombe, near Torquay.'

'It was a letter in answer to something he had sent you?'

'Yes, a poem.'

'Why should a man of your age address a boy nearly twenty years younger as "My own boy"?'

'I was fond of him. I have always been fond of him.'

'Do you adore him?'

'No, but I have always liked him. I think it is a beautiful letter. It is a poem. I was not writing an ordinary letter. You might as well cross-examine me as to whether King Lear or a sonnet of Shakespeare was proper.'

'Apart from art, Mr. Wilde?'

'I cannot answer apart from art.'

'Suppose a man who was not an artist had written this letter, would you say it was a proper letter?'

'A man who was not an artist could not have written that letter.'

'Why?'

'Because nobody but an artist could write it. He certainly could not write the language unless he were a man of letters.'

'I can suggest, for the sake of your reputation, that there is nothing very wonderful in this "red rose-leaf lips of yours"?'

'A great deal depends on the way it is read.'

'"Your slim gilt soul walks between passion and poetry." Is that a beautiful phrase?'

'Not as you read it, Mr. Carson. You read it very badly.'

'I do not profess to be an artist; and when I hear you give evidence, I am glad I am not.'

Sir Edward Clarke rose abruptly from his seat, red in the face, and addressed the judge. 'I don't think my friend should talk like that.' He turned to face his client and advised him, 'Pray, do not criticize my friend's reading again.'

'Is that not an exceptional letter?' Carson persevered.

Wilde nodded with a self-satisfied smile. 'It is unique, I should say.'

'Was that the ordinary way in which you carried on your correspondence?'

'No; but I have often written to Lord Alfred Douglas, though I never wrote to another young man in the same way.'

'Have you often written letters in the same style as this?'

'I don't repeat myself in style.'

'Here is another letter which I believe you also wrote to Lord Alfred Douglas,' Carson announced with a smile of triumph as he waved the document in the air. 'Will you read it?'

'No; I decline. I don't see why I should.'

'Then I will.' Carson announced, and proceeded to do so. *Dearest of all Boys, Your letter was delightful, red and yellow wine to me; but I am sad and out of sorts. Bosie, you must not make scenes with me. They kill me, they wreck the loveliness of life. I cannot see you, so Greek and gracious, distorted with passion. I cannot listen to your curved lips saying hideous things to me. I would sooner — than have you bitter, unjust, hating... I must see you soon. You are the divine thing I want, the*

thing of grace and beauty; but I don't know how to do it. Shall I come to Salisbury? My bill here, is £49 for a week. I have also got a new sitting-room... Why are you not here, my dear, my wonderful boy? I fear I must leave-no money, no credit, and a heart of lead. YOUR OWN OSCAR."

'Is that an ordinary letter?' Carson demanded.

Wilde pouted. 'Everything I write is extraordinary. Ask me any question you like about it.'

'Is it the kind of letter a man writes to another?'

'It was a tender expression of my great admiration for Lord Alfred Douglas. It was not, like the other, a prose poem.'

Carson stood staring fixedly at Wilde for a long moment, then shook his head sadly as he made a point of transferring his gaze to the clock on the wall, then turning towards the Bench with raised eyebrows.

'Ten o'clock in the forenoon,' Mr Justice Collins announced, and everyone breathed a sigh of relief.

Chapter Fourteen

Percy slipped the cabman five pounds and instructed him to await his return. Glad of the high collar on his overcoat, which he turned up against the strong Spring westerly that was howling around his ears, he walked up to the level crossing, then turned left down the cinder path alongside the double rail track, towards the signal box located by the side of the line that led back towards Crewe.

He climbed the steps to the box and knocked on the glass panel set into the upper half of the door. A red-faced man in his fifties, dressed in a blue serge uniform, turned when he heard the knock and beckoned for Percy to enter. As he did so, the heat from the coal-fired stove in the near corner of the box hit him like a hot flannel and he lowered his coat collar before reaching inside his jacket pocket and producing his police badge.

'Detective Inspector Enright, Scotland Yard. And you are?'

'Surprised that I've done owt bad enough ter attract the Yard.' The man grinned as he threw down the rag which he'd been using while pulling down a set of levers set into the frame in front of the windows that overlooked the lines. He indicated for Percy to take one of the two available chairs and continued to look out of a set of side windows to his left while conducting the conversation that followed. 'What can I do fer yer? Pardon the back o' me 'ead, only I'm expectin' the two forty-seven ter Llandudno any minute now on the "down" line. That's the one furthest away from us.'

'Could we start with your name?' Percy said. 'Clearly your occupation is that of signalman?'

'That's me. Ted 'Olmes, Leading Signalman these five years past. I'm responsible fer this section o' line what runs from a few miles back terwards Calverley, then onter Crewe down ter the left there an' terwards Tattenhall Box an' Chester ter the right.'

'Does your section of line include the sidings that serve the salt workings?'

'It does now,' Holmes replied as he continued squinting into the distance off to the left of the box. 'That's outta sight along the "down" side there,' he added as he continued squinting to his left. 'The "up" trains go in the direction o' London an' the "down" come *from* London. Like that express what's about ter come past — she's just cleared them sidin's yer was talkin' about. Can yer see 'er?'

'Only just,' Percy admitted. 'My eyes aren't what they used to be.'

'Well yer'll see 'er soon enough,' Holmes assured him. 'It's just a blob in the distance right now, but give it 'alf a minute an' she'll be rattlin' the winders in 'ere on 'er way ter Chester.'

'There seems to be a curve in the line back towards Crewe,' Percy observed as he narrowed his eyes to focus on the rapidly approaching train.

'That's right,' Holmes confirmed. 'That's where me "Home Signal" is, just past where the bend starts. Then beyond that, well round the bend, yer'll find me "Distant Signal". Now 'ang on just a moment.' His final words were all but drowned out by the rush and roar of the approaching express, which rattled and hissed past the box in a cloud of steam and with a "toot" of warning from its whistle as it sped over the level crossing at over fifty miles an hour. Holmes watched it disappear to their right, then pushed three levers forward into the frame before reaching up to a shelf above it and tapping twice on a small button set into a polished wooden box. 'That'll sound two bells in the Tattenhall Box, ter tell Bert Bellamy that she's enterin' 'is section,' he explained as he moved to a tall desk under a wall clock and made some sort of entry into a register lying on its sloping top. 'She's five minutes ahead o' time, so that'll please 'em at Chester. Nah, yer was askin' about the salt sidin's, wasn't yer?'

'Yes,' Percy confirmed. 'First of all, am I right in believing, from what you said a moment ago, that you can't actually see the sidings in question from this box?'

'Hardly, on account o' the curve in the line down the end o' that straight section that yer can see out there.'

'So how can trains leave the sidings, and what I'm told is the branch line down to the salt mines, without any risk of them causing a hazard for trains using the main line?'

'That's what me "Home Signal's for,' Holmes replied with a satisfied smile. When Percy looked blank, the signalman was more than happy to reveal the extent of his specialised knowledge. 'The "Home Signal" is the one just the other side o' them sidin's, an' it can be placed in "danger" settin', or just "on", as we calls it. When that 'appens, any train on the main line 'as ter stop afore it actually reaches the signal. That's company regulations. Then the engine an' wagons from the sidin's can move safely onter the "down" main line, an' 'ead straight terwards Chester. If they needs ter go the other way, towards Crewe, we can cross 'em over ter the "up" line, usin' another set o' points which connects the "up" an' "down" lines. They're controlled by levers 'ere in this box.'

'But presumably it'll be slow moving, like most goods trains?' Percy queried. 'Won't that cause delays for any passenger train that's held up by the signal?'

'Bloody right, which is why the company insists that there's no movement outa them sidin's durin' certain hours when the expresses is due through. Nor the local passenger services neither. But around this time o' day — early afternoon — it's pretty quiet, so that's when they can move stuff outta the sidin's. That Llandudno express were the last past 'ere in either direction until around four o'clock, so this is normally when I 'as me snap. I can toast bread on the fire — would yer like some?'

'No, thanks all the same,' Percy assured him with a smile, remembering the two bowls of lamb stew he'd had for dinner in his hotel, 'but don't let me stop you. We can talk as you make your toast.'

'What's this all about then?' Holmes said, as he impaled a thick slice of bread onto the end of a toasting fork, opened the fire door and held it out to toast.

'I'm investigating the possibility that a passenger carriage was hauled into those sidings one evening a few weeks ago.'

'I don't see 'ow that coulda 'appened wi'out us knowin' about it. Anyway, can't yer just go an' look forrit down there?'

'That's my next port of call,' Percy explained, 'but before I go down there I need to be fully informed of how the signals and branch line system work.'

'Then yer've come ter the right bloke,' Holmes beamed proudly. 'If they wanna pull owt in or outta them sidin's, they 'as to come ter me for the Annetts Key.'

'The what?'

'The Annetts Key. That's it down there.'

He pointed down to the end of the line of levers that Percy had seen him working a few moments earlier, and which presumably controlled the signals. Locked into its base was a curious looking metal device, approximately six inches long, with a handle reminiscent of a garden spade, but most of which consisted of a complex looking key barrel.

'That's the Annetts Key,' Holmes explained. 'When they wants ter move summat outta the sidin's, they sends a bloke up 'ere fer the key. When it's pulled outta that socket, it locks all me signal levers, so I can't let a train approach on the main line. Then the bloke goes back ter the sidin's junction and puts the key in a slot in what's called the "ground frame". That unlocks the levers, so that the points can be switched ter the sidin'. O' course, me 'ome signal's already set ter stop any train what's approachin' on the main line, along wi' the distant signal. Like I said, once that key's taken out've its socket in 'ere, it freezes all me signals.'

'Presumably someone from the salt works brings the key back when they've finished with it, and the goods train has moved off?'

'Yeah, o' course, 'cos all the system's frozen while that key's outta that lock down there on the floor.'

'And there's only the one key?' Percy asked, earning a look of mixed disbelief and sympathy from the man who'd been working the system for a long time.

'What der *you* think? If there was more than one, it'd be chaos, an' likely ter cause a dreadful accident.'

'Yes, quite. You mentioned that most of the movements out of the sidings occur mid-afternoon. Do you ever have any at night, when I assume that there are less trains on the main line?'

'None at night, ter the best o' me knowledge. O' course, them's only started back workin' that mine agin fer the past year or so, an' I 'ear as 'ow it's flooded, an' them's pumpin' it dry. So at the moment we only get two or three movements a week from them sidin's, and always in the afternoons, like I said. They doesn't work nights down there anyway.'

'You presumably work shifts in this box?'

Holmes nodded. 'Yeah, twelve hours at a time, "nights" and "days", six 'til six. We changes every month.'

'So — a month of nights, followed by a month of days?'

'Yes.'

'So, last month you would have been on night duty, is that right?'

'Yeah, an' Fred Butterworth woulda bin on the day shift.'

'Forgive me if this sounds like another silly question, but do you recall anyone making use of the Annetts Key during your night shifts last month?'

'Definitely not. Like I said, they don't work them sidin's at night.'

'Thank you very much, Mr Holmes, you've been a great help. Just one final question, if I may. Assuming for the moment that your Annetts Key remained where it is, so that your system wasn't locked, is there any other way of moving the points at the junction with the salt works sidings?'

'None that I can think of. Yer needs the Annetts Key ter work the ground frame, an' the key can't be in two places at once, can it?'

'But what if someone *did* manage to interfere with the points in some way?' Percy persisted, to which Holmes responded with a horrified stare.

'It could lead ter a mighty disaster, if a train were comin' on the down line. But so long as I 'as the Annetts Key in 'ere, it can't 'appen, can it, 'cos I can work all me signals.'

'So any train on that line would just keep coming?'

'Yeah.'

'And the remainder of your signals would be freed up for you to use in the normal way?'

'Yeah.'

Percy nodded. 'I think I've got the hang of it now, thank you very much. I'll leave you to your toast.'

''Ere, take this,' Holmes invited him as he reached inside a drawer in the desk. 'It's the gubbins on 'ow the Annetts Key works. I don't need it no more, an' yer can call back an' return it when yer've done wi' it.'

'Many thanks.' Percy smiled as he took the thin instruction booklet and opened the signal box door, exposing himself to another blast of cold air. He walked back down the cinder track towards his waiting coach deep in thought. The next step in his investigation was obviously a trip to the salt workings. But it was already mid afternoon, and hopefully the wind would have dropped by tomorrow. Time for a few pints and something to warm his stomach back at his hotel.

'Any of that brandy left?' Jack asked grumpily as he threw his overcoat down on the kitchen chair.

'It's for medicinal purposes only,' Esther reminded him, 'but I can fix you a very strong cup of tea, if that helps. There's some ginger cake left as well. Bad day?'

'You could say that,' Jack muttered as he kissed her absentmindedly on the cheek. 'How are the children?'

'Same as usual, according to Alice. She thinks that Miriam may be cutting her first tooth, which explains why she seems to be permanently dribbling. And apparently Alice's run out of games to keep Lily amused, so we need to think about enrolling her in a local school.'

'Doesn't that cost money?'

'Only a few pence a week, and apparently it's the law that we have to send her once she reaches five. There's a school only two streets away, and she could start in September.'

'I'm not sure I want our oldest daughter exposed to all that local riff-raff.'

'You obviously didn't enjoy getting out of bed early this morning,' Esther commented as she poured his tea. 'I'd better give you some extra sugar, to sweeten you up again.'

'It wasn't just that,' Jack explained. 'It was also having to sit through all this drivel about art, the meaning of words, poetry and suchlike.'

'Nothing about sodomy?'

'Not yet. I can only hope that it livens up tomorrow, or that either Carson or Wilde dies overnight.'

'That bad?'

'Really — that bad. But how was your day with Lucy?'

'I think we know who impersonated Stranmillis on that train!' Esther announced proudly.

Jack's eyebrows shot up. 'Really? Who?'

'Someone who has hopes of becoming an actor, and who was persuaded to take off with a fine suit of clothes from the theatre.'

'Won't they miss him?'

'He's the understudy, apparently. Name of Giles Holloway, and the fiancé of the girl who's the female understudy. She also obligingly disclosed that she's Patrick Ryan's niece, that he and Lord Stranmillis are the financial backers for Wilde's current play, and that they're both good friends of his. How about *that*, then?'

'Percy's right — you *do* make a marvellous detective. But that's because you're able to sit back and view things from a distance. Percy and I have to do all the leg work. And tomorrow I have to go back and listen to that boring court case.'

'Didn't you learn anything useful?'

'Apart from the fact that I'm glad Mother didn't talk me into becoming a lawyer, you mean? Not really, except that I've got another name to follow up on. A man called Allen, who tried to get money from Wilde for an indiscreet letter he'd written to his boyfriend Bosie, but then seemed to lose all interest in it, according to what Wilde said in court. I'm wondering if in fact there *was* a meeting between Wilde and Allen, but that it had nothing to do with any letter. And now that you tell me that Wilde was beholden to Ryan and Stranmillis, and in fact mixed with them socially, it's beginning to form a pattern. Quite where it all leads I've no idea, but when this actor chap gets back to the theatre, we'll obviously have to haul him in and ask who hired him to pretend to be Stranmillis.'

'According to this girl Emily Baxter it was her uncle, Patrick Ryan. From memory, wasn't he a friend of Stranmillis's from their university days?'

'Yes, and possibly a business rival,' Jack reminded her. 'But we have to ask ourselves whether Ryan was assisting his friend Stranmillis to disappear — and if so, why? — or whether there was something more sinister involved.'

'Like what?'

'I don't know, not at this stage. We'll have to wait and see what Uncle Percy can add when he gets back from Crewe. In the meantime, it's another excruciatingly dull day in court for me tomorrow. Are you going back to the theatre tomorrow?'

'Of course. I still have some work left to do, and instinct tells me that I need to keep close with Emily Baxter — the young woman I mentioned.'

Chapter Fifteen

Jack resumed his seat on the public benches with a sinking heart, but a determination to see the case through, as Justice Collins swept onto the Bench and nodded to Carson.

'I take it that you're in a position to resume your cross-examination, counsel?'

'If it please your Lordship.'

Wilde walked back to the witness box with a facial expression of studied boredom and smiled up at the public gallery, as if taking a curtain call at his theatre. Then he squared his jaw as Carson rose and began where he'd left off the previous afternoon.

'We'll move, if we may, Mr Wilde, to your relationship with Alfred Douglas, at the time when you wrote that letter we were discussing yesterday. Were you living at the Savoy at that time?'

'Yes, I was there for about a month, and had also my house in Tite Street. Lord Alfred had been staying with me at the Savoy immediately before I wrote that letter.'

'How long had you known Wood?'

'I think I met him at the end of January, 1893 at the Cafe Royal where he was sent to find me by Lord Alfred Douglas who telegraphed from Salisbury. Lord Alfred asked me to do what I could for Wood, who was seeking a post as a clerk. I do not know where he was living at that time. Taylor was living at 13 Little College Street, and I have been there to tea parties on many occasions. They were all men at the parties, but not all young men. I took Wood to supper at the Florence Restaurant in Rupert Street, because Lord Alfred had asked me to be kind to him.'

'Who was Wood?'

'So far as I could make out he had no occupation, but was looking for a situation. He told me he had had a clerkship. At that time he was about twenty-three years of age.'

'Then do I understand that the first time you met Wood you took him to supper?'

'Yes, because I had been asked to be kind to him. Otherwise it was rather a bore.'

'Was Taylor or anybody else there?'

'No.'

Carson adopted his fiercest expression as he fired a direct series of questions at Wilde, demanding to know whether or not he had been guilty of gross indecencies with Wood, all of which Wilde indignantly denied. Carson then seemed to soften his tone as he explored another line of enquiry.

'Had you a private room at the Florence?'

'Yes. I went there so that I could get a cheque cashed because the next day was Sunday.'

'How much did you give Wood then?'

'£2.'

'Why?'

'Because Lord Alfred Douglas asked me to be kind to him. I don't care about different social positions.'

'I suggest that you first had immoral relations with him and then gave him money.'

'It is perfectly untrue.'

'Did you consider that he had come to levy blackmail?'

'I did; and I determined to face it.'

'And the way you faced it was by giving him £15 to go to America?'

'That is an inaccurate description. I saw that the letters were of no value, and I gave him the money after he had told me the pitiful tale about himself, foolishly perhaps, but out of pure kindness.'

'I suggest that you gave him £30. Did you give him £5 more next day?'

'Yes; he told me that after paying his passage to America he would be left almost penniless. I gave him £5.'

'Had you a farewell lunch at the Florence?'

'Yes.'

'It was after lunch that you gave him £5?'

'Yes.'

'After Wood went to America did he ask you for money?'

'No.'

'Did he call Taylor by his Christian name?'

'Yes.'

'Did Wood call you "Oscar"?'

'Yes.'

'What did you call Wood?'

'His name is Alfred.'

'Didn't you call him "Alf"?'

'No, I never use abbreviations.'

'Did you not think it a curious thing that a man with whom you were on such intimate terms should try to blackmail you?'

'I thought it infamous, but Wood convinced me that such had not been his intention, though it was the intention of other people. Wood assured me that he had recovered all the letters.'

'And then Allen came with a letter, possession of which you knew he had secured improperly?'

'Yes.'

'What was Allen?'

'I am told he was a blackmailer.'

'Was he a blackmailer?'

'I never heard of him except as a blackmailer.'

'Then you began to explain to the blackmailer what a loss your manuscript was?'

'I described it as a beautiful work of art.'

'May I ask why you gave this man, who you knew was a notorious blackmailer, ten shillings?'

'I gave it out of contempt.'

'Then the way you show your contempt is by paying ten shillings?'

'Yes, very often.'

'I suppose he was pleased with your contempt?'

'Yes, he was apparently pleased at my kindness.'

'Were you staying at the Albemarle Hotel about 26th of February, 1892?'

'Yes.'

'At that time were Messrs. Elkin Mathews & John Lane, of Vigo Street, your publishers?'

'Yes.'

'Did you become fond of their office boy?'

'I really do not think that that is the proper form for the question to be addressed to me in. I deny that that was the position held by Mr. Edward Shelley, to whom you are referring. I object to your description.'

'What age was Mr. Shelley?'

'I should think about twenty. I first met him in October when arranging for the publication of my books. I asked him to dine with me at the Albemarle Hotel.'

'Was that for the purpose of having an intellectual treat?'

'Well, for him, yes. We dined in my own sitting-room, and there was one other gentleman there.'

'On that occasion did you have a room leading into a bedroom?'

'Yes.'

'Did you give him whisky and sodas?'

'I suppose that he had whatever he wanted. I do not remember. He did not stay all night, nor did I embrace him...'

'Did you ever give him money?'

'Yes; on three occasions — the first time £4, the second time his railway fare to Cromer, where I invited him to meet my wife and family, and the third time £5.'

'Did you think this young man of eighteen was a proper or natural companion for you?'

'Certainly.'

'Did you give him a signed copy of the first edition of Dorian Gray?'

'Yes.'

'Did you become intimate with a young lad named Alphonse Conway at Worthing?'

'Yes.'

'He sold newspapers at the kiosk on the pier?'

'No, I never heard that up to that time his only occupation was selling newspapers. It is the first I have heard of his connexion with literature.'

The laughter that this glib reply generated terminated abruptly at the fall of the judge's gavel, and Carson smiled grimly before continuing, 'What was he?'

'He led a happy, idle life.'

'He was a loafer, in fact? How old was he?'

'He seemed to me to be just enjoying life. He was a youth of about eighteen.'

'How did you make his acquaintance?'

'When Lord Alfred Douglas and I were at Worthing, we were accustomed to go out in a boat. One day when the fishermen were launching a boat on the high beach, Conway, with another lad, assisted in getting the craft down to the water. I said to Lord Alfred Douglas, "Shall we ask them to come out for a sail?" He assented, and we took them. After that Alphonse and I became great friends, and it is true that I asked him to lunch with me. He also dined at my house, and lunched with me at the Marine Hotel.'

'Was his conversation literary?'

'On the contrary, quite simple and easily understood. He had been to school where naturally he had not learned much.'

'He was a simple country lad?'

'He was a nice, pleasant creature. His mother kept a lodging-house, and his desire was to go to sea. It is not true that I met him by appointment one evening and took him on the road to Lancing, kissing him and indulging in familiarities on the way.'

'Did you give him anything?'

'Oh, yes, but no money.'

'Did you give him sums amounting to £15?'

'Never. I gave him a cigarette case in which I placed a paper inscribed "Alphonse from his friend Oscar Wilde." I called him "Alphonse," but he did not call me "Oscar." I also gave him my photograph, on which I wrote "Oscar Wilde to Alphonse." I also gave him a book called *The Wreck of the Grosvenor*.'

At this point, at Carson's request, the court bailiff held up these exhibits, which were then passed round the jury benches. Carson took a sip of water and continued, 'Were you fond of this boy?'

'Naturally. He had been my companion for six weeks.'

'Did you take him to Brighton?'

'Yes.'

'And provided him with a suit of blue serge?'

'Yes.'

'And a straw hat with a band of red and blue?'

'That, I think, was his unfortunate selection.'

'But you paid for it?'

'Yes.'

'You dressed this newsboy up to take him to Brighton?'

'No. I did not want him to be ashamed of his shabby clothes. He told me his father had been an electrical engineer, and had died young.'

'In order that he might look more like an equal?'

'Oh, no! He could not look like that. No, I promised him that before I left Worthing I would take him somewhere, to some place to which he wished to go, as a reward for his being a pleasant companion to myself and my children. He chose Portsmouth, as he was anxious to go to sea, but I told him that was too far. So we went to Brighton. We dined at a restaurant and stayed the night at the Albion Hotel, where I took a sitting room and two bedrooms. I am not sure that the bedrooms communicated by a green baize door. We returned next day. I have never taken any other boy to the Albion. I am quite certain of that.'

At this point the judge suggested that it might be appropriate to adjourn for lunch, and once the courtroom began to clear, the same man who had the previous day invited Jack to join Carson in the robbing room walked across to a point immediately below the front row of the public gallery and invited Jack to lean forward and take a piece of paper from him.

'Mr Carson asked me to give you these addresses you were enquiring about during the dinner break yesterday.'

'Thank you very much,' Jack replied as he took the paper, folded it and placed it in the inside pocket of his jacket. 'Is Mr Carson free for a moment?'

Ten minutes later Jack was back watching Queensberry's counsel consume more gorgonzola in one mouthful than Jack could contemplate in a month. Blue cheese was not his favourite smell, so he kept his distance as he asked a question he had been intending to ask at their first meeting, but kept slipping his mind.

'Inspector Enright asked me to enquire how you first became aware that Lord Stranmillis was missing.'

Carson smiled. 'Unlike my old friend Shorty Stranmillis, I occasionally revisit the town of my birth, where I retain a few friends among the local police, the "Dublin Metropolitan". When Shorty failed to show up for the meeting in Dublin, the Secretary of the Welcoming Committee telegraphed to his London address to enquire if he had changed his travel plans. When advised that Shorty had set off for Dublin as planned, the worthy gentleman assumed the worst, and contacted the local police.'

'But why did they then contact you?'

'They knew me as a fellow Unionist and were concerned in case Shorty had fallen into Fenian clutches. They also knew that I had certain highly placed contacts within the Government, and that I'd be able to sway them into commencing a search without delay.'

'So nothing to do with Oscar Wilde?'

'No, pure coincidence. But by equal coincidence I was about to contact the Home Secretary anyway, when I learned that some of the witnesses unearthed by my instructing solicitors were hinting that big names might be implicated in homosexual scandals.'

'You were obviously of the belief that some harm had befallen Lord Stranmillis?' Jack persevered. 'Did it never occur to you that he might simply have sought to disappear for personal reasons? Reasons perhaps connected with Mr Wilde?'

'That's a disgraceful suggestion, young man!' Carson snarled. 'While it's true that Shorty never married, that's no justification for an assumption that he might be — "otherwise inclined", to put it politely.'

'But it's a possibility, is it not?' Jack replied in his own defence. 'At the Yard we always maintain a policy of keeping all options open until we have evidence to justify closing them. And even if your friend was not an intimate of Mr Wilde's, he might have had other reasons for wishing to escape the spotlight — a possible business reversal, for example? It seems to me, and to Inspector Enright, I might add, that it's been too readily assumed that Stranmillis was the target of Fenians.'

'I sincerely hope that you're correct,' Carson replied coldly. 'Now, if you'd excuse me...'

'Yes, of course,' Jack replied. Then his stubborn refusal to be browbeaten overcame him, and he couldn't help adding, as he turned to leave the robing room, 'I must prepare myself for the afternoon ordeal. I can only hope that I'll manage to remain awake.'

Chapter Sixteen

Having arranged for the coachman to collect him in two hours time, Percy took mental stock of the scene before him. A dirt track led downhill slightly towards some sort of mine shaft with several buildings clustered round it, one of which appeared to be a cottage. Immediately to his right was a single rail line that ran all the way down to the buildings, with a large lake on its left at the foot of the slope. Where Percy was standing was some sort of junction, and off to its right, running parallel to the main line, east to west, was a sidings containing a dozen or so tank wagons that were presumably awaiting their removal, via the main line, to wherever they were destined to go.

With a sigh, Percy began the trek several hundred yards or so down the track, with the branch line to his right. He made careful note of the absence of rust on the line, which suggested that it was in regular use, and he looked for signs of activity in the buildings towards which he was picking his way carefully between the large stones that occasionally protruded through the loose soil of the track at his feet. Although it was a working day the mine itself appeared deserted, and he was just asking himself if anyone would be around for him to interview when there was a bark of warning, and a large snarling dog raced up from the door of the cottage, yelping an unmistakable instruction that he was to proceed no further.

Percy stood stock still as the unkempt brute dropped to its haunches and growled threateningly. He was unsure what breed it was, but it was very hairy, very dirty, and very displeased to see him. Man and dog maintained intense eye contact until a rough voice commanded the dog to come to heel, and with a lingering, wistful final glare at Percy's leg, it rose and ran back to where a man was standing at the cottage door.

'Yer can come down now,' the man yelled up to Percy. 'I've called 'im off, an' 'e's a biddable beast, so 'e won't 'ave yer 'til I tell 'im to. So who might yer be, an' what's yer business?'

Percy extracted his police badge and held it high in the air, for the avoidance of any misunderstanding. The dog might not be capable of making social distinctions, but its owner hopefully would be.

'I'm Detective Inspector Enright, Scotland Yard,' Percy announced loudly as he stepped carefully over the rail line and approached the cottage. 'I'm investigating the disappearance of your employer, Lord Stranmillis.'

'News ter me,' the man responded. 'We ain't seen 'im down 'ere in months. I takes me orders from 'Arry 'Ardcastle, the site manager.'

'So you are?'

'Jed Blower, site foreman.'

'Where are all the other workers?' Percy asked with a pointed nod towards the remaining buildings.

'There ain't none, most o' the time,' Blower explained. 'Just me an' a boy what comes down twice a week to 'elp me wi' the pumpin'.'

'Pumping?'

Blower nodded. 'That's right. The shaft over there's flooded ter about forty feet or so. At least, it were when we started a six month back. Now they reckon it's down ter twenty feet, an' by the end o' the year she'll be clear. I'll show yer, but mind where yer puts yer feet, an' keep away from the edge.'

Percy took a closer look at various idle pieces of equipment lying on either side of the path as Blower led the way down to the opening of the shaft, a circle some fifty feet in diameter with some sort of cradle hanging from a rope that was in turn attached to a crude winch on a crossbar.

'It's pretty basic right now,' Blower explained, 'but once we gets it dried out, there'll be new 'aulage gear installed at the top 'ere. Steam operated, like most o' the stuff around 'ere. That's 'ow come I gets ter be foreman o' works, 'cos I knows all about steam from me days as an engine driver.'

'You have a locomotive down here?' Percy asked as his skin began to tingle.

'In that shed,' Blower confirmed, nodding towards a ramshackle hut, whose open doors revealed the smoke box door of a small 'saddle tank' locomotive.

'So what does it haul?

Blower nodded back up the track. 'On yer way in, did yer 'appen ter see a row o' tank wagons in the sidin's?'

'Indeed I did,' Percy confirmed. 'What do they contain?'

'Brine,' Blower advised him. 'We pumps it outta the shaft wi' that pipe yer can see stickin' out've it an' it goes inter them tank wagons. When them's all full, we 'auls 'em off up ter the sidin's, then the railway people takes 'em somewhere or other an' empties 'em. Then they puts 'em back in the sidin's, an we 'auls 'em back down 'ere an' fills 'em up agin.'

'Why can't you just pump it out onto the ground out here?'

Blower gave a dismissive snort. 'Easy ter see yer no engineer. If we does that, it'll just run back inter the ground, and we'd be back where we started.'

'So you have to take it off the site in wagons?' Percy asked by way of confirmation. 'That sounds like a very painstaking task, and one that'll take forever.'

'Like I said,' Blower nodded, 'it'll be the end o' the year afore we can start minin' agin, an' even then we'll need ter keep pumpin' every day, just ter keep the water out.'

'Where does the water come from in the first place?'

'The ground, obviously,' Blower advised him. 'It's what engineers an' suchlike call the "water table". Yer gets ter a certain level below ground, and it starts ter bubble up. There must be millions o' tons o' water down there, like some sorta underground lake.'

'Like that lake over there?'

Blower nodded. 'Yeah, that's where they first started diggin' out the salt a coupla 'undred or so years back. It were closer ter the surface in them days. Then when they dropped the shaft ter get further down, it flooded, an' the level o' the water in that lake tells us 'ow much water's left in the shaft. Water finds its own level, in case yer didn't know that.'

'So while you're draining the shaft, you're also emptying the lake?'

'Yer not ser daft as yer look,' Blower grinned and Percy decided to persevere while he had some credentials left. 'What's that massive thing over there?' he asked, nodding towards what to his untutored eye resembled a huge crane on wheels.

'That's "Bessie",' Blower explained proudly. 'That's what we calls 'er, but she's really a steam crane ter move owt big. She'll be used once we gets the new 'aulin' gear fer the shaft, but fer the time bein' we just uses 'er fer owt tricky. While we're down 'ere, d'yer wanna see me locomotive?'

Percy agreed, and Blower proudly led the way into the collection of rotting timbers with a yawning metal roof that called itself a locomotive shed. Blower patted the side of the elderly locomotive that had once been green in colour, but was now beginning to display rust in places.

'She were built in Crewe almost twenty years back,' Blower announced, 'but once she's got steam up she can pull a dozen o' them tank wagons yer saw in the sidin's. It's a quarter've a mile up that slope, an' she's never failed us yet.'

'Do you have a name for her as well?' Percy asked with a smile.

Blower nodded. 'She's called "Martha" — that were me wife's name, in the days when I 'ad one. But when she died, I come down 'ere ter forget.'

Percy eyes lit on a long pole with a hook of some sort on its end, lying against the side wall of the shed. He stepped across and picked it up. 'What's this for?'

'That's me 'ook fer uncouplin' the wagons,' Blower advised him. 'Most o' the time we keeps 'em coupled tergether, but on occasions we needs ter pull 'em apart, like that time when one o' them come off the rails.'

Percy's mind wandered back to a conversation with a guard at Crewe Station, who'd advised him of the existence of specialised equipment that was normally employed to uncouple wagons, and his skin resumed its tingling.

'Could we have a closer look at that crane thing?' he asked, and Blower led the way out of the shed to where the crane sat like a huge metal crab, its jib pointing to the side from a cab set on a swivel on a wheeled platform.

'Looks quite complicated,' Percy observed, playing on Blower's vanity. 'How does it work? By steam, did you say?'

'Yeah,' Blower confirmed. 'Once she's powered up, yer can turn 'er through three 'undred an' sixty degrees, and move 'er anywhere yer likes on that bogie she's sittin' on. She'll lift damned near five ton if yer knows what yer doin'.'

'What's this white stuff on the wheels?'

For a moment Blower looked lost for words, then recovered quickly to reply, 'Salt. This *is* a salt works, after all.'

'Yes, but I don't see any salt around here,' Percy replied as he let his eyes wander down a set of track marks heading away from where the crane was sitting. They led towards the lake, on the edges of which was a thick white deposit of some sort. 'And presumably that's also salt, on the edge of the lake there?'

'Course it is,' Blower confirmed. 'Whaddyer expect ter find round the rim've a salt lake? When the water level drops, it leaves the dried salt round the edges.'

'And you say that the lake's still some twenty feet deep?'

'That's right.'

Percy turned and shook Blower's hand. 'Thank you very much for your assistance, Mr Blower. You've been most helpful.'

'Don't mention it,' Blower replied, 'an' I 'opes yer finds 'is carriage.'

Percy hurried back up the slope as quickly as was consistent with appearing unconcerned, half expecting to hear a shout of command, followed by eager panting as heavy paws came after him when Blower realised what he had given away.

Thank God the coachman had returned early, and Percy was able to sink into the safety of the padded bench inside. The horse plodded away on its return trip to Crewe Station, from where the cabman plied his trade, and where Percy was planning a return to Solomon Johnson's office to request a copy of the report of the guard who had worked the Crewe to Holyhead leg of Stranmillis's mysterious journey into obscurity. He'd need this to persuade the local force to lend him the men he needed for his return to the salt workings.

Chapter Seventeen

David and Evan Davies beached their small rowing boat onto the shingle of Trefor Beach, on the northern shore of the Llŷn Peninsula in Gwynedd, in the westernmost part of Wales. Their day's fishing had come to an abrupt halt when the bow of their vessel had bumped against something solid that was floating in the heavy swell that had been boring down from the north west for several days. It looked like a black sack until Evan reached over the side and turned it over, to reveal the body of a man. He'd yelled out in shock, and after the two men had hauled the inert, waterlogged form into the gunnels of the boat, David — the stronger of the two oarsmen — had rowed hard back to their home village, aided by the aggressively incoming tide.

As they laid their unusual catch onto the shingle, it was Evan who voiced what they were both thinking: 'Not much of a fisherman, likely. Dressed more like he was going to chapel of a Sunday morning. What's that round his face?'

'Salt,' David replied. 'And I'm thinking he's been floating for a good while. Who knows where he's come from? Best go home and tell Owen the Law what we've found, before it's us that gets the blame.'

An hour later, local police constable Owen Pugh was examining the body more carefully where it lay, discreetly covered by a tarpaulin until he removed it and began searching the pockets and clothing.

'Well, it wasn't for his money that somebody hit him on the back of the head, boyos. There must be thirty big ones here. And this label in his jacket tells me he's from London. If

London wants the body of this fine gentleman, they can come and collect it.'

Jack resumed his seat for the afternoon session. As it had been the previous day, the public gallery was less crowded after the dinner break than it had been during the morning session, and the expression on Wilde's face as he resumed his place in the witness box seemed to somehow reflect his disappointment that he was not quite playing to a full house. If Carson was experiencing a similar sentiment, it didn't show as he rose to his feet at the judge's invitation and continued his cross-examination of Wilde where he had left off.

'You told me this morning that you were intimate with Taylor, did you not, Mr Wilde?' Carson began.

Wilde frowned slightly as he replied. 'I do not call him an intimate friend. He was a friend of mine. It was he who arranged the meeting of myself with Wood about the letters at his residence, 13 Little College Street. I have known Taylor since the early part of October, 1892. He used to come to my house, to my chambers, and to the Savoy. I have been several times to his house, some seven or eight times, perhaps.'

'You used to go to tea parties there — afternoon tea parties?'

'Yes.'

Jack's stomach heaved slightly as he recalled the sordid scene inside Taylor's squalid set of ground floor rooms in Chelsea, with the revolting boy Campbell lying naked in a stinking bed. Hardly the sort of 'afternoon tea party' that Wilde was anxious to describe, unless Taylor had very rapidly gone down in the world.

'How many rooms did he occupy?' was Carson's next question, and the answer confirmed Jack's suspicion that Taylor had recently experienced a downturn in fortunes.

'He had the upper part of the house — two stories. He had a bedroom, a sitting-room, a bathroom and a kitchen. I think he did not keep a servant.'

'Did he always open the door to you?'

'No; sometimes he did; sometimes his friends did.'

'Did his rooms strike you as being peculiar?'

'No, except that he displayed more taste than usual.'

'There was rather elaborate furniture in the room, was there not?'

'The rooms were furnished in good taste.'

Again, Jack was wondering whether or not they were describing the same Taylor that he had recently visited, until Carson's next question revealed where he was heading.

'Is it true that he never admitted daylight into them?'

'Really, I don't know what you mean.'

'Well, was there always candle or gas light there?'

'No.'

'Did you ever see the rooms lighted otherwise than by gas or candles whether by day or night?'

'Yes, certainly.'

'Did you ever see the curtains drawn back in the sitting-room?'

'When I went to see Taylor, it was generally in the winter about five o'clock — tea-time — but I am under the impression of having seen him earlier in the day when it was daylight.'

'Are you prepared to say that you ever saw the curtains otherwise than drawn across?'

'Yes, I think so.'

'It would not be true, then, to say that he always had a double lot of curtains drawn across the windows, and the room, day or night, artificially lighted?'

160

'I don't think so.'

'Can you declare specifically that any daylight was ever admitted into the room?'

'Well, I can't say as to that.'

'Who was there when you went in the daylight?'

'I think Mr. Taylor only.'

'Can you recall any specific time at which you saw daylight enter that room?'

'Yes; it was a Monday in March. Nobody else was there. In the winter the curtains would naturally be drawn.'

'Were the rooms strongly perfumed?'

'Yes, I have known him to burn perfumes. I would not say the rooms were always perfumed. I am in the habit of burning perfumes in my own rooms.'

'Did you ever meet Wood there?'

'I saw Wood there only on one occasion when I met him at tea.'

'Did you ever meet a man named Sidney Mavor there?'

'Yes.'

'How old was he?'

'About twenty-five or twenty-six.'

'Is he your friend still?'

'Yes.'

'Did you know that Taylor had a lady's costume — a lady's fancy dress — in his rooms?'

'No.'

'Did you ever see him with one on?'

'No. I was never told that he had such dresses. He is a man of great taste and intelligence, and I know he was brought up at a good English school.'

'Is he a literary man?'

'I have never seen any created work of his.'

'Did you discuss literature with him?'

'He used to listen. He was a very artistic, pleasant fellow.'

'Was he an artist?'

'Not in the sense of creating anything. He was extremely intellectual and clever, and I liked him very much.'

'Did you get him to arrange dinners at which you could meet young men?'

'No.'

'But you have dined with young men?'

'Often. Ten or a dozen times, perhaps, at Kettner's, the Solferino, and the Florence.

'Always in a private room?'

'Generally, not always; but I prefer a private room.'

'Did you send this telegram to Taylor: "Obliged to see Tree at five o'clock, so don't come to Savoy. Let me know at once about Fred. Oscar"?'

'I do not recollect it.'

'Who was Fred?'

'A young man to whom I was introduced by the gentleman whose name was written down yesterday. His other name was Atkins.'

'Were you very familiar with him?'

'I liked him. I never had any trouble about him.'

'Now, did you know that Taylor was being watched by the police?'

'No, I never heard that.'

'Did you know that Taylor and Parker were arrested in a raid upon a house in Fitzroy Square last year?'

'Yes.'

'Did you not know that Taylor was notorious for introducing young men to older men?'

'I never heard that in my life. He has introduced young men to me.'

'How many has he introduced to you?'

'Do you mean of those mentioned in this case?'

'No; young men with whom you afterwards became intimate.'

'About five.'

'Were these young men all about twenty?'

'Yes; twenty or twenty-two. I like the society of young men.'

'Among these five did Taylor introduce you to Charles Parker?'

'Yes.'

'Did you become friendly with him?'

'Yes, he was one with whom I became friendly.'

'Did you know that Parker was a gentleman's servant out of employment?'

'No.'

'But if you had, you would still have become friendly with him?'

'Yes. I would become friendly with any human being I liked.'

'How old was he?'

'I should say he was about twenty. He was young, and that was one of his attractions.'

'Was he intellectual? Was he an educated man?'

'Culture was not his strong point. He was not an artist. Education depends on what one's standard is...'

'Did you become friendly with Parker's brother?'

'Yes. They were my guests, and as such I became friendly with them.'

'On the very first occasion that you saw them?'

'Yes. It was Taylor's birthday, and I asked him to dinner, telling him to bring any of his friends.'

'Did you know that one Parker was a gentleman's valet, and the other a groom?'

'I did not know it, but if I had I should not have cared. I didn't care two pence what they were. I liked them. I have a passion to civilize the community.'

'What enjoyment was it to you to entertain grooms and coachmen?'

'The pleasure to me was being with those who are young, bright, happy, careless, and free. I do not like the sensible and I do not like the old.'

'You did the honours to the valet and the groom?'

'I entertained Taylor and his two guests.'

'In a private room, of course?'

'Yes, certainly.'

'Did you give them an intellectual treat?'

'They seemed deeply impressed.'

'During the dinner did you become more intimate with Charles than the other?'

'I liked him better.'

'Did Charles Parker call you "Oscar"?'

'Yes. I like to be called "Oscar" or "Mr. Wilde".'

'You had wine?'

'Of course.'

'Was there plenty of champagne?'

'Well, I did not press wine upon them.'

'Now, after dinner, did you say, referring to Charles Parker, in the presence of Taylor and William Parker, the brother, "This is the boy for me"?'

'Certainly not.'

'And did you ask Charles, "Will you come with me"?'

'No. After dinner I went back to the Savoy Hotel, but I did not take Charles Parker with me.'

'Did you not drive him to the Savoy?'

'No, he did not come to the Savoy at all.'

'Did any of these men who visited you at the Savoy have whisky and sodas and iced champagne?'

'I can't say what they had.'

'Do you drink champagne yourself?'

'Yes; iced champagne is a favourite drink of mine, strongly against my doctor's orders.'

'Did improprieties take place there?'

'None whatever.'

'What was there in common between this young man and yourself? What attraction had he for you?'

'I delight in the society of people much younger than myself. I like those who may be called idle and careless. I recognize no social distinctions at all of any kind; and to me youth, the mere fact of youth, is so wonderful that I would sooner talk to a young man for half-an-hour than be — well, cross-examined in court.'

'Do I understand that even a young boy you might pick up in the street would be a pleasing companion?'

'I would talk to a street Arab, with pleasure.'

'And take him into your rooms?'

'Be it so...'

'When did you see Charles Parker last?'

'I don't think I have seen him since February of last year.'

'Did you ever hear what became of him?'

'I heard that he had gone into the army — enlisted as a private.'

'You saw in the papers of the arrest of Taylor and Parker?'

'Yes; I read that they were arrested.'

'You know that they were charged with felonious practices?'

'I knew nothing of the charges.'

'That when they were arrested they were in company with several men in women's clothing?'

'I read of it in the newspapers that two men, in women's clothes, music-hall artistes, drove up to the house and were arrested outside.'

'Did you not think it a somewhat serious thing that Mr. Taylor, your great friend, and Charles Parker, another great friend, should have been arrested in a police raid?'

'I was very much distressed at the time, and wrote to him, but the magistrates took a different view of the case, because they dismissed the charge. It made no difference to my friendship for him.'

'When did you first meet Fred Atkins?'

'In October, 1892. He told me he was connected with a firm of bookmakers. He was about nineteen or twenty. I was introduced to him in the rooms of a gentleman in Margaret Street, off Regent Street. I did not know him through making bets. I did not ask him to dinner on the first day I met him. I met him at a dinner given by another gentleman whose rooms I met him in first. I was friendly with Atkins on that occasion. I called him "Fred" and he called me "Oscar." He was in employment, but apologized and said he neglected his business.'

'Did he seem to you an idle fellow?'

'Well, yes. But he was ambitious to go on the music-hall stage. We did not discuss literature. I would not have allowed him to. The art of the music-hall was as far as he got.'

'Did you ask him to go to Paris with you?'

'I must explain. One Sunday I saw him and the gentleman, who has been mentioned, lunching at the Cafe Royal. I was going to Paris on my own account in reference to the publication of a book. This other gentleman was also going to

Paris about a position on Dalziel's Agency. It was suggested that we should all go together, as he had promised to take Atkins. It was arranged that we should go on a Monday, but subsequently the gentleman found that he could not go until Tuesday or Wednesday. Then, as Atkins seemed very much disappointed, the gentleman asked me if I would take Fred over. I said, "With the greatest pleasure," and I took him.'

'How long had you known Atkins then?'

'About a fortnight. We went by the Club train. I paid for his ticket, but the money was refunded to me afterwards by the gentleman. I did not suggest to Atkins that he should go as my secretary — ridiculous, it's childish to ask such a thing. I took him to the same rooms I occupied in the hotel — 29 Boulevard des Capucines. I engaged three bedrooms, having one in reserve. They all three opened on to each other. I never asked Fred to copy some manuscript for me. I took him to lunch at the Cafe Julien. He was practically my guest, as representing the gentleman I have mentioned.'

'After lunch did you suggest that Atkins should have his hair curled?'

'He suggested it himself, and I said it would be very unbecoming, and I told him it was a silly thing to do, an absurd thing. I should have been very angry if he had had his hair curled.'

'You dined with him?'

'Yes.'

'Gave him an excellent dinner?'

'I never had anything else. I do everything excellently.'

'Did you give him plenty of wine at dinner?'

'If you mean, did I ply him with wine, I say "No!" It's monstrous, and I won't have it.'

'Did you ask him to promise that he would say nothing about going to Paris?'

'No. I thought it was the great event of his life, as it was.'

'Did you consider Atkins respectable?'

'Respectable? Yes. I thought him pleasant and young. He was good-natured, and was going on to the music-hall stage. I heard him sing. He was interesting.'

'Was he alone when he came to you at St. James's Place?'

'No; I think he was accompanied by the young actor. I will swear that Atkins was not alone in the room with me.'

'Did any improprieties ever take place between you and Atkins?'

'None whatever.'

'Do you know Walter Grainger?'

'Yes.'

'How old is he?'

'He was about sixteen when I knew him. He was a servant at a certain house in High Street, Oxford, where Lord Alfred Douglas had rooms. I have stayed there several times. Grainger waited at table. I never dined with him. If it is one's duty to serve, it is one's duty to serve; and if it is one's pleasure to dine, it is one's pleasure to dine.'

'Did you ever kiss him?'

'Oh, dear no. He was a peculiarly plain boy. He was, unfortunately, extremely ugly. I pitied him for it.'

'Was that the reason why you did not kiss him?'

'Oh, Mr. Carson, you are pertinently insolent.'

'Why, sir, did you mention that this boy was extremely ugly?'

'For this reason. If I were asked why I did not kiss a doormat, I should say because I do not like to kiss doormats. I do not know why I mentioned that he was ugly, except that I was stung by the insolent question you put to me and the way you have insulted me throughout this hearing. It was a flippant answer. No indecencies ever took place between myself and Grainger. I went down in June, 1893, to stay at a cottage at Goring. I brought over Grainger as under-butler. He had asked me to get him a situation. I never on any occasion asked him to come into my bedroom. I don't know where the butler I had then is now.'

'Did you know a masseur at the Savoy named Antonio Migge?'

'Yes. He used occasionally to massage me in the morning. I stayed at the Savoy in March, 1893, but never on that occasion brought boys into my bedroom there.'

'Did you ever bring boys into your rooms at the hotel in Paris?'

'Never.'

'Or into your sitting-room?'

'What do you mean by boys?'

'Boys of eighteen or twenty?'

'Oh, yes; many called to see me.'

'Did any of them come late at night — twelve or one o'clock — and stay till four in the morning?'

'Certainly not.'

'Is it not true that there has been a scandal at the Savoy Hotel?'

'None whatever.'

'We shall see about that, Mr Wilde. Remember that we have witnesses of our own to lead, who shall tell us the truth of these matters. But now I see by the clock, my Lord, that it is rapidly approaching the hour at which the good gentlemen of the jury must be relieved of their duties for the day. If my friend has no more witnesses, I would propose to commence my opening address as the first item in this trial tomorrow morning.'

'Very well, Mr Carson. Mr Bailiff, please adjourn the court until ten o'clock of tomorrow forenoon.'

As Jack made his way out of the front door of the Old Bailey, a good thirty minutes after the main rush for the staircase, he heard a familiar voice boom out behind him.

'I trust you found that more entertaining, Sergeant?'

He stopped and turned round, to allow a smirking Carson to catch up with him.

'I must apologise for my manner at dinner time, Mr Carson, but we police officers are used to matters proceeding more quickly in the cases in which we are giving evidence.'

'That is because you only see your small chapter of the overall novel.' Carson smiled, then assumed a look of mock self-chastisement as he added, 'Dear me, I seem to have adopted Mr Wilde's literary outlook on life. I hope that it's the only bad habit of his I've acquired.'

'He seemed to walk straight into your gunfire,' Jack observed. 'He was denying things he hadn't even been accused of, such as being alone in hotel rooms with young men.'

Carson allowed the smirk to widen. 'The advantage of exchanging copies of our pleadings in writing to counsel for the other side, without having them formally read out at the start of the trial. Wilde knows what we're going to get from *our* witnesses, and he feels obliged to deny it all in advance, since it's his only opportunity to go into the witness box. But as you rightly point out, it creates a great air of suspicion when he appears to be denying events of which only he could be aware.'

'It makes my job seem much simpler by comparison,' Jack conceded. 'I don't think I'd have the patience to play a witness like a fish, the way you are called upon to do.'

'Hopefully we'll be hauling him in tomorrow morning.' Carson smiled as he made to walk to the open door of the cab that was awaiting him. 'We may even succeed in doing so without calling a single witness. And so I bid you a good afternoon.'

The supper things had been washed and put away, and Jack and Esther were settling down to their late night cocoa ahead of retiring for the night, when they were alarmed to hear a heavy pounding on their front door. Jack placed his trouser braces back over the shoulders of his shirt and went to answer the summons in his stockinged feet, while Esther brushed down her nightgown and listened in surprise as Jack demanded to know why Percy was making enough noise to awaken the entire building, quite apart from their three sleeping children.

'Any tea in the pot?' Percy demanded gruffly as he stalked determinedly down the hall carpet and into the kitchen. He saw how Esther was dressed, and his face softened. 'Sorry. Were you preparing for bed?'

'Why the late hour?' Jack asked. 'Come to think of it, aren't you supposed to be in Crewe?'

'I was, until I caught the last Euston train in order to get back here for an early start tomorrow, armed with a letter of authorisation from Bray to stick under the noses of those bone-heads in charge of the Cheshire force. I haven't even been home yet.'

'So you won't have eaten?' Esther asked.

Percy shook his head. 'But don't worry about me,' he reassured her, 'I can swallow some of Beattie's poison when I get home.'

'You'll do no such thing,' Esther insisted as she lit the gas oven and bent down to lift a casserole dish from inside it.

'There's plenty of brisket stew left, and to judge by Jack's face when I served it he won't mourn its absence on the leftover dinner table tomorrow. Now sit down, and let me make you some cocoa.'

'So what's the problem in Cheshire?' Jack asked.

Percy grimaced. 'I think I know what happened to Stranmillis's railway carriage, and where it can be found, but the bovine plods that constitute the Cheshire Constabulary are demanding something in writing from the Yard before they'll agree to drain a salt lake, sour the surrounding land, and delay the reopening of a potential source of local employment.'

'This threatens to be a long night,' Jack muttered.

'What was that about a lake?' Esther asked as she served Percy a generous portion of stew in one of her best bowls, cut him several thick slices of cottage loaf, then reached for the notepad and pencils that she kept hidden on the top of shelf of the kitchen cupboard in case Lily was tempted to draw fairies all over her carefully compiled notes of the case.

'First things first,' Percy explained between grateful mouthfuls. 'The guard on the Crewe to Holyhead leg of Stranmillis's train journey reported a brief delay at a set of signals near a place called Beeston, which we know from Jack's researches is the place where Stranmillis has his estate, and his recently re-opened salt workings. Further researches at Crewe, and with the signalman at Beeston, revealed the continued existence of a sidings and branch line leading off the main line down to the mine workings a few miles or so east of Beeston.'

'And that's where you think the Pullman was taken?' Jack asked.

Percy nodded, while Esther was adding eagerly to her notes. 'I then visited the salt workings themselves and confirmed that they have a locomotive that's in full working order, and more than capable of heaving a single carriage down the branch line into the salt works.'

'The lake?' Esher prompted him.

Again Percy nodded. 'When I got down to the mine site, I met up with the resident foreman — and his very unpleasant guard dog — and was shown round. Just to the front of what will become the new pit head, as we may call it, is a large salt lake, which I was advised is the result of the flooding which has also affected the mine shaft, and was the reason why salt extraction was originally abandoned there. But now they've brought in pumping gear, and the foreman reckons that there's only twenty feet or so of salt water — "brine", they call it — left to pump out, then the mine can re-open. Meanwhile you have a twenty foot deep salt water lake in which you could easily, and conveniently, hide a Pullman carriage.'

'The locomotive pushed it off the line, you mean?' Jack enquired.

Percy shook his head. 'That wouldn't have sent it far enough in to hide it. They have a steam crane on the site, and because they weren't expecting any police investigation they didn't bother to conceal the fact that said crane had recently travelled down to the lake. If it were positioned between the line and the lake, it could have been used to lift the Pullman from the track, swing it through one hundred and eighty degrees, and drop it into the lake.'

'You'd need a large crane,' Jack objected.

Percy nodded. 'Believe me, it's a monster, and capable of lifting a Pullman carriage.

'Did you question the site foreman about all this?' Esther asked.

Percy frowned. 'When he was armed with a dog that could take on a horse? What do you think? I was there on my own, remember. But he gave himself away good and proper, and that's when I beat a hasty retreat. When I was leaving he said that he hoped that we found his Lordship's carriage, when I'd not mentioned anything about the circumstances of his disappearance. And certainly not anything about a carriage.'

'So he was obviously involved?' Jack concluded.

'It couldn't have been done without him,' Percy confirmed, 'particularly not since, in addition to any other duties he may have, he's the locomotive driver.'

'But to detach the Pullman from the train in the first place,' Esther pointed out unnecessarily, 'they needed to halt the train.'

'Indeed,' Percy nodded, 'and it seems from what the signalman told me that it could have been done using a special device called an "Annetts Key". Here's a set of instruction on its use for you to study, Esther, but to keep it brief, this key can be employed to change the points at the junction between the main line and the sidings. What I can't work out is how they did it without the knowledge of the signalman on that stretch of line, who quite frankly is too stupid to have lied convincingly when I questioned him. He told me, what's more, that when the Key comes out of the socket in his signal box, it effectively disables all his signals. That couldn't have happened without his knowledge, yet he denies any use of the key during his night shifts last month, when the coach disappeared.'

'Not *last* month,' Esther reminded him as she glanced down at her notes. 'This is April, and the coach disappeared on the twenty-second of February.'

Percy stared back at her for a few seconds, then smacked the ball of his hand against his forehead and let fly a string of oaths that even made Jack blush.

'Sorry,' Percy said with a red face, 'but I just realised what a stupid mistake I made when talking to the signalman. He may not have been the one on the night shift when the train must have been held up briefly — it could have been his opposite number! They work twelve hour shifts, rotating monthly, and I forgot to ask if that was a calendar month or a block of four weeks. You can see now why we need a third head on this case, to avoid us making misleading assumptions.'

'Like the fact that this key had to be taken from the signal box in order to work the junction?' Esther added unassumingly, then caught the expression on Percy's face. 'Well, presumably it could be duplicated?'

Percy's mouth dropped open.

'Block your ears — he's going to swear again.' Jack grinned.

'Double what I just said — Esther, you're God's gift to an overworked detective!'

'Well, *this* one anyway,' Jack replied territorially as he left his seat in order to put his arm round Esther and give her a kiss.

'So if we assume that the key used to work the points was a duplicate,' Esther persevered with an embarrassed blush, 'then the only evidence you need is from the signalman who was presumably persuaded, in all innocence, to signal for the train to stop.'

'And hopefully I'll get that when I go back up there tomorrow,' Percy confirmed. 'Now then Esther, since you seem to be the top of this evening's bill, have you and Lucy got anything for me?'

'I almost hesitate to mention it,' Esther whispered modestly, 'but we're pretty sure we know who "Bunbury" was — you know, the man who took over Stranmillis's identity on the train and the boat from Holyhead?'

'Yes?' Percy prompted her.

'His name is Giles Holloway, and he was the male understudy in Wilde's latest play. He took off a month ago with a set of gentleman's morning clothes, telling his fiancée Emily Baxter, who's also in the cast, that he was undertaking an important part in another production somewhere out west. The really interesting point in all this is that the man who hired him for the part was no other than Patrick Ryan, who just happens to be Emily's uncle. It's all tying together nicely, isn't it?'

'Particularly when you throw in a fact that came out in the trial,' Jack added, 'namely that Wilde had a visit from a man called Allen, who's a career blackmailer. Wilde was uncommonly guarded about what they talked about — preferring to let us all think that it had something to do with an indiscreet letter that Wilde had written to his boyfriend, Queensberry's son. But my nose tells me that it was to do with something else, and it also seems, from what Esther found out from Emily Baxter, that Wilde was indebted to Ryan and Stranmillis — Stranmillis in particular — for the finance for his latest production. No doubt that's already been handsomely repaid with interest, but it might be interesting to see if there's any link between the three of them and this blackmailer.'

'I think Emily Baxter trusts me,' Esther added, 'and she mentioned well-attended Summer holiday house parties at Ryan's country estate, at which Wilde was present. I'll see if I can get hold of a guest list. But let's not forget that another of our assumptions all along has been that Stranmillis *chose* to disappear. Because there's been no body discovered, we've been assuming, probably quite rightly, that the Fenians had nothing to do with it. But there might have been others who wanted Stranmillis dead. Perhaps his body's in that railway carriage.'

'We'll soon know, when we pull it out,' Percy reminded them. 'Now I really must go. My grateful thanks for that delicious supper, and as usual for the produce of that fine brain of yours, Esther. And of course you, Jack, for your courage above and beyond in attending what according to the newspapers is a most tedious trial.'

'I've been to more entertaining events, certainly,' Jack confirmed. 'Including a few hangings. But I've persevered thus far, and now it's my natural stubbornness that's keeping me going. Carson hinted that it might all be over by tomorrow evening, anyway.'

Chapter Eighteen

Jack was on the front row of the public gallery well before the appointed hour of ten o'clock when the knock came on the communicating door between the Bench and the corridor to announce the entry of the judge and the commencement of the third day of the proceedings. Wilde's counsel Sir Edward Clarke rose for long enough to confirm that he had closed the case for Wilde, and Mr Justice Collins invited Edward Carson to 'open' for Queensberry.

Carson rose to his full height, adjusted his wig in a gesture that was more theatre than necessity, cleared his throat and began, his rich Irish brogue worthy of an ancient bard. 'May it please you, my Lord, gentlemen of the jury. In appearing in this case for Lord Queensberry I cannot but feel that a very grave responsibility rests upon me. So far as Lord Queensberry is concerned, in any act he has done, in any letter he has written, or in the matter of the card which has put him in the present position, he withdraws nothing.

'He has done all those things with a premeditation and a determination, at all risks, and at all hazards to try to save his son. Whether Lord Queensberry was right or whether he was wrong, you have probably to some extent information on which you can found a judgment. I must say for Lord Queensberry, notwithstanding the many elements of prejudice which my learned friend, Sir Edward Clarke, thought fit to introduce into the case in his opening speech, that Lord Queensberry's conduct in this respect has been absolutely consistent all through, and if the facts which he stated in his letters as to Mr. Wilde's reputation and acts are correct, then not only was he justified in doing what he could to cut short what would probably prove a most disastrous acquaintance for his son, but in taking every step which suggested itself to him to bring about an inquiry into the acts and doings of Mr. Wilde.

'Gentlemen, from beginning to end Lord Queensberry, in dealing with Mr. Oscar Wilde, has been influenced by one hope alone — that of saving his son. What is Mr. Wilde's own case? The prosecutor has said that up to a certain date he was on terms of friendship with Lord Queensberry, and therefore there were no circumstances rendering his Lordship liable to the accusation that what he had done in the present case was done from malice arising out of disagreement. Lord Queensberry came to know of Mr. Wilde's character, of the scandals in connexion with the Savoy Hotel, that the prosecutor had been going about with young men who were not co-equal with him in position or in age, and that he had been associating with men who, it will be proved beyond doubt, are some of the most immoral characters in London.

'I refer above all to the man Taylor, a most notorious character — as the police will tell the Court — who occupied rooms which were nothing more or less than a shameful den. Whether Taylor was or was not a procurer in this sense, the fact remains that on Tuesday last — 2nd April — he was in company with Mr. Wilde at the latter's house in Tite Street and that he has not been produced by the prosecution. Taylor has fact been the right-hand man of Mr. Wilde in all the orgies in which artists and valets have taken part; and, if opportunity had only been given of cross-examining him, it might have been possible to get from him at least something as to what was going on at Fitzroy Square on the night of the raid there last year.

'Taylor is really the pivot of the case for the simple reason that when the various witnesses for the defence are called and examined — as unfortunately will be necessary — as to the practices of Mr. Oscar Wilde, it will be found that it was Taylor who introduced the young men to the prosecutor. Mr. Oscar Wilde has undertaken to prove enough to send Lord Queensberry to gaol and to brand him as a criminal, but it is remarkable that the only witness who could have supported Mr. Wilde's assertion of innocence has not been called. Yet Taylor is still a friend of Mr. Wilde, and nothing, said the prosecutor, has happened to interrupt their friendship.'

Jack was surprised to hear this when he recalled the conversation he'd had with the much impoverished Mr Taylor, who had been offered money — or so he said — to testify at the Wilde trial. Then again, he hadn't specified who had been intending to call him as a witness, and in view of what had emerged during the evidence so far it might well be the case that Wilde's counsel was not now prepared to risk putting Taylor in the witness box, where Carson could tear him to shreds.

Carson now had Jack's full attention as he continued: 'It will be painful to be compelled to ask the various witnesses that will be called to describe the manner in which Mr. Wilde has acted towards them; but, before the case is ended, you will be obliged to hear a good deal more of the extraordinary den which Taylor kept in Little College Street. Therefore, it is above all things necessary, when we have so much proved by his own admissions, that Mr. Wilde should bring any witness he can to bear out his own explanations. We have heard a great deal of the gentleman whose name was written down. On each occasion when it was convenient to introduce somebody, this was the name which Mr. Wilde gave because he was out of the country. But Taylor is still in the country. Why has he not been called?

'Let us contrast the position which Mr. Wilde took up in cross-examination as to his books, which are for the select and not for the ordinary individual, with the position he assumed as to the young men to whom he was introduced and those he picked up for himself. His books were written by an artist for artists; his words were not for Philistines or illiterates. Contrast that with the way in which Mr. Wilde chose his companions! He took up with Charles Parker, a gentleman's servant, whose brother was also a gentleman's servant; with young Alphonse Conway, who sold papers on the pier at Worthing; and with Scarfe, also a gentleman's servant. Then his excuse was no longer that he was dwelling in regions of art but that he had such a noble, such a democratic, soul that he drew no social distinctions, and that it was quite as much pleasure to have the sweeping boy from the streets to lunch or dine with him as the greatest litterateur or artist.

'In my judgment, if the case had rested on Mr. Wilde's literature alone, Lord Queensberry would have been absolutely justified in the course he has taken. Lord Queensberry has undertaken to prove that Mr. Wilde has been "posing" as guilty of certain vices. Mr. Wilde knows no distinction between a moral and an immoral book. Nor does he care whether the article is in its very terms blasphemous.

'Passing now to *The Picture of Dorian Gray*, it is the tale of a beautiful young man who, by the conversation of one who has great literary power and ability to speak in epigrams — just as Mr. Wilde has — and who has his eyes opened to what they are pleased to call the "delights of the world." If Dorian Gray is a book which it can be conclusively proved advocates the vice imputed to Mr. Wilde, what answer, then, is there to Lord Queensberry's plea of justification?

'The turning of one of Wilde's letters to Lord Alfred Douglas into a sonnet was a very thinly veiled attempt to get rid of the character of that letter. A more thinly veiled attempt to cover its real nature has never been made in a Court of Justice. I have some difficulty in understanding why my learned friend, Sir Edward Clarke, has referred to that letter at all. Perhaps he thought the defence had the letter, and that it would be better to give an explanation of it; but if that is so, it is futile because, for the letter which the defence did produce, my learned friend has no explanation.

'My learned friend has referred to "a man named Wood" as being supposed to have taken out of the pocket of Lord Alfred Douglas correspondence which had passed between him and Wilde. But who is Wood? Why, he too is "Fred," one of Wilde's bosom companions, a friend of Taylor, one of the Little College Street lot! What, then, was the cause of the strained relations between Wilde and Wood? Why did Wilde give Wood £16? When I state that, previous to the possession of those letters, Wood had been carrying on certain practices with Wilde, you will have the key to the whole situation.

'That is one reason why Wilde would be anxious to get the letters at any cost, and when Wood came to levy blackmail, then Mr. Wilde became very anxious that the man should leave the country. So he paid his passage and, after a farewell luncheon, he shipped him off to New York and, I suppose, hoped that he would never see him again. But, gentlemen, as a matter of fact, Wood is here and will be examined before you.'

Above the excited hum of expectation that reverberated around the courtroom, Carson raised his voice for more dramatic effect, and continued, 'I am not here to say anything has ever happened between Lord Alfred Douglas and Mr. Oscar Wilde. God forbid! But everything shows that the young man was in a dangerous position in that he acquiesced in the domination of Mr. Wilde, a man of great ability and attainments. Against that letter written by Mr. Wilde to Lord Queensberry's son, Lord Queensberry protested; and I wish to know, gentlemen, are you, for that protest, going to send Lord Queensberry to gaol? Lord Queensberry was determined to bring the matter to an issue, and what other way was open to him than that which he had chosen?

'Before you condemn Lord Queensberry I ask you to read Wilde's letter and to say whether the gorge of any father ought not to rise. I ask you to bear in mind that Lord Queensberry's son was so dominated by Wilde that he threatened to shoot his own father. Gentlemen, Lord Queensberry did what he has done most deliberately, and he is not afraid to abide by the issue which he has raised in this Court. When you have heard Wood's evidence, the whole story of the payment of those sums of money by Wilde, and the mystery of those letters, will be explained; and the suggestion that they were valuable manuscripts, which Wilde desired to obtain, will be dissipated. As a matter of fact, Wilde knew that we had all the evidence, and he preferred to discount it as far as possible in advance.

'I have dealt as fully as I intend to deal with the question of Mr. Wilde's connexion with the literature and the two letters which have been produced in this case, and I almost hope that I have sufficiently demonstrated to you upon that matter that so far as Lord Queensberry was concerned, he was absolutely justified in bringing to a climax in the way he did this question of the connexion between Mr. Oscar Wilde and his son.

'I have unfortunately a more painful part of the case now to approach. It will be my duty to bring before you young men, one after another, who have been in the hands of Mr. Wilde, to tell their unhappy tales. It is, even for an advocate, a very distasteful task. But let those who are inclined to condemn these young men for being dominated, misled and corrupted by Mr. Wilde remember the relative position of the two parties. Let them say whether those young men were not more sinned against than sinning. I am not going in any great detail now to criticize the evidence of Mr. Oscar Wilde in relation to the several transactions on which he was cross-examined. But there are some general observations applicable to all the cases that have been raised against Mr. Wilde. There is in point of fact a startling similarity between each of them on his own admission which must lead you, gentlemen, to draw the most painful conclusions.

'There is the fact that in no one of these cases were these parties on an equality in any way with Mr. Wilde; they are none of them educated parties with whom he would naturally associate, and they are not his equal in years. But on the other hand, gentlemen, you will have observed a curious similarity in the ages of each of them.

'Mr. Wilde has said that there is something beautiful, something charming about youth which led him to adopt the course he did. But was Mr. Wilde unable to find more suitable companions, at the same time young and charming, in the ranks of his own class? Why, the thing is absurd. His excuse in the witness-box is only a travesty of the facts. Who are all these young men — these lads? There is Wood. Of his history Mr. Wilde has told us that he knows nothing. So far as Mr. Wilde knew, Wood was a clerk out of employment. Who is Parker? Mr. Wilde professed the same ignorance as to that youth. Who is Scarfe? Exactly in the same way Mr. Wilde knew nothing of him. He only knew that he was out of employment. Alphonse Conway he picked up by chance on the beach at Worthing.

'All the young men introduced to Mr. Wilde were of something like eighteen or twenty years of age. The manner of their introduction, and the way in which they were subsequently treated with money and presents, all lead up to the conclusion that there was something unnatural in the relations between Mr. Wilde and these young men.

'Take the case of Parker. How did Mr. Wilde get to know that young man? Parker was a gentleman's servant out of employment; and what idea could Taylor have had of Mr. Wilde's tastes when, on being invited by Wilde to ask his friends to a birthday dinner, he introduced as his guests a groom and a valet? If it were true, as undoubtedly it was, that Taylor first met the two young men in a restaurant in Piccadilly, why did he — if he knew that Mr. Wilde was an artistic and literary man, and, what was more, an upright man — bring the couple to dine with Mr. Wilde? There can be no explanation of the facts but this: that Taylor was a procurer for Wilde, as he undoubtedly was.

'Parker will be called to tell his unfortunate story — his story that he was poor, out of place, and that he fell a victim to Mr. Wilde. Upon the first occasion that Mr. Wilde met Parker, the valet, he addressed him as "Charlie," and Charlie addressed Mr. Wilde, the distinguished dramatist, whose name at the time, was being mentioned in the highest circles in London for his plays and his literary work, as "Oscar."

'I do not wish to say anything about Mr. Wilde's theories as to putting an end to social distinctions. A man of noble and generous instincts might be able to break down all social barriers; but there is one thing plain in this case, and that is that Mr. Wilde's conduct to the young men introduced to him was not instigated by any generous instincts. If Mr. Wilde wanted to assist Parker, if he were interested in him, if he wanted to find him employment, was it doing the lad a good turn to take him to a restaurant and prime him with champagne and a good dinner? Was that the work of charity and sympathy one would expect a man in Mr. Wilde's position to extend to another man like Parker? All the ridiculous explanations of Mr. Wilde will not bear one moment's explanation as to what he was doing in his suite of rooms at the Savoy. The Savoy is a large place, with plenty of room to move about in, and there is no doubt that, without leading people to suspect anything, Mr. Wilde could have brought young men into his rooms.

'Parker will tell you that when he went to the Savoy with Mr. Wilde he had whisky and sodas and iced champagne — that iced champagne in which Mr. Wilde indulged contrary to his doctor's orders. Parker will furthermore tell you of the shocking acts he was led by Mr. Wilde to perpetrate on that occasion. Mr. Wilde was asked in cross-examination, "Is it not true that there has been a scandal at the Savoy Hotel?" "None whatsoever," said Mr. Wilde. But about that very extraordinary thing Lord Queensberry has referred in his letter dated 6th July, 1894.

'It might have been that no one had seen Mr. Wilde turned out into the street, but such kind of gossip could not have arisen without going abroad and being reported in the circles in which Lord Queensberry mixed. The wonder is not that the gossip reached Lord Queensberry, but that, after it was known, this man Wilde should have been tolerated in society in London for the length of time he has. Well, I shall prove that Mr. Wilde brought boys into the Savoy Hotel. The masseur of that establishment — a most respectable man — and other servants will be called to prove the character of Mr. Wilde's relations with his visitors. Is there any wonder that reports of a scandal at the Savoy should have reached Lord Queensberry, whose son was living a portion of the time at the hotel?

'Mr. Wilde has not ventured to deny that Parker has dined with him, has been in his company, and has lunched with him at his rooms and at the Savoy. Mr. Wilde, seeing the importance of these facts, has made a clean breast of it. "Oh, yes," he said, "they were perfectly innocent, nay, more, they were generous actions on my part." It is remarkable that Mr. Wilde has given no account as to what he was doing in those rooms at the Savoy. Parker will tell you what happened on arriving there. He has since enlisted in the army and bears a good character. Mr. Wilde himself said that Parker is a respectable man. Parker will reluctantly present himself to tell you his story.

'As to the boy Conway, Conway was not procured by Taylor — he was procured by Mr. Wilde himself. Has there ever been confessed in a court of justice a more audacious story than that confessed to by Mr. Wilde, in relation to Conway? He met the boy, he said, on the beach at Worthing. He knew nothing whatsoever about him, excepting that he assisted in launching the boats. Conway's real history is that he sold newspapers at Worthing at the kiosk on the pier. What a flippant answer it was that Mr. Wilde gave to the question, "Did you know that Conway sold newspapers?" when he replied, "I did not know that he had previous connexion with literatures". Perhaps, in that, Mr. Wilde thought he was clever at repartee, and was scoring off counsel whose duty it was to cross-examine him. But here are the facts.

'After helping Mr. Wilde to get out his boat, an intimacy sprang up between them, and within a day or two Conway was taken by Mr. Wilde to the house he was occupying. If the

187

evidence of Mr. Wilde was true — and I sincerely hope it is not — Conway was introduced to Mrs. Wilde and her two sons, aged nine and ten. Now, it is clear that Mr. Wilde could not take about the boy Conway in the condition he found him in. So what did he do? And it is here that the disgraceful audacity of the man comes in.

'Mr. Wilde procured the boy a suit of clothes to dress him up like a gentleman's son, put some public school colours upon his hat, and generally made him look like a lad fit and proper to associate with Mr. Oscar Wilde. The whole thing in its audacity is almost past belief. Why, if the defence had proved the fact, instead of getting it from the mouth of the prosecutor, you would have said it was almost incredible. But why did Mr. Wilde dress up Conway? If Mr. Wilde were really anxious to assist Conway, the very worst thing he could have done was to take the lad out of his proper sphere, to begin by giving him champagne luncheons, taking him to his hotel, and treating him in a manner in which the boy could never in the future expect to live.'

It had become obvious to everyone in the courtroom that Wilde, seated at a table to the rear of his counsel, was engaged in animated conversation with the instructing solicitor who sat next to him. That solicitor, in turn, leaned forward to clutch at Sir Edward Clarke's sleeve, to speak urgently with him. Clarke picked this moment in Carson's opening address, while he had paused to take a sip of water, to rise to his feet and address the judge.

'My Lord, I am receipt of urgent and important instructions from my client, which I need a moment or two to discuss further with him. I see that we are now but twenty minutes short of the dinner adjournment, so if I might seek your Lordship's indulgence for an early adjournment, during which

I can take full instructions that might have a bearing on the outcome of this matter?'

'Yes, of course,' the judge replied with a smile. 'If anything, I would have anticipated this a little sooner, Mr Clarke, but certainly you may have your adjournment. Two o'clock, Mr Bailiff.'

The court rose to a background of excited chatter, and Carson remained standing with a broad smile on his face, then turned and gestured for Jack to join him outside.

Jack found Carson in the main hall downstairs, surrounded by his legal team, who were chattering excitedly.

'What's going on?' Jack demanded of Carson, who grinned wolfishly and placed a heavy hand on Jack's shoulder.

'I kept my part of the bargain, Sergeant. There can be no doubt that Wilde is about to abandon his action and will have the unique privilege of paying my fees in this matter. I now call upon you and your colleagues to do your bit — find me Lord Stranmillis.'

Chapter Nineteen

Carson clearly wasn't the only one anticipating a capitulation by Wilde, Jack quickly discovered as he walked back up the well-worn wooden steps to the public gallery for what he hoped would be the final time. The seats immediately adjacent to the door were crammed with eagerly chattering newspaper reporters, who were obviously hopeful of a swift exit once the outcome of the trial was determined, and anxious to be the first out into the street to file their copy for the evening editions.

As he watched the jury members being led back onto their benches with hopeful smiles, Jack looked hard for any sign of Wilde himself. But he left it until the very last moment, and slunk back into court, taking an obscure seat in a corner, just as the judge was ushered back onto the Bench and looked hopefully down at Sir Edward Clarke. Sir Edward rose slowly, and announced that in view of the evidence that had been led — and which Carson was proposing to lead — he was left with no other option but to concur in a verdict of 'Not Guilty' being recorded against Lord Queensberry, in the sense that, whatever might be the truth of the matter, his Lordship had been justified, not only in describing Wilde as having 'posed' as a sodomite, but in having brought this behaviour on his part into public knowledge.

The jury were directed to enter a verdict of 'Not Guilty', which they did with obvious relish, and when a spattering of tentative applause broke out in the public gallery at this outcome, the judge demanded silence with the assistance of his much-used gavel. Then it was on to the matter of costs, and to no-one's surprise, but Carson's visible pleasure, the entire costs in the matter were awarded against Wilde, since he had instituted the proceedings.

Jack caught the next bus down to Whitehall feeling like a man released unexpectedly from a lengthy prison sentence, but he was unsure how to spend the rest of the afternoon. Uncle Percy would barely have reached Crewe, even assuming that he had been able to acquire the necessary paperwork from Chief Superintendent Bray, so there were unlikely to be any wires from him regarding the search he was planning to conduct at the salt works. However, Jack could hardly take the afternoon off so blatantly, particularly since the sudden and early end of the trial would be all over the evening papers. Instead, he could occupy his time writing up his report on the salient points of the trial so far as they would assist ongoing investigations into the extent of Wilde's little coterie of shirt-lifters.

As Jack walked past the uniformed officers on security duty at the front entrance, one of them called out after him.

'Sergeant Enright? Chief Superintendent Bray wants you to report to him as soon as you get in.'

Jack made his way up two flights of stairs into the wing of the Yard building that contained its most senior operational officers. Bray was bent over some papers as Jack tapped on the door, then stood there deferentially until Bray became aware of his hovering presence and waved him in.

'How's the investigation going?'

'I'm just back from the Bailey, sir,' Jack advised him, silently congratulating himself on not having sloped off for the rest of the day. 'Wilde threw in the towel after the dinner break, and he's now officially a posing sodomite. As for the search for Lord Stranmillis, I'm awaiting a further progress report from Inspector Enright.'

'I may have been a little precipitate in signing that authorisation this morning,' Bray grumbled as he handed over a single sheet of paper for Jack to read. 'They've found a body in North Wales which may well be the chappie in question.'

Jack quickly ran his eyes over the telegram that had been dispatched the previous day from a police station in somewhere called 'Carnarfon', then frowned. While he was seeking the words with which to politely disagree with a very senior officer, Bray added an explanation.

'It took a while to land on my desk, until they put two and two together with the reference to the "Oscar Wilde Theatre Group". Presumable that's the same Oscar Wilde?'

'Yes, sir, but I don't think, from the description, that the man whose body's been found is Stranmillis. In fact, I think I know who it really is.'

'And what makes you say that?' Bray enquired in an irritated tone, having clearly been happily contemplating a swift conclusion to the second matter referred to the Political Branch by Carson.

'This report describes the body as being that of a young man in his twenties, approximately six feet in height,' Jack explained. 'Stranmillis was in his late forties, and only five foot four. But if, as the report states, the man's clothing contained a label claiming it as the property of Wilde's company, then I believe that the body will prove to be that of an actor from that company who's been missing for as long as Stranmillis, and who stole some clothing from its Wardrobe department on his way out.'

'What's the man's name?' Bray demanded, presenting Jack with a dilemma. He could hardly say 'My wife's been investigating that aspect of the case, entirely unofficially and at the personal request of my uncle,' so he opted for 'I don't recall at this precise moment, sir, since I've taken to working on certain aspects of the case at home in the evenings, and my notes are there, but I can let you know first thing tomorrow.'

'Presumably someone at this theatre can identify the man if I get a photograph of the body sent down here?'

Jack experienced a cold shudder at the prospect of advising an aspiring young actress that she no longer had a fiancé. But he smiled appreciatively, and undertook to have the body formally identified as soon as the photograph became available.

'So assuming that your uncle has left you with the primary task that was assigned to the two of you,' Bray continued, 'have you identified any prominent homosexuals among the Cabinet or the royal family?'

'Not as yet, sir, but I acquired a few more names during the trial, and I'll be following those up.'

'Make sure not to be side-tracked by Percy Enright.' Bray grinned kindly. 'He's very good at side-stepping the difficult stuff, then demanding support from his juniors when he gets into difficulties. An excellent officer in some ways, but *very* impetuous, as you probably know from being related to him.'

'You're home early, and you're smiling,' Esther commented as Jack closed the front door behind him. 'Have you been fired or promoted?'

'Neither,' Jack smiled. 'Wilde abandoned his prosecution of Queensberry.'

'Why would he do that? And get those boots off before you walk down the hall carpet. I've spent all morning getting mud off it.'

'Who knows, but if I'd been him, I'd have done the same, rather than have all these pathetic young boys telling the court how Wilde plied them with money, clothes, wine, meals and so on before taking them to bed.'

Esther grimaced. 'But presumably that means that you've finished your part of this business?'

'How do you mean?'

'Well, weren't you supposed to be standing by in case the trial resulted in the dropping of some embarrassing names of people in high places? Now that the trial's over, that surely can't happen.'

'No,' Jack conceded, 'but there's now something else to look into that might result in a few names being dropped into the mix.'

'Such as?'

'Are you still posing as a seamstress at the theatre?'

Esther's face set in a disapproving frown as she replied. 'First of all, I never have to "pose" as a seamstress, since I am one, as your recently repaired suit trousers can testify. Secondly, who do you think was at home all morning cleaning *your* mud off *our* hall carpet?'

'I'll take that as a "no".' Jack grinned, content to have got her briefly energised for what he had to tell her.

'I go back there perhaps twice a week,' she advised him, 'since I've done all the major repair work that was originally required, and now only go in to do running repairs as and when they're needed. Unlike your sister, who seems to have taken to the role as if she wasn't originally planted there by Uncle Percy. I think she sees herself as established in the profession of her dreams.'

'That girl in Wilde's company — Emily something or other?'

'Emily Baxter. What about her?'

'She's still there?'

'Of course, it's her big chance to become a fulltime actress, although the woman she's replacing is due back tomorrow, so she'll have to revert to being the general dogsbody around the place.'

'And it was her fiancé who we think may have impersonated Stranmillis on the train at Crewe?'

'Yes.'

'And he was put up to it by Patrick Ryan?'

'So far as I can recall, yes. That was your last question before you tell me what this is all about.'

'I think he's been murdered.' Jack opened up, as Esther sat listening in mounting horror. 'A body was pulled out of the sea yesterday, somewhere on the coast of Wales. It was a young man approximately six feet tall, and the suit he was wearing belonged to Wilde's theatre company. I'm having a photograph sent down tomorrow, and hopefully it will be a front view, because according to the brief report I read he had suffered a massive blow to the back of the head. I had a quick look at a wall map in the tea room before I left, and I'd hazard a guess that he was knocked unconscious before being heaved off the ship that he had boarded posing as Lord Stranmillis. So unless your actress's fiancé has been in touch recently, I think she just got unengaged.'

'How can you be sure?' Esther queried, her hand to her mouth.

'I can't, obviously,' Jack conceded, 'but we need Emily to identify the man from the photograph, and I thought you might oblige.'

Esther went slightly pale, and shook her head. 'I'm not sure I'd be able to do that, Jack. She's such a sweet girl, and just about to realise her dream of becoming an actress. She'll be devastated, and don't you police officers do that sort of thing all the time?'

'I wasn't suggesting that you do it alone,' Jack reassured her. 'But it would be nice for you to be there when I show her the photograph, in case she goes all hysterical or something.'

'You surely don't propose to do it in the theatre, and expose who I really am?'

'I don't think there's any more need for you to keep your connection with this case secret,' Jack suggested, 'and after the disgraceful stuff that came out in court about Wilde's private life, I don't think that the play will be running for much longer. Not with an audience, anyway. I suppose Lucy will blame me for that.'

Esther had fallen uncharacteristically silent as she contemplated what Jack was asking of her. 'I'll do what you ask, but only if the photograph you were talking about isn't too dreadful. To be told of the loss of a loved one is bad enough, but to be shown a photograph of the body is ten times worse. And I suggest that we take her somewhere public, like a cafe or somewhere. There are plenty in that part of Victoria, and if we're in a public place she'll be less likely to go hysterical.'

'That would be all to the good,' Jack nodded, 'since I'll have some other questions for her that might not go down very well.'

'Such as?'

'Such as can she put her hand on her heart and swear that her uncle's not capable of murder. Because if not, who did it?'

Percy was at the head of the forces of law and order as they made their way down the rough track towards the salt works. He was one of the only two not in police uniform as they headed towards the cottage occupied by Jed Blower and his dog. The other man in civilian clothing was a dog catcher employed by the local authority. He was the first to justify his place in the party as the cottage door opened, and the hound in question hurtled towards them with excited yells, then lowered itself onto its haunches a few feet away from them and growled a warning. The dog catcher — a man called Reilly — reached inside the hessian bag slung over his shoulder and, with a gloved hand, extracted a dead rabbit that he threw at the dog's feet.

After studying it for a few seconds, the dog crawled forward on its stomach and grabbed the rabbit in its jaws, before holding it tightly between its front paws and crunching it, bones and all, in its powerful jaws. As the newly arrived party watched on anxiously the dog slowly rolled onto its side with a slight whimper, and remained motionless. Then came a yell from the cottage door, and as they looked up they were confronted by the sight of Jed Blower pointing some sort of long-barrelled firearm in their direction.

'If yer killed me dog,' Blower yelled, 'then yer next fer the chop. I've got two shots fully loaded, and the geezer wi' the ferrety face gets the fust un!'

'Assuming that was a reference to me,' Percy shouted back calmly, 'then let me assure you that "Toby" isn't dead. As for your two shots, you won't need the second one, because as soon as you loose the first, these gentlemen behind me will give you the benefit of their own collection of firearms. They have six shots between them, and you're enough of an engineer to calculate the odds.'

Blower had decided to lower his gun, and the procession completed the last few yards towards his cottage heaving a collective sigh of relief. Percy raised his police badge high in the air and smiled sarcastically at Blower.

'You didn't make any effort to inspect this properly during my last visit, Mr Blower, so I assume that you accept my identity. If not, let me assure you that these gentlemen behind me didn't hire their uniforms from a theatrical costumier. You're under arrest.'

'What for?' Blower demanded.

'Resisting arrest, and assault with a deadly dog.' Percy smiled back. 'That's only by way of the opening chorus, but when we get that lake drained we can probably add fraud, receiving a stolen Pullman carriage, and possibly murder.'

'Murder?' Blower yelled in disbelief. 'I ain't done no murder!'

'That remains to be seen, does it not?' Percy reminded him. 'Or perhaps you can advise me in advance whether or not, when we extract the railway carriage from that lake, we'll find the body of Lord Stranmillis?'

Chapter Twenty

Jack halted at the front entrance to the three storied residence, then checked the address he had been given by Carson. If Samuel Allen was the blackmailer that he was rumoured to be, then he must be at the top of his profession, if this was how he lived. The narrow but neat little street on the fringes of Shepherd Market was the residential choice of writers, artists and theatrical types, not low-life operators such as Allen, chiselling a few pounds here and there from victims no wealthier than he was, but with horrible secrets that they desperately needed to keep hidden. Then again, if Allen specialised in blackmailing those of an artistic leaning, then he was surrounded by them in this somewhat pretentious offshoot of its better class neighbour Mayfair.

Allen had the effrontery to describe himself on the gold name plate at the front entrance of this block of apartments as a 'Commercial Consultant', but then this was no different from a high class prostitute advertising her 'discreet personal services', as some of those who were known to live in this area actually did in the personal pages of the grubbier newspapers that it was almost a confession of vice to be caught reading. While the hypocrisy of the man might be breathtaking, it would give Jack immense personal pleasure to acquire evidence against him that would puncture his facade, destroy his lucrative trade in other peoples' misery and, as an added bonus, have him locked away in Pentonville for a few years.

But that wasn't why he was standing outside, feeling like a beggar at the gates of Caesar's palace. Jack was here because he had a strong suspicion that the man calling himself a commercial consultant had consulted with Oscar Wilde, ostensibly in the matter of the missing letter to 'Bosie' Douglas, but in reality with some other purpose in mind. Given Wilde's lifestyle and sexual preferences, and given his lauded place at the dinner tables of the wealthy, the ennobled and the downright perverted, it might be the case that Allen was prepared to oblige Wilde in some way or other — financially, or in the form of willing young men — in return for information that Allen could then use to his advantage regarding others of a like persuasion to Wilde's who would be prepared to pay handsomely for his — that is, either Allen's or Wildes' — silence. Or perhaps even both of them.

Was it possible that Wilde had abandoned his action against Queensberry, at considerable financial cost, because he had been warned off pursuing it and risking the prospect that Carson would call a witness who would blow the cover off someone really significant in British public life? After all, the weekend house parties that Wilde and his little boys' club frequented were hardly hosted by, or for the benefit of, your average man in the street.

Jack entered the elegantly tiled entrance hall and climbed the stairs to the first floor, as directed by the name plate at street level. He rang the bell, and after a short delay a manservant of some sort opened the door and looked down his nose at Jack.

'You have business with Mr Allen?'

'I hope so,' Jack replied with an eager expression.

'Is he expecting you?'

'No, since the nature of my business is such that it would have been indiscreet to write in advance.'

'I'll present your card, and enquire if he'll see you,' the flunkey advised Jack in a bored nasal tone as he held out his hand, presumably anticipating a calling card.

Jack tried his best to look embarrassed and confused. 'Again,' he replied, 'it would be unwise of me to leave evidence of my visit here, should the nature of your master's business be such as I have been advised that it is. You may advise him that a Mr Jackson wishes to engage his services, should they be as rumoured.'

'Wait there,' Jack was instructed as the door was closed in his face. Wondering whether Allen would be prepared to risk admitting someone from the street who might well be a hired assassin, given the nature of his business, Jack was relieved when the door was re-opened after less than a minute, and he was ushered down a heavily carpeted hallway and into a drawing room, where the man himself sat behind a small desk.

The room was richly furnished, with oil paintings on the walls, heavy drape curtains overlooking the street below, and several luxurious easy chairs dotted around the room. Allen himself was the epitome of a wealthy man on a day of rest, although it was a Friday, and he rose casually to lean across the narrow desk and shake Jack's hand with warm confidence as he gestured him into the visitor's chair.

'In what way may I be of assistance to you, Mr ... Jackson?'

'It's a very sensitive matter,' Jack mumbled convincingly as he looked down at the table rather than meet Allen's eye.

'Most of the matters I handle are,' Allen replied confidently, and Jack allowed his assumed alter ego to look up and take a closer look at his quarry. He was in his late thirties, apparently, and comfortably attired in a blue velvet smoking jacket with a matching cravat, with a smooth complexion, and sporting a monocle in his left eye socket. His face was almost elegant in its slimness, and the blue eyes gave nothing away except the suggestion created by the light wrinkles that surrounded them that this man was wont to smile a good deal.

It fell embarrassingly silent until Allen removed his monocle, twirled its gold chain thoughtfully in his hand, and broke the ice.

'I believe that you wish to consult me regarding an affair of the heart,' he suggested, and Jack nodded with what he hoped was the appropriate amount of reluctance.

'You are very perceptive, sir,' he mumbled.

'In my profession, one is required to be,' Allen replied.

'I am advised, sir, that the nature of your profession is such that affairs of the heart can be, shall we say, managed to satisfaction.'

'A man or a woman?' Allen demanded bluntly.

'A lady,' Jack confessed. 'A lady, what is more, who is married, but unhappily.'

'Her husband being…?'

Jack shook his head vigorously. 'Forgive me, sir, but we are not yet sufficiently acquainted for me to divulge that information.'

'But it is he whose attitude you wish to see adjusted, in the matter of his wife's affectionate disposition towards yourself? Or is the lady herself proving importunate in her demands?'

'Indeed, sir, you have reached the nub of it, in your first suggestion.'

'I usually do,' Allen boasted as he leaned back in his chair with an air of self-satisfaction. 'There are two types of client who occupy the chair in which you are now seated. Those who wish to relieve themselves of an embarrassment, and those who wish to inflict it on another. You, I suspect, require both such services.'

Despite himself, Jack was impressed by the man's powers of perception, and there could be no doubt that he was capable of moving smoothly in the highest of social circles with the lowest of agendas. He almost had Jack convinced that the story he had invented for the occasion was genuine. It was time to play out more line to catch this most oily of fish.

'If I may be frank, sir,' Jack wheedled, 'I must confess that in the past twelve months or so, I have become enamoured of a certain lady a few years older than myself, the wife of a very wealthy and prominent man around this city whose name would be instantly known to you, were I to divulge it at this stage. My affection for her is reciprocated, and in our less restrained moments we have indulged in matters of a carnal nature of which we should be thoroughly ashamed, although we are not. But in her defence, I should add that she has been starved of any pleasures of that nature for some time now, due to her husband's fondness for other fleshly pursuits.'

'He would not be the first husband to take his pleasures with certain obliging ladies, one of whom even resides on this staircase,' Allen commented.

'Regrettably, for my beloved, that is not his nature. He is — how may I put this? — he is inclined towards sexual partners of the other gender.'

'He's a queer, is that what you're getting at?' Allen demanded bluntly.

Jack did his best to blush. 'Is that what they are called? Men who prefer boys? Young boys?'

'That's one word for them, certainly,' Allen confirmed, 'but where is this leading?'

Jack dropped his gaze to the desk as he gave out the rest of his prepared story. 'To my considerable shame, regret and embarrassment, certain love poems that I had written for the lady proved so acceptable to her that she kept them in her handbag, where they were discovered by her maid, who lost no time in passing them on to the lady's husband, thereby gaining herself a certain financial reward. The husband is now threatening to employ them in a most disagreeable way, namely as evidence in a divorce action.'

'And you wish me to secure the return of these importunate scribblings? How much are you willing to pay for their return, should I agree to approach this man on your behalf?'

'I had not thought in terms of money,' Jack replied with suitable modesty, 'since I am not a wealthy man.'

'But you must have realised that I would require a fee for my services?' Allen replied with a less friendly facial expression. 'Why do you waste my time, sir?'

'I had hoped,' Jack replied deferentially, 'that when I give you certain additional information regarding this man, and his activities with young men at weekend house parties in certain Home Counties country estates, you might be able to persuade him to hand the missives to you in return for not revealing his proclivities to his employer, given his position.'

'His employer being...?'

'The Government. He is a senior public servant whose name is household.'

'Really?' Allen's face lit up in confirmation that Jack had secured his quarry. 'Pray who is this man?'

'Before I divulge his identity,' Jack replied guardedly, hoping that the prize he was dangling in front of Allen's eyes was enough to encourage less discretion on his part, 'how can I be satisfied that you possess the ability to persuade him to part with these letters?'

'You have presumably been advised of my previous successes?' Allen replied as his eyes narrowed in warning. 'Otherwise you would not be here. Might I enquire who recommended my services to you?'

Jack hesitated for what he judged to be the appropriate few seconds before replying. 'I had no direct recommendation as such, but I read of you in the newspapers, regarding your involvement with Mr Oscar Wilde.'

'My name was mentioned but briefly in that disgraceful travesty of a trial,' Allen grimaced, 'and Oscar was poorly advised to give in when he did. He is a good friend of mine, and I feel for him in the public humiliation that he has suffered.'

'It was not disclosed at the trial that you were his friend,' Jack replied with genuine surprise. 'It was mentioned only that you sought to return a certain letter to him in exchange for money. You were unkindly described as a blackmailer, although that is a term that I deprecate. However, it was your experience in returning lost letters that led me to believe that you might be of assistance in my matter.'

'That was a minor matter, compared with some of the business transactions I have negotiated during my twenty or so years in this business,' Allen boasted expansively. 'Some of the leading lights of this nation of ours have consulted me in their anxiety to draw the veil of charity over their indiscretions. I have regularly been consulted by associates of Oscar Wilde in such matters, and it may well be that I have been present at one or more of those weekend house parties to which you referred. Who, pray, is the cuckolded husband to whom you referred earlier?'

'If I supply you with his name, and further evidence of his fondness for young boys, there will be no charge to me for your services? If I adjudge you correctly, you will be charging your fee directly to the gentleman in question, in addition to securing the return of my love poems?'

'Indeed I will,' Allen grinned, 'and it is I who am indebted to you for bringing this matter to my attention.'

'And how do I know that you will not retain these documents so important to me, and charge me for their return?'

'You don't,' Allen replied with a smirk, 'any more than I can rest assured that you were not sent here by a certain Mr Ryan.'

'And who might he be?' Jack hoped that his suddenly increased heart rate was not audible through his waistcoat.

'If you know the man to whom I refer, then you do not need to enquire,' Allen replied peevishly, as if he had said too much. 'But if you do not, then why should I reveal further information about him? What is this additional evidence that you wish to bring to me?'

'Something known only to his wife, my lover.' Jack smiled as an idea came to him. 'We shall both present ourselves to you in the course of the next few days. And so I take my leave.'

He thought he detected a look of relief on Allen's face as he rose from his chair and headed for the door. Was it perhaps that Allen had been fearful that Jack had come armed for the occasion? And had he been referring to the *same* 'Mr Ryan'?

Chapter Twenty-One

Percy watched anxiously as the long lengths of soft piping were connected to the powerful pump that the engineers from the locomotive works had carefully brought down the track, pulled by two horses. Men had been feeding coal into it from the copious pile that had serviced the original pump that now lay, discarded, to one side of the shaft. It was now ready, and as one of the men in overalls gave the 'thumbs up' sign to his colleague, he turned a wheel, and the steam engine hissed into life as the pipes swelled with the first of their load of brine, and Percy watched the first few gallons passing down the long network of pipes until the bulge disappeared into the far distance.

Once the pump was fully engaged, the engineers transferred their attention to the crane that sat at the entrance to the shaft building, and after only a few minutes it was up and firing, and they slowly moved it out into position, with the brine lake on one side and the railway branch line to its rear. The combined noise from two steam devices was almost overpowering, and certainly prohibitive to normal conversation, so Percy beckoned to the senior constable on duty and walked with him a few hundred yards further back up the track before attempting to speak.

'How long do you think it'll take until we see the roof of the Pullman carriage?'

'Assuming that it's down there,' the constable replied, 'the engineers reckon a couple of hours or so. Apparently they reckon that they can pump out five feet an hour.'

'Can I borrow the police wagon for a short trip back into Beeston?'

'You're the Inspector,' the constable replied deferentially. 'As a matter of pure formality, what do you need it for?'

'I'm off to see a man about a signal,' Percy replied. 'By the time I get back, hopefully you'll have a railway carriage for me to inspect. If I'm gone for a while, tell the men to drain it, but not to go inside.'

Back at Beeston signal box, Percy was relieved to see the familiar grinning face of Ted Holmes as he beckoned him inside. The weather was a little warmer than it had been on his previous visit, but the stove in the corner was burning as brightly as it had then, and the heat was almost overpowering. Holmes was seated in the far corner reading a newspaper, and presumably there were no trains due immediately, so this would make it easier.

Percy took the seat indicated by the imperious wave of Holmes's hand, and smiled.

'I was a little remiss during our last conversation,' Percy advised him, 'in that I failed to obtain precise information regarding your shift workings. When you told me that you switched from days to nights every month, I assumed that you meant calendar months, and in any case I was particularly seeking information about an incident that I believe occurred on the evening of the twenty-second of February last. I don't suppose you can remember whether or not you were on duty that evening?'

'I don't 'ave to,' Holmes replied with a smile, 'since it'll be noted in this Train Register.' He stood up, moved the sloping wooden desk, and began to turn back the pages of the register, which lay in its permanent place on top of the desk. 'What were that date agin?'

'February the twenty-second,' Percy replied. 'I believe it was a Friday.'

Holmes found the page, then smiled as he turned to face Percy. 'There it is. Fred Butterworth were on duty that night, an' seemin'ly 'e 'ad a problem wi' the crossin' gates out there. Read it fer yerself.'

He handed the book down to Percy, who squinted as he reminded himself that Beattie was right to nag him about going to see the doctor about his eyesight. But by holding the oily-feeling book a few more inches away from his face, he could just make out the shaky handwriting of a man employed more for his signalling skills than his literacy. *7.38pm. Cart stuck on crossing. Both Distant fixed at warning, Home and Starters at stop. Down Holyhead delayed fifteen minutes while Fireman and Guard helped move the cart.*

'It's a bit vague,' Percy complained, as he finished copying the entry into his notebook, and handed it back to Holmes.

Holmes looked at it again and replied reassuringly. 'It says what it needs ter say. There were a delay when summat got stuck on the level crossin' that yer can see from me winder. It were cleared, but the "down Holyhead" train were 'eld up fer fifteen minutes, an' that's the bit what were important fer the railway company ter know about.'

Percy got up and stood in front of the windows. Down to his right he could see the level crossing that had been in front of him when he turned left down the cinder path to the signal box. The gates were currently open to the narrow country lane that traversed the line at this point, blocking access to trains wishing to proceed through the crossing.

'If a train wants to travel through that crossing down there,' Percy enquired, 'what actions do you have to take? Walk down there and close the gates to road traffic?'

'Not any more,' Holmes grinned. 'A coupla years back they put in that wheel on yer right. I just 'as ter make sure that there's nowt comin', then I turns that wheel an' the gates'll close fer road traffic. Then once it's open ter trains I'm free ter work the signals ter allow it through.'

'So when the gates are open to road traffic, you can't work the signals?' Percy asked as the light began to dawn.

'That's right,' Holmes confirmed. 'If there *is* a train comin', it'll be met wi' a caution signal, follered by a stop. Once I've turned the wheel ter close the gates ter the road traffic, the signals can then be shifted so as ter tell the train driver that it's safe ter proceed.'

'So for as long as those gates are opened for road traffic, any trains in your section will be halted by signals, have I got that right?'

'Yeah. It's when the gates clunk back inter place for train traffic that the signals is freed up, but I still 'as ter work 'em, so as ter call the train through. That's not done automatic, like.'

'Perfect,' Percy muttered out loud, and Holmes agreed with him, not realising to what he was referring. 'It's better than the old system, anyway. I were worn down in them days, goin' up an' down the stairs ter open an' shut the gates by 'and.'

'Just remind me again,' Percy requested. 'The signal I can see out there is which one?'

'That's the "Starter" signal for the down line ter Chester,' Holmes advised him.

'And the other two that Mr Butterworth referred to in his log entry?'

'They'd be the "Distant" and "Home" signals in each direction.'

'Just think about the down line for a moment,' Percy requested. 'There are two signals further east of here — which is which?'

'The "Distant" signal's the one furthest away — about 'alf a mile back from the salt sidin's that yer was so interested in.'

'And the other one — the "Home" signal?'

'Just afore the sidin's, comin' from the east. About another 'alf mile closer to where we're standin'.'

'So for as long as the level crossing down there was set for road traffic, the signal furthest east from here would be set to warn the train to slow down, while the signal just ahead of the sidings would command it to stop?'

'That's right, yeah.'

'And nothing could be altered until the crossing gates were altered to allow trains to pass through?'

'Correct.'

'Where will I find this Mr Butterworth?'

'Same place as yer'd've found me if yer'd come after six,' Holmes advised him. 'We gorra pair o' shared cottages up the road back there. Yer musta passed 'em on yer way down, if yer come direct from Crewe. Them's called "Railway Cottages", an' yer can't miss 'em.'

'Thank you, Mr Holmes.' Percy smiled as he headed for the door. 'I'll be sure to advise Mr Johnson how much assistance you willingly gave me.'

'A pleasure,' Holmes assured him.

Percy found Fred Butterworth in his back garden, digging the drills for his seed potatoes. He was a slightly built man in his late fifties, to judge by appearances, and he straightened up his back with evident relief as he looked down at Percy's extended arm containing his police badge.

'Yer must be the bloke what were enquirin' down at the box earlier this week,' Butterworth observed as he reached into his jacket pocket for his pipe and began to fill it. Percy decided to do likewise, if only to establish a rapport between them before asking Butterworth to dredge his memory.

'A couple of months ago you had an incident at the crossing down near your signal box,' Percy reminded him. 'Just after seven thirty in the evening, when a cart got stuck on the crossing — remember that?'

''Ardly likey ter forget it, am I?' Butterworth grimaced. 'We 'ad the down 'Oly'ead express stood at the 'ome signal while we got the bloody thing off the tracks.'

'What happened, exactly?'

'Well, I 'adn't got the two bells fer the express, so I reckoned it were in order ter let a cart across what I could see comin' down the road, even though it were only pulled by a single 'oss, an' bugger me if the bleedin' thing didn't shed a wheel, right there in the middle o' the tracks. I shouted down to the blokes what were wi' the cart' ter try and get it cleared off the line, but I couldn't go an' help 'em, 'cos just then I gets the two bells — that's "train entering section", but o' course it 'as to slow down and stop at me 'ome signal. Then the fireman comes down to see what the delay is, as the Rule Book says 'e must, and he gets the guard to help, and between 'em they managed ter lift up the axle an' put the wheel back on. Then they pushed it off the tracks, so as I could open the gates fer the express. By the time the fireman and guard had got back to the train, it were fifteen minutes late. I wrote it all out in the train register.'

'Yes, I read that,' Percy assured him. 'And while all this was happening, that express would have been standing at a signal further east?'

'Yeah — the "'Ome" signal, near the branch line ter the salt mine.'

'And there were two men with the cart?'

'Yeah.'

'Were they locals?'

'No. The one what done the most o' the talkin' spoke funny, like 'e weren't from round these parts.'

'Irish?'

'Wouldn't know. But not local.'

'Thank you for all that.' Percy smiled. 'Now I'll let you get back to your potatoes.'

Thirty minutes later Percy was back at the salt workings, watching the last of the brine splashing out of the Pullman coach that had been hauled onto the bank of the lake and was sitting upright on its bogie. One of the engineers standing to its side called over to him.

'When we open that door, the rest o' the water'll come rushin' out, so stand back.'

'Very well, do it,' Percy instructed, 'but don't be surprised if a body floats out.'

Both carriage doors were opened at the same time, and fountains of greeny-white water poured from the sodden sides of the former Pullman wagon, and out with it came various items such as glasses, bottles, and two heavy portmanteaux — but no body.

'You were wrong about the body,' the senior constable murmured at his elbow.

Percy turned and glared at him. 'It was only ever a possibility, but the presence of those two heavy bags suggests the existence of a body somewhere else, possibly in the lake. So you have to pray that it turns up somewhere else, or the man himself chooses to reveal his continued existence to the authorities, or you'll be sending mermaids in diving suits in there to find it. Now get your men to scour every inch of the inside of that wagon, and send me a list of everything you find in there. Then go through that cottage in search of something that looks as if a garden spade gave birth to a mortice lock.'

'And you?'

'Me, I'm going back to London, and some decent food for once. You've achieved something at least — I never thought the day would come when I'd look forward to my wife's cooking.'

Chapter Twenty-Two

'I might have known I wouldn't be allowed a day off,' Jack grumbled as he walked away in disgust from the open front door, leaving Percy to follow him down the hallway. Jack pushed open the kitchen door to reveal Esther and announced, with heavy sarcasm, 'He followed me home — can I keep him?'

'Not if he's intending to stay to dinner.' Esther smiled as she turned her head from the sink. 'The mince will barely stretch two ways, let alone three.'

'Will it help if I go and get something from Farringdon Market?' Percy asked. 'Or, if you prefer, we can all go down to Whitehall for a meat pie. We're both supposed to be at work anyway.'

'I'll do you a deal,' Jack offered. 'We share our Saturday dinner with you, and you absolve us from attending Sunday dinner in Barking.'

'Would that I could, on a permanent basis, including absolution for myself,' Percy grinned, 'but as it happens I'll be spending Sunday sending wires all over the north of England.'

'Applying for a transfer?' Jack asked as he slid into a chair at the kitchen table.

Percy shook his head. 'No — looking for Stranmillis's body.'

'You think he's dead?' Esther joined Jack briefly at the table.

'Any risk of a cup of tea?' Percy asked as he took the third seat. 'We have a lot of information to exchange. At least, I hope it'll be an exchange, and not a monologue from me.'

'I'll put the pan on to boil,' Jack offered.

'So what makes you think Stranmillis is dead?' Esther asked eagerly as Jack filled the pan and lit the gas.

'I found the Pullman carriage exactly where I suspected it might be found,' Percy announced proudly.

'In that lake?' Jack said over his shoulder.

'In that lake indeed,' Percy confirmed, 'in twenty feet of salty brine, where it had remained hidden since it was diverted from the Holyhead Express.'

'How did they manage that?' Esther asked, intrigued, and Percy treated her to one of his insufferable smiles of triumph and condescension.

'It's quite complicated, but to explain it in simple terms, they caused a diversion at the level crossing by the signal box that controls the stretch of line that includes the points that lead to the sidings. While the train was held stationary at a signal out of sight of the signalman who was too preoccupied getting a broken down cart off his level crossing, they unhooked the Pullman, and presumably at that point transferred the tail light to the luggage van. And as the signalman told me, the guard was too busy helping to shift the cart to know what was going on at the back of the train. Then, when the train pulled away, they used a duplicate Annetts Key which was discovered yesterday inside the cottage of the site foreman. Employing that key, they changed the points and towed the Pullman into the salt works sidings using the locomotive that's kept in the salt works for towing wagons to the main line. It then hauled the Pullman down to the salt lake that's formed at the site over the years, before they employed a crane they have conveniently available as part of their normal equipment to lift it into the lake. We partly drained the lake two days ago and fished the Pullman out of the lake.'

'What did you find in the carriage?' Jack placed the tea things in the middle of the table. 'Anything significant? No body, obviously.'

'No, but six heavy bags full of clothing,' Percy advised them. 'What does that tell you?'

'That Stranmillis wasn't reunited with his luggage,' Jack replied.

Esther looked puzzled. 'But wasn't it all part of his plan to reclaim all that clothing at some stage? The whole point of him using the Pullman in the first place was to transport his chosen belongings to wherever he intended to hide himself. So why did he instruct them to leave it all in the carriage when it went underwater? I dread to think what state that clothing must be in after a month in salt water.'

'Think it through,' Percy invited them as he poured himself a cup of tea and looked pointedly at where the biscuit tin would normally be located. Esther took the hint and retrieved the tin from the cupboard above the stove, well out of child reach, placing it in the middle of the table with an exasperated shake of the head in Jack's direction.

'Either he didn't intend to catch up with his clothing, or he was double-crossed,' Jack announced proudly.

'And why would he go to the trouble of putting all his clothes in the Pullman, if he didn't intend to collect them later?' Esther challenged him. 'But he wouldn't have been the only one to be double-crossed, would he?'

'Clearly you have something to tell *me*,' Percy prompted them.

Jack nodded. 'The actor who was employed to impersonate Stranmillis on the boat across to Dublin is now playing the role of a corpse in a mortuary somewhere in Wales. The description fits the man who was engaged to that actress at Wilde's theatre, and I checked on the map. I reckon he was heaved overboard from the vessel on which he'd used Stranmillis's ticket. Why kill him when he'd already fulfilled the role allocated to him in all this? It all fits with a massive double cross that involved Stranmillis.'

'It could have been Stranmillis himself who organised his death,' Esther pointed out. 'Either way, Jack and I were planning on going down to the theatre again on Monday and giving his fiancée — Emily Baxter — the bad news, and enquiring of her whether she can suggest anyone who might have wanted him dead for reasons other than his part in the Stranmillis disappearance.'

'Why wait until Monday?' Percy asked. 'What's wrong with today or tomorrow?'

'The theatre's closed on Sundays,' Esther advised him, 'and today is the matinee performance, the final day when Emily's stepping into the role left vacant while the main actress gets over her illness. That gives me the excuse to return to the theatre on Monday and make the alterations needed to the stage costume that the two women have been sharing. Then Jack and I were planning on taking her out to morning tea and breaking the news to her as gently as we can. While we're at it, we can ask her about other reasons why her fiancé might have been killed.'

'And we'd better not lose any more time over that,' Jack added, 'even if it means that Esther will have to reveal her real part in all this. Rumour has it that the play won't be running much longer anyway, after the revelations about Wilde's private life.'

'Indeed, we haven't even touched on that yet,' Percy reminded them as he selected his fourth biscuit. 'I only read about it in the newspapers, but you were there, Jack. Why did Wilde give in so easily?'

'I don't know officially,' Jack replied, 'and obviously neither he nor his counsel sought to consult me in the matter. But Carson had a whole busload of young men waiting in the wings to tell horrific tales about how Wilde had plied them with presents, meals, champagne and suchlike, then seduced them. If I'd have been Wilde, I'd have given in too, rather than have all that aired in public. I think that Stranmillis may have been the victim of blackmail, which would explain why he chose to disappear, before somebody else perhaps decided to make his absence more permanent.'

'What makes you suspect blackmail?' Percy asked.

'Well, during the trial there was a reference to a shady character called "Allen", who allegedly tried to blackmail Wilde regarding a love letter he'd sent to Bosie Douglas. I paid Mr Allen a visit, unofficially of course.'

'You broke into his house, you mean?' Percy demanded with a look of concern.

'No, I pretended to be a client,' Jack reassured him. 'There's no doubt that Allen is a blackmailer, but a very successful one who specialises in the wealthy and the well placed in society. His rooms on the fringe of Mayfair are more appropriate for a successful lawyer or banker, and he was boasting about his many connections, plus his friendship with Wilde — contrary to the picture that Wilde sought to paint in court — and he as good as offered to blackmail anyone I cared to name.'

'Talking of house calls, fancy a trip to Cambridge Terrace before we come back armed with dinner, courtesy of Farringdon Market?' Percy asked Jack.

'Why is that address familiar?'

Percy looked unimpressed. 'Esther's right — you have a memory like a colander. Cambridge Terrace is the town house of the possibly late Lord Stranmillis. He's hardly likely to be home, and we should have subjected it to a minute inspection at the very start of this business. We may find something there that points the finger at the root cause of the initial disappearance, and perhaps even the reason for his possible demise.'

'You still think he may have been done in?'

'It begins to smell that way. And talking of smells, this pipe of mine has spent too long in my jacket pocket. Let's head out and bring back something alluring for dinner.'

The factotum who answered Percy's commanding summons at the house on the eastern fringe of Regents Park somehow seemed to have been expecting their arrival, and looked only briefly at the police badges they held up in front of his face before stepping back and inviting them in.

'We haven't heard from the master for several weeks,' the man advised them. 'I'm Lancaster, the master's manservant, and I helped him pack a number of bags of clothing before he set off on his trip to Ireland. Is he in some sort of trouble?'

'Do you have any reason for believing that he might be?' Percy demanded.

The man shook his head. 'No, except that he seemed a bit distracted when he was planning his Dublin trip, then I received a telegram from the man he was supposed to be meeting over there, to say that he hadn't arrived. It's unlike him to be away from London for so long a time, and not to be in touch with instructions regarding his wardrobe. Although most of it went with him, and he gave me a massive tip just before he got into his coach for Euston that morning. He also gave one to Preedy, the coachman, almost as if he wasn't expecting to return. Anyway, assuming that you're here to conduct a search, where would you like to start?'

Two hours later they'd been carefully through the master bedroom, three spare bedrooms, a sitting room, a drawing room, a kitchen with attached scullery, and several rooms on the top floor that were allocated to live-in domestic staff. That left just a study of some sort, and as they closed the door behind them and contemplated the neatly maintained collection of desks, chairs, bookshelves and cabinets, Jack gave voice to his innermost thoughts.

'In view of all the filth I heard during the Wilde trial, and what I had the misfortune to witness in that Molly House, I half expected to find some women's dresses in the wardrobes upstairs.'

'You're guilty of assuming that he was a Mary-Anne, are you not?' Percy smiled. 'And for all you know, he took his fancy dress with him. Remind me to enquire what was in all those clothing bags in the Pullman. If I'm correct in one of my deductions, he dressed as a woman in order to leave the carriage at Crewe, but I assume that when he changed back into a man in the Waiting Room he carried the ladies' attire back out in the bag he was carrying. If it's in the Pullman, then we know he got back on board it. I hope so, because if not he could have hopped on board any other train at Crewe — possibly one back here to London.'

'Let's see if there's anything here to give us a lead,' Jack suggested, 'since I hear the call of Farringdon Market. Do they do cooked lamb roasts, can you remember?'

'You'll settle for fish and chips again, I assume?' Percy began opening the drawers to the main desk that sat in pride of place

221

in front of a window with a commanding second floor view of Regents Park.

Jack wandered over to what looked like a writing desk in front of the bookcase, most of whose volumes seemed to be about Irish history — a curious taste in literature for someone who hadn't been back to the land of his birth for several years. Jack was about to reach out for one particular volume that promised to be illustrated when there was an excited shout from Percy.

'Look at this, Jack my boy! All Stranmillis's bank records for the past couple of years, with a *very* interesting series of cash withdrawals in recent months. Fits the blackmail theory, does it not?'

'So might this,' Jack replied distractedly as his eye fell on a blotting pad lying face up on the desk. It contained a few smudgy remnants of items that it had recently been employed on, and one in particular seemed to possess a nagging familiarity. It was an address of some sort, but because it was the blotted version of the inked original, it was written backwards.

'What have you got?' Percy walked over with a handful of bank records.

'This blotter pad,' Jack advised him as he nodded down at the item in question. 'There's some sort of address that looks vaguely familiar, but it's written backwards, since it's obviously the inked impression left when it was blotted, presumably by Stranmillis.'

Percy picked up the blotting pad and walked over to the mirror on the far wall. As Percy held the blotter up before the mirror Jack gave a yell of delight as he was able to read the address the right way round in the mirror image.

'That's Allen's address! You know, the man I visited — Wilde's friend, the blackmailer?'

'Of course I remember,' Percy advised him. 'You have the only colander brain in the family. But it further confirms the blackmail theory, does it not? Stranmillis chose to bow out of public life because he could no longer tolerate paying Allen's price for his silence.'

'That's one theory,' Jack conceded. 'Another is that if we don't go home bearing dinner in the next hour or so, I'll need to leave the country to escape Esther's nagging.'

Chapter Twenty-Three

'Perhaps Stranmillis isn't dead,' Jack suggested to Percy as they sat in the latter's office on the Sunday morning, awaiting replies to the telegraph enquiries that Percy had launched northwards the previous afternoon.

'Let's look at the facts as we know them,' Percy suggested. 'Stranmillis organises a very clever and complex operation to secure his apparent disappearance, after clearing his bank account of all but a token amount of money sufficient to keep that account operational, and also plans to take most of his clothes with him. In order to make his escape possible, he switches identities at Crewe, and plans to head off to who knows where, leaving instructions for his clothing to be forwarded to him in due course, once he's re-established himself in a new identity somewhere where he's not well known.'

'All of which suggests that he's very clever, very determined, and very wealthy,' Jack argued. 'But that's *all* it suggests. What makes you think he's been murdered?'

'Well, for a start, why was the Pullman lobbed into the lake, containing all his precious clothes?' Percy queried. 'Not only would that not have been done on his instruction, but it must have been done by those who knew that he wouldn't be requiring them. Nor did anyone steal them, which suggests a far more important motive, namely that of disposing of the man himself. Then there's the sheer number of people involved in the operation — two at the railway crossing, at least one — if not more — at the salt workings, and the substitute Stranmillis who was a hired actor, at an absolute minimum. Also, if it was known that he was travelling with a large amount of money in cash, the temptation for murder and robbery would have been almost overwhelming.'

'Aren't those two motives inconsistent?' Jack argued.

Percy smiled. 'You *are* still awake, aren't you? But either way, the man's probably dead.'

'So where did he go after Crewe, and where's his body?' Jack challenged him.

'Put yourself in Stranmillis's shoes.' Percy smiled as he filled his pipe with his favourite 'Navy Plug' and applied a match. 'You want to get away completely. Where would you go?'

'Abroad, clearly,' Jack replied. 'Perhaps America — can't you get there by ship from Liverpool?'

'One of the reasons why I sent a cable to the Liverpool Constabulary, who even as we speak are likely to be contacting the shipping lines for convenient sailings at around that time, with tickets booked by either "Lord Stranmillis" or a "Mr Bunbury". Also the Liverpool hotels, for overnight accommodation acquired under either name.'

'Liverpool can be reached by train on the LNW Railway, certainly,' Jack conceded, 'but so can Manchester, and — by way of connecting services — anywhere in Scotland, where Stranmillis has an estate, remember. Or even, as you pointed out yesterday, back to London via Rugby, which gives access to the whole of the Midlands. You're looking for a needle in a haystack.'

'I've sent the same request to Manchester,' Percy advised him, 'and if neither of those cities has heard of him we might consider what you're suggesting. At least I'm not just sitting waiting for him to walk in here and shout "boo" — like this chap.'

'This is for the Sergeant, sir,' the uniformed constable advised them as he laid a sealed envelope on the desk in front of where Jack was seated. After thanking and dismissing him, Jack opened the envelope and smiled.

'At least Esther and I can go ahead with our plans for tomorrow, although I'm not looking forward to showing this to the woman who was planning on making a life with him.'

He slipped the photograph across the table to Percy, who found himself staring at the somewhat ethereal image of a pale face that had presumably once been handsome, the ghostly image of which was rendered even more spectral by the deposits of salt in the eyebrows and moustache, and around the eye sockets and nasal cavities.

'This your man from the Welsh coast?' Percy asked. 'The one who impersonated Stranmillis on the train from Crewe? I don't envy you the job of showing that to his beloved. That's one aspect of this rotten job of ours that I've always hated. Do you really think that she can take our enquiries much further?'

'No idea at this stage, but this photograph will give her a powerful incentive to help us find whoever launched him into the Irish Sea.'

'Anything from the examination of the body?'

'Just confirmation of the cause of death. In the usual medical terms, of course, but it reads to me like a smack on the back of the head with an iron bar. I bet they have plenty of those available aboard an ocean-going vessel. And apparently he had thirty pounds on him, so robbery wasn't the motive.'

'Quite. But doesn't it strike you as curious that they did away with him, when he'd already fulfilled his part of the operation?'

'They would hardly have done it *before* then, would they?'

'Very funny. But my point is that somebody clearly wanted to tie up all the loose ends, and all we've learned about

Stranmillis so far suggests that he wasn't a murderer, so why did someone *else* want to cover their tracks? The man who hired him perhaps — Ryan, wasn't it, according to the poor man's fiancé?'

'I've just remembered something! When I spoke with that blackmailer Allen the other day, he revealed that he was apprehensive that I might have been sent by Ryan.'

'Just adds weight to my argument.' Percy smiled in his self-satisfied way. 'If Ryan is the violent type, which Allen's reaction tends to suggest, and Ryan hired his niece's boyfriend with every intention of having him done away with, then he could well be capable of organising Stranmillis's demise.'

'Aren't the two of them good friends?'

'So were Henry VIII and Cardinal Wolsey, once,' Percy pointed out. 'Read some history, instead of that rubbish by Dickens. And even if only one man was responsible for the killing on board the boat to Dublin, that's one more to add to the collection, and it suggests a sizeable team, possibly with an Irish connection.'

It fell silent until a man hurried down the corridor towards them with a message. Percy scanned the incoming wire urgently, then threw it down on his desk with a frustrated noise.

'No passages booked to New York on either of the vessels leaving at around that time, at least not under either of those names.'

It was late in the afternoon, during their tenth game of 'hangman', that a cable arrived that caused Percy to leap from his chair in excitement.

'One for the patient plodder! A hotel in Liverpool reports the curious behaviour of a man calling himself "Sir John Bunbury", who paid cash in advance for two nights, failed to use the room on the second night, and was being closely observed for possible Fenian connections because he spoke with a faint Irish accent and had no luggage other than one large carpet bag which, when opened by the hotel's security manager, proved to be full of ladies' clothing.'

'When was this?'

Percy's smile grew even wider. 'The twenty-second and twenty-third of February — precisely when Stranmillis might be expected to have jumped a train at Crewe, and headed for Liverpool. Presumably he planned to pay for a crossing to New York or somewhere in cash, the following day or shortly thereafter.'

'So you'll be heading for Liverpool?'

'No *we* will, but by separate trains, I suspect. You have to speak to the dead man's actress fiancée tomorrow, and I have some important questions to ask of a man currently missing the daylight in Crewe. The bloke who was in charge of the salt workings — I gave orders for him not to be granted bail, and he's being held on a suspected murder charge, which is probably a little harsh. But now he can earn his redemption. May I borrow that photograph of Stranmillis with his two university pals? I have a feeling that it will come in useful.'

The other customers in the cafe in Cathedral Walk, a neat little alleyway to the rear of the St James Theatre, looked the other way out of politeness as the pretty young girl cried her eyes out, with the occasional scream, on the shoulder of the older woman and the stern looking man who was with them.

'I *knew* in my heart that something was wrong,' Emily gasped between sobs, 'but I could never have imagined in a thousand years that someone had killed him! I just can't bring myself to believe that anyone could *do* such a thing to such a gentle, loving soul like Giles. Do you have the remotest idea why?' she pleaded as she gazed through her tears at a grim-faced Jack.

Jack braced himself to give the only answer he could. 'How well did your fiancé Giles get on with your uncle — the one who hired him?'

'Pretty well, or so it seemed,' Emily gurgled through her tears as she wiped her nose on the handkerchief she was handed by Esther, being one of several she had brought along for the occasion. Then the penny dropped with Emily, and she stared at Jack with eyes wide with shock and disbelief. 'Do you honestly believe that it could have been Uncle Paddy who had Giles murdered? I know that at first he was a bit suspicious of him, mainly out of a desire to protect me, I thought, but once we became engaged he seemed to accept him, and went to considerable lengths to make him welcome at our Summer house parties.'

'Those parties,' Jack persevered. 'Was there anyone else there who might have intended harm to either Giles or Lord Stranmillis?'

'Why are you asking about him?' Emily asked, confused but by no means lacking the ability to put two and two together.

Jack sighed and opted for the entire truth. 'Lord Stranmillis has disappeared, and he went missing at exactly the same time that Giles accepted your uncle's offer of an acting role "somewhere out west", as you described it to Esther. The "somewhere out west" turned out to be Crewe, in Cheshire, where Giles was hired to impersonate Lord Stranmillis as part of his Lordship's desire to disappear for a while — possibly for ever. Do you know any reason why he'd want to do that?'

'Not really,' Emily replied in an uncertain voice. 'Although at my twenty-first party he seemed to be having some sort of argument with another of the guests. I can't remember the guest's name, and the argument was only brief, then they seemed to get over it. Dermot — Lord Stranmillis, that is — left the party early that particular weekend, which was unusual for him. He normally stayed on until the Monday morning, after breakfast, but he left on the Sunday afternoon. However, he seemed all right during my big party on the Saturday night; his argument with whoever it was had taken place around lunchtime on the Saturday.'

'This was your twenty-first party, you said?' Esther asked, and Emily nodded. 'Attendance was by invitation?' was Esther's next question, and again Emily nodded.

'Yes, but there were a huge number of people invited. I remember, because I did the seating plan for the tables at my birthday dinner, and it took ages. One of my hobbies is calligraphy, and I did the table plan in old English copperplate, using a special pen and coloured inks.'

'Do you still have it?' Jack asked eagerly.

Emily nodded. 'I'm pretty sure I kept it, because I was so proud of it. Do you want me to see if I can dig it out?'

'Yes please,' Jack urged her, 'since from what you were saying it sounds as if the person that Lord Stranmillis was arguing with was one of those guests.'

'Why are yer 'oldin' me on a murder charge?' Jed Blower demanded as he sat across a rickety table from Percy Enright in the only interview room that the local police station in Crewe possessed. 'I ain't done no murder, an' yer knows it.'

'I don't know anything, other than what you're prepared to tell me.' Percy smiled encouragingly. 'But what you *do* tell me may help to clarify matters regarding how that Pullman carriage finished up in your brine lake — and *why*.'

'It were 'is Lordship 'imself what ordered me ter do it, an' if — like yer said — it were 'is own private carriage, then where's the 'arm done?'

'Tell me the whole story,' Percy demanded, and Blower obliged without any apparent hesitation. Mind you, Percy reminded himself, he'd had a day or two to dream up the story he was about to deliver.

'Well, it were like this,' Blower began. 'I were in me cottage one day, feedin' the dog, when 'is Lordship turned up in 'is coach. 'E told me as 'ow a train from Crewe were gonna be deliverin' 'is private carriage down ter the top o' the sidin's one night, an' when that 'appened me an' the boy was ter tow it down ter the lake an' use the crane ter chuck it in.'

'A rather unusual instruction, you'd have to admit,' Percy commented.

Blower nodded. 'Particularly since it were gonna be delivered after dark, an' we was ter chuck it in the lake as soon as it arrived.'

'How did you know which night it was to be?'

'I were given the date by 'is Lordship.'

'He came to the salt diggings personally in order to give you this instruction?'

'Yeah. That were pretty unusual — in fact it were the first time — since I normally got me orders from 'Arry 'Ardcastle, the site manager.'

'So that was the first time you'd ever seen his Lordship?'

'Yeah.'

Percy reached inside his inside jacket pocket and extracted the university reunion photograph that he'd been given by Jack, then placed it in front of Blower with a question.

'Do you recognise anyone in this photograph?'

'Yeah, that's 'is Lordship, on the right.'

'You're quite certain of that?' Percy said with a beaming smile that he couldn't prevent, given its spontaneity. 'Not the one in the middle?'

'The short one? No — it were definitely the one on the right. Did yer find 'is body in that railway carriage? If yer did, I knew nowt about it, 'onest ter God.'

'No, there was no body in the carriage, Mr Blower, and you're no longer suspected of murder. In fact, given what you told me regarding your authorisation to dump the carriage in the lake, I'm not sure that we can charge you with anything, except perhaps having a dog out of control. You'll find Toby at the local dog pound when you're released later this morning, although you'll probably have to pay a nominal fee for his upkeep for the last few days. And I strongly recommend that when you get him home you keep him chained up.'

'We could have had dinner in that cafe,' Esther reminded Jack, 'or you could have gone back to work and left me to come home on my own. Why did you want to come with me?'

'I wanted to talk to you where we wouldn't be overheard.'

'What about?'

'I never thought I'd hear myself saying this, but I need your cool independent brain to think us through what we do next.'

'I'm not sure what we can do, until Emily gives us that guest list. I'll obviously be turning up to the theatre every day until she does, but what did you have in mind after that?'

'Well, it may be that I'll be taking you to meet a blackmailer.'

'I beg your pardon?'

'We know that Stranmillis was paying money to a blackmailer — a man called Samuel Allen, who I visited a few days ago in the guise of the lover of the wife of a senior public figure whose husband was threatening her with divorce after he found some compromising letters in her handbag.'

Esther giggled, then apologised, 'I'm sorry, but you just reminded me of a funny line in Wilde's play, which I saw them rehearsing a scene from one day. One of the heroes explains to this frosty lady that he was an orphan who'd been found, as a baby, in a handbag at Victoria Station. The lady replies "A handbag?" in this screamingly funny voice. Anyway, sorry, carry on.'

'As I was endeavouring to explain,' Jack replied grumpily, 'I was adopting this false character in the hope of getting this Allen bloke to drop something out by accident about the extent of his blackmailing activities. At the time I was fishing for possible big names that might be at risk of disclosure by Wilde during the trial, but now I'm thinking along other lines. If Stranmillis was being blackmailed by Allen, that may be the reason why he decided to disappear, and he got his very old friend Ryan to supply the actor to impersonate him after the train left Crewe, where Stranmillis had conveniently hopped off. According to what Uncle Percy and I have learned, he was heading to Liverpool, where we think he may have been intending to jump on a boat to America. For all we know, he already did, and Uncle Percy's up there making the necessary enquiries at a hotel where we know he was staying on the night he changed trains.'

'Get to the bit where you tell me why we have to visit a blackmailer.'

'Bear with me while I develop this theory,' Jack requested, 'since I need you to double think it with me. It may be that the reason why Stranmillis decided to make himself scarce was something to do with this argument he had with someone during Emily's party weekend. We know that the argument wasn't with Ryan, else she would have named him. According to her it was one of the other guests, and I'm wondering if it was this bloke Allen.'

'We don't even know that Allen was at the party,' Esther objected.

'But we will when Emily produces that seating plan, won't we? And we'll also have a list of other people it might have been. What I'm proposing is that we go through the list of guests and pick a name — someone very prominent in Government circles. Then we go back to Allen, and you pretend to be that man's wife, and my lover, in the hope that Allen confirms that either he — Allen, that is, or the man whose wife you're pretending to be — was the one who fell out with Stranmillis. My money's on Allen, and that the row was all about Stranmillis refusing to pay any more blood money to him, and that prompted him to make it look as if he'd died or something.'

'So, what's Stranmillis's dark secret?'

'He's unmarried, and a close friend of Oscar Wilde — close enough to finance his latest play. What do *you* think?'

'I've already expressed my opinion that just because a man remains unmarried does not automatically mean that he's — well, one of "those".'

'No, but he could be, or there could be some other secret he'd want to keep hidden. Maybe something about how he made his millions, who knows? But the regular cash withdrawals from his bank account, and the fact that he had Allen's address, all point to blackmail, given Allen's known talents in that department.'

'So Stranmillis decides that he's paid Allen all that he intends to pay — then what?'

'He tells Allen that he's getting no more, and Allen threatens to go public on whatever he's got on Stranmillis, so his Lordship decides to go to America, and enlists his lifelong friend Ryan in the subterfuge.'

'But why not just do precisely that — go to America? Why make it look as if he's disappeared?'

'To put everyone off the scent, obviously. If it's something really infamous, Stranmillis's name would be all over the newspapers, and he'd be hounded wherever he went, including America. But if he stages his own disappearance, then reappears in another country using another name, he's off the hook. We know that he hired a hotel room in Liverpool under the name of "Sir John Bunbury", which is one of the characters from Wilde's play, or so you told me.'

'How do you account for Giles Holloway's murder?' Esther demanded.

'I admit that's a bit of a puzzle,' Jack conceded, 'but from what Emily told us it's unlikely that her uncle Paddy Ryan had anything to do with that. It may well be that Stranmillis himself ordered that, to cut any remaining links to his disappearance.'

'If so, he must have been pretty desperate,' Esher pointed out. 'He's not only walking away from all his business interests, all his friends, and his entire past, but he's prepared to commit murder to keep his disappearance ruse secret. What on earth could he have been running from?'

'We might find that out when we visit Mr Allen.'

Jack returned to his office at the Yard two hours later, to be advised that he had an urgent cable. It was from Percy, and it read: 'I've located your body for this week. Join me at the Adelphi Hotel in Liverpool.'

Chapter Twenty-Four

'Why did you drag me all the way up here, only to tell me that I can't even view the body?' Jack demanded peevishly as he and Percy sat propping up the Residents' Bar in the Adelphi Hotel. 'And how can we be sure that it's Stranmillis's anyway?'

'The jacket he was wearing when he went coal-mining was not only totally unsuitable for the occasion, but it had the label of his London tailor in it. That tailor's garments are so exclusive that they actually contain a client identification number as part of the label, and a quick cable to London generated confirmation that the jacket was made for Stranmillis last November. As for not seeing the body, even the police doctor had to delay his examination for long enough to spew in a bucket at his side. Cause of death was a whack on the head, probably several weeks ago, and consistent with his Lordship's last night having been spent here in the Adelphi, before he sallied forth onto the docks to pay in advance for what he believed would be his accommodation on a cargo freighter bound for Cork.'

'The same freighter in which his body was located?'

'Indeed, but travelling in the humblest of steerage berths, under fifty tons of coal in the bunker.'

'So how was the body discovered?'

'From its smell, apparently. It's a long story, but two of the deckhands on the vessel were suspected of being Fenians, and had attracted the attention of our own Liverpool counterparts. They believed that the two Irish gentlemen — and I employ that term loosely — had been over here buying guns, and just before the vessel was about to cast off they jumped on board, arrested the men in question, and began a search of the vessel for the suspected guns. They were halfway through digging down into the coal bunker — an obvious hiding place — when they were almost gassed to death by the stench of rotting flesh. The rest you can work out for yourself.'

'Again, and before you buy me that second pint, what the Hell do you need me up here for?'

'To be present when one of the two deckhands in question — a Mr Brady, apparently — tells us a little story in exchange for not being charged with murder, then hanged by the neck until dead. He claims that he and his chum were simply disposing of a body that had already been created, and chose the coal bunker in the belief that they'd be safely back on Irish soil before the pile got too low.'

'That sounds like shit, even to me,' Jack snorted. 'A more likely version of events is that Stranmillis was croaked when he boarded the vessel on the twenty-third, and has lain there ever since. It's too much of a coincidence to suggest that he was brought back, weeks later, to the very vessel that he'd been planning to board. Has the master of the vessel confirmed that Stranmillis was booked to travel to Cork with him?'

'He has indeed, except he knew him as "John Bunbury", and he claims that after his passenger paid for his fare, he left the ship to return to his hotel. But the good captain can't explain why he didn't cast off when he was scheduled to do, except in terms that he was awaiting a shipment of guns. He's prepared to put up his hand for that, rather than "Accessory to Murder", which is the alternative that I offered him.'

'So if he hadn't been greedy and waited for the guns, the idea was to heave Stranmillis over the side halfway across the Irish Sea, or perhaps into the ship's furnace?'

'Probably, but we may have to deny ourselves all the gory details if we're to complete our part of this job we were lumbered with.'

'Which is, remind me again?'

'To find out who betrayed Stranmillis, and what it was that he knew that led to his untimely demise.'

'Esther and I found out yesterday, from Giles Holloway's former fiancée, that Stranmillis had an argument with someone who was also a guest at her twenty-first birthday party. We're awaiting the guest list from that party, but my money's on that nasty little blackmailing type Samuel Allen, whose address you saw written in that mirror. I think that Stranmillis refused to pay Allen any more, Allen threatened to expose his guilty secret, and his Lordship chose to leave the country.'

'As, in the event, he did, but in a different manner to the one he intended,' Percy pointed out. 'But if he was leaving town solely in order to preserve himself from a red face, why was he killed?'

'Because his exposure would result in the exposure of someone else?'

'But *think* about it,' Percy countered. 'If Stranmillis's secret was also someone else's secret, then that someone else had an interest in ensuring that Stranmillis made an effective disappearance.'

'What more permanent and effective disappearance can you imagine than death?' Jack replied. 'Or could it be the case that there was only one person with the secret, and it wasn't Stranmillis? If our dearly departed peer of the realm knew something about someone in a high place, and was blackmailing him then that someone had a perfect motive for doing him in, did they not?'

'Then why was Stranmillis paying money to Allen? And why would someone offer to help him disappear, rather than simply send a couple of toughs round to his house with a meataxe?'

'We don't know what the cash withdrawals were for,' Jack reminded him, 'and we've been assuming blackmail because sodomy is all the rage this season, and Stranmillis never married. He may have been paying Allen to put the squeezers on someone *else* for reasons of his own. And may I suggest that his success in obtaining Government contracts has been way above the expected average? Whoever it is either got tired of it all, or panicked, or whatever, and told Stranmillis to leave town for the good of his health.'

Percy fell silent for well over a minute as he considered what Jack was offering by way of a case theory. Finally a grin broke across his face, and he leaned forward to slap Jack on the back.

'I'm proud of you, Jack my boy! Never too proud to listen to your wife when it comes to something important.'

'I thought that up all by myself!' Jack objected, 'and we've no way of knowing, at this stage, how much of all that is accurate.'

'Which is why tomorrow's interview with Mr Brady is so important,' Percy reminded him.

'I wasn't sure if you'd be here today,' Emily Baxter whispered as she sidled up to Esther behind a rack of stage costumes that Esther was examining for the fourth time that morning. 'Here's that table plan I promised you. The ink's faded a bit in places, but you can still make out all the names.'

'Did you manage to remember which one was arguing with Lord Stranmillis on the Saturday morning?' Esther asked hopefully.

Emily shook her head. 'I didn't know all of them well. Uncle Paddy used the occasion to invite people who were important to his business or personal interests, but I was able to narrow it down to three or four, and I've written their names down on this separate sheet. Had it been someone I knew well I would have remembered, but I'm pretty sure that it was one of those on this separate list.'

Esther glanced at the list and realised that she at least had something to occupy her time while Jack was away in Liverpool. She could go to the reference section of the London Library in Westminster. She knew that the Library was the biggest source of reference books in London, and hopefully the names on the list she'd been given would be those of people so famous or important that she'd be able to find information on them. It was worth a try, and with Alice and her niece happily occupied for the day looking after the Enright brood, she could start right away. She thanked Emily for her assistance, and lost no time in taking the short bus journey from Victoria to Westminster.

By the time she was obliged to leave the tiny enclave near the front window where she'd spent three hours reading about important people in a series of books supplied to her, along with paper and pens, by a librarian who had hopes of inviting her out to supper, Esther had the basic information she had been seeking on all but one of the men named by Emily as having been the one with whom Lord Stranmillis had been arguing on her birthday weekend. Now she would have to await Jack's return before they could progress the matter any further.

Percy Enright glared across the table at the burly deckhand with the scared eyes as he launched into his best threatening manner with Jack seated to his right.

'Right, Mr Brady,' Percy announced, 'this had better be good. From where I'm sitting now I can just imagine the noose tightening around your fat neck as the trapdoor drops from under you. Please convince me that you had the body of Lord Stranmillis delivered to you, rather than having to go to the trouble of creating it yourself.'

Brady swallowed hard, and his voice was barely above a croak as he bargained for his life. 'I have this old friend — Aiden Driscoll. Him an' me, we grew up together in this terrible church orphanage in a place called Murragh. Sure an' 'twas an evil place, an' those what had the terrible misfortune ter be raised there formed blood bonds that was never meant ter be broken. Him an' me ran away when we was thirteen, an' we hung around the dockside in Cork until we was old enough ter take ter sea, an' from then 'til now we bin workin' the cargo steamers back an' forth ter Liverpool. He was wedded ter me sister Bridey 'til she up and died from typhoid a while back, an' he's still me best friend.'

'Very touching, Mr Brady, but get on with it,' Percy growled.

Brady swallowed hard again and continued, 'Well, a few weeks back he come ter me on me boat. I was workin' the *Mary Flynn* — that's the boat that ye found the body on — while he was on its sister ship, the *Connaught*. He comes ter me wi' this sad tale o' how he was with this woman o' no account when her husband kicked in the door, an' there was this terrible stramash. He clattered the ponce over the noodle, an' 'e died. So he comes ter me wi' his face on the floor, askin' if I could assist him in the wee matter of disposing o' the evidence. Well, weren't him an' me sworn blood brothers, so me an' Brian Kilpatrick took a leg each, while Aiden took the moothy end, an' we heaved the maggot inter the coal bunker. It was empty then, but we was due ter take on a bunker full the next day, an' we knew that the chancer would be buried like a hen's egg up a duck's arse. The *Connaught* was already coaled up, yer see, so 'twas better that we used the *Mary Flynn*. I swear by Jesus, Joseph an' all the holy angels that I had no idea the man was top drawer, since his wife was common as peat in Mayo, or so Aiden telt me.'

Percy frowned heavily as he replied, 'If — and I emphasise *if* — your story is true, Mr Brady, then it would seem that your bosom friend Mr Driscoll sold you a packet of fairy floss. But such has been my experience of juries that I may not be the only one prepared to buy your unlikely story in exchange for an easy life, so we'll charge you simply with interference with a corpse, and you can take whatever sentence comes your way. As for Mr Driscoll, we already have him identified as one of the local Fenian organisers, so I expect that he'll meet the hangman long before you do.'

'Was that right?' Jack asked as Brady was led out, manacled at the wrists and ankles, but bringing down verbal blessings upon Percy and his loved ones, and a fervent hope that the patron saint of policemen would watch over him for his remaining days. 'Is Driscoll *really* a local Fenian boss? If so, then Carson was correct, and Stranmillis was done in for political reasons.'

'How many more conclusions are you going to jump to in this case?' Percy treated him to a sceptical frown. 'While it is undoubtedly the case that his Lordship departed this life at the hands of Fenians, it may have been for different reasons. The Brotherhood have been known to accept private work on the side.'

'Meaning?'

'Meaning that in addition to campaigning for a free Ireland, they boost their available funds by undertaking private jobs. It may well be that someone in a vulnerable position in London who was under threat from Stranmillis tried to make his demise look political.'

Jack thought for a moment, then looked up in horror. 'Carson?'

Percy shook his head. 'Carson and Stranmillis were on the same side, politically, and it was Carson who started this entire ball rolling. If he was behind Stranmillis's death, why seek the services of Scotland Yard to ferret out the truth?'

'Good point,' Jack conceded. 'But then who else?'

'Another good point. We're no further ahead than we were at the very start of all this, except that we know that Stranmillis was lured to his death by a promise that he could safely disappear from public view. The change of trains at Crewe, the disconnection of the Pullman carriage at Beeston, and the passage on a coal steamer to Cork, were all part of a plan that Stranmillis believed would lead to a new life, whereas in fact it was intended all along to result in his obscure death in the Liverpool docks. What we need to do now is investigate more deeply into who organised that double cross — was it the person who arranged for all the subterfuge, or someone who took advantage of a gift horse when they became aware of it?'

'I still don't understand why anyone would seek to kill a person that they were obtaining blackmail money from.'

Percy tapped his nose in a familiar gesture. 'Don't assume that it was Stranmillis who was being blackmailed. What if he was the blackmailer? Wouldn't that make more sense?'

'Of course it would, as I pointed out yesterday, but why was he making regular payments to Samuel Allen?'

'Allen's a blackmailer, is he not?' Percy reminded him. 'If the purpose of the blackmail wasn't financial — if Stranmillis was gaining some other advantage by threatening to expose his victim — then clearly he'd need to pay Allen for his services in keeping the pressure on the victim, would he not?'

'I clearly need to visit Mr Allen again,' Jack observed. 'And this time I'll take Esther with me.'

'You'll do nothing until we've discussed this further,' Percy insisted. 'All three of us, that is. Time we took the train back to London, Jack my boy.'

Chapter Twenty-Five

Four days later Jack and Esther were shown into Allen's sumptuous home office and Jack introduced Esther as 'Lady Molyneux, the lady about whom we spoke during my last visit.'

'Indeed, and delighted to be making your acquaintance, your Ladyship,' Allen oozed as he shook her hand and waved her into the second visitor chair in front of his desk. 'I'm advised that you can supply me with certain information regarding your husband's ... er, "personal habits", shall we call them? — which will enable me to oblige Mr Jackson here in the matter of the return of certain embarrassing documents that were stolen from your handbag.'

'At no cost to either of us?' Jack prompted him.

Allen nodded. 'Indeed not. So, pray tell me what your husband would wish to have concealed from public knowledge.'

Esther did her best to look embarrassed. 'It was my invariable practice to attend a bridge session at the home of Lady Claridge on Tuesday afternoons. On this particular Tuesday I arrived to discover that her Ladyship was unwell, and so I returned home, only to find my husband in ... in ... "circumstances" with one of our young footmen that left me in no doubt as to what had been transpiring. The footman was dismissed, but with a good character after he confessed to me that his "activities" with my husband had been going on for several months, whenever I was at bridge. My husband and I never resumed our marital relationship, and then I had the good fortune to meet Mr Jackson here, who was gracious enough to be attracted to my fading beauty, and he and I developed a relationship that remains important to me. But the scandal of divorce is something that I cannot contemplate, so if it were possible for those documents of passion to be retrieved we would both be extremely grateful.'

'The name of this servant, if I might make so bold?' Allen enquired.

'William Somers,' Esther lied on cue.

'And your husband's full name?'

'Seymour Molyneux. *Sir* Seymour Molyneux.'

'The same Sir Seymour Molyneux who occupies the post of First Secretary to the President of the Board of Trade?'

'Yes.'

Allen smiled sickly, then reached out and rang a hand bell on his desk. Almost immediately the door to the room opened, and two burly men stalked through it, each armed with a heavy club.

'You will forgive my lack of hospitality, Mr Jackson and whoever your delightful accomplice is, but in my line of business one always requires associates with certain specialised abilities. I am well acquainted with Seymour Molyneux, and had you taken more detailed instructions from Paddy Ryan, you would have learned that Molyneux is not married. However, you were correct in your assessment of his sexual preferences, which is why Mr Ryan was obliged to take certain steps to ensure that such preferences did not become general knowledge.'

'So it *was* Ryan who arranged for Stranmillis to disappear, was it?' Jack asked, seemingly unperturbed by the presence of Allen's thugs in the doorway.

'Did he not advise you of that, before sending you here in an attempt to discover whether or not I knew?' Allen smirked. 'How remiss of him not to recall that it was I who was employed as the go-between for Stranmillis and Molyneux. And I assume that the plan was that when you returned with the necessary confirmation he would have me removed in the same way as his former boyfriend Stranmillis, employing some more of his Irish playmates? Well, as you can see, the pair of you will not be in any position to report back to him after my colleagues here render you unconscious for long enough for your late afternoon dip in the Thames.'

'We are not the only ones who got it slightly wrong,' Jack replied with a wide smile as he drew the revolver from his jacket pocket and pointed it in the direction of the doorway. 'It is fortunately equipped with six shots, there are only three of you, and I am accredited a fair marksman. However, I must follow orders. Esther, would you do the honours?'

While Allen remained behind his desk with a gaping jaw, and his two bully boys stood uncertainly in the doorway, Esther walked to the window that commanded a view of the street below and waved her handkerchief as she looked down with a smile. A minute later came the sound of pounding feet on the staircase from the street, followed by the unmistakeable noise of splintering wood as the front door gave way to the fifteen pound metal 'enforcer', and three uniformed constables obeyed Jack's command to buckle the two bodyguards, who offered no resistance.

Percy appeared in the doorway with a smile and looked across at Jack enquiringly. Jack nodded.

'I assume you want the credit as usual, so buckle Mr Allen here for Accessory to Murder, unless he's disposed to give us the whole of the story that he's so far only confessed to half of. It was indeed Ryan who was behind it all, so you owe me a tenner. However, Stranmillis *was* a Mary-Anne, so the account's squared.'

'I guessed some of that!' Esther protested.

'Ah yes, but for a civilian to engage in a wager with a serving officer in the Metropolitan Police regarding an ongoing investigation is contrary to law, and therefore unenforceable as a contract,' Percy smirked. 'But you *do* qualify for a cream cake in that fancy tea shop I noted on the corner.'

'I assume that this will be the last of the fish and chips?' Jack asked sadly on the Saturday following, as they met for dinner in the Clerkenwell rooms.

Percy nodded. 'Regrettable in one way, but cause for celebration in another.'

'Did Allen prove forthcoming?' Jack asked, while Esther lowered the oven door and slipped the parcel inside.

'Sang like a canary, rather than become entangled in a murder investigation.' Percy smiled. 'He's only a slimy blackmailer, at the end of the day, albeit a very successful one. He freely confessed to putting the weights on Molyneux to award all those lucrative contracts to Stranmillis rather than have his fondness for ladies' clothing made public knowledge — a matter discovered by his fellow fetishist Stranmillis during those parties at Bosie Douglas's place in Surrey, of course. So there was a connection with Wilde, after all.'

'And armed with that knowledge, what did you get out of Ryan?' Esther asked as she placed the bread and butter on the table.

'As much as I need to have him charged with murder, including a confession.'

'Why would anyone freely confess to a capital offence?' Esther said disbelievingly.

'Because it doesn't necessarily have to end on a trapdoor,' Jack explained as he sat down and began brandishing a knife and fork suggestively, looking pointedly at the oven. 'There's such a thing as a "recommendation for clemency", which is best obtained in return for telling the whole story from the very beginning. It's called "co-operating with the authorities".'

'And Ryan co-operated most obligingly,' Percy advised them. 'Not only did he admit to having organised his friends in the Fenian Brotherhood to dispose of Stranmillis — and bear in mind that he's a lifelong Catholic, whereas Stranmillis was reviled by anyone hoping for Irish Home Rule — but he told us why.'

'To obtain all the Government contracts that Stranmillis had been getting as part of his blackmail, using Allen as the hired go-between?' Jack suggested.

Percy nodded before turning to stare at the oven.

'All right, all right, I get the message,' Esther advised them testily. 'But while you're both congratulating yourselves, don't forget that I was the one who picked out Molyneux as the likely blackmail target.'

'He was the only senior Government figure on the list!' Jack pointed out. 'Stranmillis was hardly likely to be blackmailing a Catholic Bishop, the headmaster of a public school or an operatic tenor. *And* you nearly got us killed by failing to note that Molyneux was unmarried.'

'I never said I was perfect.' Esther grinned, before bending forward to open the oven door.

'So, at a guess, Molyneux offered Ryan first pick of future Government contracts in exchange for getting Stranmillis off his back?' Jack suggested.

Percy nodded, then smiled as he saw Esther placing the sauce bottle on the table. 'So what have I left out, Esther?'

'The reason why Stranmillis was persuaded to make himself scarce, which presumably had something to do with the upcoming Wilde trial?'

'Isn't she truly splendid?' Percy asked rhetorically as he cut into his first piece of fish. 'You never asked that, Jack.'

'You never gave me the opportunity,' Jack replied sulkily. 'But go on — show off, as usual.'

'Esther said it all,' Percy explained. 'Stranmillis apparently had a particularly embarrassing hobby when he was with rent boys.'

'That disgusting little stinkpot Campbell told me that,' Jack interposed. 'He liked to dress up as a woman while Campbell...'

'Yes, thank you, Jack,' Esther interrupted. 'No more of that, unless you were hoping to *wear* your fish and chips.'

'Anyway,' Percy continued with evident amusement, 'the last thing he wanted was to be around when Campbell advised the court of that, as he was persuaded he was about to do. He wasn't, as it happens, and in the event of course he didn't give evidence at all, but it was enough to scare Stranmillis, so that when Ryan offered to organise his escape route, he couldn't bring himself to say no.'

'So — all over and done with,' Jack sighed contentedly. 'We can look forward to a few days off after a job well done.'

'I'm not sure you can,' Percy said quietly.

'How do you mean?' Jack and Esther said in unison.

'Well tomorrow's Sunday, and we missed worshipping at your mother's shrine last week. She's been in touch with Beattie, and I *really* think you should make the effort tomorrow. Apparently, your mother's been meddling again, and you need to prepare yourselves for a shock.'

'I can't believe that you're not ecstatic!' Constance Enright complained after carefully clearing her mouth of the lemon syllabub that had been specially bought in for the Sunday dinner that they had been all but commanded to attend. 'I'm offering you a four bedroom house, free of all encumbrance, and all you can do is sulk! At least Esther looks more excited. Aren't you, dear?'

'More taken by surprise than anything,' Esther replied diplomatically as she squeezed Jack's hand under the table cloth. 'But it was indeed most generous of you.'

'I had a motive of my own, clearly,' Constance admitted. 'With you all installed in the old Bentley house, I'll clearly get to see more of my grandchildren. Plus you and Jackson, of course. Jackson, have you *nothing* to say — not even "thank you"?'

'Thank you for the thought, obviously,' Jack muttered gracelessly, 'but how many times have I tried to advise you that I'm required to live in London as a condition of my employment?'

'Your employment with the Metropolitan Police, certainly. But what if you were to join the Essex Constabulary? I suppose it's too much to expect you to give up policing and pursue a more respectable career, but did you really think I hadn't already taken care of *that* as well? Percy was most obliging in that regard.'

Jack shot a furious glare across the table at Percy, who looked down uncomfortably at his empty bowl. 'It was only a character reference, and I wasn't obliged to lie or anything,' he muttered.

'So what have you got for me?' Jack demanded angrily. 'Am I to become the next Chief Constable of Essex?'

'Not yet, anyway,' Constance replied, as if unaware of the ironic tone in which the question had been delivered. 'But they need a new Detective Sergeant in Chelmsford, and with your new house being so convenient for the station...'

'So you had me apply for the job, without me even being aware of the fact?' Jack protested angrily.

Constance shook her head. 'Not directly, no, but after Percy wrote that wonderful reference for you, the job's yours. The fact that Chief Superintendent Charles's wife and I became good friends during that Ladies' Guild National Conference that I attended in Ipswich was merely the introduction.'

'So you're suggesting that I take up a new role supervising men who'll be well aware that my mother got me the job?' Jack demanded, red-faced.

'You're clearly overcome by the excitement, and no doubt the suddenness of it all,' Constance suggested. 'Why don't you and Esther take a turn in the garden and start planning your move? Esther dear, I think you know what Jackson needs to be reminded of, in the way of his duties to his family.'

'She's really gone *too* far this time, the interfering old...' Jack began, until Esther put her fingers to his lips, then replaced them with her own, as they stood hidden from view behind the potting shed.

'Did *you* know anything about this?' Jack demanded as they separated.

'Not until Percy came over with those fish and chips yesterday, and whispered it to me in the doorway while I was showing him out.'

'How can I possibly get out of this, given that she's already bought the bloody house?' Jack said, almost in tears. 'And I bet she used the last of my family trust money to do so!'

'Do you really *want* to get out of it?' Esther questioned softly.

252

Jack looked down at her in amazement. 'Are you serious?' he demanded.

Esther nodded. 'We need to move anyway, now that we have three kids. London's getting grubbier and more dangerous by the week, and even you described the local children that Lily would be attending school with as "riff-raff". Out here, the children could play in the open air, just like you once did, and you could grow vegetables in the garden. Chelmsford's less than an hour away by train, and the station's only a few doors down.'

'Has Mother been bullying you onto her side?'

'No, Jack — I just want what's best for our family, and this way we could enjoy a much better life, and you'd still be a police officer.'

'You mean that you actually want to make this suggested move just for yourself, and not simply because you're scared to say no to Mother?'

'Your mother stopped frightening me some time ago, Jack. This would be for *us*. And with four bedrooms, well — who knows?'

A NOTE TO THE READER

Dear Reader,

Thank you for your latest investment in the exploits of Jack, Esther and Percy Enright, who certainly live through some interesting times.

Oscar Wilde not only authored a series of plays that were so successful that they're still in the repertoires of modern theatre groups — he also authored his own downfall when he unwisely sued the Marquess of Queensberry. This was late Victorian England, a nation that prided itself on its rigid morality, and the last thing it needed was someone jumping up and down exposing his own preference for sexual partners of the same gender. The Establishment was both shocked and nervous at what was coming out in the newspaper reports of a trial that should never have been launched, had Wilde been properly advised.

To put matters in context, it should be remembered that homosexuality in those days was not even mentioned in a polite society that preferred to believe that it didn't exist. It was regarded as so alien to Queen Victoria's cosy little tea-party world that some medical specialists were even looking for a cure for it! As one of my characters in this book points out bitterly, if a cure had existed, there would have been long queues of men — and even women — prepared to pay for whatever was available.

Little wonder that there was panic in Establishment circles when the reading public began to learn of a network of gay men and boys, some of them being paid for their services, and the existence of bordellos that catered for 'deviant' tastes, as they were considered to be in those days. This panic was not simply a reaction to the bad image of Her Majesty's Empire that such practices created; it was in response to a growing realisation that such 'perverted' behaviour could be found at the very highest levels of society, not excepting the royal family, some of whose princes were beginning to investigate what might be on offer as a refreshing change from the 'norm'.

Given that Percy Enright was heading up a new department within Scotland Yard euphemistically labelled 'The Political Branch', dedicated to wiping highly placed noses when their behaviour threatened to blot the copybook of the rich and privileged, he was the obvious choice when it came to finding out how far up the social scale the moral stain had spread. And since his nephew Jack owed his very continued existence within the police force, and his new Sergeant rank, to Percy, it was also par for the course for Percy to call in the favour when someone was required to work undercover and learn what was to be learned about the seedy underworld of 'rent boys', 'molly houses' and blackmail at the highest levels of society.

The higher they come, the larger the price that blackmailers could demand, so from the very start it seemed that the mysterious disappearance of Lord Stranmillis during a train journey, along with the private railway carriage in which he was travelling, might somehow be connected with a blackmail attempt against a peer of the realm who had social connections with Oscar Wilde. But since Wilde's world was the theatre, of which Percy had no experience, he had no qualms about dragging in Jack's amateur dramatics sister Lucy, who he'd shamelessly exploited on a previous occasion when her talents matched his investigative needs. And since Lucy's undercover role required someone skilled with needle and thread, why not complete the family circle by making further demands on

Jack's wife Esther, ignoring her excuse that she now had responsibility for three children?

I was able to incorporate into this latest novel extracts from the trial transcript of *Wilde v Queensberry*, but of course the remainder of the story is fictitious. However, I like to think that it accurately relives what must have been the shock to the nation when it was revealed that one of the darlings of its theatre wasn't quite what he should have been. He was certainly what he seemed, but not what he should have been.

As well as writing these novels, I enjoy the feedback from readers, some of whom have now become social media friends. Feel free to review this latest one on **Amazon** or **Goodreads**, and perhaps send me a 'hi' on my Facebook page:

DavidFieldAuthor.

Happy reading!

David

davidfieldauthor.com

Sapere Books is an exciting new publisher of brilliant fiction and popular history.

To find out more about our latest releases and our monthly bargain books visit our website:
saperebooks.com

37223572R00151

Printed in Great Britain
by Amazon

POISON IN

AUGUST RAINE

For my Sunflower

A Cure For The Itch

Book I

CHAPTER 1

As the bus drew to a halt and the doors swung open, none of the waiting passengers made to board. It had been the same at the last few stops. Nodding resignedly, the driver pulled away, likely knowing he'd have the same problem at the next stop. And the next stop. And the one after that. There were plenty of empty seats, but the bus may as well have been standing room only. People were afraid of one another. Nobody wanted to catch the Itch by sitting next to another passenger.

I knew that was nonsense, as they should, but despite countless advertising campaigns debunking the myth the Itch was contagious, the lasting effects of the hysteria it created were still present. Professionals never greeted with a handshake. Reunited friends never hugged, no matter how long they'd been apart. Having witnessed the symptoms of the Itch, I could understand the stigma, even if I didn't share in it.

I left the bus just after crossing the river on Bridge Street. As I got off, one of the five people waiting dashed on, which frustrated those who'd missed a seat. From there, I headed to Spinningfields. I used to like the area – old redbrick architecture merging with modern towers of glass and steel – but it had changed a lot in recent months.

Before the Itch, a lot of the buildings in Spinningfields were offices or restaurants. To cope with the rising number of patients, the government had started converting available space into hospital wards. Concert venues, offices, and conference centres had all been given a medical makeover. Nowadays, every other building was being used to treat the sick. The temporary signs placed at entrances to these makeshift hospitals were looking worn, which was a damning sight. It seemed like the only buildings spared the transformation were those already dedicated to combating the Itch, one of which was my employer, Rathbury-Holmes.

The company specialised in pharmaceuticals. Their laboratory was nestled amongst the other blocks rising above Hardmann Square. It was vastly different at night. The mob that had been occupying the paved square for months now had disbanded for the evening. There was no point campaigning if there was no one to listen. Even so, the memory of their abuse rang in my ears. That was the main reason I was there; somebody had to find out what had happened to their loved ones.

The guard behind the front desk gave me a puzzled look as I approached. Determined not to give myself away, I kept my face impassive.

"How come you're here so late?" he said, checking the monitor in front of him.

"Frank asked me to come in to sort some stuff. Call him if you want?" I said, nodding towards the phone. The guard thought for barely more than a blink before shaking his head softly.

"I'd rather not," he replied.

Frank – my boss – had a formidable temper, and the guard clearly knew he wouldn't appreciate being bothered in the evening. I'd received the full brunt of his rage earlier that day. A halfway decent manager would have handled the situation very differently. I was still struggling to believe he'd asked us to drop the investigation. How could I? Seven people were dead. And I was determined to find out why.

As I rode the lift to the fifth floor, I reached for the necklace I was wearing. It was only simple – a piece of string with two bottle caps hanging from it – but it meant more to me than anything else. If anyone had known why I wore it, they might have thought it was nothing more than a painful reminder. I didn't think of it like that, though. To me, it was motivation.

I left the office lights off, keen to draw as little attention as possible. My desk was exactly as I'd left it earlier, speckled with stationery and paper I'd scattered in anger. Frank's office was on the other side of the room. Someone was moving around inside, so I tucked myself behind a pillar and waited for them to leave. Initially, I was worried it might be him but realised it was probably one of the cleaners finishing up for the evening. In all the years I'd worked for him, I couldn't think of a single instance when Frank had stayed a minute later than he had to. Plus, the person in there was much too slim to be Frank.

Once the sound of footsteps had faded, I peered from behind the pillar. I was alone. Eager not to waste any more time, I dashed over to Frank's office. Of course, the door was locked, but I'd expected as much. After a few seconds, I found a video on the internet explaining how to use the lockpick I'd bought online. It took several attempts, and at one point I was sure I'd jammed the lock, but the door eventually swung open.

As I entered, I vividly recalled our discussion from earlier.

"I told you to drop this," Frank had yelled. His flabby cheeks were beetroot red, a combination of his anger and unhealthy eating habits.

"And I told you there was an issue before the trial."

"Are you suggesting this is my fault?"

"I never said that," I'd replied, although I certainly felt it was Frank's fault. After all, he'd approved the protocol, despite my warning.

"If you'd thought there was a real concern, you should have-"

"A real concern? You saw the data. You knew what the risks were. And yet, you pushed the trial. We were supposed to be helping those people. Now, seven of them are dead. Their blood is on your hands."

"Those people were dying anyway. They've only themselves to blame," he'd roared.

In my frustration, I said a lot of things I probably shouldn't have. Worse, though, was the volume with which I'd spoken. Everyone in the office must have heard my tirade. But I didn't care. He deserved what I'd said and worse. How could he be so callous? True, those people were in a critical condition, but that certainly didn't make their lives expendable.

I'd considered going to a news agency, or perhaps plastering what Frank had said all over social media. But in those scenarios, other people at the company might suffer; countless innocent people who'd worked on the project. I wouldn't let that happen, just as much as I wouldn't let Frank get away with what he'd done. So, I'd decided to sneak into his office and look for anything that might explain why he'd pushed the trial.

His desk was clinically tidy. Everything was either perpendicular or parallel to everything else. How someone could be so careful with office stationery but so careless with people's lives was astounding. Slowly, I moved a photograph of his gigantic rottweiler, taking note of how it aligned with everything else, and then flipped his keyboard – just as Frank did every morning. Sure enough, his password was taped to the underside.

Arranging his emails into date order, I scrolled to roughly three months ago, which was around the time I'd first voiced my concerns about the trial. Annoyingly, he hadn't opened any of the messages I'd sent him. That was enough to land him in serious trouble – it proved he'd ignored my warning – but I wanted more. I wanted to know why he'd knowingly endangered the patient's lives and, ultimately, killed seven people.

I was busily scrolling down the list of emails, but something beneath the desk was making it difficult to sit comfortably. Irritably, I reached under and pulled out a small duffel bag. The zip was open, revealing a small digital timer.

It was counting down, seconds away from zero.

CHAPTER 2

My whole body seized. I couldn't even blink. As I gawked at the timer, paralysed, valuable seconds slipped away. When I finally regained control of myself, my mind raced to make up for lost time. Dozens of thoughts ran through my head, battling for consideration. I couldn't just leave the bomb. But then, what else could I do? Surely, I wouldn't be able to disarm it. The window? No, there might be people outside. In the end, with only three seconds left, I did the only thing I could and raced for the door. I barely made it out of the office before I was launched off my feet.

The ringing in my ears was so piercing I didn't hear the guards approaching, and so was shocked when they hoisted me to my feet. As my vision bled back into focus, I realised the blast had propelled me surprisingly far. Thick smoke had already filled the room, blocking-out the few lights that hadn't been damaged by the explosion. Smouldering wreckage was scattered across the office.

The guards escorted me down the fire escape and out of the building. By the time we made it to the evacuation point on Hardmann Square, I could stand without assistance. From there, I could see flames burning through the windows on the fifth floor. Passers-by were already gathering, pointing at the smoking remnants of Frank's office littering the square.

The guards were asking me something, presumably about the explosion, but I struggled to hear what they were saying. When an ambulance arrived, a paramedic examined me, by which point I was growing impatient. There were more pressing matters on my mind than bandaging a few cuts and scrapes.

Why was there a bomb in Frank's office? And who had planted it? A blizzard of possible answers flurried inside my skull, each as unbelievable as the next. Given the time, I couldn't imagine it was an attempt on Frank's life. Anyone who wanted to hurt him would surely know he wouldn't be there so late in the evening. But why else would someone want to destroy his office?

"You're a lucky man, Mr Bright," said a voice, disrupting my concentration.

I'd been so wrapped up in my thoughts I hadn't noticed the woman standing outside the ambulance. Although she was smiling politely, something about her tone put me on edge.

"Excuse me?" I asked.

"A few more seconds and they'd have been cleaning you off the plasterwork. Well… what's left of it, at least."

"Sorry, who are you?"

"DCI Dunhill," she said, pulling a badge out of her jacket pocket. "What were you doing up there?"

"I work here."

"Awfully late, isn't it?"

"We're awfully busy."

It wasn't meant to sound sarcastic but, unfortunately, it came across that way. Her eyes narrowed, fleetingly, before she schooled her expression.

"Why were you here?" she asked, smiling.

"Why are you asking?"

"Just routine questioning."

After a little consideration, I decided not to tell her why I'd been snooping around the office after hours. Although I was convinced something wasn't right, I was a long way from telling anyone my theory. Instead, I told her I was following up on something I'd forgotten about that day. She went on to ask if I'd seen anything suspicious whilst I was in the office. I mentioned there had been someone in Frank's office when I'd arrived, at which she nodded sceptically. At least she wrote something down, though. Finally, she tucked her notepad back into her jacket, asked me to contact her if I thought of anything else, and then bade me a good evening. After that, I hurried away, eager to get home.

I'd been extremely lucky – and not simply because I'd survived an explosion. It was clear the detective suspected me of planting the bomb, and who could blame her? I was caught at the scene. Plus, there was the slanging match I'd had with Frank that afternoon. Although I'd been released, I had a feeling I hadn't heard the end of this. For certain, there would be consequences when Frank found out.

The flat I rented was in a block at Salford Quays, overlooking the water near MediaCity. It cost more than I could really afford, but I wouldn't have traded it for anywhere else. The city lights strewn across the murky urban skyline were stunning. There'd been a time when I'd have come home from a tough day and poured myself a drink. Surviving a bombing would have warranted a particularly large, strong one. And a lot of them. Now, there wasn't a drop in the house. Once, I'd relied on booze to rinse away my fears, worries, and anxieties, but I'd never do that again.

As soon as I got home, I took a seat on the balcony and, free from distraction, thought about why someone had planted the bomb. I spent all night thinking about it, fuelled by single-minded determination. There was no shortage of people who wished Frank harm. As project leader, he'd given a statement to the media after the trial had failed. Unfortunately, Frank wasn't known for his sensitivity. After essentially saying he thought the victims deserved their fate, it wasn't surprising people were baying for his blood. Now I'd had time to think about it, the idea that someone wanted to harm him had a lot more credibility.

Although I knew that Frank wouldn't be at work, it was possible the bomber might not have. Or perhaps they'd intended it to detonate the following morning when Frank sat at his desk but made a mistake when setting the timer. There was even a chance I might have triggered it when I sat down. And yet, another motive seemed likelier.

After everything that had happened during the trial, a lot of people at the company were asking questions of those involved. Fingers were being pointed. People were passing the blame higher and higher up the Rathbury-Holmes corporate ladder. Of course, the accusations were meaningless without any proof of negligence or wrongdoing. But perhaps that was why the bomb had been planted. Had someone blown up Frank's office to hide incriminating evidence? Was Frank responsible for the blast?

Whether he was capable, I couldn't be sure. However, I was certain someone was trying to hide something and had a sneaking suspicion Frank was involved.

When it got too cold on the balcony, I came inside and sat in the kitchen. There was a newspaper on the small dining table. It was a few weeks old now, but I wanted to keep it. It was an article about the trial.

"*The families of those affected by the drug trial were attempting to take the matter to court*" it read. "*But today, a judge has dismissed the case against Rathbury-Holmes. A spokesperson for the company, known for producing chemicals such as CPT, Noxisolv, and a wide variety of pharmaceutical products, confirmed they are continuing to develop a cure for the sickness, but would not comment further.*"

I wasn't sure exactly what was said in court but knew it had something to do with the investigation that followed the trial. At first, it was all hands to battle stations. Everyone was pitching in, trying to work out why the trial had failed. But after only a few weeks, we'd been forced to cease our efforts. Frank concluded that *the deaths were unavoidable,* and we needed to *move on*. Those were his exact words. And his testimony, I suspected, was part of the reason the case against the company hadn't gone to court.

Of course, I'd protested at the time. I couldn't believe we were stopping without knowing why it had happened. Frank had ignored me, but I hadn't given up. I'd refused to believe this was simply a terrible accident. I knew something wasn't right. So, I'd continued investigating the trial. Gripping my bottlecap necklace, I was filled with fresh determination to find out what really happened during the trial and who was trying to hide the truth.

As the approaching sunrise set fire to the horizon, I rubbed my eyes, took an ice-cold shower, and dressed. It had been another sleepless night. Truthfully, I never slept more a few hours anyway but lately, it had been getting harder to close my eyes at all. Whilst I ate breakfast, I checked the news. A quick scan showed the bombing had already been extensively reported on. Thankfully, I wasn't mentioned in any of the articles I read. Police had searched the rest of the building and found no other explosive devices. There were several theories about who might have been responsible for the blast, none of which I considered likely. There was also the daily update on the Itch, but I chose not to read that.

Once I'd eaten, I left the flat and headed to the bus stop. It was a short walk along the water's edge. I could see the Lowry Theatre opposite. The striking architecture was another reason why I'd chosen to live at Salford Quays. Everywhere I looked, there was something to catch my eye. As I crossed the water, I saw people swimming. Few things terrified me as much as water. I hadn't been more than ankle deep since I was a teenager. The last time my family had been whole. To anyone else with the same fear, it might have seemed crazy to live quayside. The view from the flat had trumped my fear. Just.

Like yesterday, people refused to get on the bus when it arrived. I earnt myself some concerned and amazed looks as I stepped on; the person I sat beside looked truly mortified. Early on, Itch sufferers were outcast like plague bearers in medieval villages.

Crude and vulgar slogans were painted on doors to warn others to stay away. For one of my neighbours, the abuse had been so extreme he'd been forced to move. Public attitude had improved since then, but only a little.

Before the cause was known, wild theories were almost as prevalent as the sickness. Terrorists unleashing biological or chemical weaponry. Newly evolved, hypervirulent microorganisms. There were even those who believed it was divine retribution. When the cause was finally announced, it was far more unexpected.

The bus crawled along, caught in sluggish traffic. It took a lot longer than expected to get to work. I could have taken the Metro, which would have been much quicker but, since the sickness, services had been reduced; it wasn't surprising with over 300,000 sufferers. Loss of workforce had been felt by almost every industry. Fewer drivers meant public transport ran on a reduced timetable. Fewer checkout workers meant there were longer queues in supermarkets. Everywhere had similar problems and, although things were improving, no one really knew when society would fully recover.

As expected, the mob had gathered outside the office. There were perhaps 30 people carrying signs and banners with words like *Injustice* and *Criminal* written on them. They were hurling abuse at everyone who entered the building. A few weeks after the trial, a group of unknown assailants had managed to break into the office. They'd caused a lot of damage, ransacking most of the laboratories and offices in the building. But it was the banner they'd hung from the windows that had done the most harm. It was a picture of Frank, which I was told had been taken from his LinkedIn profile. The photograph had been heavily edited and was extremely unflattering. A single word was written beneath it: *murderer*. Although no arrests were made, it was clear who the culprits were.

When they'd first gathered at the site, I'd responded every time I passed them, hoping to convince them I was on their side. But they never listened. Although it was difficult being called a *heartless monster*, I did my best to ignore them, focussing on proving what had really happened to their loved ones.

From my desk, I could see a wooden board had been used to seal what was left of Frank's office. A few doors down, there was a piece of tattered paper with his name on it. Naturally, people were eyeing the board suspiciously, chattering amongst themselves about what might have happened.

"Temper finally got the better of him, then?" Lizzy asked as she sat at the desk opposite mine.

Lizzy Chao and I had started the company within a few days of one another and had been friends ever since discovering our mutual love of food. I'd lost count of the number of times we'd gorged ourselves to the point of bursting. Although I laughed at her comment, it passed quickly. When I told her that I'd been in the office at the time, her expression changed to something between surprise and admiration.

"Was it you?" she asked conspiratorially. When I didn't reply, she added, "Because I totally understand if you've finally cracked."

"I think somebody is trying to hide something."

"Or maybe they've had enough of his-"

Before she could finish her thought, Frank appeared beside my desk. I kept my face passive as I looked up at him. His chubby cheeks were pale pink, suggesting a rage was imminent.

"My office. Now," he snarled.

"Step lively, private," Lizzy said as I passed her. If not for my impending scolding, I might have laughed.

There was something almost predatory about the way Frank paced as he waited for me to take a seat. The room was much smaller than his other office but just as well-kept. In the short time he'd been in it this morning, he'd already organised the stationary on the desk, the files on the shelves, and ensured that the two blinds across the windows were adjusted to the same level.

The springs in his chair groaned as he lowered his wide frame onto it. Whenever he was angry, he pursed his lips. He was so overweight that it almost looked like he was pouting.

"Well?" he asked.

"Sorry?" I replied, unsure how else to respond.

"The constabulary was good enough to call round in the middle of the bloody night," he sneered. I suspected it probably hadn't been that late but decided not to comment. "They told me that you were snooping around in my office. Care to explain?"

"I was looking up information about the trial," I said resignedly. "I wanted to know why you approved it."

I was convinced he already knew the reason I was there, but his reaction suggested otherwise. His cheeks ran from pale pink to beetroot red. Veins bulged in his neck and forehead. He jowls quivered as his temper built towards an outburst.

"I don't bloody believe this," he roared. "What the Hell is wrong with you? Do you not understand simple instructions? Or are you just deliberately disobeying them?"

"Aren't you going to ask me about the bomb?" I asked. Was he really going to overlook the fact his office had been destroyed?

"Don't try to change the subject."

"I'm not. I just thought you'd be more concerned about someone planting a bomb under your desk."

"You're a bloody disgrace."

"Excuse me?" I said, struggling to maintain my composure.

"You think you can come in here and do whatever the Hell you like. Well, I've had enough of it."

"I don't think that," I said, fighting to keep my voice level.

"Then, why, after I told you to drop it, do I find out you're still looking into that bloody trial?"

"Because people died, Frank," I said, my anger finally boiling over. "In screaming agony. Can you imagine what it must be like to spend your final hours in that much pain?"

The initial symptoms were common; headaches, sweating and dizziness. A lot of sufferers simply thought they had a cold. Some also suffered from mood swings or lethargy. But as time passed, they all started to feel mild skin irritation. That's why people had started calling it the Itch. Within as little as a few days, though, that mild irritation progressed to burning agony. Many had died from complications as a result of the pain, including heart attacks and, in the worst cases, injuries they'd inflicted on themselves. Sufferers were given daily doses of pain medication to control their symptoms, but that couldn't last. Currently, the only long-term treatment was a medically induced coma.

Recently, the Health Secretary, Rupert Prophett, had given a public address, in which he'd told stories about patients with the sickness. A young woman who'd doused herself in hydrogen peroxide and scoured her body with wire wool to stop the Itch. She'd died from chemical burns a few days later. A man who'd taken a power sander to his forearm. His flesh was so badly shredded he'd damaged a nerve and lost the use of his left hand – luckily, that meant he hadn't been able to damage his other arm.

Foolishly, I'd expected my words to have an impact on Frank. But when he spoke, his tone was indifferent.

"And as I said before; they were already dying," he said.

"How can you say that?" I replied. "They trusted us to help them. They weren't sacrificing themselves for the greater good. Did their lives really mean so little to you?"

"There's a reason Dose is illegal. As far as I'm concerned, they've only themselves to blame for the condition they were in."

Although a cure hadn't been found, scientists at Rathbury-Holmes believed they'd identified the cause of the Itch; a recreational drug called Dose. It was banned a few years ago, before the first cases of the

Itch, but at the peak of its popularity, it was suggested that there were more Dose users than smokers in the UK. Now, almost 300,000 Dose users were suffering from the Itch. And the number was rising every day.

Without thinking, I took hold of the bottlecaps on my necklace. My mind was drifting dangerously close to memories I really didn't want to think about, so I shook my head to refocus. Fortunately, Frank didn't seem to notice.

"What if you're wrong?" I asked.

"What the Hell are you talking about?"

As patiently as I could, I explained my theory about why the trial had failed. Even after being told to drop the investigation, I'd spent every minute of my working day reviewing the data we'd obtained. I'd also tried to find information about the seven victims of the trial. I'd managed to speak to six of the seven families, but the seventh family had categorically refused to speak to me.

The scene was always the same. A grieving widow or distraught parents showing me a memorial to the person they'd lost. They told me how stunned they were when the sickness was diagnosed. Everyone was surprised to hear someone they cared about had taken a banned substance. I knew that feeling all too well. It hadn't been easy, but I'd learnt as much as I could about the people they'd lost.

I'd hoped to find a pattern, something that linked the victims. But if there was one to be found, it had eluded me. Two of the victims were over 50, but three were less than 20, so age seemed unlikely. Their addresses were spread across the country. None of them worked in the same industry. Although they all had existing health conditions, they were extremely diverse, from sexual health problems to anxiety. I couldn't imagine any of their ailments could have been fatal.

After all that, I'd arrived at the only conclusion that made any sense; we'd incorrectly identified the cause of the Itch. Of course, it wasn't easy to admit that. In fact, if anyone had suggested it before the trial, I'd have thought that they were completely insane. Clearly, Frank was still of that opinion.

"Have you lost your mind?" he asked. "Do you really think anyone could have been stupid enough to make a mistake like that?"

"You did," I challenged. "You pressed the trial when you knew there was a risk it wouldn't work."

"Who the Hell do you think you are?" he said, his voice rising threateningly. I wasn't going to be intimidated.

"Why did you do it? What, were they just lambs for the slaughter?"

"Don't act so saintly, Jack. You know how this works. You presented a risk, but the potential benefits outweighed that. It's called risk assessment. All managers have to do it."

"So, they were expendable, then?"

"A few casualties would have been a small price to pay if we'd found a cure. The company has invested millions in this already. We're in too deep to quit now."

I'd expected several answers – corporate pressure, personal glory, divine foresight – but had never imagined he could be so callous as to risk lives because of the financial cost. There were plenty of four-letter words festering on the tip of my tongue, but I held them back.

"You should be ashamed of yourself," I snarled.

"I couldn't give a monkey's what you think. As far as I'm concerned, your opinion means…"

Dramatically, he snatched a mug in his chunky fingers, fixed my eyes, and then tipped the mug upside down. I wasn't entirely sure what the gesture was supposed to mean, so was glad when he clarified by saying, "Nothing."

"Why are you so against this? You must know I'm right," I said.

"No, Jack," he said, slamming his mug down. "All I know is that you're disobedient, stubborn and, quite frankly, out of control. So, effective immediately, you're suspended."

"You can't be serious?"

"*Without* pay," he sneered.

I couldn't believe it. Was he really so thoughtless that he was going to ignore what I'd said? Surely, he knew I was right. All the data supported my theory. When two security guards arrived to escort me from the building, though, I realised he was ignoring everything I'd told him. Heads turned as I was marched across the office. Hushed chatter followed me through the room. When Lizzy saw what was happening, she came rushing over.

"Woah, stand down, soldier," she said as one of the guards chivvied me along. "What's going on?"

When I told her what had happened, she looked outraged. Momentarily, I thought she was going to stomp into Frank's office and start yelling, but I told her not to bother. It was pleasing to see that she wanted to help, but I didn't want her to get involved. There was no sense in her getting suspended, as well.

By some miracle, I made it out of the building and arrived at the bus stop before I started cursing. As a stream of four-letter words tumbled out of my mouth, a few people looked in my direction, but I ignored them. I'd never liked Frank but to approve the trial because of money was beyond despicable; it was downright wicked. Could he really have been so callous and, if so, why? And, if his motivation was entirely financial, why had someone destroyed his office? As I rode the bus home, my temper continued to simmer, threatening to boil over at any second.

To resolve some of my frustration, I decided to go straight from my flat to the gym. There were plenty of facilities within walking distance of my flat, but most were part of a chain, and all were crowded around the clock. I didn't like having to wait to use the equipment. I needed sweat and fatigue. So, I'd opted to join a boxing club in Old Trafford. The owner had converted an old factory several years ago. It was rundown and smelled of stale sweat. The roof leaked when it rained. Everything was battered and worn. But at least I didn't need to wait to use the equipment.

When I was younger, I could barely climb a flight of stairs without getting breathless. I'd started getting fit whilst at university and went whenever I had to let off some steam. Over recent months, I'd spent a lot of hours there and, although I was far from peak fitness, I'd certainly noticed an improvement in my health. On that occasion, I got on a treadmill, and ran further than I ever had. By the time I stepped off, I could barely stand. At least I was too tired to be angry at

Frank.

Once I was back at my flat, I stood on the balcony, looking towards the city, and thinking about what I was going to do. It was early evening when my phone rang.

"What happened?" Lizzy asked as soon as I answered.

Reliving my conversation with Frank was infuriating. When I'd finished, Lizzy used several expletives to voice what she thought of him. I couldn't help smiling as I listened. She and I had worked together on the cure and subsequent investigation into why the trial had failed. Although she'd also continued working on it after Frank ordered us to drop it, she hid her tracks better than I had. When I was found out, Frank demanded to know if anyone else had ignored him, but I hadn't said anything. I knew that Lizzy would have done the same for me.

"Do you think Frank planted the bomb?" she asked when she'd stopped cursing his name.

"I don't know," I said.

If he wanted to get rid of information, there were easier ways than blowing up his office. Files could be lost, misplaced, or simply spoiled with a mug of coffee. But there was something about the way he'd reacted during our meeting. At the time, I'd thought he was angry. Looking back, though, I realised there was something more to his mood, something irrational that could easily have been fear. Was he worried I was close to uncovering something incriminating?

"Want me to sprinkle milk powder on his chair,

again?" she said, which distracted me.

A few years ago, Frank had made some extremely offensive remarks about Lizzy's heritage. Although she'd raised the issue with HR, there was no way to prove what he'd said, and Frank had gone unpunished. After that, she'd taken the matter into her own hands. Ever since then, she'd been enacting her vengeance through a series of practical jokes. They ranged from the simplistic, such as hiding things around his office, to more elaborate pranks like subscribing him to a host of pornographic publications, which she had delivered to work so that security would see them before dropping them on his desk.

"Much as that would cheer me up, I don't think it's a good idea," I said, chuckling as I remembered how long it had taken to get the smell of spoiled milk out of his office after the last time. "I'm sure he's hiding something. I think that's why he didn't want me around anymore."

She made a joke, suggesting that he was probably just fed up with me coming into work and ignoring him all day. I was still laughing after I hung up the phone but quickly turned my mind to more pressing matters. I'd been through the project files for the trial so many times that I had them committed to memory. If there was anything suspicious in there, I certainly hadn't found it. But that didn't mean there was nothing to find.

I decided not to let my anger at Frank divert me from my original goal. Whilst it didn't take much to convince me he was capable of blowing up his office, I had to stay focussed, and so spent the evening thinking about where I might find proof of what had really happened during the trial. In the end, only one place came to mind. Unfortunately, it wasn't going to be easy. I was probably one of the last people they wanted to speak to.

When I got up the next morning, it took me a while to remember I didn't need to go to work. It was strange. Since starting at the company, I'd never had any sick days, so my only previous absences were annual leave. It was even stranger, though, when I took the bus to Spinningfields and headed towards the office. I had no intention of going inside but knew that was where I would find who I was looking for. Or, at the very least, someone who could help.

As soon as I approached the mob, the jeers began. Unlike every other day, though, I had to endure it. I needed their help.

"Look, I need to speak to someone," I said.

"Go back to killing babies," someone yelled.

"How do you sleep at night?" somebody else shouted. One person simply yelled a four-letter word, which polarised the group a little.

"Did anyone here know Dylan Keeling?" I asked.

Dylan Keeling was the seventh victim in the trial. So far, I hadn't managed to speak to anyone in his family. I knew without asking that his family wouldn't be there. They'd never attended these rallies. I suspected they didn't want to be reminded of his death. But perhaps someone in the mob had known him. A friend or colleague, maybe.

"How can you say his name?" a woman yelled.

"You make me sick," another cried. Once again, the four-letter word sounded, much louder than anyone else. Under different circumstances, I might have laughed.

"Look, do you see that?" I roared, pointing up at the remnants of Frank's office. "I think somebody is trying to hide something. Why else would someone go to the trouble of targeting a single room in a building this size? I know what most of you think of me but, I swear, I'm trying to find out what happened. And to do that, I need to speak to someone about Dylan. If anyone knew him, please, I've got a few questions that could-"

A torrent of abuse drowned the rest of my words. They booed, hissed, shouted and, in one case, spat at me. When I could stand it no longer, I walked away, quietly seething. Whilst I knew they had every right to be angry, it was maddening that so much of their anger was directed at me. I was heading back towards the bus stop, eager to work out some of my own anger at the gym when somebody grabbed my arm. I braced, ready for physical abuse, but it never came.

"Her name's Kelly," said a woman sheepishly. "She was Dylan Keeling's girlfriend. They were living together when he got sick."

"Do you know where? Or how I can get hold of her?"

"No," she said, shaking her head. "But she's doing the charity run on Saturday."

"Thank you."

"If you speak to her, just think about what you're going to say," she said, her voice suddenly serious.

"Course," I said, although I wasn't really sure what she meant.

"She's been through a lot," she added. "Bear that

in mind, yeah?"

Before I could reply, she'd walked away to join the mob. Speaking to Kelly was the next step in my investigation.

CHAPTER 3

Since the Itch had become a national crisis, huge amounts of money were required for research and treatment. A group of companies, including Rathbury-Holmes, had organised a race to raise funds that weekend at Heaton Park, which wasn't far from the city centre. Places had been reserved months in advance, but I wasn't going to let that stop me. If there was ever a chance I could speak to someone about Dylan, this was it. Although the likelihood of Kelly knowing whether Frank had planted the bomb was slim, she might be able to tell me something about Dylan that would explain why the trial had failed. Before then, though, there was an issue I would need to resolve. I had no idea what she looked like. I didn't even know her full name.

That afternoon, I sat at my laptop, wondering how to find Kelly. Social media was the obvious answer, even if that made me a little uncomfortable. I certainly wouldn't like someone to spy on me through their computer screen. But that would still be difficult without knowing her surname. Firstly, I went on Facebook and found a group created to promote Saturday's race. Within a few minutes, I'd found half a dozen people called Kelly in the group. I checked each profile and eventually found a heart-breaking post about Dylan. Her full name was Kelly Cooper. After a few more minutes, I'd also found a picture of her number for the race on Sunday, which would be useful for making sure I had the right person.

Lizzy met me at the gym that evening. We used to spend a lot of our free time together, but she'd recently moved in with her boyfriend, which meant we'd seen each other less and less outside of work. As well as being one of the sharpest minds I knew, Lizzy was also superhumanly athletic, annually competing in all sorts of endurance races and physical challenges. Currently, she was training to run 40 miles across the Pennines.

"Eurgh, you little stalker," she said after I told her how I'd tracked down Kelly.

"Thanks. That makes me feel much better," I said, hammering the punch bag for a few more seconds before dropping my hands.

"So, what's your plan?" she asked, stepping up to the bag and throwing a few lightning-fast jabs.

"Honestly, I think I'm just going to have to wing it," I admitted.

I'd considered a few possible options. Pretend to be an old acquaintance or friend of Dylan's. Perhaps a co-worker. Unfortunately, none of those ideas would work because, eventually, I needed to ask Kelly some personal questions about Dylan; questions that a friend or colleague would surely know the answers to.

"Good luck with that," Lizzy said, confirming that it wasn't a particularly good idea.

Whilst we took turns beating the bag, we also talked about the bombing. Whilst she speculated about Frank's involvement, I did my best not to let her lead me astray. True, she wasn't one to make deductions without careful consideration and, when she did, she was usually correct, but first, I wanted to find out why the trial had failed.

"Do you really think Frank could do it, though?" she asked. "Explosives aren't easy to come by."

"I'm sure you wouldn't have any trouble," I said jokingly.

Lizzy had once told a story about an experiment in a laboratory practical at university, which had resulted in an ear-splitting explosion. When asked about it, she'd insisted it had been an unfortunate accident. The truth was she was trying to make nitroglycerine and hadn't expected the mixture to react so violently.

"My interest in that area was purely academic," she said matter-of-factly, although she was grinning. "I just meant it's not the sort of thing they stock at the local supermarket."

"No, but he could buy the ingredients there," I countered. "Not to mention, there's plenty of stuff he could use in the labs."

"When was the last time you saw Frank in a lab coat?" she joked, before adding in a more serious tone, "Do they even make them in his size?"

"Fair point," I said with a chuckle.

By the time we'd finished our workout, I could barely move. In complete contrast, Lizzy had barely broken a sweat. After showering, I met her outside and walked her to the bus stop. I joked I couldn't let a young lady walk alone at night, but we both knew she didn't need me to look after her. Before stepping on to the bus, she said the same thing about Kelly as the woman earlier.

"I know she's been through a lot," I said as reasonably as I could. "And yes, I'll think about what I'm going to say." I was a little peeved my closest friend thought I was going to take such a sensitive conversation lightly.

On Saturday morning, I got up and left the flat early, dressed in my running gear. First, I took the blue line into the city centre. After alighting at Piccadilly Gardens, I walked across the grassy lawns to Lever Street. It was a soggy day, which meant there were very few people sitting outside. I left the spacious square for a narrow side street. The buildings seemed taller as they got closer together. I found a photography shop, where the owner printed an A4 copy of a race number I'd downloaded from the Facebook group I'd found. I fixed it to the front of my t-shirt. It seemed unlikely people would be checking numbers, so I wasn't concerned about being found out. From there, I walked to the nearest bus stop and headed north out of the city centre.

The tall buildings were slowly replaced with two storey terraces. At every stop, more runners boarded the bus. Before long, all but a handful of passengers were dressed for the race. When I saw the trees that surrounded the park, I got off with the rest of the racers and headed to the entrance. Giant signs hung on each side of it. I followed the group along the tarmac path. Even from a distance, it was clear there were a lot of people in attendance. Every few seconds, an almighty cheer spooked the birds from the treetops.

The race started and finished in an enclosure at the edge of the forest in the centre of the park. There were stands arranged around the edge, each bearing the logo of a sponsor. Rathbury-Holmes had the largest stand, their lavender and turquoise emblem towering above those beside it. Briefly, I worried someone from work might be attending and that they would recognise me. Those concerns were quickly dispelled when I saw the sheer number of people waiting to run.

There were easily a few hundred, perhaps even a thousand milling around. The odds of bumping into the true owner of my number were, therefore, in my favour. Even so, I kept my hoodie zipped up, with only the race logo visible on my illicit number. A quick conversation with one of the runners confirmed the first digit of my number – which matched Kelly's – indicated the group we would be running in.

Before I could start looking for Kelly, an instantly familiar voice sounded from speakers around the park.

"Good afternoon, ladies and gentlemen," said Rupert Prophett.

As well as being the Health Secretary, Prophett was the local MP, so it made sense he would attend an event like this. He was standing behind a podium on a stage next to the starting line, above which hung an inflatable arch.

"I'm absolutely delighted to see so many of you here today. It really is a testament to the spirit of this city. Now, I've never been one for speeches, so I shall keep this brief. We all know why we're here. We know what we're fighting against. Many of you, I'm sure, have been personally affected by this hideous sickness. To you all, I'd like to say a tremendous and heartfelt thank you. Every penny raised here today will go towards combatting the sickness. There aren't enough hours in the day to express my thanks here and now. But in appreciation of your efforts, I will match the total raised here today."

Whatever he said next was lost in a deafening cheer. People were hooting and yelling, applauding. It wasn't hard to see why Rupert Prophett had held his post for so long. The people of Manchester adored him.

"No amount of words or promises can bring back those we've lost. But together, here today, we can make a difference. We can prevent further loss. We can and will find a cure for the Itch. Whether you walk, run, jog, sprint or crawl your way around the course, every person that competes today is fighting it. And anyone worried about running a slow time, I can assure you, you won't be the slowest."

As he stepped out from behind a small podium, I noticed that he was also wearing a number. Once again, the crowd erupted. They were chanting his name. I didn't feel like I was watching a politician but a rock star. Whilst the first group gathered at the start of the race, I made my way into the middle of the park.

Not knowing how long I had before our group would start, I quickly looked for Kelly. The second and third group had commenced before I spotted her. She looked to be on her own, eyes focussed on the start line, but there were so many people around her I couldn't be sure. In the fervour before the race, there didn't seem any risk of being spotted, so I unzipped my hoodie and tied it around my waist. As the runners from the fourth group gathered by the starting line, I picked my way through them to where Kelly was standing. Taking my chance, I reached out and tapped her on the arm.

"Kelly?" I asked.

"Do I know you?" she replied suspiciously.

"I need to ask you some things," I said.

"Who are you?"

"I need your help."

"First, you can tell me who you are."

I grappled with what to say. If I told her who I was, or more importantly, why I wanted to know about Dylan, there was every chance she'd refuse to speak to me. But it was equally likely that she wouldn't want to speak to a stranger about her deceased boyfriend and the circumstances of his death. In the end, I knew I had to tell her the truth. As soon as I told her where I worked and what I wanted to ask her, though, her expression soured.

"You're disgusting, you know that?" she yelled.

"Please, I just-"

"It was bad enough when you were hounding me on the phone, but now you're seeking me out in public. At a charity event to raise money for the sickness that killed my partner. What's wrong with you?" she said, so loudly that people were looking at us.

"Look, I'm on your side," I said, which thankfully silenced her. "I've been trying to prove what happened in the trial, but I need your help. I've spoken to all the other families. Now, I need to ask you some questions about Dylan. Look, I understand this is probably the last thing you want to talk about, but you might be able to help prove what happened. If you don't like what I have to say, then, I'll leave you alone. Just give me five minutes."

For a long time, she stared at me with narrowed eyes, chewing her cheek thoughtfully. Anxiously, I waited. Before she'd replied, the announcer began counting down to signal the start of our race.

"If you can keep up, we can talk," she said. And with that, the race began.

For thirty seconds, I matched Kelly's pace. Beyond that, though, it was clear I was going to have my work cut out.

"Well?" she asked, already pulling ahead.

"Firstly, I just want to say that I'm so sorry for-"

"Stop wasting your five minutes and tell me why you're here."

Naturally, I was a little shocked by her forwardness, but, at the same time, it was a relief to be able to get straight to business.

"I think somebody made a mistake," I said.

"There's an understatement."

"Not during the trial"

"When?"

"During early development. I think there was some false information used to develop the cure."

"You've said *think* a lot," she observed.

"There's a chance that Dose isn't causing the Itch," I said, lowering my voice so that the other runners didn't here.

Over the last few years, there'd been plenty of hypotheses questioning how Dose might have caused the Itch, but all had been disproven. Drug withdrawal: unlikely because of the high concentration of Dose detected in most Itch patients. Harmful breakdown products: also, unlikely because Dose wasn't easily metabolised. Chronic toxicity, adverse reactions, unexpected chemical properties, and mimicking cell signalling were also rejected. Some had suggested that the effects might be psychological – that patients weren't experiencing an itch – but as the number of victims rocketed, that hypothesis had been quickly disregarded.

Based on that information, there was already a pretty overwhelming case against Dose as the cause of the Itch. Also, there was the disastrous outcome of the trial. Early clinical development showed the active ingredient in the cure was totally effective against Dose. So, why had it been so ineffective when administered in the trial? As ludicrous as it might seem, I was almost certain someone had made a mistake; that something else was making people sick. And on top of that, the bomb in Frank's office suggested someone was trying to hide the truth. Unfortunately, I couldn't prove any of this.

"Is this a joke?" she asked.

By now, we'd entered the forest. The ground was

soft, and my feet were already covered in mud. Kelly was clearly a runner, and there were only a handful of people ahead of us. I wasn't entirely sure I'd be able to keep up with her for five minutes but kept going regardless.

"Why would I joke about this?" I replied.

"Why would you track down a grieving person to ask about their dead boyfriend?"

"Because I need proof. I need to ask you some questions about Dylan."

"Like what?"

As with the other families, I asked Kelly about Dylan's personal life. At 34, he was roughly in the middle of the group. He was a plumber and the only one in the group who worked in that field. He'd lived his entire life in Manchester. Although one other victim lived in the area, they were separated by some miles. The only link came when I asked her about his underlying health.

"Cancer in his liver," she said. "A few years ago."

"Did he have any problems after treatment?"

"That's enough," she said. To my surprise, she stopped running. "I don't know what you're doing. I don't know why you're asking these questions. And I certainly don't know why you think anyone would want to have this discussion for a second time, but-"

"Second time?" I said. As far as I knew, nobody had managed to speak to anyone in Dylan's family. There was certainly no record of any such communication.

"Somebody else from your company," she yelled. "I told him everything I know. So, if you've got questions, ask him. Now, if you don't mind, I'm getting back to my race."

"Who was it?" I asked.

She looked aghast. I couldn't say I blamed her. I would have been equally annoyed if someone had pestered me like this, particularly about such a sensitive subject. As I often did in situations like this, I reached for my necklace, fighting against memories I didn't want to deal with at that moment. Fleetingly, I thought Kelly wasn't going to answer.

"His name was Frank. I recognised him from the news. Utter scumbag. Right, I've been more polite than you deserve. So, now, I want you to leave me alone. And if you come near me again, I'm calling the police."

A moment later, she disappeared amongst the other runners. I stared after her. Several runners looked back at me to see if I was alright. Eventually, I started jogging at a more comfortable pace. It didn't seem right not to finish the race, even if I shouldn't have been running it. Whilst I ran, my mind raced, too. Why had Frank kept his meeting with Kelly from everyone in the office? What had they discussed? Had she revealed something that might explain why the trial had failed?

When I crossed the finish line, there was no sign of Kelly. Whilst the other runners celebrated and posed for pictures, I slipped away. It would take over an hour to get back to my flat by public transport. Eagerness to act on what I'd learnt, plus the prospect of a long journey in sweaty clothing prompted me to call a taxi.

As I rode the taxi home, I called Lizzy. She was about to go to the gym, so couldn't talk right away, but I agreed to meet her there. Her workout was sure to be tough and I wasn't sure I'd be able to keep up with her, but I couldn't wait to tell her what I'd found out, so redirected the driver. When I arrived, she was already on the treadmill. Reluctantly, I joined.

"She said Frank's name?" Lizzy asked once I'd finished telling her what Kelly had said.

"She said it was somebody called Frank from the company. She also said he was a scumbag," I replied, already struggling to keep up.

"Certainly sounds like Frank."

Frank had a reputation around the office as an ogler. According to Lizzy, he'd sexually harassed most of his female co-workers. Lizzy was in a small minority that had escaped his lustful gaze. She said it was because he thought she was gay, but I thought it was because he was afraid of what she'd do to him if she caught him staring.

"But why would he lie about speaking to her?" she mused, increasing the speed on her treadmill. I did the same. If I was going to get a workout, I might as well make sure it was a good one. "Maybe somebody was posing as him to get information."

"No," I said, gasping for air. "Recognised him from the telly."

"So, what are you going to do now, then?"

By now, we were no longer jogging but sprinting. I tried to reply but couldn't get my words out. Talking would have come at the expense of breathing and, currently, my need for air outweighed my desire to speak. Thankfully, Lizzy hit the stop button after a few minutes. Once we'd both stepped off the treadmill, I took a minute or so to catch my breath.

Lizzy waited patiently, hardly looking as though she'd run at all.

"I need to know why he lied about meeting her," I said when I could breathe normally again.

There were no records of any conversation with Kelly in the investigation file. Frank's PC had been destroyed, along with everything else in his office. And after what Kelly had told me, it was looking increasingly likely Frank was responsible for the bomb. But if that was the case, and he'd taken such extreme steps to hide something, there was no way he'd be careless enough to keep a record elsewhere. I considered asking Lizzy to see if she could find anything but decided against it. The last thing I wanted was for her to get in trouble.

"What if we force his hand?" I said. "What if we make him think Kelly knows he's lying about speaking to her?"

"Do you think she'll want to help?" she asked sceptically.

"She doesn't have to," I said, grinning shrewdly. "I could write a letter or an email. From Kelly. Address it to Frank."

"How are you going to make him believe you? Or... believe her? If Frank knows you're involved, he'll just ignore the message."

"So, I make it convincing, then. Keep it vague. Tell him I know something. Something bad. Threaten to reveal it if he doesn't meet me."

"Blackmail," she observed. I thought that she was going to put an end to the matter, but then, she added, "How can I help?"

On Monday morning, Lizzy went into work with the letter I'd drafted. I'd written it on Sunday and sent her a copy. Of course, she'd made extensive changes, which she insisted I should review. After we'd agreed on the content, she'd printed a copy and planted it on Frank's desk. In the letter, I wrote that I – Kelly – had discovered Frank was lying about the failed trial and, if he didn't meet me outside the town hall that evening, I would tell the police what I knew. I kept the letter deliberately vague to tempt him to act without revealing my deception.

Roughly half an hour before we were due to meet, I left the flat and took the Metro to St. Peter's Square. When I arrived, I headed towards Albert Square, which was where I'd arranged to meet Frank. I'd chosen there because it was easy to get to but, upon further consideration, I probably should have picked a more intimidating location like a warehouse or alleyway. Then again, all I needed was him to turn up. His presence would confirm there was something he didn't want people to know.

I waited across the road from the square, which gave good views whilst maintaining my distance. Glancing at the town hall's clocktower, I saw I was a few minutes early. With nothing else to do, my eyes wandered over the impressive spires and turrets of the town hall. It was one of my favourite places in the city, likely because the Christmas Markets were held in the square every year. As I looked around, memories surfaced, prompting me to grip my bottlecap necklace. Last year, I hadn't visited the markets. It hadn't seemed like a time for celebration.

When the clock struck seven, I fixed my eyes on

the square, scanning every face. It probably wasn't necessary – Frank's bald head and large physique weren't difficult to miss – but I did it anyway. Five minutes passed, and then ten. After a quarter of an hour, I started to doubt whether he would show. Half an hour later, any hope Frank would arrive had vanished entirely. Frustrated, I headed back to the Metro and went home.

The instant I arrived, I threw on my gym kit and headed right back out the door. Lizzy was at the gym, too. She was doing an abs workout, which I didn't particularly want to join, so instead, I did some circuits involving the punch bag.

"Maybe he didn't read the letter," I said as I finished explaining what had happened.

"Possibly. It wasn't where I left it on his desk, though" she said whilst doing crunches beside me. "Do you think he might have seen you?"

"I doubt it," I said. I was confident my vantage point was sufficiently secluded.

In between exercises, we discussed the reasons why he might not have shown. In the end, we both agreed the letter hadn't been enough to trick him into revealing his hand. Neither of us was sure what to do next.

"You could speak to Kelly again. Ask her if she's willing to state he spoke to her. That would prove he's withheld information."

"Probably do more harm than good," I said, recalling her parting words.

When I got home, I had a hasty meal and then went to sit on the balcony, gazing towards the city. I was trying to think of a reason Frank would lie about speaking to Kelly. Based on the answers to the questions I'd asked her, there was nothing to suggest there was anything suspicious about Dylan's death. Was it possible I'd overlooked something in her responses that had aroused Frank's concern? If that was true, I couldn't think what it might be.

I was still thinking about it when an urgent knock rattled my front door. It was too firm to be a friendly caller. Concerned, I waited for the visitor to announce their identity.

"Open the door, Mr Bright," said DCI Dunhill, the detective who'd interviewed me outside Rathbury Holmes.

"How can I help?" I said as I opened the door. Two hulking police officers were standing beside her, who made me feel a little anxious.

"I had a very interesting conversation earlier," she said, strolling around the flat, regarding things like a shopper browsing the shelves. What could this be about? Did she know about my attempt to trap Frank? Was that why he hadn't turned up? Had he figured out my trap and called the police? It seemed unlikely. How would he have known it was me? And why would Dunhill have followed up on something so trivial? I concluded it could only be related to one thing.

"I already told you that I had nothing to do with the bomb," I said.

"I remember. And no, it's nothing to do with that," she said, which surprised me.

"Then why are you here?"

"Mind if we have a look around?" she asked, although she was already perusing the titles on my bookcase.

"Don't you need a warrant for that?" I said irritably.

"You're quite right," she said. Reaching into her jacket, she pulled out a folded piece of paper. "Our invitation" she added dryly as she handed me the document. Hesitantly, I took it from her and started reading. It seemed legitimate but, if it hadn't been, I wouldn't have known.

Before I could say anything, Dunhill and the two officers started opening cupboards and drawers. They checked behind the units, under cushions and even under the rug in the middle of the living room floor. It happened so quickly that, by the time I found my voice, the two officers had disappeared into my bedroom.

"What are you doing?" I demanded.

"Working," she replied simply.

"Ma'am," one of the officers yelled from my bedroom.

"Excuse me," Dunhill said, slinking passed me.

I was starting to lose my patience. Surely, she couldn't treat me like this. If it wasn't about Frank or the bombing, why was she searching my flat? And how had she come by a warrant so quickly? Keen for some answers, I went to confront her. We met in the hallway. Her eyes were menacingly narrow. She was carrying a clear plastic bag, which she held out for me to see.

"What's this?" she asked.

Puzzled, I looked a little closer at the white plastic tubes inside. There were perhaps 50 of them, each about the size of a lipstick. At first, I didn't recognise them, but then, I saw the small letter D embossed on the surface of each device. I was almost too scared to speak, simply gawking at the bag.

"They aren't mine," I said finally.

"Are you aware that possession of this drug is-"

"I swear, that's not mine."

"Course not. Until we know for sure, though, you'll be coming with us," Dunhill said. The kindness in her voice was more unsettling than if she'd been yelling at me.

I recognised the speech as one of the officers started reading me my rights but forgot the words almost as soon as I heard them. Whilst the officer spoke, he pulled my arms behind my back and handcuffed my wrists. Where the Hell had the drugs come from? I'd been at home for most of the day, and they certainly weren't there earlier. So, when had they appeared? And who had-

With that final thought came a disturbing realisation. For reasons I didn't know, someone had broken into my flat and planted the drugs. And although I wasn't sure of it yet, I had every reason to believe they must have called the police.

"Somebody's trying to frame me. They must have broken in whilst I was out."

Nobody listened.

CHAPTER 4

As the officers led me from the flat, I tried to explain they were making a mistake. If they were listening, they gave no sign. Neither spoke as they forced me into the back of a waiting police car. The handcuffs dug painfully into my wrists. I was so preoccupied I didn't really pay attention to where I was being taken. But as the buildings started to shrink away from the car, I realised we were leaving the city centre.

By the time I arrived at the police station, I was too anxious to register anything about my surroundings. I was taken to a grey room with grey walls and a grey table. The officers that were escorting me sat me on a grey chair. There was a cup of something that looked like tea on the table. If I'd been calm enough to take a sip, I'm sure it would have tasted grey. Thankfully, though, I was no longer handcuffed.

When the door opened, and DCI Dunhill entered, my back was damp with sweat. With the elegance of a snake, she slid into the seat opposite me. Her eyes remained fixed on the folder in her hands, which she'd been reading since she walked in. Although I knew it was absurd to think so, I couldn't help feeling as though she didn't know I was there.

After a moment, she placed the folder on the table in front of her, along with a small recording device. Once she'd introduced herself and the two hulking police officers for the recording, she finally looked at me, smiling so sweetly I briefly forgot what was happening. After I said my name for the recording, she consulted her notes again, drumming her fingers thoughtfully on the table.

"Where do you live, Mr Bright?" she asked eventually.

"You already know where I live," I replied.

"What's your address?"

"Why? What am I supposed to have done?"

"Are you aware that the possession of Dose is punishable by up to-"

"I've already told you; I've never seen that before. Somebody must have planted it in my flat. Shouldn't you be checking the scene of the crime? There's bound to be evidence of a break-in."

"Do you rent or own?" she said, ignoring my questions.

Why was she asking about my flat? Did she suspect my landlord might have planted the drugs? I highly doubted the kindly Mr Baker would be capable of something like that. And besides, what reason would he have for doing it? In all the years I'd lived there, I couldn't remember exchanging anything other than pleasantries with him. I'd probably only met him a handful of times, too. After I told her how much my rent was, she consulted her notes again, drumming the table as she did so. Each tap of her fingertips sounded like the thump of a gavel.

"What do you do for a living?" she asked.

"You already know that too."

"No, I know where you work. I want to know what you do there."

"I'm a scientist. I work in the new product development team."

"A lot of money in that, is there?"

"I get by," I replied, wondering why that was relevant.

"Well, there must be for you to afford such a nice place to live. Unless you've some other source of income," she purred.

"What are you suggesting?" I asked. Although I had a fairly good idea what she meant, it was too ridiculous to give credence to.

"You're a scientist, Mr Bright. I'm sure you can work it out."

Admittedly, my flat was expensive, but did she really believe I was dealing drugs to pay for it? It wasn't as if I was living in a multi-million-pound luxury apartment.

"Why were you suspended from work?" she asked, which caught me off guard. Clearly, she'd done some digging already.

"Professional disagreement," I said.

"Can you be more specific?"

"It was about a project I was working on."

"Sounds pretty trivial."

It was clear from her tone she didn't believe me. I considered telling her my theory about the cause of the Itch and the trial. It didn't seem wise to make a claim I had absolutely zero evidence to support, but what choice did I have? Resignedly, I started explaining. She remembered the trial, of course. When I told her why I was looking into it, she seemed sceptical.

"I think somebody made a mistake," I said, defending my position. "I've been trying to find out what really happened. I thought maybe there would be something linking the victims of the trial."

"What do you think happened?" she asked.

"I don't believe Dose is causing the Itch," I said hesitantly.

"Excuse me?" Dunhill replied. One of the officers by the door smirked.

"That's why the cure failed. Something else is making people sick. Plus, I think somebody is trying to hide the truth," I said.

"Who?" she asked. I was pleased to see that she sat forward, her expression suddenly attentive. But I wasn't sure how to answer.

At present, I had no concrete evidence Frank had done anything illegal. If I was mistaken, what impact would that have on his reputation? And my own? He might be a terrible boss, but that didn't justify dragging his name through the mud without just cause. In the end, I gave the only answer I could confidently support.

"I don't know yet. But I've got a strong reason to believe it's Frank Badder."

"Your boss?" she asked, to which I nodded. "I guess he suspended you?"

"Yeah, because he's a-" I began but caught myself. It seemed unwise to say what I really thought of him, so I continued in a calmer tone. "Yes, he did, which is why I started suspecting him. I think he wanted to get rid of me because I was getting close to the truth. Who knows? He might have planted the drugs in my flat."

"Awfully inconvenient for you," she replied sarcastically.

"If you don't believe me, check the bags. I can

guarantee you won't find my fingerprints on them. Without that, how can you prove they're mine?"

Something like anger flashed behind her eyes, but it was gone as quickly as it had appeared. She flicked through the folder in front of her, drumming the table again. Once she'd found what she was looking for, she slid the folder across the table so I could see it.

"Who's that, Mr Bright?" she asked triumphantly.

I felt as if the air was being sucked out of the room. No matter how deeply I inhaled, I couldn't get enough air to my lungs. As I stared down at the photograph in the folder, my mood swung from murderously angry to inconsolably upset. Reflexively, I reached for my bottlecap necklace.

"What does he have to do with this?" I asked.

"He was a dealer, wasn't he?"

"That's not true."

"But he was diagnosed with the Itch, correct?"

"That doesn't make him a drug dealer."

"When there's that much smoke, it's a safe bet something's burning."

The words that erupted from my mouth were uncharacteristically hostile; not to mention, extremely rude. Throughout my tirade, though, Dunhill's face remained entirely passive. Once or twice, she checked her watch or ran a hand through her silvery hair but, otherwise, didn't indicate she was even listening.

"This is ridiculous," I said, finally calming down. "You can't honestly believe this? Look, I want to make something absolutely, irrefutably, one hundred percent crystal clear; I am not, nor have I ever been, a drug dealer. And until I've spoken to a lawyer, I'm not saying another word to somebody that is making such a wild accusation."

After my rant finished, I stared at Dunhill, almost daring her to challenge what I'd said. No matter what had happened in the past, I knew he was no more a drug dealer than I. And there was absolutely no way I was going to let DCI Dunhill – or anyone else, for that matter – accuse either of us of that crime. If I'd expected her to be fazed by my outburst, though, I was very much mistaken.

"I'm not in the habit of making wild accusations, Mr Bright," she said, fixing me with a deathly stare. "If I were, I wouldn't be a very good detective, would I? Jack Bright, I'm charging you with possession with intent to supply the banned substance, Dose," And with that, she got to her feet and left the room. Too stunned to speak, I shut my eyes, willing myself to wake up from the hideously vivid nightmare I was having. But, of course, I didn't wake up.

I'd never dealt with the police, so had no idea what was going to happen to me. TV shows made it seem as though prisoners were processed almost immediately. In fact, I spent the next two days trapped in my cell awaiting trial. Although I'd seen everything that happened to me in crime films, nothing was believable. Even the residual ink on the end of my fingers wasn't enough to convince me they'd taken my fingerprints. They must have taken someone else's. That person was the criminal, not me.

As I didn't have a solicitor – and hadn't the faintest idea how to get one – I was appointed somebody to give me legal advice. It transpired there was no evidence of a break-in. The police had found 20,000 tubes of Dose in my flat. Even more disturbing was the traces of the drug found in other rooms. There was paraphernalia, too, including scales, several pay-as-you-go phones, and a duffel bag full of money. Whoever was framing me had been thorough. Upon hearing the charges and the evidence against me, the solicitor had advised me to put in a guilty plea.

"If you're found guilty – and you likely will be – you could be facing a long sentence; 10, maybe even 15 years," he'd explained. 15 years – almost half my life – for a crime I hadn't committed. The solicitor had left without an answer from me. Even now, hours later, I had no idea what I was going to do.

I was shocked and, frankly, annoyed at Dunhill for being so unresponsive to my theory. Understandably, such a suggestion seemed absurd without supporting evidence but, surely, she had to investigate it. Wasn't it her job to find proof of a crime? Based on my current predicament, it was pretty clear she wasn't willing to give any thought to my idea.

Without a clock, it was impossible to gauge how long I'd been in the cell, which made me more anxious; if I couldn't handle a single night, how would I handle 10 years? Or longer? I spent most of my time sitting on the edge of the mattress, which was so firm it was a wonder anyone was ever able to sleep on it. The profanity scratched into the peeling paintwork didn't help. Wearily, I kneaded my eyes with the palms of my hands, far too anxious to fall asleep, even for a few minutes. When that didn't help ease my mind, I got to my feet and started pacing. Very quickly, though, I started to worry whether that would look suspicious, and so sat back down on the mattress.

I was still sitting the following morning, running my fingertips around my bottlecap necklace, when an officer opened the door to my cell. After placing me in handcuffs, he led me through the station to a car. Over the last few days, I'd heard dozens of prisoners being taken to trial for Dose offences. I suspected that was why it had taken so long to get a trial.

As we pulled away, I rested my head against the window, trying to work out what I was going to do. The sky was iron grey and threatening rain. Even after only a brief interaction with DCI Dunhill, plus the damning advice the solicitor had given me, it seemed almost impossible there was a way out of this, but I had to try.

The driver grumbled about such a tedious duty, suggesting it shouldn't be part of his job to ferry criminals to trial. He continued complaining until we reached the city centre. The officer beside me made noncommittal noises throughout the conversation, clearly of a different opinion to the driver. We were heading along Fairfield Street and had just passed beneath the wide railway bridge that led to Piccadilly station when a massive jolt sent the car into a sideways skid. It happened so quickly that nobody said a word, the only sound that of the tyres howling against the tarmac. After ricocheting off something, we skidded in the opposite direction for a split second before the car rolled.

I had no idea how many times we flipped. It felt as though I was trapped in a tumble dryer filled with broken glass and other debris. When we finally came to a standstill, the car was in the middle of the road.

My head felt as though it was only barely attached to my body. Every breath lodged in my lungs, my chest swelling painfully as I sucked in more and more air. Frantically, I scoured the scene around the car, trying to understand what had just happened, but the street seemed unusually quiet. Then, I turned my attention to my police escort.

Neither officer was moving. From my seat, I could see a nasty cut on the driver's temple. Blood had already soaked his collar. Although the officer beside me wasn't visibly hurt, his head was hanging limply. Gingerly, I checked myself for injuries. Miraculously, I could only find a few scrapes and bumps. And then, as I sat back in my seat, unsure what to do, I realised my passenger door was slightly ajar.

Hurriedly, I unbuckled my seatbelt; as I was handcuffed, it wasn't easy. Once I was free, I twisted around so I could kick the door open. It took a lot of force. There was so much broken glass on the street it looked like it was covered in frost. Once I was out, I saw a van a short distance away. The bonnet was heavily crumpled. In the cabin, I could see the driver stirring. He must have lost control and struck the police car. A small crowd had gathered, some of them heading over to help the van driver. They kept their distance from me, which was understandable.

My eyes darted from the crowd to the police car, suddenly conflicted. If I stayed, I was almost certainly going to prison. Fleeing would only add to the charges against me. *But only if I was caught*, I thought. Whilst the officers were unconscious, I might have a chance. In seconds, my mind was made up.

It wasn't easy, but I managed to open the driver's door. Next, I searched his pockets until I found a set of keys. Getting the handcuffs off was nightmarishly difficult. When I felt the tumblers move, I quickly shook them off, rubbing my wrists. Then, after yelling at the crowd to call an ambulance, I started running.

At first, I was a little unsteady on my feet but broke into a normal rhythm after a few strides. By now, I could hear sirens. The sound echoed off the tall buildings, which made it seem as though it was coming from all around me. For all I knew, I was running towards an approaching police car. But I didn't stop.

I knew I needed somewhere to hide but, as I raced along the street, I realised I had no idea where to go. The police would surely check my flat, and I didn't have any family to help. On a bridge overhead, I could see the train tracks leading to and from Piccadilly station. With nowhere else in mind, I headed there. Perhaps if I left the city, I could find somewhere to hide for a few days and regroup.

I'd just laid eyes on the ornamental brickwork of the main station building when I remembered the police had taken my wallet. Then, I noticed a police van parked in the taxi rank outside the station. I should have known there would be a police presence at one of the busiest train stations in the country. Did they already know about the accident? Were they looking for me? I didn't hang around to find out, hurrying back in the other direction.

For some respite, I left the main road and ran down a side street. Once I was sure I hadn't been followed,

I took refuge under a bridge so I could think. The ground floor windows of the nearby buildings had bars on them, and I was unpleasantly reminded of my brief time in police custody. I couldn't stand another night in a cell. I had to prove I'd been framed. But how and where would I find answers? And more pressingly, how long would I be able to evade capture?

The police had taken my phone. I had no money. I wasn't sure who I could trust. I couldn't go back to my flat. It was unlikely Dunhill would follow up on my theory about the Itch and Dose. So, somehow, I had to prove something else was making people sick and someone was lying about the true cause. Firstly, though, I needed somewhere to hide.

The only name that came to mind was Lizzy. She was my closest friend, but I didn't want to involve her. If the people responsible for framing me found out she'd helped, surely, they'd do the same to her. And now I was a wanted man, would she be willing to help me? On top of that, there was her boyfriend, Kieran. How would he feel when he found out Lizzy was harbouring a fugitive? As it was the only idea I had, though, I dug down to my last reserves of energy and started running towards her address.

I ran for about 15 minutes through the rabbit warren of side streets in the city centre. I passed modern high rises, followed by old warehouses, and then finally arrived in Ancoats to the northeast of the centre. It took another 10 minutes or so to find the street I was looking for. The houses were all terraces, with identical PVC fascia and neatly trimmed squares of lawn. When I saw her house, I let out a shaky laugh. My relief was quickly replaced with panic, though. It was early evening, so she must have finished work. Most nights, she went straight to the gym. Despairingly, I knocked on her door. There was no answer.

The distant sirens felt like they were all around me, which made it difficult to think. After a moment to collect myself, I ran to a narrow alley that linked Lizzy's street to the next. There, I waited. It was all I could do. Occasionally, people walked past. I did my best to seem calm but wasn't sure I managed it. To keep my mind occupied, I toyed with my necklace but had to stop that when unwanted memories began to surface.

I'm not sure exactly how long I'd been waiting, but the streetlights were on when Lizzy returned home. And she wasn't alone. She and her boyfriend, Kieran, were laughing together as they entered the house. I was still unsure whether I could trust him – or Lizzy, for that matter – but had no other option. With great restraint, I managed to wait five minutes before knocking at their door. I was sure it would have seemed odd if I'd knocked right away. Thankfully, Lizzy answered.

"You look awful," she said. It was a fair assessment. I hadn't had a shower in almost three days.

"Can I come in?" I asked. Or rather, demanded.

As soon as she stepped back, I rushed past her. For the first time since my arrest, I was able to relax, if only a little. Lizzy stood behind me, presumably waiting for an explanation. My eyes fell on a photograph of Kieran on the wall. It was taken on the day he'd become a police officer. I tried my best to ignore it.

"Where's Kieran?" I asked anxiously.

"Unpacking upstairs. Why?"

"Who is it?" he called, almost on cue.

"Jack from work," she replied.

"Hi Jack from work," he replied. Lizzy rolled her eyes.

For about a minute, Kieran and Lizzy had a conversation about whether I would stay for dinner. As patiently as I could, I waited for them to finish.

"Do you want something to drink? Or a shower?" she said. Despite the joke, her voice was serious.

We headed to the kitchen, where she poured me a glass of water. I drank it all in only a few giant gulps. They'd only recently moved into the house, and there were still boxes labelled *Kitchen – Misc.* scattered around the room.

"I need your help," I said eventually.

"I can see that," she replied. "What's wrong?"

"Somebody is trying to frame me," I said. There was no way I could tell her the full story, but she at least needed to know that. "They must have broken into my flat earlier today."

"Is this a joke?"

"Do I look like I'm joking?" I said frantically.

"Do you have any idea who it was?"

"I can certainly guess."

"Frank? Do you really think he could do something like that?"

"It makes sense. I mean, a few days ago, his office was destroyed by a bomb. The following day, he suspended me from work. Then, I find out he's lying about speaking to Kelly and now, I'm on the run from-"

"On the run?" she said. Internally, I cursed. I should have been more careful about what I was saying.

"I just mean- I didn't mean that," I said hurriedly. And then, an unsettling thought occurred to me. "This has happened before. Someone else at the company."

"Are you sure?" she asked dubiously.

"It was a project scientist a few years ago. He was arrested for something around the time the Itch was linked to Dose. Don't you remember?"

"Wilson Loveday?" she asked in a disbelieving tone.

"Yes, that's him. What if he was framed, too?"

"I think you might be getting a little carried away," she said. But my mind was made up.

"There has to be a connection. Don't you remember his trial? The evidence? The suspicious circumstances. I think he was working with Frank at the time, too."

I was certain this was no coincidence. If I was right, and Frank had framed Wilson, he might have resorted to those methods again. He'd already made it clear he was willing to lie to keep his secrets. Wasn't it possible, even likely, that he'd do something so devious to keep the truth buried? I was giddy with excitement, but Lizzy shared none of that.

"You need to speak to Kieran," she said reasonably.

As if in slow-motion, I watched her heading towards the staircase. My mind scrambled for a way to stop her. In the end, though, all I could think to do was block her path.

"What's going on, Jack?" she asked.

"I'm in trouble," I said.

"I think you need to tell me what's really going on."

"I can't."

"Why not?"

As I looked at my closest friend, I realised she deserved to know the truth. If she was going to help me, and potentially put herself in harm's way, I had to tell her what I'd done. But as much as I wanted to, I couldn't bring myself to speak. It was an unfortunate coincidence that at that moment, my face appeared on the TV. Lizzy must have read the horror in my expression and followed my gaze. Before she could say anything, I headed for the door.

"Jack, wait," she said.

"I'm sorry. I shouldn't have come here."

Upstairs, I could hear the muffled sounds of Kieran unpacking boxes. Surely, it was only a matter of time before Kieran found out what I'd done. And then, there was only one possible outcome.

"Let's just think about this. There must be something we can do. Maybe Kieran can help," she said. I'd never heard her sound so flustered.

"No," I said. "I need to go. Look, no matter what they say, I swear I had nothing to do with it."

And before she said anything else, anything that might tempt me to stay, I left.

CHAPTER 5

For perhaps a mile, I ran as fast as I could. Not knowing where else to go, I headed back to the city. Eventually, I had to stop to catch my breath. Gasping for air, I ducked behind an electrical substation. Sitting with my back against the smooth green plastic, I thought hard about what I was going to do next.

I knew that someone was trying to frame me and had a fairly good idea who that was. But without proof, it was my word against Frank's. I didn't have a phone, money, or a place to sleep. Surely, it was only a matter of time before I was spotted. If I was going to prove my innocence, I would need help. With that final thought, a name came to mind. It wasn't someone I thought of as a friend – in fact, we were coldly indifferent to one another – but, with no other options, she was the only person who might be able – and willing – to help.

Although we weren't friendly, I had a fairly good idea where she'd be. Unfortunately, it was a very public place, with nowhere to hide if the police arrived. On a positive, though, there would be a crowd, so I'd be tough to spot. Surely, I was more noticeable hiding in an empty street. Proceeding at a gentler and less conspicuous pace, I headed towards Piccadilly Gardens.

Night had firmly fallen, and the city lights were glowing brightly. It seemed unwise to leave the gloomy suburbs for floodlit roads teeming with evening commuters, but there was nothing I could do about it. After zigzagging my way through narrow side streets, I arrived at Portland Street, which was only a few hundred metres from my destination. It was much wider – not to mention, busier – than the rest of my route, and I felt vulnerable.

After hurriedly dashing across the road, I made my way to Piccadilly Gardens. Previously, I'd thought that the sprawling grassy lawns were a nice place to relax in the busy city centre. Now, though, it seemed exposed and dangerous. I heard the chanting as I approached. There was a crowd of people waving signs and placards surrounding the fountain at the centre. Unlike the other people around the square, who gave one another a wide berth, the crowd was pressed together, closely knit with arms linked. There was a banner hanging above them, which read *Don't Dose us with lies*. The crowd were chanting the slogan tunelessly. She was standing on a podium in the middle of the crowd, yelling more loudly and enthusiastically than anyone else.

Although Dose had been linked to the Itch, the lack of a cure had people questioning whether it was the cause. Despite numerous awareness campaigns about the dangers of the drug, protesting the ban was common. When they first occurred, police presence was high. Countless arrests were made, but convictions never stuck; people were obviously smart enough to abstain from using the drug before publicly endorsing it. And few people endorsed it as strongly as the woman I'd come to see.

The sight of her was enough to make me hesitate. Vividly, I recalled the last time I'd seen her. I was certain she'd remember it too, which only made me less eager to approach her. But as the sound of sirens steadily built around me, I realised it was the favourable choice; not by much, but enough.

She caught sight of me as I made my way through the crowd surrounding her. Her initial reaction was something like astonishment, but it was quickly replaced by the disinterested look I'd expected. Rapidly, I started thinking I'd made a mistake but was too anxious to turn back.

"Well, this is a surprise," she said. Her tone made it clear that she wasn't surprised but annoyed to see me.

"Erin, I need your help."

"I'm sure you can polish your own microscope," Erin said, before resuming her chanting.

"This is serious," I hissed, eager not to be overheard. "Look, I'm in trouble, and I don't know who else can help."

"I'm sure you'll think of something."

"Please. I don't-"

At that moment, a police car raced past, sirens blazing. Hastily, I spun to hide my face. Once the car had passed, I turned back, by which time Erin looked curious.

"What's going on?" she asked.

"I can't explain right now."

"Then, I can't help right now," she replied, shrugging lazily.

"It's about the Itch," I said hurriedly. "Something isn't right. Look, I can't talk about it here. Please, can we just go to your flat? I'll explain everything, I promise. I just can't stay here."

For a moment, she simply watched me, as if trying

to detect a lie. I waited for her decision as patiently as I could, trying not to betray my urgency. Eventually, if a little resignedly, she nodded.

"Fine," she said, before walking away through the crowd.

Although it was a relief to get away from wide-open space to a narrow street, I couldn't help checking over my shoulder every few steps. When we arrived at a junction or had to cross a road, I checked for police cars as subtly as I could. Erin must have noticed I was acting strangely but didn't say anything.

Erin rented a flat in the Northern Quarter. It was an old redbrick building, which had been renovated into trendy cafes, bars and restaurants on the ground floor, and studio apartments above. Although most of the venues were open, the night was still early, so there weren't too many patrons who might later be used by the police as eyewitnesses. She led me to a narrow door hidden in shadow, which opened to reveal a windowless staircase lit by a chandelier.

Even though I'd never been in her flat before, the inside seemed to suit her personality. The walls were bare brick, the floorboards polished wood. Exposed girders stretched across the ceiling. Black and white photographs hung around the room, most of them depicting women in raunchy poses. None of the furniture matched, although it was all old and faded. Everything felt cluttered. Although it was clean, every surface had an ornament on it. Her books were haphazardly stacked, some with the pages pointing outwards. By comparison, my flat was clinically bare. The only thing that looked remotely organised was her extensive CD collection, which occupied floor to ceiling shelves along an entire wall.

On the right side of the room, there was a kitchen fenced off by a high worktop with a doorway out of the living room opposite it. Erin headed into the kitchen and poured a glass of water. I was anxiously peering out of the windows at the street below, making sure that we hadn't been followed when she came to stand in the living room.

"You've got until I finish this," she said, indicating the glass in her hand. "Fire away."

It was hard enough without added time pressure to describe the events of the last few days; so much had happened I was struggling to remember it all. With no better starting point in mind, I began with the drug trial and proceeded from there. By the time I started telling her about what Frank had said after the bombing, there were only a few mouthfuls of water in her glass. And she was showing no signs of drinking any slower.

"Sounds like you're looking for absolution," she said, taking another long swig.

"What's that supposed to mean?"

"You're feeling guilty about what happened in the drug trial. Yeah, I know what happened," she added as I threw my hands up in exasperation. "And I think you're looking for mistakes or faults to make yourself feel better about what happened instead of taking responsibility for your actions."

"How long have you been waiting to say that?" I said before I could stop myself. It was a mistake.

"You asked for my help, remember? If you're going to be like that, you certainly won't get it. If you thought there was an issue, why didn't you say something?"

"I did."

"Then, why don't you go to the police?"

Although I'd suspected I would have to tell her why I couldn't go to the police, I wasn't prepared for it. After a heavy sigh, I started explaining. She listened as I told her about the drugs in my flat, the charges against me, and how much trouble I was in. When I'd finished describing how I'd escaped from the police, she was glaring at me.

"Jesus, Jack," she said.

"I didn't do it."

"That's beside the point. They're going to be looking for you. And now I'm implicated."

"Well, you've never held much regard for the law before, have you?"

I knew that it wasn't fair to say, and might not even be true, but I had to try whatever I could to get her on my side. Unfortunately, it didn't work. Almost instantly, her expression soured.

"Protesting the ban and escaping police custody are not the same," she said, anger plain to see in her face. "And besides, you've no idea why I'm doing this. As far as I can tell, you're just trying to cover your own arse."

"I'm sorry. I shouldn't have said that," I said, backpedalling. "Look, I wouldn't have come to you if I had anyone else."

"Oh, thanks. That's much better."

"Someone is trying to get rid of me. And I think I know who it is. I think he's trying to hide something."

"And what do you think he's hiding?" she asked dubiously.

"I think you might be right. I think there's a chance Dose isn't causing the Itch. I'm sorry I didn't tell you earlier, and I understand if you want me to leave. But before you make up your mind, just think about what this could mean. If someone is lying about the cause of the Itch, I have to find out who they are and make sure they're held to account. Please. I haven't got anywhere else to go."

Once again, she was silent for a long time, which left me teetering on a knife-edge. If she refused to help, there was no one else I could turn to. It would only be a matter of time before the police caught up with me.

"Fine," she said eventually. "You can stay."

"Thank you."

"I'm not doing this for your benefit," she said poignantly. "I'm doing this because – if you're right – I want to know what's making people sick."

"That's fair."

"And if you're lying, I can always call the police," she said wickedly.

I spent the night in Erin's spare room. Much like the rest of the flat, the room was shabby chic. There was a bookcase made from an old ladder and other items fashioned into furniture. Shortly after I'd arrived, she'd returned to the protest and, with nothing else to do, I'd gone straight to bed. Of course, I hardly slept and, when I finally drifted off, I awoke after only an hour or so. My brain felt like it was fizzing, overflowing with thoughts and ideas.

Yesterday, I was facing trial for a crime I hadn't committed. There was an overwhelming amount of evidence against me. Surely, escaping police custody had compounded my situation. I'd never broken the law. Never even littered. Apart from a half-hearted rebellious phase in my teens, which I spent doing very little besides sleeping and loitering at the local park, I liked to think I'd always been a decent person. But that had changed. It didn't matter that I'd been framed. By escaping, I'd broken the law. It was so strange to think that, by trying to make things better, I'd unquestionably things worse.

The thought of what would happen to me was terrifying. I found myself thinking about my childhood. Mum had always encouraged us to be adventurous, to embrace life to its fullest. Rock climbing. Paragliding. Scuba diving. Thinking about the latter made me shudder. Of course, I was grateful for the opportunities I was given, but I never enjoyed those activities. Frankly, I was a little bit of a coward. But I'd always given them a go, no matter what daredevil feats Mum had planned. She used to tell us we couldn't let fear of the unknown keep us prisoner. If we did, we'd never leave the house. Meditatively, I pressed the bottlecaps against my lips, staring at the ceiling as her words echoed in my mind. I wouldn't let fear get the better of me. I had to prove I was innocent.

When I couldn't bear to lie in bed any longer, I got up and headed to the living room. Erin looked like she was just finishing some exercise. Music was playing. Although it wasn't familiar, I liked the song.

"It's a great album. Track six is mind-blowing," she said when I told her. "Sleep well?" she said without looking at me.

"Not really," I replied.

"It's not much, but it's better than prison," she said.

"I didn't mean… never mind."

I could have corrected her – told her that, with everything I'd been through over the last few days, I was much too anxious to sleep – but didn't want her to think I was arguing. I took a seat at the kitchen counter. She poured herself a glass of water, and then took the seat next to me.

"Do you have any proof that Dose isn't the cause?" she asked. "Or that someone tried to frame you?"

"Not yet," I said, shaking my head softly. "I think I know where to look, though."

Automatically, I reached for my phone, but the police had confiscated it when they'd arrested me. Erin begrudgingly handed me hers and, once I'd found what I was looking for, I handed it back to her.

"Who's Wilson Loveday?" she asked, reading from the screen.

"Don't you recognise him?" I asked in astonishment.

"Just answer the question," she replied wearily.

"He used to work at Rathbury-Holmes. But he was arrested a few years ago for possession of Dose," I explained.

It was national news at the time; a senior manager at a global pharmaceutical company caught with the drug that was causing the Itch. Erin didn't seem to think it was important, though.

"Plenty of people have been arrested for that. Thanks, Mr Prophett," she said disdainfully.

As a strong opponent of the Dose ban, it was no

surprise Erin wasn't a fan of the Health Secretary, Rupert Prophett. He'd received criticism from both sides of this debate. Some thought he wasn't doing enough to combat the sickness, whilst others – like those who shared Erin's opinion about Dose – thought there wasn't enough evidence to ban the drug. Quite frankly, I wasn't sure there was much more he could be doing to combat the Itch.

Before his career in politics, he'd worked for Rathbury-Holmes. I'd met him a few times and found him to be quite likeable. Besides an unusually strong aversion to physical contact – which was likely because he'd worked for such a long time as a microbiologist in the pharmaceutical industry – I certainly thought better of him than I did of my present company. As I needed her to see my point, though, I kept my thoughts to myself. Plus, it sounded like there might be more to her words, something personal, perhaps, which I didn't want to delve into.

"Wilson identified the link between Dose and the Itch," I said, which roused her curiosity. "He insisted he'd been set up, but there was a lot of evidence against him. I think he had a lot of problems with money, too. Gambling, from what I can remember."

"So, you think he was framed, too?" she said, to which I nodded. "How does this help you?"

"Because I think my boss, Frank, might have had something to do with it."

"Does this have anything to do with you being suspended?" she asked.

"No," I said irritably. "You don't know him like I do."

"Colourful history," she said as if discussing a

scandal, before adding in a more sincere tone "How are you going to prove it, then?"

"I need to speak to Wilson."

"And how are you going to do that?"

"He's being held at the Fairbank Recovery Facility," I said, recalling what I'd read on her phone. "It's in the Peak District, I think. I need to see him."

I'd expected Erin to say something or, at the very least, give some indication she'd heard what I'd said. It was frustrating, then, when she remained silent, simply staring at me.

"That's probably not the best idea," she said eventually. Naturally, I asked why. By way of an answer, she handed me her phone again. There was a news article on the screen.

"*Greater Manchester police are investigating an incident that occurred on Wednesday morning, in which a prisoner escaped custody,*" the article began. "*The prisoner was being taken to trial for drug offences when the vehicle he was travelling in was involved in a traffic collision. GMP has released a statement, which identified the prisoner as 32-year-old Jack Bright. Two officers were injured in the collision, but Bright's condition is not known. GMP has refused to comment further at this time.*"

Vividly, I recalled seeing my face on the news at Lizzy's house. There was no telling how many people had seen the article since then.

"That certainly complicates matters," I said, running a hand through my hair.

"There's an understatement," she said.

"I have to speak to him."

"And how are you going to do that? There's bound

to be some sort of security check. Now that your name is all over the news, you'll never make it inside."

"I'm not just going to give up," I said. For encouragement, I grabbed the bottlecaps around my neck.

"I never said that. I just think you need to think before you act."

I was in a difficult position – and it wasn't simply because I disagreed with Erin's point. When I was arrested, the police had taken all my personal possessions, including my wallet and phone. Without those, the only way I could get to Fairbank was on foot. Given the distance and route I'd have to take, that wasn't an option. I had to concede, then, I would need help getting there, and so, unenthusiastically, agreed to think about what I was planning to do – if only to end the conversation.

After a quick breakfast, Erin left for work. I knew from previous meetings she worked in hospitality, although I wasn't exactly sure what she did. Before leaving, she'd explained she'd be coming and going a lot due to shifts or protesting the Dose ban, so there was a strong chance I was going to be alone in the flat for long periods of time. There wasn't much in the flat to keep me occupied, but that didn't matter.

As soon as she left, I started thinking of ways to get to Fairbank. Hitching a ride was risky because the driver might recognise me. Taxis posed the same problem. And in any case, I didn't have any money to pay for a ride, which ruled out all other forms of public transport. But perhaps I wouldn't need a ride. Perhaps Erin had a car or bike I could borrow. I combed the flat, checking every drawer, jar, cupboard, pot, and any other place someone might keep their keys. I searched everywhere except her bedroom; I had to have some boundaries. Whilst I was rifling through a dresser in the living room, I noticed a small cupboard on the wall near the front door, roughly the size of a bird box. When I saw a car key inside, my mind was instantly made up. Almost as an afterthought, I grabbed a set of door keys, as well, and headed out the door.

CHAPTER 6

Luckily, there was parking below the building, so I easily found Erin's car. Although she was quite a bit shorter than me, I didn't need to adjust the seat to fit behind the steering wheel. I was, however, greatly shocked by the deafening volume of the music when I started the engine. Once again, I liked the song but switched it off so I could concentrate. Without an address, I wasn't exactly sure where to go, but picked somewhere on the built-in satnav – which may or may not have been close to Fairbank – and then set off.

I'd barely made it to the street before guilt set in, but I pushed the feeling away, eager to keep a clear head for what was to come. The traffic in the city centre was diabolical but, after I'd escaped the trudging procession, the cityscape slowly gave way to the countryside. I drove through a few large towns, and then the road was completely deserted, rolling over the hilly landscape. Raindrops streaked across the windows. All I could see beyond the edge of the road was swirling grey mist.

Whilst I drove, I thought about what I would say to Wilson. Of course, I couldn't reveal why I thought we were connected, but could easily steer the conversation to the company. Specifically, I needed to know about his dealings with Frank. The consensus from anyone who worked with him was that he was brutish, stubborn, and rude. Perhaps Wilson could prove he was also capable of framing someone.

Leaving the main road, I turned onto a very narrow lane, bordered with dry stone walls. It was so narrow I had to pull into a ditch to let a hulking 4x4 pass. The road continued rising and falling with the undulating terrain. After realising I wouldn't be able to find Fairbank on my own, I stopped some drenched dog walkers, who pointed me in the right direction.

Eventually, I arrived at an ornate gate. I was about to pull up to the call box beside it but hesitated. Something about the heavy gates unsettled me; not to mention the CCTV camera sweeping across them. When I thought about it, I realised it wasn't a good idea to arrive in Erin's car. If anything happened, it would incriminate her. Instead, I carried on a little further up the road, following the wall which ran around the grounds of Fairbank, until I found a mud track that was almost completely hidden by thick hedges and dense canopy.

After parking the car, I headed back to the front gate. I'd checked the boot for an umbrella or coat but didn't find one, so zipped my jacket right up to shield myself from the rain.

"Can I help you?" said a voice through a callbox.

"I'm here to see a patient," I replied. "Wilson Loveday."

"Head through the gate. Someone will meet you outside the house."

A moment later, the gate opened, and I hurried through. The trees thinned until the driveway emerged alongside Fairbank. The house was a magnificent limestone building, with bay windows and a slate roof that glistened in the fresh rain like the scales of a serpent. A sloping lawn led down to woodland at the end of the garden. As I neared the house, someone came rushing out to greet me with an umbrella.

"Good afternoon. I'm Suzanne Walters," she said. I offered a hand, but she ignored it. I should have known better; most people still didn't shake hands. "I understand you're here to see Mr Loveday. If you'd like to follow me, please. You need to sign in beforehand."

The inside was just as grand as the outside. The entrance hall was long with dark wooden beams along the length of it. The walls were covered with portraits, most of which were of stern-looking men in military dress. There was a rug on the floor, which – although it had been worn to threads in places – was exquisitely woven. Pieces of dark wooden furniture were placed around the edge of the room.

She led me into a small office, where I was prompted to fill out my personal details in a visitor book. I used a fake name and address, just in case. When she asked me how I knew Wilson, I panicked and said that he was my uncle. She didn't challenge me about it. After that, I followed her to his room. We chatted a little about the terrible weather. Even though I'd only parked a few hundred yards from the entrance, I was soaked to the bone. Although she offered me a towel, I declined. For some reason, I thought it might become evidence.

I could hear classical music, twinkling piano and oozing cello. Suzanne started humming along. We climbed to the first floor, where there were additional rooms behind closed doors. She told me Wilson had a personal carer, who would be visiting to check on him shortly. It might complicate matters – I would have to be careful about what I said in front of someone else – but there was nothing I could do about it.

"Here you are," she said, indicating one of the rooms. "I'll leave you to speak in private."

Once she'd disappeared down the staircase, I opened the door. It was fair to say Wilson's room was the grandest patient room I'd ever seen. It was furnished in a similar style to the rest of the house, with pale walls and dark wooden furniture. There was a writing desk by the bay window, through which I could see across the garden towards the hills in the distance. Someone was sitting in the chair by the desk, gazing across the grounds. The view was obscured by streaks of rain on the window. His shoulders were hunched forwards, and he had a blanket over his legs.

"Mr Loveday?" I said as I closed the door. At the sound of my voice, he turned, smiling brightly.

"Crikey!" he cried. "I almost never get visitors! I shall put the kettle on," he replied, lumbering to his feet.

"You don't have to do that."

"You'll have to forgive the mess. I'm afraid you haven't caught me at my best," he said, shaking his head as he shuffled across the room. "I'm all sixes and pears at the moment."

There was something almost child-like about the way he spoke, each word carefully pronounced.

"Mr Loveday," I said, a little louder.

"Well, that doesn't sound right," he mumbled, shaking his head again. "Sixes and apples? Sevens and…"

As I watched him pouring from an empty teapot, two things came to my mind. The first was that I wasn't sure he'd be able to tell me anything useful. The second was that there was clearly something seriously wrong with him. And I was convinced it wasn't caused by Dose abuse.

"Do you need any help, Mr Loveday?" I said, edging towards him.

"No. I'm fine, thank you," he replied, nodding quickly. "Oh, and please call me Wilson."

"Okay," I replied. "Do you mind if I sit down, Wilson?"

"Where are my manners? Of course, please do."

"Thanks," I said, taking the seat opposite Wilson's.

"Do I recognise you?" he asked.

I'd been afraid of this. Although we'd never worked together, there was a chance he might have seen me around Rathbury-Holmes. As it turned out, he thought I'd sold him a second-hand car in the early eighties – before I was born. When I said otherwise, he was mortally embarrassed, but I assured him no offence was taken.

"My secretary has been away, and I'm useless without her," he admitted. "How can I help?" he asked, handing me an empty mug, and taking his seat.

When I saw him up close, I stifled a gasp. His eyes were cloudy, making the red rings around them stand out more. He didn't seem to care that his nose and mouth were oozing. But it was his pallor that startled me most. His veins stood out like ink marks on his skin. It was clear that he was seriously unwell. And yet, he seemed unconcerned by his condition.

"Would you like to play?" he said, indicating a chessboard on the table beside him. Although it appeared to be set up to play, several pieces were missing. I agreed to a game, though.

What followed was a combination of chess, checkers and – most unusually – snap. When two matching pieces were adjacent, Wilson cried-out and removed the pair from the board. Whilst we played, he talked about how rarely he received visitors. It was heart-breaking to hear even his wife and daughter hadn't been to see him.

"I actually wanted to ask you some questions about your work," I said, eager to steer the conversation to the Itch.

"Fire away."

When I mentioned the report that he'd written about the link between Dose and the sickness, his expression changed from worried to curious to happy and back to worried again. I gave a little more context – mentioned the company and his arrest – but that only made him more agitated.

"Hmm," he mumbled. "I'm afraid you might have the wrong chap."

"It was a really important piece of work. Are you sure you don't remember anything about it?"

"Well, I- it's- do you know, I'm afraid I don't. Perhaps my secretary can- could- I- do you know where she is?"

"It's alright. Don't worry," I said, trying to reassure him. "Do you remember someone called Frank Badder?"

It was clear the name registered. Wilson's already pallid face lost what little colour remained. His lower lip trembled. Mechanically, he reached into one of his desk drawers, pulled out a piece of paper and started writing feverishly on it. Throughout, he stared out of the window, scribbling more and more feverishly.

"Are you okay, Wilson?" I asked. He was muttering something under his breath. *Badder*.

As I watched him, I noticed that he didn't appear to have any scars. Like a reflex, I gripped my necklace, battling against memories. Even in the early stages of the Itch, sufferers showed signs of the sickness: sores or scratches or even small cuts. If he'd taken Dose, and the drug caused the Itch, why didn't he have any injuries?

"You remember him, don't you?" I asked.

"Badder," he mumbled, over and over. Although it was clear Wilson was suffering, I had to press him.

"Did he do this to you?" I asked.

As suddenly as he'd started, Wilson stopped writing and, without looking away from the window, handed me the piece of paper. Slowly, I took it from him and read the letters and numbers *DEV/08/045*. He'd traced over it so many times that the paper was almost worn through.

"Why are you giving me this?" I asked, trying to keep my voice level.

"Giving you what?" he asked. I repeated myself, showing him the paper. It seemed to distress him, but I couldn't stop. I asked him two or three more times but, instead of answering me, he peered at something out in the garden.

"Wilson, did Frank Badder do something to you?"

"Who?" he asked curiously.

"Frank Badder. Do you remember him?"

"I'm afraid you've got the wrong chap," he said serenely. "My name is Wilson. Wilson Loveday."

Truly, Wilson had lost his mind. But despite not being able to tell me what had happened to him, he might have given me a clue. And it was clear from Wilson's reaction that Frank might be involved.

"Hooray! More visitors," he cried gleefully, clapping his hands softly. At first, I wasn't really sure what he meant until I heard the sirens. In the distance, I could see the eerie blue glow of a police car approaching up the driveway.

Hastily, I got to my feet and raced to the door. Perhaps I should have said something to Wilson before I left but, in all honesty, I wasn't sure he'd register I was leaving. At the top of the stairs, I listened for sounds from the foyer. Suzanne was talking to someone, her voice drifting up the stairs.

"-looked familiar but said he was here to see his uncle," she said, clearly flustered. And then, I heard a voice that chilled me to the bone.

"If you recognised him, why did you wait so long before calling?" asked Dunhill.

"Well, I- I guessed he must have visited before."

"Did he show you any identification?"

"No. But-"

"Do you usually let people see patients without checking their ID?"

"No," Suzanne said in a small voice. Dunhill made a mocking noise that suggested she was pretending to think.

"So, why didn't you check this time?"

I didn't have time to think. Seconds before they started climbing the stairs, I dashed through the nearest door. Luckily, the room was empty. Pressing my ear to the door, I listened intently as two sets of feet walked past. It sounded as though Suzanne was struggling to speak. Having been under Dunhill's scrutiny before, I couldn't help but feel some sympathy.

"Is he dangerous?" Suzanne asked.

"Do you really want me to answer that?" Dunhill replied, laughing harshly.

Suzanne stammered for a few seconds, clearly flustered, before eventually saying something I didn't hear. Whatever it was, Dunhill was displeased.

"Which room is he in?" Dunhill demanded.

"This one here," Suzanne said, rushing to catch up. "The patient's name is Wilson Loveday."

There was a forceful knock on the door, followed by Dunhill saying Wilson's name. The rest of what she said was cut off by the door opening and closing. Almost immediately, I peeked through a crack in the door, checking each direction before opening it fully. I descended the stairs two at a time, walking more quickly than an innocent person would. My feet banged loudly on the polished wood. When I saw the front door was ajar, I sighed, quickening my pace. But as two police officers appeared outside, my footsteps faltered. Then, my eyes shot back up to the first-floor landing. Dunhill's voice was drifting along the corridor.

"You think you made a mistake?" she asked sarcastically. "How on Earth do you make a mistake like this?"

With the entrance blocked, I ducked under the staircase. It might not have been the best hiding place, but with Dunhill fast approaching, I had no other choice. As she descended, two more people entered the room. I guessed they were the two officers from outside.

"Check every room" Dunhill ordered. "I want statements from staff and patients as well. If it's Bright, I want to know why he's been here."

The disdain with which she said my name confirmed what I'd suspected after our most recent meeting. What I wasn't sure of, though, was the reason for her vendetta against me. Yes, it was her job to catch criminals, but this was something more than that. It felt like she was particularly keen to catch me.

"Ma'am," two voices replied in unison. Booted feet bounded up the stairs above my head.

"Excuse me?" Suzanne asked nervously. "Is everything alright?"

"Did anyone else speak to him?" Dunhill asked acidly. From the direction of her voice, I guessed she was stood in front of the entrance.

"He- he will have spoken to- to security."

"Well, are you going to call them?"

Footsteps rushed away from the foyer, leaving Dunhill alone, muttering something that sounded like *incompetent* under her breath. In an almost leisurely way, she strolled around the foyer in a loop. At one point, she came dangerously close to spotting me. Thankfully, somebody came bounding in through the front door, drawing her attention.

"Did you check his ID?" Dunhill asked.

"I didn't get chance," mumbled the guard from the gate.

"Unbelievable. I supposed you were worried about

a *lickle wain*, were you?" Dunhill said mockingly.

"We've got security footage at the entrance, though. Would you like to see it?"

"Yes, I think that would be helpful," Dunhill snarled.

The guard led her out of the room, their voices fading as they left. Sensing my chance, I was about to race for the front door but barely made it out from my hiding place before I heard heavy footsteps descended the stairs. Cornered, I rushed to the nearest door, closing it just as the two officers started searching downstairs.

Somehow, I had to find a way out of the building. The main entrance was too risky, but there had to be at least one other way out of the room. Fear mounting, I peered through the window. There was a slim patch of lawn. The trees that surrounded the house were only a few metres away. If I could make it to the woods, I might be able to find my way back to Erin's car.

Optimistically, I tried to open one of the windows, but it would there was a safety latch preventing it from opening more than a few inches. The other window also had a latch on it. With voices approaching in the foyer, terror bubbling inside my stomach, I picked up a heavy antique lamp from a table and was about to smash one of the windows, when I noticed a small red button on the wall. A fire alarm. Without hesitation, I pressed the small glass panel.

The siren was instantaneous. Cautiously, I opened the door to peek into the foyer. Even after only a few seconds, it was chaos. Police were arguing animatedly with staff. Dunhill arrived a moment later. After exchanging heated words with the officers, as well as staff, Dunhill left through the main entrance, shortly followed by the officers and staff. Once the foyer was empty, I took my chance.

Using the lamp as a lever, I tried to force the safety latch on the window. It took more effort than I expected. After a few unsuccessful shoves, I put my whole weight behind it. The bracket made quite a lot of noise as it broke away from the window frame, but I was sure it was masked by the alarm. A little clumsily, I climbed through the window, dropped to the ground, and then ran towards the trees.

I scrambled through the undergrowth, vaguely in the direction of Erin's car. I had to find my way back to the mud track. From there, it would be much easier to find where I'd parked. I had no idea when the police would realise what I'd done – if they hadn't already. At any moment, I might hear them yelling. Although I was no longer in earshot of the fire alarm, I didn't slow down. More than once, I lost my footing in the leaves and other detritus on the woodland floor.

Up ahead, the ground sloped downwards to a muddy slip of road. After sliding down the bank, I jogged a few yards, trying to get my bearings. I'd never had much sense of direction and had no idea if this was the track where I'd parked. Ultimately, I picked a direction and started running. Mud and leaves clung to my trousers. My shoes were full of muddy water, squelching with every step. Through the swirling haze of rain, I saw a car. I waited until I was certain it was Erin's before breaking into a sprint. I checked my pockets for the keys. After checking those in my jacket, I searched all my pockets a second time. The keys were missing.

Had they fallen out when I'd slipped in the woods? Or had I dropped them in Wilson's room? Frantically, I scoured the mud around the car but, after a few minutes, hadn't found them. Without the keys, I'd have to escape on foot. But the police would surely find the car when they searched the area. Would that lead them back to Erin? Would she be-

Slowly, I leaned towards the window, spying the small keyring dangling from the ignition. Hardly daring to believe my luck, I tried the door. It opened. I practically leapt inside, cursing my idiocy as I started the engine. Mud spewed from the wheels as I floored the accelerator. The tyre tracks on the road were deep, and the ride was extremely bumpy, but I kept my foot down until I saw the road. Once there, I turned away from Fairbank and drove as fast as I dared in the opposite direction, not caring that I had no idea where I was going.

CHAPTER 7

Although the rain had eased, the winding roads were soaked. Every mile or so, I had to remind myself to drive slower. After escaping the police at Fairbank, it would have been extremely careless to get caught because I'd lost control and crashed. Moments after slowing, though, my foot pressed down on the accelerator. I decided to follow signs for the A6, which eventually led me to a sign for the M60. It wasn't until I joined regular traffic on the ring road around the city that I maintained a reasonable speed.

By the time I pulled into Erin's parking space, it was mid-afternoon. Eager to get back to the relative safety of her flat, I raced up the stairs. I'd barely turned the keys when the door flung open. My immediate thought was that the police had tracked me down, and I was preparing to sprint away when I realised it was Erin.

"Where the Hell have you been?" she snarled.

"I had to speak to him," I replied.

"So, you stole my car?"

Despite my needs, I couldn't deny I'd been wrong to take her car without asking. If I hadn't been careless enough to leave the keys in the ignition, I might have had to abandon it. All I could manage to say, though, was "I didn't know how else to get there."

"Oh, well, that's perfectly reasonable," she said, slamming the door.

"What do you want me to say?" I said.

"You could start by apologising."

"I told you I needed to speak to him."

"How does that justify stealing my car?"

"I didn't steal it. I borrowed it."

"Jesus, Jack. What the Hell's wrong with you?"

"What's that supposed to mean?"

"Between the bomb, the drugs, escaping police custody, and now this, I'm starting to wonder how innocent you are," she barked. "You're going to a lot of trouble over this; more than most people would. Maybe you're not trying to prove what happened. Maybe you're just trying to clear your name."

"Do you really think that?"

"Why shouldn't I?" she asked, throwing up her hands in exasperation.

"Because I was the only person who told them not to go through with it," I roared.

I was filled with anger and would have carried on yelling if Erin's expression hadn't softened. She no longer looked accusatory but curious, perhaps even concerned. There was only one thing to do. Previously, I'd only once described the trial in detail. It was during an official review by senior management, which had been almost unbearable. I'd been making every effort not to go through it again, but it seemed like this was the only way to convince Erin I was innocent. So, I started telling her what happened.

"New drugs go through a lot of testing to make sure the compounds are safe before they're given to people. Everything went well in early development; better than we could have hoped. There were no adverse side effects or unexpected toxicity. Plus, the compound removed all traces of Dose in cell studies. The cure looked like it was going to work, so we moved to human trials. We tested a small group and had no issues, so we moved to a mid-sized group; a few hundred people. That was when we noticed the issues. One of the test subjects reported their symptoms weren't fully eliminated by the treatment. I raised the issue, but Frank ignored me. At the next phase, we tested thousands. Looking back, I'm surprised more subjects weren't affected. I have absolutely no idea how or why it happened, but the cure did nothing for them. I should have done more to stop it but…"

At that point, I trailed off, my mind back at the trial. It had taken place at the Royal Infirmary in the city centre. I'd been there when the trial took place. I could remember watching the medical staff through a window into the isolation room. They'd been wearing protective clothing – masks, overalls, gloves – but the quarantine wasn't for their benefit. Skin protected the body from contagions like bacteria and viruses. Unfortunately, the patients' skin was so severely damaged it no longer kept them safe.

Although I knew a lot about the seven victims now, I didn't know any of their names at the time. Or any of the other test subjects, for that matter. I had no idea where they were from or how old they were, either, but it had to be that way. If I'd known anything about them, there would be a connection between us. And even a link as tenuous as where they were from would have made the trial almost impossible to bear. The only thing I knew about them was that they'd all been receiving almost constant pain relief before the trial.

When it began, subjects were given the cure, and then slowly weaned from their pain medication. The trial had only been running for a few seconds when the screaming had started. It had followed me from the ward and stayed with me ever since. I'm certain there was nothing I could do to forget that sound. The official cause of death was cardiac arrest. But it was pain that killed them. Because of the Itch.

"I didn't know," Erin said softly.

"I should have done more to stop the trial," I said, shaking my head.

To begin with, I just wanted to know why Frank had ignored me; why he had endangered the lives of those patients. Now, though, I wanted to get to the bottom of this. I wanted to know what was making people sick and prove someone was lying about it. And if Frank was to blame, I would make sure he was held to account.

"I'm sorry," she said, a little begrudgingly.

"Yeah, me to," I replied.

As it happened, she'd come home during her break to bring me some lunch, so I felt doubly guilty for stealing her car. She told me she worked as a chef in an Asian-fusion restaurant nearby. Although I'd never eaten there, I vaguely recalled colleagues raving about it. I wasn't sure what was on the tray she handed me, so took it without comment. It was delicious.

After eating, I told her what had happened at Fairbank. When I mentioned Wilson's condition, she agreed something was wrong with him; something other than Dose addiction. She was even convinced when I suggested someone might have poisoned him to keep him from talking. Her enthusiasm fizzled, though, when I showed her the paper that he'd given me.

"Doesn't look like... well, anything," she said disappointedly.

"It's the number of a project at Rathbury-Holmes," I said matter-of-factly. "DEV means development, followed by the year and a sequential number. He started writing it when I said Frank's name. You should have seen the way he changed. It was like he was possessed."

Suddenly engaged, she asked me what the project was about. Unfortunately, I didn't know. There were so many projects at the company I couldn't possibly have known about them all. In fact, I hadn't long since started working at the company at the time of this project. But I was certain that the number was important. It looked like he'd tried to *carve* the numbers into the paper. Perhaps that was the only way he could think to send a message.

"I need to see the project report," I said. "I've no idea how, though. There's no chance I'll get into the building without being recognised."

Of course, I knew there was at least one person inside the company who might be willing to help. With the way I'd raced away from her house, though, I wasn't sure whether Lizzy would want to get involved. Her boyfriend, Kieran the police officer, was another reason not to contact her.

"Well, before you go planning any more covert ops, you need a shower," she said, wrinkling her nose. "And some clean clothes."

Erin had to leave to finish her shift but returned that evening with a bag full of clothes, which she'd bought from a charity shop. Although I insisted I would repay her, she refused my money. When I saw the selection, I was a little relieved she hadn't charged me. Everything was worn and faded, and mostly denim. There were a lot of studs, too.

After showering for the first time in almost a week, I chose the least outrageous items I could find and dressed, simply glad to be clean again. Erin made a comment about the band on my t-shirt but – as I'd never heard of them – I could only smile awkwardly in reply.

"Do you know how you're going to get the report?" Erin asked as she prepared dinner. I'd offered to help, but she wouldn't even let me in the kitchen whilst she was cooking. Probably for the best, I thought.

I'd spent most of the day thinking about it and had come up with a plan. Erin listened as I told her my idea. She was slicing vegetables, thinner than I would have thought possible with such a large knife. Once I'd finished, she paused mid-slice.

"You're kidding? That's your plan?"

"It's the only way."

As I couldn't get to the report myself and wasn't willing to ask Lizzy for help, I had only two options: breaking in or infiltration. I certainly didn't have the knowhow to break in, so I chose the latter. My plan was to pose as a delivery person. The laboratories used such large quantities of a variety of chemicals that deliveries were daily. Security was always wary of hazardous chemicals, so was unlikely to inspect empty cardboard boxes if they were labelled *toxic* or *corrosive*. Once inside, I'd log on to my PC and access the online document repository through our intranet.

"How is a disguise going to fool security?" she said. It was a fair point, but one I'd already considered.

"I'll need someone to come with me. They can provide the paperwork, sign in, and then we'll head to my office to find the report."

"Who's going to help?" she asked.

That was something I hadn't considered yet. Before I could ask her, she shook her head. I knew without having to think there was nobody I could ask. But Erin might.

"So, just to clarify," she said, exasperatedly. "You want me to ask one of my friends to pose as a delivery driver to help you sneak into this place and steal a confidential report?"

"I know it's not ideal," I said.

"There's an understatement."

"If you've got a better idea, I'm all ears. Otherwise, this is the only way I'll get that report."

She said nothing whilst she prepared two plates of food. I was starting to get a little frustrated when she said, "I might know someone who can help."

After we'd eaten, she disappeared for a moment with her phone pressed to her ear. About 10 minutes later, a man arrived at the flat. Despite being summoned so late at night, he couldn't have appeared any less interested in what was going on. As soon as he'd walked in, he'd taken a seat by the window and was currently reclining, both hands stuffed down his boxers. Erin introduced him as Bowker. He didn't ask for my name.

Whilst I told him my plan, the impression he wasn't paying attention was cemented in my mind. Surprisingly, though, he had something to say as soon as I'd finished.

"Off his head, man," he sneered. "Pure laughs that."

"Settle down," Erin said warningly.

"Boy wants his head checking."

"Bowker, stop," she said.

"What? Why?" he barked.

"Stop," she repeated. "What do you need?" she asked me.

Rathbury-Holmes received deliveries from several suppliers, but ARC provided most by far. Drivers wore dark blue polo shirts and hi-vis jackets. Once I'd finished explaining, Bowker scoffed again.

"If you don't want to help, why are you here?" Erin asked him.

"Back off," he drawled. He paused for a moment, glowering at Erin, and then at me. "I'll do it. Ain't gonna be no cocktail party, though, man. Better not piss your panties when we get inside."

Not long after that, Bowker left to gather what we needed. Once he'd gone, I asked Erin how she knew him. My first impression of him wasn't great, and I found it hard to believe that she would be friends with someone so obnoxious.

"He's protesting the ban, too," she said. "I know he's… difficult, but he's good to have around."

Erin and Bowker had been at school together. Although they hadn't been friends, Erin knew him by reputation. It wasn't too hard to imagine what Bowker was like as a schoolboy. After finishing his studies, he'd enlisted in the army, where it sounded like he'd served with some distinction. Unfortunately, his passion for troublemaking had outweighed his desire to follow orders, and he'd been discharged for reasons she didn't know. Given the help he was providing, I could agree he was a useful person to know, even if he was a little dislikeable.

"He was kicked out around the time the ban was implemented. I'm not even really sure he believes in the protest. I think, after serving, he just wanted to do something rebellious. A big, fat middle finger to the Law."

Bowker certainly seemed like the type to join the protest for sheer enjoyment rather than principles. I began to think perhaps he wasn't the right person to help. Without an alternative, though, I knew I would have to take who I could get. I also realised, then, that I had no idea why Erin was protesting the ban. Previously, she'd said something about the number of arrests for Dose possession. It wasn't so much what she'd said, but her tone that made me think perhaps she'd been personally affected by it. Perhaps I should have asked her, but I wasn't sure we were close enough to talk about something like that. The thought drew my fingers to the bottlecaps around my neck. If she asked about those, I wouldn't want to tell her.

Bowker returned to the flat the following evening with the uniform I'd asked for. We had to leave late to ensure the offices and laboratories were empty. At around seven o'clock, I followed him down to the car park, where a plain white van was waiting.

Ordinarily, ARC vans bore the company logo, but there wasn't much I could do about that now.

It was only a short journey to Rathbury-Holmes, but it felt long. I suspected that was partly due to my anticipation, but certainly wasn't helped by the tense silence in the cabin. After setting off, I'd tried engaging Bowker in conversation, but he simply ignored me. Even when I gave him directions to the loading bay, he said nothing until the security guard spoke to him through the call box.

Once we'd parked, Bowker got out and waited for security to meet him. From the cabin, I listened to what was being said. At first, the guard was concerned about the hour, but Bowker fed him a story about a high number of deliveries. When asked about our delivery, Bowker opened the van to reveal stacks of boxes, labelled with foreboding skulls and bones. They were all empty but, as expected, the guards didn't inspect them.

The guard escorted Bowker inside to sign in. A few minutes later, he returned with a visitor's badge for each of us. In silence, we stacked the boxes on a trolley, taking care to make them appear heavier than they were, before heading to the lift. We rode to the fifth floor, and then I led us to my former office. At every corner, I quickly checked to make sure there were no CCTV cameras; something I'd never done before. Bowker smirked every time I did it, but I ignored him.

Frank's office was still sealed with a wooden board. I wondered how long it would stay like that. Repairing the damage was sure to take a lot of work, which would probably cost more than the company could afford at the moment. As far as I was aware, every penny of funds was going into the search for a cure.

When we reached my desk, I loaded the online document repository and sorted through the files until I found *DEV Reports*. I was so focussed that the sudden sound to my side startled me.

"What are you doing?" I asked Bowker as he rifled through the drawers beneath one of the neighbouring desks.

"Back down," he snapped.

"Don't touch anything," I said warningly.

"You gonna stop me?" he snarled, advancing.

"If anything is out of place, someone will know we've been in here," I explained. "So, unless you're going to put everything back in exactly the right place, don't touch anything."

He considered what I'd said, and – eventually – stalked away, grumbling under his breath. Ignoring whatever his reply was, I returned to my search. Scrolling through the indexed files, I skipped ahead to roughly where I would find what I was looking for. 042. 043. 044. 046?!

But that was impossible. Once uploaded to the intranet, documents couldn't be removed; it was a failsafe for data integrity. Puzzled, I checked the adjacent folders to make sure it wasn't simply in the wrong location. After that, I did a search through some of the other folders. But there was no sign of the file.

Someone obviously wanted to make sure the report wasn't read. Removing it from the repository wouldn't have been easy. There were probably only a handful of people in the organisation with the user rights to do it. But who was it and – more importantly – why had they removed it?

Before I could answer either question, an ear-splitting siren pierced the silence. Panicked, I leapt to my feet, looking for Bowker. As far as I could tell, he wasn't in the office. After calling his name several times, I checked the adjoining offices, eventually spotting him in the laboratory. To my astonishment, he had a cigarette between his lips.

"What the Hell are you doing?" I demanded.

"I ain't even done nothing," he snapped.

I was about to tell him about the chemical detection system, which was activated when an unknown compound was detected in the laboratory. Before I could say more than a few words, though, he'd bolted for the door. I followed, peeved he hadn't waited.

The fire alarm echoed off the bare concrete walls of the fire escape stairwell. When we made it to the bottom, Bowker checked to make sure the car park was empty. Satisfied, we raced to the van. We were moving before I'd shut the door. As we sped towards the exit, I noticed a security guard racing towards us. But he was a long way behind and quickly disappeared as we crashed through the loading bay barrier, racing back towards the Northern Quarter.

"What the Hell were you thinking?" I snapped.

"Leave it," Bowker replied.

"Do you have any idea what would have happened if they caught us?"

"Didn't, though, did they?"

I realised there was no point in arguing with him. Whatever I said, he would surely bring it back to the fact we'd escaped. Even so, I was furious. By now, security knew we were imposters. Surely, I wouldn't get another chance to try to infiltrate the company.

"What happened?" Erin asked as we got back to her flat. I could hear sirens drifting through the window.

"Fire alarm," I said.

"How?" she pressed.

Briefly, I considered telling her the truth but hesitated. Although Bowker had triggered the alarm, I wouldn't have been able to get inside without his help. In the end, I decided to say it was just an accident. When she asked Bowker, he simply shrugged, which annoyed her. The two of them argued, their voices resonating through the flat, until Bowker gave an offensive gesture with one of his fingers, and then left.

After that, Erin let out a long sigh, running her fingers through her hair. She asked me what happened, her tone probing. Resignedly, I told her.

"Unbelievable. Sometimes, I feel like he actually wants to get into trouble. Look, I'm sorry. I knew he was reckless but... well, I thought even he couldn't be that stupid. Did you at least get what you were looking for?"

"No," I said grimly. "It's missing. Somebody has removed it."

"You're kidding? Is there a hardcopy?"

"Yeah, in the archive. But that'll be even harder to get."

Access to the archive was heavily restricted. Card keys were only given to certain personnel, who were required to personally sign in and out of the room. It was kept under constant surveillance, too, so even if I were able to get in, I'd be spotted almost immediately.

"Well, it could have been a lot worse," she said once I'd finished. Something about her tone annoyed me. It sounded like she wanted to say I-told-you-so.

"How could it have been worse?" I snapped.

"I get that you're annoyed, but don't take it out on me."

"I'm not," I said, before repeating myself in a calmer tone. "Alright, I am annoyed. But it's not fair to- I didn't mean- sorry."

"Solid 2-star apology there," she said. But at least she said it with a smile. "Well, I think I need a drink."

The sound of ice against glass and a faint trickle of liquid was enough to make me shudder. My fingers closed around the bottlecaps on my necklace. For the first time since I'd drained my last-ever-glass, I craved the numbness of a drunken haze. The lack of concern. The absence of anything except for the familiar burn. It was lucky she didn't offer me one. I wasn't sure I could have turned it down.

"Is there anybody at the company who could help?" she asked, sipping from her glass. "Maybe get into the archive."

Initially, I said no, but quickly backtracked. People accessed the archive every day to look at historical data. Surely, nobody would get suspicious if Lizzy went to look at the original copy of the report.

"Can you trust her?" Erin asked after I'd told her my thoughts.

"Only one way to find out," I said grimly.

CHAPTER 8

Although we were close friends, I hadn't committed Lizzy's number to memory, which Erin found hard to believe. I didn't think there was anything wrong with relying on my phone to store contact information but had more pressing matters on my mind, so didn't debate the subject with her. Erin offered to meet her on my behalf, which might have worked if I hadn't already told Lizzy that I'd been framed.

"She'll never trust you," I said.

"What if I tell her you've asked me to meet her?"

"I'm not sure that'll work."

"What do you suggest, then?"

"I need to see her."

There were two reasons I suggested that. The first was that it seemed like the only way I could convince her to help me. The second was, quite simply, that I wanted to see her.

"But can you trust her?" she asked. "What if she calls the police?"

"I trust her more than anyone else," I said.

"I'll try not to let that get me down," she said pointedly. "What's your plan, then?"

The ideal meeting place was obvious. She was guaranteed to visit the gym after work. It was a quiet area, too, so I wasn't likely to be seen. If she didn't want to help, I could simply turn around and walk away. The only issue was getting there. Thankfully, Erin agreed to give me a lift.

Lizzy often trained long into the night, but I

wanted to see her as she arrived, and so headed out shortly before she was due to finish work. We arrived shortly after five o'clock in the evening. And then, we waited. I was too anxious to make conversation, but that didn't seem to bother Erin. Silently, she watched something through her window that I couldn't see.

As soon as I saw Lizzy approaching, I scrambled out of the car and raced towards her. I shouldn't have been surprised when she stepped back, fists raised. Thankfully, she lowered her hands when she recognised me. Her expression remained guarded, though.

"Jesus, Jack. What the Hell are you doing here?" she asked.

"Nice to see you, too," I said. Although my voice was light, I was a little stung by her reaction.

"Kieran told his superiors you'd been to the house. The police have questioned me about your whereabouts."

"What did you say?"

"What do you think? I said I didn't know where you were."

A tense silence formed, stretching for at least a minute. Eventually, I took a step closer. Almost instinctively, Lizzy stepped back.

"Is it true?" she asked.

"How can you ask me that?" I replied.

"Is it true?"

She was angry. Her fists were clenched, and her eyes were narrowed. But I was angry, too. I couldn't believe she would suggest something like that. I was about to tell her she was being ridiculous – that, of course, I wasn't dealing Dose – and that the suggestion was an insult. But then, I realised why it was so difficult for her to hear this.

Shortly before we'd met, Lizzy's stepfather had been arrested. Although she'd told me a few details, I didn't have the full picture. It didn't seem right to pry, so I'd never really asked her about it. From what I knew, his charges were related to Dose. She hadn't seen him since. I suspected that was the main reason she'd agreed to help me prove what happened during the trial. Anyone else would have thought the suggestion that Dose wasn't the cause of the Itch was insane.

"Lizzy, you have to believe me," I said. "The drugs aren't mine. And I think I can prove it. That's why I need your help."

Hastily, I told her about Wilson and how he'd reacted to Frank's name. She remained uneasy throughout. As I started recounting my disastrous mission to retrieve the DEV-45 report, she looked surprised.

"That was you?" she said. She went on to say staff had been told about the incident the following day. As I'd feared, they were bringing in new security measures to prevent recurrence.

"I have to see what's in the report," I said. "You didn't see Wilson. The way he reacted when I said Frank's name. He practically engraved the project number into a piece of paper. And then, he almost immediately had no memory of doing it. He didn't even know who Frank was. I think there's something seriously wrong with Wilson. I think it involves Frank. And I think the answers are in this report. But somebody has removed the online copy. I need to see the original."

Even if they hadn't tightened security, there was a strong chance I wouldn't have been able to see it. Surely, the person who'd framed me wouldn't have let that happen. As was so often the case, I needed Lizzy's help. We stared at one another. Her expression wasn't positive. I was preparing for rejection. Although I'd partially expected her to say no, it wouldn't be easy to hear. Lizzy was the person I thought I could rely on more than any other. It was a relief, then, when she smiled.

"I'm pissed you didn't call," she said. "But yeah, I'll help."

Like Erin, Lizzy was also astonished I couldn't recall her number. What made it worst was that she knew mine. I told her it didn't matter, though, because the police had taken my phone.

"So, what? I just send up smoke signals when I'm ready to see you again?" she asked, grinning.

As much as I wanted to see Lizzy in person again, I knew it was too risky. I'd wanted to see her this evening but, in future, it would be best to talk over the phone. If either of us were spotted, there would be trouble. Without a phone of my own, I gave her Erin's number and asked her to call when she'd found the report.

"It's good to see you," I said, smiling.

"You, too."

"Take care of yourself, okay?" I added, the smile falling from my face.

"Keep it together, Bright," she teased.

Perhaps I should have told her why I was worried – that, if the person responsible for the coverup found out she was helping me, she might end up in a similar predicament. But I decided against it. It didn't seem fair to burden her with that information and, in any case, it was doubtful anyone would know she was helping me. After a brief hug, we parted, and Erin drove us back to her flat.

Neither of us spoke, which made the journey a little awkward. It was perhaps because of how different my feelings for Lizzy and Erin were, but I tried not to dwell on it. I might not have been as close with Erin as I was with Lizzy, but Erin was helping me hide from the police. For that, I was willing to overlook the unpleasantness of our past. For now, at least.

Back at her flat, Erin made noodles in a spicy broth, which was delicious. She put some music on, which saved the need for conversation whilst we ate. Once I'd finished my meal, though, the awkwardness returned. I was about to excuse myself when Erin broke the silence.

"We need to talk," she said.

"What about?" I asked warily.

"Danny."

Although I'd suspected she might bring him up, it was difficult to hear his name. I gripped my necklace, unsure what to say. Eventually, I shook my head.

"There's nothing to talk about," I said.

"I need you to know how sorry I am about-" she said.

"Erin, stop," I said as patiently as I could. "Look, I really don't want to talk about this right now. I know I said some things I probably shouldn't have. And I understand if you're angry about that. If you want to talk about it, we can. But not right now, okay?"

From her stance, plus her expression, it was clear Erin wasn't happy to let the subject drop. Thankfully, though, she shrugged and nodded. Shortly afterwards, she went to her room. With nothing else to do, I went to mine.

The following morning, I awoke to find Erin doing a morning workout again. It reminded me that I hadn't been to the gym for a few days, so I resolved to do some exercise once she'd left for work. The tension between us was impossible to ignore. Perhaps I could have said something to alleviate it but, honestly, I had no idea what might help. In the end, I simply made breakfast and ate in silence. Erin was happy for me to use her kitchen, but made it clear I could only do so when she wasn't in it.

Erin and I said nothing to each other all morning. I was a little relieved when she finally left for work. With the run of her flat, I picked a compilation album of punk tracks from her CD collection and did some circuit training in the living room. The music reminded me of my teens, during which time I'd had a brief, angsty rebel phase. But that also reminded me about what I'd lost. I used the memory to push myself as far as I could. Once I'd finished, I was exhausted but felt fulfilled. I took an icy shower, and then made some lunch. Unlike the rest of her flat, the kitchen was spotlessly clean. Everything was neat. There was no clutter on the countertops. I wanted to keep it that way, so made some pasta, which I ate from the pan to limit the amount of washing up I'd have to do.

As Lizzy could only contact Erin, I had to wait until she returned. Not knowing when that would be, and not being thrilled at the prospect of simply whiling away the day, I put the TV on and slumped on the comfiest-looking beanbag in her living room. There was a news broadcast on, which was an update about the Itch. The number of confirmed cases was well over 300,000. A woman appeared on screen, describing how her daughter had used a wood plane to peel her skin off. The girl had died from blood loss. Throughout the broadcast, I gripped my necklace tightly.

I was about to change the channel when a face I recognised appeared. It was Dylan's girlfriend, Kelly Cooper. Instantly, I sat forward, my full attention on the news broadcaster's voice.

"The 28-year-old was reported missing by colleagues on Tuesday morning," the broadcaster said. "She was last seen at Heaton Park on Sunday, where she participated in a charity race to raise money for the cure to the Itch. Kelly's partner, Dylan Keeling, was one of seven people who was killed during a drug trial of a prospective cure by the pharmaceutical giant, Rathbury-Holmes. Eyewitnesses reported she left the event around three P.M. by bus and is believed to have changed somewhere in the city centre before making her way back to her home address in Levenshulme. Anyone with information about her whereabouts is urged to contact Greater Manchester Police."

My temper rose. I took a deep breath, followed by several more, but it didn't help. Before I could stop myself, I threw the TV remote across the room. I stood with my hands behind my head, fighting my rising anger. There could be only one explanation for

Kelly's disappearance. I'd thought Frank had ignored the letter I'd sent him, in which I'd posed as Kelly, but it was clear he hadn't. I was now certain he was hiding something. But I also knew I was at least partly to blame for her disappearance.

My letter must have forced his hand. Thinking she knew something incriminating about him, Frank must have eliminated her. To even think such a thing made me shudder. But try as I might, I couldn't convince myself a less grim fate had befallen Kelly.

Erin returned home that evening with trays of food. The smell was almost irresistible, but I wasn't in the mood to eat. I was sitting at the kitchen counter. My rage must have been obvious because she faltered when she saw me. Before she asked, I told her what I'd seen on the news and my thoughts about Frank's involvement. I left out the letter I'd sent him, not wanting to reveal my involvement.

"Jesus," she said. "Do you think they suspect him?"

"I don't think so. They're still asking for information. I think they'd have said if there were any suspects," I said.

"She might turn up."

"I hope so."

As usual, we ate in silence. Unlike previous occasions, though, it wasn't entirely unwelcome. I was still so angry and didn't think I'd be able to hold a civilised conversation. Besides, there was only one thing on my mind; proving what Frank had done.

When Erin's phone rang, she handed it to me. Hearing Lizzy's voice brightened my mood. If only a little. I was looking forward to good news but, as soon as she started explaining, I knew I wasn't going to get it.

"So, I checked the archive," she said slowly. "The report is missing."

"That doesn't make sense," I replied. "Did you ask to see who'd taken the copy?"

The people who managed the archive kept a record of everyone who withdrew documents in case any went missing.

"No record," she said. "It was archived after completion and hasn't been touched since."

"Is there any data related to it? Or a draft copy saved on the network?"

"I found some charts and tables, none of which have any bloody headers. There are some scans of analytical worksheets, too, and an excerpt from a textbook about chyrolic compounds."

Chyrolic compounds were common in pharmaceutical products. Their structure was similar to naturally occurring chemicals in the human body, which meant they had high efficacy with low toxicity. But another chyrolic compound came to mind: Dose. When I asked Lizzy if the report was linked to the drug, though, she was dubious.

"I asked a couple of people involved in the Dose project. They didn't recognise the reference or the data," she replied. "I could ask around and see if anyone knows-"

"No," I said suddenly.

It was bad enough she'd already spoken to the people involved in the Dose investigation. With the news of Kelly's disappearance, I didn't want too many people to know what Lizzy was looking into;

least of all, Frank. I tried lying about my concerns, but Lizzy saw right through my ruse.

"You saw the news, then?" she asked. "You know, I don't need you to protect me."

"I know," I said. "I just- I don't want anything to happen to you."

"But I want to be infamous, too," she said in a mocking tone. Despite the implications of her joke, I couldn't help laughing.

"I'm not sure relationships between criminals and police officers last long."

"Star-crossed romances always have a happy ending, right?" she asked brightly.

"Just be careful," I said, laughing despite my sentiment.

"I always am," she replied, more sincerely, before hanging up.

Erin listened without comment as I explained what Lizzy and I had discussed.

"What now, then?" Erin asked.

"Now, I need to think about how to get hold of a phantom report."

"Maybe try writing to Santa?" she said, smiling. Although she was joking, it gave me an idea.

"That's not a bad idea," I said slowly.

"Oh, Jack. Didn't anyone ever tell you?" she teased.

"His name is Berglund," I said, ignoring her taunt. "Klas Berglund."

"Klas Berglund?" she exclaimed. Her tone was no longer amused but confused.

Klas Berglund had made a name for himself as a fashion designer. Unlike many of his competitors,

Berglund didn't want his brand to be enjoyed by only the super-wealthy, instead opting to make his products affordable – bordering on *cheap*. Although I wasn't particularly keen on his clothing, he had legions of loyal customers who always had his latest designs.

It wasn't just his clothing line that made him so popular, either. Berglund was also a keen campaigner for human rights, ensuring all his products were produced ethically and that the manufacturers were paid fair wages. He was extremely vocal on controversial subjects like fur in fashion and self-image.

"He's got a knack for procuring hard-to-obtain items," I said. The reluctance in my tone was plain to hear.

"I feel like I'm missing something here," she asked, uncertainly.

"The man you know – the man from the TV and the news – that isn't the real Klas Berglund. It's just a costume; a disguise to mask his true personality. He thrives on desperation. He wants people to need him; to be so absolutely lost they're willing to do anything. But no matter how much you want something – no matter how much you think you need it – I can guarantee you'll regret making a deal with that man."

"This might be a personal question, but why do you know someone like that?"

Without thinking, I gripped my necklace, squeezing until the caps dug into my palm. It was a personal question, but she already knew the answer. Slowly, she realised. Comprehension spread across her face. She opened her mouth to say something but closed it quickly. Although she knew about my reasons for asking, I certainly wasn't going to tell her what I'd asked him for.

Using Erin's phone, I called Klas's assistant, Michael. I'd called him so many times in the past that I had his number committed to memory. Erin was good enough not to comment on the fact I knew Michael's number but not my best friend's. As always, Michael sounded suspicious when he answered, but relaxed when he realised who was calling.

"Long time, Bright," he said. I'd always struggled to place his accent. Listening to him now, I thought he sounded Scandinavian, but couldn't be sure.

"I need to see him," I said. It was always important to use the word need when making plans with Berglund. He would only meet desperate people.

"Time for your medicine?" Mikael asked. Even over the phone, I could tell he was smirking.

"Kicked the habit," I mumbled, checking to make sure Erin wasn't listening.

"Shame. The boss enjoyed you. So, how can we help?"

After telling Michael what I wanted, he gave me a time to meet him, and then hung up. Erin had been listening from a seat at the kitchen counter. Something about the way she was sitting – perched on the very edge of her stool – suggested she'd taken her seat in a hurry. I didn't draw attention to it, though.

"When are we meeting him?" she asked.

"You're not coming," I said, a little crossly.

"The Hell I'm not. If this report can prove Dose

isn't the cause of the Itch, then I want to know about it."

"Then, I'll tell you when I get back," I said, not knowing why she was pushing this.

"Well, I hope you're meeting him locally. Because you're not borrowing my car again," she said, smiling shrewdly. Regrettably, it wasn't local. But I wasn't going to cave.

"I can walk," I said. "Look, Erin, I'm not messing around. Klas Berglund is debauched, sadistic, and manipulative. He preys on the weak, the vulnerable, and the needy. He's not interested in money or sex or anything like that. All he wants is to revel in the misery of others. He is the lowest form of life I've ever had the displeasure of meeting and, I'm sorry, but I won't expose anyone to him without good reason."

"Wow," she said, suddenly serious. "Okay, I won't come."

CHAPTER 9

In the run-up to my meeting with Berglund, Erin read about his exploits. A quick search online showed that his clothing line was doing a roaring trade, endorsed by a musician neither of us had heard of. He recently held a charity gala to raise money for research into the cure for the Itch. There was also something about his hometown in Sweden, which he'd visited to unveil a statue in his honour. She told me all this, wondering if perhaps I was exaggerating about him. I wished I were.

Whilst searching, she also found something about me. She showed me the interview with DCI Dunhill, in which she was updating the public about the search for a *potentially dangerous drug dealer*. Although she didn't use my name, it was obvious I was the subject of the interview.

"Whilst I'm sure the public are concerned about the whereabouts of the escapee, I want to assure everyone we are committed to bringing this individual to justice," she said. "At present, I'm unwilling to discuss the investigation at length but will provide an update when it's appropriate to do so. In the meantime, I ask everyone to rest assured we are doing everything possible to ensure all involved are bought to justice. Combatting drug crime is one of the highest priorities of Greater Manchester Police. All perpetrators will be held to account for their crimes and face the full penalty for the misery they've brought on others."

A flurry of bitter thoughts about Dunhill entered my brain, most of which she probably didn't deserve. She wasn't the only person Frank had duped and – until the truth came out – I had to accept she'd done nothing wrong. I wondered if she'd act differently when she found out I'd been framed. During my arrest, I'd gotten the feeling she simply didn't like me. Hearing the animosity with which she spoke during the interview, I had the same feeling she was crusading for my arrest.

Since hearing about Kelly's disappearance, there was no doubt in my mind Frank was responsible. That also meant he might know not only why the trial had failed, but also what was causing the Itch. He hadn't just lied. He'd hurt people to keep his secret. The thought of it made my blood boil. Along with my necklace, I used my anger as fuel and wouldn't stop until Frank had been held to account. It kept me focussed. I was going to need to keep a sharp mind if I was meeting Klas Berglund.

When the day of my meeting finally came, I felt wretched. My head was throbbing, which I put down to stress. No matter how many remedies I tried to treat it, nothing worked. I'd spent most of the day lying on my bed with the curtains drawn. Around mid-afternoon, Erin brought me a cup of herbal tea, which she assured me would help. It didn't, but I sipped it anyway, not wanting to appear rude.

Just before midnight, Erin and I headed down to her car. It was a pleasant night. The air was warm. For some reason, though, I couldn't stop shivering. I put it down to nerves and tried to think of something to calm myself down. Nothing came to mind.

After 20 minutes, the redbrick buildings of the city centre were replaced by an industrial landscape of concrete and metal. Most of the factories and warehouses were closed for the day, which made the area much eerier. I directed Erin to a train station, which was really nothing more than a tiny ticket office alongside a single track.

"What now?" she asked.

"I wait for my invite," I said.

We'd been waiting for perhaps quarter of an hour when the streetlamp beside the ticket office began to flicker. It struggled for a few seconds, before going out completely. Then, from the darkness of the tracks, a shadowy figure emerged.

"Don't follow us," I said as sternly as I could.

"Alright," she mumbled.

"I'm serious," I said, eager to convey the gravity of the situation. She nodded, folding her arms, and reclining in her seat. Satisfied, I left the car and headed to meet the figure.

"Bright," he said by way of a greeting.

"Michael," I said.

For a moment, he said nothing. Then, he pointed over my shoulder.

"Who's your friend?" he asked.

"No one," I replied.

"Excuse me?" Erin snapped.

I hadn't realised she was standing behind me. With Michael in earshot, I couldn't explain why I'd been so dismissive in the car. I would have to explain later why it wasn't wise to bring someone – *anyone* – to meet Klas… by which time my warning would be redundant.

"I told you to wait in the car," I hissed.

"That hurts," she said, huffing in mock indignation. "I'm Erin, by the way," she added, offering a hand to Michael.

"Pleasure," he purred, before disappearing onto the track.

"At least he's friendly," she said.

"Is this a joke to you? Didn't you hear what I said about Klas?"

"I'm not a little kid. I can look after myself," she said firmly.

I felt as though I was talking to Lizzy. Under any other circumstance, I would have agreed Erin seemed more than capable of looking after herself. Then again, she'd never met Klas Berglund. Michael had disappeared back onto the track. Without another word to Erin, I headed after him. She followed.

Our footsteps crunched on the stones underfoot. It was difficult to see where I was treading, and I stumbled more than once. Erin didn't have any problem. We followed Michael for several hundred yards until we came to a rusted metal shipping container alongside the track. There were no markings on the outside, which was perhaps why Erin seemed dubious about it. When Michael unlocked the container, he revealed a staircase leading below ground. Fluorescent lights ran along the ceiling, which cast a dim glow over the steps.

Naturally, Erin was astonished. The first time I'd visited Klas, I'd reacted in the same way. If only I'd known what I knew now about him. Silently, Michael stood aside and allowed us to enter. Once we were inside, he closed the container door, and then ushered us down the staircase. The echoes of our footsteps made it sound as though there were more than three of us.

There was a wall at the bottom of the staircase, with a metal door at the centre like the hatches I imagined a submarine would have. Dried cement oozed between the bricks, which made it look as though the wall had been constructed in a hurry. When Michael knocked, a small window slid open on the door. A moment later, the door swung open, and we were shepherded through.

"Are you carrying anything?" I whispered.

"What? Like a weapon?" she muttered back. "Sorry, I left my AK back at the flat."

"They're going to check you."

Inside, there was a small brick chamber with a door at the opposite side. A single bulb hung above us, bathing the room in a dreary glow. Once we'd entered, Michael closed and bolted the metal door. Without preamble, he turned to me and ran his hands roughly over my arms and legs, checking every pocket, fold, and seam.

Once he was satisfied, he moved onto Erin, starting from her ankles, and working his way up. His hands lingered for a lot longer as he checked her body. He traced his hands up the outside of her thighs and then slid them around her waist. From there, his palms moved down her back and cupped her buttocks. He grunted contentedly as he did so. From there, he moved up her back, keeping her body pressed close to his. Whilst his hands felt underneath her arms, he winked at her. Impressively, she didn't react.

As I watched, appalled, a memory slithered into my brain like Michael's hands moving over Erin's body. The night we'd met. Why the Hell was I bringing that up? Those feelings were long gone. They weren't even ancient history. They were prehistoric. Besides, the last thing I needed was a distraction.

After checking the front of her body with equal enthusiasm, he cast a quick glance up at the corner of the room, where I could just make out the blinking LED of a security camera. There was an angry buzzing sound, followed by a heavy clunk. The door opposite swung open, and Michael led us through.

The room beyond was filled with people dressed in the outlandish style I associated with Berglund's label: fir, sequins, and skin-tight leather. Interspersed around the room were podiums, fashioned to look like ancient pillars, with a nude model posing on top of each one. Most people were congregating around a podium. Music was playing, although it sounded like nothing more than the noises of electrical equipment.

"Where are we?" Erin asked.

"Underneath an old factory. It closed years ago. I think Klas bought the plot and tore down the factory so he could build this place. I guess it's a bit like a casino. He likes games of chance and gambling, so I'll probably have to play to get what I want."

"You don't sound sure."

"Sometimes he asks for other things," I said bitterly. "Look, just don't say anything, okay? Don't make any jokes. Don't comment on anything you see or hear. Don't accept anything that's given to you. Don't offer to do anything. And, above all, don't agree to any deals he makes."

"I won't," she said.

Looking around, I felt strangely disoriented, not to mention, a little nauseated. The strobe lights made my head throb. Michael led us to the centre of the room, where plastic curtains hung from the ceiling. They were cloudy white like a shower curtain. As we passed through them, the music was oddly muted.

We'd entered a square space that had been decorated to look almost like a living room from the 1960s. The furniture was outrageously designed and looked as though it would be uncomfortable to sit on. Everything was covered in black and white shapes and geometric patterns. Berglund was reclining on a beanbag chair in the middle of the floor.

He was wearing a fur jacket, which was open over his bare gut. His trousers were so tight they looked like they'd been painted on. Despite the gloom in the room, he wore a pair of enormous sunglasses. To complete the look, he had perhaps the most ridiculous haircut I'd ever seen, his hair almost perching on top of his head like a helmet.

"I almost thought it was too juicy to be true," Berglund said.

"Mr Berglund," I replied curtly. Klas insisted guests referred to him in this way.

"You're looking well," he drawled.

After taking a moment to find his balance, he stood facing Erin and me, absentmindedly tracing circles around his belly button with a jewelled finger. It was an unpleasant action, somehow sleazy and carnal. And yet, I knew he wasn't motivated by something as primitive as sexual desire. He did it to make those in his presence uneasy.

"How long has it been?" he said with a chuckle.

"A while," I said.

"A gripping article came to my attention recently. You have been a busy boy, haven't you?"

"You shouldn't believe everything you read about people," I replied. Although my tone was civil, he saw through it to the jibe beneath. Too late, I realised I shouldn't have said it.

"How can I help?" he sneered, his tone suggesting that he wasn't feeling particularly helpful.

Of course, he already knew why I was there; I'd told Michael over the phone, and he must have passed on the message. When I told Klas about the report, he laughed uproariously.

"Anything else? Priceless artworks? Nuclear launch codes, perhaps? A small island in the Caribbean?"

He was trying to goad me. He wanted me to lose my temper; to show him how desperate I was. To keep my nerve, I gripped my necklace, exhaling slowly, before replying.

"No, that's all," I said simply.

"You are sure you wouldn't prefer something with a little more *punch*?"

Once again, he was trying to get a rise from me. He remembered my previous visits, just like Michael had. But I'd long since mastered those cravings.

"If you can't do it, just say so, and I'll find another way. Otherwise, state your terms."

The pause that followed was so tense I hardly dared to breathe. Berglund and I stared at one another as if we were the last two people alive in a terrible battle, each ready to finish the other off. Furtively, I glanced around the room, suddenly noticing the sheer number of guards surrounding us in the shadows.

"I don't recognise this one," Berglund said finally. With a start, I realised he was staring at Erin.

"So?" I replied, hoping I sounded dismissive.

"Well, does she have a name?" he enquired, slithering a little closer.

"Seems like it'd be more polite to ask me," she said calmly. Reflexively, my body tensed. Berglund slid the sunglasses off his face, revealing two eyes that were almost entirely black.

"And you are?" he said in a dangerously low voice.

"This is Erin," I interrupted before she could reply. "Look, can you get what I need or not?"

As the words tumbled out of my mouth, I heard the strain in my voice. The longing. And so, too, had Klas. With a cunning grin plastered on his flabby face, he nodded slowly.

"Easily," he purred.

"What do you want for it?" I asked.

Klas strolled around the room, tracing a finger around his belly button. It was common for him to make his clients wait. The longer they stewed, the needier they became. He walked a lap around the room, before sitting on his beanbag chair. Then, he raised one of his bare feet in the air.

"This little piggy went to market," he cooed, wiggling his toes at us. "This little piggy stayed at home. This little piggy had roast beef, and this little piggy had none. And this little piggy..." He paused, wiggling his big toe. "...would like a bubble bath."

"You're disgusting," I hissed, earning a single bark of laughter from Berglund.

"Oh, Jack, I wasn't asking you," he drawled, his eyes drifting in Erin's direction.

I felt like hooks had been sunk into my skull, twisting my face towards Erin. I resisted but was sure Klas had seen the effort it cost me.

"What's going on?" Erin asked.

"He wants you to drink a mouthful of champagne, and then suck his toe," I explained.

This was Klas's game. His clients were offered a degrading or dangerous task, which was designed to test their resolve. If they refused, it showed they weren't desperate enough, and he wouldn't do business with them. Accepting without comment wasn't much better. It showed they were willing to go further for what they needed, which wasn't something I wanted Klas to know. The best thing to do was haggle and agree on a new deal. It showed enough neediness that he would still do business, without giving him too much information. But Erin didn't know any of this.

"Okay," she said.

"No," I exclaimed, further weakening our position.

"Why not?" she hissed in my ear.

"Do we have an agreement or not?" Berglund asked, his voice so full of happiness he sounded as though he was singing.

"I told you, I can make my own decisions," she said angrily.

"You don't understand. It isn't-"

"We need to see that report. And if this is all it costs, I'm happy to pay," she said, before adding

"Well, not happy, but willing."

"Come, now, or the offer expires," Berglund chimed.

"Don't," I hissed, but she'd already squeezed past me.

"I'll do it," she said.

As she approached him, Berglund held up a glass filled with fizzy liquid, his toe wiggling excitedly. Taking the glass, she sniffed it. And then, briskly, she tipped the contents it into her mouth.

"Don't let all the bubble burst," Klas murmured. Erin sank down to her knees, shuffling a little closer to where Berglund was sitting. Decisively, she took hold of his ankle, staring at his toes as they wiggled gleefully. Tilting her head back slightly, she parted her lips and tucked his toe between them.

Erin waited for an indication that it was over, Klas's foot hanging out of her mouth. After a while, I started to wonder if that would come. Eventually, she let his toe fall from her lips, drooling champagne over the floor.

"Bravo," Klas said.

"Well?" I snapped.

"Oh, yes. Very well done."

"Do we have a deal or not?" I demanded.

"Happy to oblige," Klas purred.

"Let's go," I said to Erin.

"Feel free to stop in any time," Klas said. "Tata for now."

I told them Erin's address so they could deliver the report there, and then Michael led the two of us out of the room. We walked quickly. Michael stood to one side to allow us through the hatch. As I passed him, he muttered something in a language I didn't understand. I could guess what it meant.

Once we were above ground, I stormed back to the car, not caring if Erin was following. She called my name, but I didn't reply. By the time she caught up with me, we were almost at the station.

"Hey. Slow down," she said.

"Hurry up," I snapped.

"Why are you being like this?"

"I told you not to come," I said, whirling to face her. "I told you Klas wasn't to be trusted. And yet, you decided to come anyway. I told you not to make any deals or bargains with him. And yet, the first opportunity that arose, you did exactly that. Do you have any idea what you've done?"

"You were the one who was saying we needed this report. And yeah, I made a deal with him. But it could have been a lot worse. Who cares if all I had to do was suck his toe?"

"You haven't got a bloody clue, have you?" I yelled. "Did you ever wonder why I said don't make a deal with him? It's because he wants to push people to their limits. And by obliging so willingly, you've shown him how far we'll go to get this report."

"Why does that matter?"

"Because he *didn't push us to our limit*. So, yeah, you might have walked away with a win. But that won't matter to Klas. We didn't earn our prize, so I can guarantee he won't honour our agreement."

CHAPTER 10

Erin carried on yelling at me until we made it back to her car, but I was too angry to respond. The drive back was unpleasantly tense. We were both seething. Under different circumstances, I might have realised I was being unreasonably harsh on Erin; after all, Klas deserved my fury far more than she did. But I couldn't convince myself to forgive her for what she'd done. When we got back to her flat, Erin headed straight to her room. Although I wasn't tired, I went to my room and lay on the bed.

As the sun rose the next day, I shuffled to the edge of the mattress, massaging the sleep from my eyes. Over the past few days, I'd slept less and less. Last night, I couldn't have slept for more than an hour.

"Hey," Erin said from the door.

"Hey," I replied simply.

"This was in the letterbox this morning."

She was holding a plain brown envelope. It was thick. I tore it open. It wasn't surprising to see that he'd acquired the report. Erin looked optimistic, but when I showed her the contents, she realised what I'd meant about Klas. Crudely, someone had redacted all the key information from every page. Even the title had been removed. There was a handwritten note on the corner of the first page. *Feel free to drop by for the rest. K.*

"Do you remember what I said last night?" I asked.

"Is this where you say *I told you so*?" she replied.

She was frustrated, but I knew it wasn't because of me, so kept calm.

"Do you remember?" I said, to which she nodded.

I'd told her how Klas liked to test people; how he enjoyed seeing people at their lowest. As I told her how we should have handled the situation, she frowned.

"Why, though? That doesn't make any sense. Surely, doing something so disgusting showed we were desperate."

"No. By agreeing so easily, it showed him we were getting a good deal" I explained. "And, because of that, he now knows he can push us further. That's why he's done this. He knows how much we need the report. And he knows that we'll do whatever it takes to get it. He doesn't do things for physical pleasure or material gain. All he wants is to see how far people are willing to go to get what they want; to know that, without raising a finger, he can make people do anything he asks."

"So, you are saying *I told you so*?"

"No," I replied calmly. "I just wanted you to know why I reacted the way I did."

Erin left for work around lunchtime. She said nothing as she left. To be honest, I wasn't sure I minded. I spent all day reading the report, trying desperately to glean something from it. But Klas had been thorough. Although there were still signatures on the first page, he'd removed just enough content to eliminate any useful details from it. The pages of the report were spread across the kitchen counter. I was sitting on one of the stools, staring at the paper, wondering how I'd ever find out what was written there when an idea occurred to me from seemingly nothing. Tearing through the paper, I searched for the cover page. It took me a few minutes but, as soon as I saw it, I knew I'd found something significant.

That evening, I practically tackled her at the front door. Understandably, she was annoyed by that, but I was too impatient to explain myself.

"I need to use your phone," I said.

"Nice to see you, too" she replied.

"Just give me your phone."

"Why?"

It didn't seem fair to get annoyed at her again for a second time in less than 24 hours. As patiently as I could, then, I showed her the cover page, indicating the signatures. In the days before he was a politician, Rupert Prophett had worked at Rathbury-Holmes. He'd approved the report. As he was the current Health Secretary, there was no way I'd ever be able to speak to him. Wilson Loveday and Frank – my former boss – had proofread it, but I was certain neither would tell me anything useful. That left the author, Dina Mulchandaani.

"So, you want to talk to her?" she asked.

"That was my plan. But I think there's a problem, which is why I need to use your phone."

When she handed me her phone, I hastily googled Dina's name. The top result was exactly what I'd expected.

"Dina Mulchandaani – deceased" I explained after passing Erin her phone to read. "She disappeared just after signing this. Police found some of her clothing on the coast. They concluded she took her own life."

"How does that help?"

"Her father was convinced something wasn't right. There are still posters up around the office asking for information. He thinks someone killed her."

"So, why is this important?"

"What if Dina knew something? What if – like Wilson and Kelly and me – somebody wanted her out of the way? But instead of framing her, they killed her and made it look like a suicide."

"Okay," Erin said slowly. "How does this help?"

"I have to talk to her father. He might know something."

"I feel like we've been down this road before," she said resignedly.

"This is different," I said. "He created a website. There's a mobile number. I can call him and ask what he knows about Dina's death."

It was clear that Erin was reluctant, and I could understand why; I certainly wouldn't want to be hounded for details about my brother's death. But unless we could miraculously find a copy of the report from some other source, Dina's father was the only chance we had. Looking less than thrilled about it, she finally nodded and handed me her phone again.

"Hello?" came a dreadfully hollow voice over the phone.

"Hi," I said simply, before realising I had no idea what to say. "I'm- I wanted to talk to you about your daughter."

"If you're one of those sick *crime tourists*, you're wasting your time. I'm not discussing anything about my daughter's death just so that you can get your sick kicks."

"I- what?" I replied, unsure that I'd heard

correctly. Would people really contact a grieving father, simply to discuss the gory details of his daughter's death? If so, how was I going to convince him I was any different?

"Don't call this number again," he snapped.

"No, it's nothing like that," I said, floundering. But with no time to think about what to say, I simply carried on blabbering. "Look, I believe what you said about Dina. We worked at the same company. I knew her. I think something might have happened to her. Please, I need to talk to you about what happened."

It was the first thing that I could think of, and, in all honesty, it wasn't necessarily true. In all the years we'd worked together, I could only think of a handful of instances when we'd been in the same room – let alone spoken to one another.

"I'll only discuss it in person," he said bitterly. "If you're telling the truth, and you really believe me, then you can look me in the eyes and say so. And if you are lying, I'll know."

Although it was a step in the right direction, it wasn't feasible; if he recognised me, I couldn't guarantee that he wouldn't call the police. Then again, if I wanted to speak to him, what choice did I have?

"Okay, I'll meet you," I said quickly. Beside me, Erin shook her head in disbelief, but I waved her aside.

"Meet me outside the Lowry in an hour," he said curtly. And, before I could reply, he hung-up.

CHAPTER 11

Erin wasn't happy about the meeting. For almost half an hour, we argued about whether I should go. Her evidence against was sound but, each time she suggested a reason not to, I simply said that I needed to know what Dina's father knew about her death. Maybe she'd told him something about the report, and if so, I had to hear it. As the other people named on the report – Frank, Prophett and Wilson – weren't likely to be much help, Dina's father was my only option. In the end, Erin conceded. She even offered to drive me to the Lowry, although she added she was only doing it to make sure I didn't do anything reckless.

I felt strangely detached from the pedestrians we passed. They were going about their day-to-day lives, heading to work or meeting friends, maybe. In contrast, I was on my way to question a father about the circumstances of his daughter's death in the hopes of clearing my name and, potentially, revealing the truth about a conspiracy that had affected hundreds of thousands of people. Plus, I was on the run from the law. It was fair to say my life had changed drastically over a very short period.

In that moment, I felt as though the weight of everything that had happened was pressing against me, forcing the air from my lungs. Part of me – a significant part, I suspected – seriously considered giving up. Throwing in the towel. Marching into the police station and announcing myself. They could take me away and I wouldn't have to think about any of this again. I shook my head, driving that thought away, annoyed I'd even let it enter my mind. Abandoning hope was dangerous. My education in that particular area was extensive. No matter what, I wouldn't submit to despair. I wouldn't let myself simply give up.

Erin drove into the multi-storey car park at the Lowry Outlet, which wasn't far from the theatre. She also lent me her mobile, *just in case*. I wasn't sure I wanted to know what she thought might happen, so took it without comment. Thankfully, it was midweek, so there weren't too many cars or people milling around. Regardless, I kept my head down and avoided eye contact, suspicious of everyone around me. *That's what being framed will do to you*, I thought bitterly.

I took the stairs to the ground floor, which brought me out alongside the water. From there, it was only a short walk to the theatre. Even after only a short absence, it was strange being back at the Quays. I could see my flat in the distance and began to wonder what sort of state it was in. Surely, the police had searched it from top to bottom after I was arrested.

When I arrived at the theatre, I stood to the side of the square in front of it, watching every face that passed. It was after lunchtime, so the nearby restaurants were almost empty. After a while, I started thinking about the last time I'd been there. I'd never been to the theatre since moving only a few hundred metres away but distantly recalled watching a play at the theatre with my family when I was younger. I'd long since forgotten the title or whether I'd enjoyed it,

pg. 133

but I remembered my brother making jokes throughout. Hastily, I pushed the memories away.

10 minutes passed, and then 15. I'd been waiting for nearly 20 minutes when I started to wonder if Dina's father had changed his mind. My suspicions increased when the phone in my pocket started ringing.

"Hello?" I said, preparing for disappointment.

"I wanted to be sure," said a voice from behind me.

I spun quickly to see a skeletally thin man glaring at me. Combined with the soundlessness of his arrival, there was something unsettling about him. My unease worsened when he refused my outstretched hand; I should have expected as much, though. I introduced myself as *Danny*, eager not to reveal my identity. He didn't give me his name, so I simply called him *Mr Mulchandaani*.

He led me away from the square outside the theatre towards the water. I followed in silence, wondering whether I should say something. Eventually, he stopped walking and leaned against a rail that ran around the water's edge. I stood beside him, still waiting. My eyes fell upon the water. Even though I was standing behind the rail, the sight of the inky black depths made me shudder. To settle myself, I focussed on the opposite bank, where I could see the futuristic architecture of The Imperial War Museum.

"Why are you here?" he asked finally.

"I think someone hurt your daughter. And I think the same thing might have happened to other people, too" I replied.

I'd given a lot of thought to what I'd say to Mr

Mulchandaani, particularly about why I wanted to know about his daughter. I told him a little about Wilson, too, but thought it best not to reveal too much. Although I barely said anything, it seemed to appease Mr Mulchandaani.

"Dina loved swimming," he said, gazing across the water. "Do you like swimming?" I couldn't lie, but didn't want to upset him, so simply shrugged. "She came here every weekend. That's one of the reasons they suggested she might have gone to... why she might have done what she did. I never believed it, though."

"I know this must be upsetting for you," I said, noting the hitch in his voice.

"I'm not upset; I'm angry. I'm angry that someone did this to my daughter."

"Do you have any idea who it was? Or why they would do that to her?"

He shook his head. Although I'd never worked with Dina personally, I knew she was well-liked by her colleagues. As her father described how kind, caring, compassionate and friendly she was, I started to feel guilty for forcing him to relive these memories. His voice was overflowing with rawness, which only made me feel worse. When he'd finished, I was almost certain no one would've wished her any harm; at least not for personal reasons. But then, that raised an important question.

"I'm sorry to ask this but, why are you so sure someone hurt her?"

"If I'm honest, I wasn't, at first," he said. "Grief made it difficult to believe anything else, though. I'd have probably believed anything to explain what happened. But when it passed, and I could think again, murder was the only thing that made any sense. She was happy. She was well-liked. Ambitious. She had no reason to do that to herself. There was no note, either. Do you really believe a loved one would take their own life without leaving a note for their family? Without saying goodbye?"

Any doubt in my mind dissolved instantly. Mr Mulchandaani believed, beyond all doubt, that someone had murdered his daughter. Now, I wanted to understand why they'd done it.

"Did you ever talk to her about work?" I asked, steering the conversation.

"Of course. Why?"

Briefly, I told him about the report that she'd worked on before her death.

"I think it might be important, but I'm not sure why. Did she ever mention anything about it? Or did she ever tell you about a problem at work?"

"Problem?" he muttered, almost to himself. Slowly, he reached into his pocket and took out a mobile phone. With the skill of someone that wasn't particularly familiar with technology, he tapped the screen, before eventually handing it to me. There was a short email on the screen.

"*Frank, I think we need to discuss this, RE: DEV45. Could be an issue for approval. Regards, Dina*"

"How did you get this?" I asked.

"The police gave me her belongings after they finished their investigation. This was in there."

"Do you know if they followed up on this message?"

"They said he had an alibi," he said, although I'm

not entirely sure he believed it was true. "Is it important?"

"I'm not sure."

He was silent for a moment, staring down into the water. I kept my eyes on the opposite bank.

"You've had run-ins with him before, haven't you?" he asked.

"Sorry?" I stammered.

"I recognise you from the newspaper. Something about an explosion in his office," he said. "Jack something or other. The police are looking for you, too," he added.

"Look, it's not what you-"

"I'm not going to turn you in," he said. "But, if you're looking into Dina's murder, I want to be sure your doing it for her and not a vendetta."

"Honestly, I don't know," I said hesitantly. "It's true; I don't like Frank. But I've got strong reason to believe he's covering something. He might've hurt people, too. If that's true, I can't let him get away with it. I couldn't prove it before, but this changes things."

Frank had ignored Dina's warning, shortly after which something terrible had happened to her. Was Frank involved? Had Dina discovered the true cause of the Itch whilst working on DEV-45? And was Frank now covering up what she'd found? As I handed the phone back, Mr Mulchandaani shook his head.

"Take it," he said softly. "It's just a painful reminder for me. It'll be more useful to you. Just... just find out what happened to her."

As Erin drove us back to her flat, I explained what Mr Mulchandaani had said, but was careful not to mention that he'd recognised me. I also reminded her about the discussion I'd had with Frank before I was arrested. Even though it was only a few days ago, it felt like a distant memory. Whilst I spoke, Erin listened without saying a word and carried on doing so for a long time after I'd finished.

When we got back to the flat, I showed her the message that Dina had sent to Frank.

"Do you have any idea what she was talking about?" Erin asked.

There was a diagram that had been hastily scrawled and attached to the email. It showed a chemical reaction but was missing much of the detail so I couldn't work out what any of it was. Slowly, I shook my head.

"I've got to speak to Frank," I said. "He must know something about this."

"I'm just not sure that's a good idea," she said. "Meeting Wilson and Dina's Dad was one thing, but Frank *knows* you. Plus, you two hardly sound like best buddies. How can you be sure he won't call the police when he sees you?"

"If we were alone, I could-"

"You'd better not be about to suggest kidnapping."

"Of course, I'm not," I said, although some small part of me might have been considering it.

"What, then?"

"No idea," I said, shaking my head.

"What about Berglund?" she suggested.

"What about him?" I countered.

"He managed to get hold of a confidential report in less than 24 hours. Surely, he can find dirt on Frank. Something to make him cooperate."

"No," I said eventually. My voice was calm, but I couldn't mask the anger in my expression.

"You really can't stand Klas, can you?" she mused. I wanted to tell her to mind her own business but bit my tongue.

Erin left for work that evening, leaving me alone in the flat again. After checking the report for what felt like the thousandth time, I went to my room and did some press-ups and sit-ups. It felt good to exercise. It took my mind off everything, if only for a little while. Once I'd finished, I took a shower, helped myself to some curry from the fridge, and then sat back at the counter to recheck the report.

The following morning, Erin told me she was going to a protest, so would be gone for most of the day. Despite my assurances that I wasn't planning any day trips, she took her car keys and spares for the flat. With nothing else to do, I picked up the report and tried to think of ways to remove the ink from the pages without affecting what lay beneath. I found some nail polish remover in the bathroom, which unfortunately removed everything from the small area I tested it on.

I was checking the cupboard under the sink, looking for some sort of stain remover or cleaning product, when a knock at the door disturbed my concentration. It sounded much too heavy to be a friend. Besides, they would surely know that Erin was at a protest. Who was it, then? Had the police tracked me down? Were they here to arrest me?

"It's me," Bowker yelled. I went to the door. I wasn't exactly relieved. Less anxious was probably a better term.

When I told him Erin wasn't home, he simply said she'd asked him to come, so I left him in the living room whilst I continued looking for something to remove the ink from the report. I'd barely resumed my search when there was another knock at the door.

To my surprise, Bowker answered it.

"Who are they?" I asked as two men entered, each an identical copy of Bowker, right down to his ridiculous haircut. But Bowker simply told me to *simmer* – whatever that meant – and went to sit in the living room.

Within minutes, he and his entourage were cackling like a pack of hyenas. A moment later, one of the men started playing music on his phone. To me, it sounded more than sound effects than a tune, but they appreciated it. When I asked Bowker what they were doing, he made a joke about my sexuality, which prompted more hysterical laughter. Suddenly, my temper rose.

"Can you turn it down?" I asked, fighting to keep my voice level.

"Must be on his period," one of them sneered.

"Just turn it down," I said, hoping I sounded demanding.

A hush rippled through the room. Bowker's fists were balled at his sides, his eyes narrowed and fixed on me. Slowly, he strode towards me, eyes locked on mine. Despite the urge to take a step back, I stood my ground. He stopped a few inches away from me, close enough that I could see the muscles around his eyes twitching.

"You want to pay them words some mind" he snarled. "This ain't no playground."

"Could have fooled me," I retorted, glancing at his friends lounging in the living room.

"Needs schooling, man!" barked one of the men. The other murmured some agreement.

"Fixing, more like," Bowker purred.

The men grinned at one another as Bowker reached into his pocket. For a dreadful moment, I thought that he was going to pull out a weapon. But when he removed his hand, he wasn't holding a weapon, just a small white tube. I recognised it instantly.

"Partaking, or what?" he hissed, offering me the tube. The others had closed in around me like predators getting ready to strike.

"No," I said firmly.

It happened before I could register movement. One of Bowker's friends grabbed my arms. Once I was restrained, Bowker advanced, holding the tube up to my face. I pressed my lips tightly shut, so he pinched my nose. I held my breath as long as I could but eventually had to open it. As he slotted the tube between my lips, I thrashed wildly. But it was no use. I had to inhale.

I'd never given any thought to how taking Dose might feel. Even before the sickness, I wasn't particularly interested in trying it. As such, I had no idea what to expect. I was still wondering how long it would take to kick in when I felt the effects.

It wasn't easy to describe. At first, I thought it was calming me down. My breathing slowed. I could no longer hear the thump of my pulse in my ears. But after a few seconds, I realised it was more than that. Somehow, my mind felt clearer. The chaotic jumble of thoughts that had been rattling around in there was gone – not lost, just moved somewhere for later consideration. Now, all that remained was how to escape. And in that moment of lucidity, I realised Bowker's goon had loosened his grip.

Wildly, I swung my fist, catching Bowker on his cheek and sending him crashing to the floor. After spitting the tube from my lips, I raked my fingernails down the face of the man holding me, and he let go. Freed, I backed away from them. Throughout the struggle, the third man had been a safe distance away. Now, though, he joined the others, the three of them surrounding me in a ring. I was confident I could defend myself against one attacker, perhaps even two. But there was no chance I could hold off three men. I was backing away from them, unsure what else to do when the front door opened.

"What the Hell is going on?" Erin snarled.

"Nothing," Bowker grumbled, fidgeting under her gaze.

"Who are they?" she demanded.

"Who's rattled her cage?" one of them muttered.

"Was I talking to you?" she barked, rounding on the man that had spoken. Despite being much bigger than she was, he recoiled.

"They're just-" Bowker mumbled.

"-just leaving?" Erin snarled. "Yes, I see that. Ta for now chaps."

"What's her-"

"You've got 10 seconds," Erin roared. "After that, you'd better hope you aren't here anymore."

"Is she for real?"

"One, two-"

She didn't make it to three before Bowker started shooing the men out of the door. They argued a little, but Bowker didn't listen. Once they had left, he turned to look at Erin.

"They were-"

pg. 142

"Are you dragging?" she demanded. Bowker shifted nervously from foot to foot. "Have you been fucking dragging?"

"Just one," he said in a small voice.

"In my house?" she roared. Bowker started to say something, but Erin shouted him down. "No. You do not come to my house and fucking drag."

"It was just-"

"What made you think this would be okay?"

"Didn't even-"

"Is this the first time?"

"What?"

"Is this the first time?" she repeated, very slowly.

"Yeah," Bowker said, looking away as he replied.

"I certainly hope so," she snapped. "If I ever catch you doing this again, it's going to be more than just harsh words exchanged. Now, get out."

Bowker stared at her grumpily before throwing his arms up in the air. He mumbled something. In reply, Erin cupped her hand around her ear, but he didn't say anything else. For a long time, Erin and I didn't speak. I could tell that she was trying to catch my eye, but I wouldn't look at her. Eventually, she sighed.

"I'm so sorry, Jack," she said gravely.

"You're sorry?" I spat. Despite my best efforts, I was reliving a memory that I'd been trying desperately to suppress; the argument that Erin and I had a year ago.

CHAPTER 12

The memory began with my brother, Danny, on the night before he'd died. We'd had a few drinks at my flat. I'd kept the bottlecaps around my neck ever since. The difference in his appearance that night versus the next day in a hospital bed still haunted me. In a matter of hours, the Itch had made him almost unrecognisable. The thought of what his final moments must have felt like had given me nightmares for months afterwards.

Erin used to work with my brother. That was how we'd been introduced. When I saw her at his funeral, she'd given me the customary sad smile and kind words, just like everyone else. It was a few days afterwards that I'd seen her at one of the protests. It wasn't fair to say that his death was her fault. Danny had made his own choices. And yet, I couldn't contain my outrage.

She'd tried to console me – to explain that Dose wasn't as bad as I'd been told – but I hadn't listened. With what had just happened, all that anger came rushing back.

"I understand you're upset," she said reasonably.

"Too flipping right I'm upset. Your boyfriend and his thugs almost-"

"He's not my boyfriend," she interjected, nettled.

"You invited him in, though," I countered.

"No, I didn't. I had no idea he'd be here," she said loudly. If she was lying, her tone made it extremely difficult to tell. But that didn't matter.

"I'm leaving," I said.

"Where are you going to go?" Erin asked, sounding as though she was no longer interested in the conversation. I hadn't given that any thought whatsoever. Hastily, I made a mental list of all the places that I could go but was alarmed that very few names came to mind.

"Anywhere is better than here. Not to mention, safer."

"Where are you going to go?" she said.

This time, there was a knowing tone in her voice. Of course, she must have known I didn't have any family. She and Danny were friends for a long time. And I'd already told her I didn't really have any friends I could turn to. As much as I wanted to argue with her, there was nothing I could say. But despite that, I wasn't willing to spend another second in Erin's company. Fuming, I stormed out of the room. Happily, she didn't follow.

Although it had been dark for hours, there was no way I could sleep. My head was overflowing with thoughts, most of them too chaotic to make sense of. How could I have been so naïve? Did I really think someone so actively protesting the Dose ban wasn't also dealing the drug? And then, there was Bowker. If Erin hadn't returned, what would he and his goons have done to me?

It was clear that Erin must be high-ranking. How else would she have been able to command such respect from those thugs? Was she the head of a drug ring? Furious, I gripped my necklace in my hand, remembering what she'd said to me when I'd confronted her after Danny's funeral. I couldn't believe that I'd been desperate enough to come to her for help.

It was morning when there was a knock at the door. I ignored it, but the door creaked open.

"I need to talk to you," Erin said, her tone oddly formal.

"Don't bother," I replied. For a moment, she looked uncertain but eventually started speaking in a very deliberate tone.

"I had no idea he was going to do that."

"When I told you I'd been arrested, you almost turned me away," I said. "You were worried that you'd be implicated. Is this why? Were you worried they'd find out you're selling Dose?"

"In case you've forgotten, I wasn't the one who-"

"Is that why you're protesting the ban? To legitimise your little earner. Retire early and live it up on your ill-gotten gains."

Her eyes swelled. She clenched her fists. Instantly, I knew I'd said the wrong thing.

"How dare you," she snarled. "You don't know a damn thing about why I do what I do. Not that it's any of your business, but that's not why I protest. I'm protesting because the ban tore my family apart. You may have only just realised that Dose isn't the cause of the Itch, but I've known for a long time. The people I care about most have been taken away from me without good reason. That's why I protest."

Distantly, I remembered the feeling I'd gotten when she mentioned the arrests for Dose possession. It had seemed personal to her.

"I'm sorry," I said, looking away from her.

"You might blame me for Danny's death, but I

didn't kill him. And neither did Dose. It isn't the cause of the Itch. You have to understand that. Otherwise, what the Hell are you doing here?"

It wasn't what I'd expected her to say and, as such, I had no idea how to respond. We stared at one another for a moment, both breathing heavily. I couldn't deny her point.

"Do you have any proof that Dose isn't the cause?" I asked.

"No," she said angrily, before continuing in a calmer voice. "Nothing that isn't anecdotal, at least. But I think you can find it."

Despite agreeing with her, what she was asking was easier said than done. The only way to find proof was speaking to Frank, which posed a serious problem. I couldn't trust him. Even if I could speak to him, I had no way of knowing if he was telling the truth. Plus, there was every chance he might call the police as soon as he saw me. And of course, he'd made it clear that he was willing to protect himself. He'd lied and hurt people already. But it was a risk that I would have to take if I wanted answers.

"Can you give me a lift?" I asked.

Hurriedly, I told Erin about Frank's passion for golf. Given the terrible weather we'd had recently, I found it hard to imagine he'd be playing at the weekend, which meant he'd be at the driving range. He'd mention it recently at work, and it wasn't far from Erin's flat. If I could catch him outside – maybe on his way from or to his car – I might have enough time to speak to him privately.

At first, she didn't seem sold on the idea; after all, there was a strong possibility I'd be recognised by another golfer. Plus, there was the risk that Frank would simply call the police as soon as he saw me.

"I'll convince him not to," I said.

"How?" she asked.

"I'll think of something."

Erin continued to voice her concerns, but, eventually, she agreed to help. It was a good job, too, because I had no idea how I'd manage without her. On Sunday morning, she drove me to the driving range. True to form, it was a wet and drizzly day. The sky was streaked with inky black clouds like a blanket of smoke. Although it was warm in Erin's car, I couldn't stop shivering. What made it worse was the sweat coating my face and back. To combat the cold, I pulled the zip of my jacket up as far as I could, burying my chin inside my gilet. Erin asked if everything was alright, but I simply nodded.

As expected, I saw Frank's ostentatious 4x4 in the car park; I recognised his personalised number plate, *ROTT3R* – a tribute to his beloved rottweiler. I asked Erin to park a short distance away, close enough that I could still see his car but far enough that he wouldn't necessarily spot me waiting for him.

We'd been waiting for about a quarter of an hour. Neither of us had said a word since we'd parked when I decided to ask something that had been nagging at me all night.

"Have you ever taken it?" I asked.

"A few times," she replied. "Never really enjoyed it."

I was fairly sure she was telling the truth. But that raised another question. How did she know Dose wasn't causing the Itch? Once again, I found myself wondering about her reason for protesting, specifically her disdain for the arrests made because of it. Before I could ask her about it, I saw Frank waddling across the car park. Given the chill in the air, I was surprised to see how much he'd sweated. Large rings were spreading out from his armpits, plus a streak from his neck to his buttocks.

I waited until he was only a few cars away before getting out and speed walking towards him. I was still some distance away when someone from the driving range called over to him. As he stopped to engage the man, I dropped to my knees, pretending to tie my shoelace. The two of them were arguing vigorously. At one point, I thought Frank was going to look right at me, so dropped my head. After a few seconds, I glanced in his direction. To my frustration, Frank had marched off and was already putting his clubs in the boot of his car.

Acting on impulse, I waited until he was squeezing himself into the driver's seat before rushing towards him. Just as he closed his door, I slotted myself onto the front passenger seat. I was darkly satisfied to see the shock on his face, no matter how fleeting it was. Quickly, his expression was overflowing with barely contained rage.

"What the Hell do you think you're doing?" he snarled.

"We need to talk," I replied.

A string of expletives left his flabby mouth, promptly followed by several threats of violence. He reached for the door handle. Worried that he was about to get out, I quickly thought of a way to make him stay. I wasn't proud of my idea but was sure it would work.

"If you want this to be a civilised chat, you'll stay where you are," I said. "Otherwise, step out and see what happens."

"Are you threatening me?" he scoffed.

If I came to it, I had no doubt that I would beat Frank in a fight. The problem was that a fight would draw a lot of attention. I had to say something that would make him stay in the car. There was only one thing that I could think of.

"I know what you did to them," I said. I was pleased to see a spasm of surprise chase across his chubby cheeks.

"What?"

"I know that you hurt those people."

"I've no idea what you're talking about," he said. But his flustered expression said otherwise.

"Shall I jog your memory? Kelly. Dina," I said.

Their names made his eyes widen in horror. It took tremendous restraint to suppress a smile.

"What do you want?" he asked eventually.

"I want to know about a DEV trial."

When I told him the reference, his round face crumpled in confusion. There were so many folds that it looked like his skull was collapsing.

"Why are you dragging that up?" he asked.

"Dina flagged a problem which you ignored. Shortly after that, she was found dead. I also flagged a problem which you also ignored. A few months later, the police arrested me."

"Are you suggesting that I murdered Dina? Just to stop her whinging about some minor issue that might have derailed a multi-million-pound project? And that

I've done the same thing to you?"

"I'm way beyond *suggesting* it. I've got proof that you've ignored warnings about potential issues. Plus, I think whatever Dina highlighted was more than just a *minor issue*; I think it's the real reason people are getting sick. I think you've hidden the true cause of the Itch and, when I pointed out that there might have been a mistake, you tried to cover your tracks again."

Once again, I'd expected my words to have more impact and – once again – I was disappointed. After a few seconds, he chortled, before guffawing idiotically.

"You don't know what DEV-45 was for, do you?" he said. The smugness in his voice made me wary, but I admitted that I didn't know. "It was CPT. I take it you know what that is…?"

Cyclo-phosphomorphic toluthorazine; otherwise known as CPT. It was a novel preservative, which Rathbury-Holmes had introduced a few years ago. Given its effectiveness against a wide range of microorganisms, CPT was one of the most commercially popular preservatives in the country. It was used in almost every industry, from pharmaceuticals to food. In fact, I'd probably be hard-pressed to find a product that didn't contain CPT. But there was still something that didn't add up.

"What about the trial?" I asked. "If Dose was really the cause of the sickness, why did those people die? The cure was one hundred per cent effective during pre-clinical trials. So, why wasn't it one hundred per cent effective in human tests?"

Yet again, I felt as though I'd delivered a hammer blow. Expectantly, I waited for Frank to start floundering; to reveal that he was lying. But what he said filled me with doubt.

"By this time tomorrow, you'll realise you made a mistake."

"Maybe I should have a word with the police," I said, scrambling to recover my advantage. "I'm sure they'd be very interested to hear what I have to say about you."

"You can't prove a thing," he said, his usual arrogance returning.

"Are you sure you want to take that risk?"

"Are you?" he challenged. "Last I checked, you're still a wanted man. You can't torch me without getting burned yourself. Now, I'm only going to say this to you once. This better be the last time you try to drag me into this. Because, if I have to tell you again, I'll make sure you regret it."

I stared at him, almost daring him to force me out, but realised that wasn't a good idea. A scuffle would draw attention, which I really didn't need. Nodding slowly, I stepped out of the car. As he sped away, he glared at me. I met his gaze with equal fury. After he'd left the car park, I headed back to Erin's car. She looked at me, expectantly, but I shook my head. When I told Erin what he'd said, she looked almost as angry as I'd been.

"He admitted killing them?" she asked, outraged.

"Not in as many words," I said. "You should have seen how he reacted when I said their names, though. He definitely knows what happened to them."

I knew Frank was right about the police, too. They would never convict him without evidence and, although he'd indicated committing a crime to me, I couldn't go to the police. Gripping my necklace, I sat back in my seat, thinking hard.

We'd been driving for about 10 minutes when Erin started accelerating unexpectedly. At first, I thought nothing of it, but as we continued gathering speed, I began to wonder what she was doing.

"That car has been following us since we left the driving range," she said, nodding at her rear-view mirror. Curious, I peeked in the wing mirror beside me.

It was a glossy black saloon. Although the glare on the windscreen made it difficult to see inside, I could just about see two people in the front seats. From their size, I guessed they were men.

"Turn right up ahead," I said.

After telling her to turn right again, Erin worked out what I was suggesting. If we looped back on ourselves, and they did the same, it would confirm that they were following us. Sure enough, the car matched our loop. And what was more, the driver had accelerated.

"Wonderful," Erin said, speeding up. "I swear to God if you've got me into-"

"Wait, slow down," I said.

"Not quite sure you understand how a pursuit works."

"Trust me."

Although grumbling about how untrustworthy I'd proven to be, she pushed the breaks until our tail was just a few car lengths behind.

"Look for a car park. Or something with an entry barrier," I said.

"What?" she yelled. "I'm not going to-"

"Just trust me," I said. She opened her mouth but faltered. After letting out a short, angry breath, she said, "You'd better know what you're doing."

It took another 10 minutes or so, but we finally saw a sign for a multi-storey up ahead. As we pulled onto the entry slip, the car behind did the same. At that distance, I could now see two burly figures, eyes fixed on our car. Erin wound down her window to collect a ticket, but I told her to wait.

"What are we going to do?" she hissed. "Wait until they get bored and leave?"

"Just wait," I said.

"Are you serious?"

"Yes."

The cars behind must have wondered what was happening, but I insisted Erin waited until a car approached the exit on the other side of us. Once again, she knew what I was suggesting as soon as I started to explain. She took our ticket and pulled through the barrier. Meanwhile, our tail pulled up and waited for a ticket. Beside us, the exiting car had passed through. Then, once our tail was through the barrier, Erin slipped into reverse. In a display of expert driving, she managed to reverse out of the exit and join the traffic on the main road.

"Nicely done," I said appreciatively.

"Don't celebrate too soon," she said, indicating the mirror again.

A car was peeling away from the queue to enter the car park and was racing in our direction. This time, Erin floored the accelerator.

"What now?" she demanded.

"Can you lose them?"

"I think you're confusing me with a getaway driver."

By now, we'd entered the city limits. The traffic was denser. Plus, there were a lot of pedestrians on the pavement. I flinched as Erin slipped in and out of gaps that were barely wide enough for her car.

"Have you got anything that I could use to get rid of them?" I asked.

"Sorry, I left my shotgun at home," she said sarcastically.

"Anything at all."

"There might be some stuff under my seat. I doubt it'll be any use, though."

Gracelessly, I clambered into the backseat. Erin cursed as my rear pressed against his shoulder. There was an ice scraper and can of de-icer. There was also another bottle of luminous blue liquid. It was antifreeze.

"Do you have a lighter?" I asked.

"The car does." she replied. "Why?"

"I've got an idea. Head away from the city."

"Once again, that doesn't sound like a good-"

"Just do it."

I got the impression that her sudden change in direction was a way of expressing her anger. After hauling myself out of the footwell, I asked her to depress the lighter. We'd left the main road and were now driving through an industrial estate. The street was lined with trees, beyond which I could see the roofs of warehouses and factories. In the distance, I could just about see the metalwork of Old Trafford stadium. The lighter popped out, and Erin passed it to me without a word. When she saw the bottle of antifreeze, though, her expression darkened.

"What the Hell are you doing?" she asked.

"Improvising," I replied. It was all I could think to say.

Rather clumsily, I opened the bottle, careful not to spill any on myself. Erin protested when I asked her to slow down, but I told her that I needed the car to be close enough to hit it. Cursing, she pressed the brakes. The car was little more than a foot away from us when I wound down the nearside window. After I dropped the lighter into the bottle, I threw it at their bonnet.

At first, nothing happened but, after a few seconds, the driver slammed the brakes on. As we vanished around the next corner, I could see the heat haze from the invisible flames covering their windscreen.

"I think we lost them," she said. "I can't believe that worked."

"Don't mess with a chemistry nerd," I said, a little disbelievingly. To my surprise, Erin laughed.

When we got back to her flat, we sat at the kitchen counter discussing what had just happened. Erin suggested that it might have been the police, but I pointed out that, if it had been, they'd have turned on their sirens when we tried to lose them at the car park.

"Frank must have sent them," I said. "Why else would they have followed us?"

Before Erin could reply, I was on my feet, fists balled at my sides. More than anything, I'd wanted to punch Frank's flabby face until he'd admitted what he'd done; force him to confess to his crimes. It had taken all my restraint to get out of his car. Now, though, my temper had resurfaced. The goons he'd sent after us were fuelling my anger.

"Jack?" Erin asked.

"What?" I snapped.

"Easy." she replied.

"Sorry. I- that wasn't fair. I'm just a little annoyed."

"A little?" she asked mockingly.

"Sorry," I repeated.

I told her that, usually, I smashed a punchbag to work-off my frustrations. I'd expected her to make a joke about that; I could admit that I didn't seem like much of a fighter. It was a surprise, then, when she said, "Have you ever heard of Tai Chi?"

"What, like meditation?"

"Sort of," she said with a grin. "I can show you if you like?"

"Why?" I asked, more bluntly than I meant to.

"Help soothe that sourpuss," she said, pinching my cheek.

"Not a good idea."

"Don't worry. I'll be gentle."

"I'm not worrying. I'm being sensible."

I protested for a while longer before eventually allowed myself to be led into the centre of the room. She started off with a few very basics moves, mainly how to stand and moving from foot to foot. I was starting to think this was going to be a total waste of time, but her demonstration continued to get more complicated. Eventually, I was stumbling around like a lame horse, tripping over my own feet and crashing into the furniture. Within minutes, I was flustered and sweating.

"How are you feeling?" she asked.

Surprisingly, I felt much better. I was turning to face her, but unfortunately, hadn't realised how close she was standing. Before I could stop myself, I crashed into her, and we tumbled to the floor, a tangled mass of arms and legs. My elbows struck the floor first, which sent a shock through my arms to my head. I rolled onto my back, rubbing my elbows. Erin was lying on her side just next to me. I was about to apologise when I saw that she was smirking.

"You're right; that wasn't a good idea," she said. It didn't sound unkind, but sympathetic somehow.

"I tried to warn you," I replied.

She shuffled into a sitting position and put a hand to her head, at which point she stopped smiling.

"Are you okay?" I asked, suddenly serious. She nodded, only once, but it was enough to make her wince.

"I think I hit my head," she said as she rubbed her skull. I shuffled over to her side.

"Let me see," I asked. She looked like that was the last thing she wanted me to do. "I'm not going to bite," I said mockingly. Slowly, she lowered her hand and turned her head.

I'd had a little first aid training through work, and so I put my hands on her cheeks and peered into her eyes, checking the response of her pupils. Carefully, I stroked a strand of hair behind her ear so that I could see both of her eyes. But as I picked out the flecks of green in her otherwise blue eyes, felt the warmth of her cheeks and saw the dimples forming as her lips bent into a grin, my pulse quickened. We gazed into one another's eyes, my hands still clutching her face, inches from my own.

"Looks good," I said, a little awkwardly.

"Such a charmer," she said with a grin.

"I mean, I can't see anything wrong," I said, hurriedly dropping my hands.

After we'd finished, she fetched a bottle of liquor from one of the cupboards in the kitchen and poured herself a glass. The tumbler was almost full to the brim. She offered me one, but I declined. She pressed, suggesting it might help my mood. When I told her I didn't drink, she looked briefly embarrassed, but I told her not to worry. I really didn't want to get into that right now. Thankfully, Erin starting cooking not long afterwards.

Whilst she chopped ingredients, I thought about what had just happened. How my pulse had quickened, not as a result of my exertion but when our eyes had met. Inches apart. Close enough that I could smell her shampoo. I remembered her smile and other memories too. Although Danny's death had put her in my crosshairs, there was a time when we'd been quite close. In fact, there might have been a chance we'd-

I shook my head. That was the last thing I should be thinking about. Those thoughts would only complicate matters. By now, the flat was filled with a deliciously spicy aroma, which helped me get back to reality. Once Erin had added everything to a pan, she left it sizzling and picked an album from her extensive collection. I recognised the opening track right away. The album was Abattoir Blues/Lyre of Orpheus by Nick Cave and the Bad Seeds. It was one of my favourites.

"Dad used to call this *lethal poetry*," I said.

"Reminds me of him."

"Shit," she muttered. "I'm so sorry. Do you want me to-"

"No, no. It's a good memory."

In his last few months, there hadn't been many of those. It was nice to have something positive to hang on to. He never watched TV but would spend hours listening to music.

"What happened to him?" she asked, a little awkwardly. "Danny never really talked about it."

Honestly, neither of us really talked about it much. We'd never been particularly good at sharing our feelings and were even worse at discussing bad memories. It seemed like a long time ago, but the wound was still raw.

"Sorry," Erin said, rousing me from my thoughts. "That was- you don't have to-"

"Heart attack," I replied.

I wasn't sure why I told her. The only other person I'd told was Lizzy. Of course, she didn't know the full story, and I certainly wasn't going to tell Erin. But for some reason, I wanted to tell her the abridged version.

"Not long after Mum," I went on. "Broken-hearted. Literally."

"Jesus."

Lizzy had reacted in a very similar way. I'd told Lizzy more of the story, more than I was willing to share with Erin. The holiday. The accident. The press coverage. I felt like it had been scorched into my grey matter. A brand, a permanent reminder. The worst memory. We'd all struggled, but Dad was inconsolable. Childhood sweethearts. 38 years together. I understood why he couldn't carry on. But that was no excuse for what he did. Less than two years after Mum's death, my brother and I had to bury another parent. Technically, we'd only buried one, but I did my best not to think about that.

"Jack, I'm-" Erin said. But words never came. I couldn't blame her. If I were in her position, I wasn't sure what I'd have said.

"It was a long time ago," I replied.

She sighed. Even her breath was full of sympathy. She wanted to help, wanted to say something. But I knew nothing would help. Nothing would change what had happened.

"Time for a top-up," she said, shaking her glass. "Sure you don't-"

"No, I'm fine," I replied quickly. Booze was the last thing I needed.

"Change of tunes too, I think."

Nick Cave's melancholy baritone was replaced by a maudlin Country & Western track, which Erin quickly skipped. The next song was an equally gloomy 80s ballad. I made a joke about feeling much better. Erin cursed the shuffle function, claiming it was working against her. Eventually, a Ska band I didn't recognise came on. Bedouin Soundclash, according to Erin. Although it wasn't necessarily something I'd listen to, it definitely improved my mood. Her dance moves helped too.

Whilst she tended a pan on the hob, Erin coolly steered the conversation to music, and we chatted about some of our favourite bands. I was grateful. It was also grateful for the dances she did whenever the track changed. Only a few hours ago, I'd been murderously angry, but now, I was actually enjoying myself.

The conversation naturally drifted from music to films and books. Erin and I had very similar tastes. We were both particularly fond of anything set in a dystopic future where the protagonist had to fight almost insurmountable odds to survive. Internally, I drew comparisons to my own situation.

We eventually found our way to zombie apocalypse films. Whilst we ate, we each made our case for the greatest of all time. Erin's choice was Anna and The Apocalypse, whilst I'd gone for 28 Days Later. Erin was busy contesting whether mine was a valid choice when a song interrupted her.

"Oh my God!" she said. "Do you remember this?"

The track was familiar, but I didn't know the name, so simply shrugged. Erin's face split into a knowing grin. I thought a little harder. Realisation struck me with the force of an anvil dropping from a rooftop.

"Christ," I groaned.

A party. Danny's birthday, maybe. He never needed an excuse for a gathering. That was the night Erin and I met. By that point in the evening, I was mortally drunk. Back then, I drank with abandon. Perhaps that was why I was so struck by her beauty. Normally, I wouldn't stare at a anyone because I knew how uncomfortable that would make me feel. But when I first saw her, I stared. Gawked, in fact.

"What was the line?" she asked.

The same song was playing when I'd walked over to her. On my brother's advice, I'd quoted the line, thinking I was being charming. Unfortunately, I'd misinterpreted the lyrics. Erin had erupted with laughter when she told me the song was actually about a stalker. Danny also found it highly amusing. Rather than relive the shame of it, I told her I couldn't remember what I'd said.

"That might be the worst first impression ever," I said, putting my face in my hands.

"You turned it around pretty well."

I was a little surprised by that. As I recalled, I'd made more of an arse of myself as the night went on. I suspected she was probably being polite. After reminiscing about a few other events from that evening, I excused myself for the night. I wasn't tired, just didn't want to think about embarrassing myself anymore.

Sleeplessness was all too familiar. But there was something different that night. Every time I closed my eyes, I was transported to the party. Unquestionably, I'd made a fool of myself. And yet, from that moment, Erin and I had spent most of the evening together. Of course, the following morning had brought sobriety and shame. Except for the day of Danny's funeral, we hardly spoke since, and hadn't at all after that until a few days ago. Once again, it seemed I was overthinking, as had always been my habit.

Throughout the night, Erin barely left my thoughts. Just as I managed to get her out of my head, I awoke to find her stretching in the living room. To distract myself – and hide the colour in my cheeks – I asked to use her phone to call Lizzy. It took her a while to answer and, when she did, she was annoyed. Since living with Erin, I'd lost track of the days. It might have been a weekday. Other reasons why she wouldn't want me to call her occurred, but I didn't want to think about those.

"Sorry," I said hurriedly. "Look, I need you to ask around about that report."

Her tone quickly changed.

"I thought it was too dangerous to-"

"I spoke to Frank again," I said, cutting her off.

"What? Why? What if he tells the police?"

"I don't think he will," I said. "No matter how cocky he seemed, he knows I'm on to something. Plus, I think he'd rather deal with me in his own way."

When I told her about the car chase, she cursed me for being foolish enough to meet him. She was, however, quite impressed when I told her how I'd gotten rid of them. I relayed what Frank had told me about DEV-45 and asked Lizzy if she could confirm it. She was more than happy to help, on the condition that I didn't do anything needlessly reckless.

Whilst Erin was at work, I tried my hand at some Tai Chi. Somehow, I didn't enjoy it as much without her, so opted to do a simple workout instead. After that, I returned to stripping the ink from the report that Klas had provided. When that didn't work, I dedicated myself to understanding why Wilson had given me the report.

I had two theories to expand on. The first was that, unfortunately, he'd utterly lost his mind, and had simply recovered a random fragment of information. But the way he'd written it – or rather, inscribed it into the page – led me to think that it was more than a sporadic moment of clarity. He'd also reacted when I said Frank's name. On top of that, there was Frank's admission that he had hurt Kelly and Dina. Surely, that was grounds to suspect he'd also had some involvement in Wilson's condition.

My other theory, then, was that CPT was causing the Itch. Dina had found a problem, which she must have flagged to Wilson and Frank. Realising that they both knew the truth, Frank had eliminated them both. But although these events made sense, and Frank had all but admitted hurting Dina, everything else about that idea was utter nonsense. If CPT was causing the Itch, why were only Dose users affected? Why weren't the people that used products containing CPT also getting the Itch?

More for something to do, I went through one of Erin's kitchen cupboard and arranged the items into those with and without CPT. There were far more that contained the chemical. I was still rummaging through her cupboards when she returned that evening. Hastily, I tried to explain my method, but before I could say more than a few words, she showed me her phone.

"You need to see this," she said.

The urgency in her voice was concerning. I took the phone and read the screen. It wasn't until I'd reread it four or five times that the words finally sunk in. *A Cure for The Itch*.

CHAPTER 13

There was a video on the screen of a public announcement made earlier that day. It was from the Health Secretary, Rupert Prophett.

"For almost four years, scientists have worked tirelessly to produce a cure for the sickness known as the Itch" he began. "Today, it is my immense pleasure and privilege to announce that, following the collaborative effort of half a dozen industry-leading companies, a cure will soon be available. The drug has successfully completed the final phase of human trials, and a full-scale production batch is currently being manufactured by the Manchester-based firm, Rathbury-Holmes. The first samples will be distributed to hospitals in the coming days to allow treatment of the worst cases. There will be an official launch for the cure this weekend at the Manchester Central Convention Centre. Despite the breakthrough, though, I urge everyone to continue avoiding consumption of the recreational drug Dose. The British public has endured so much over recent years, but I'm confident we can now conquer this sickness once and for all."

As soon as he finished speaking, people came rushing towards him, microphones outstretched. But he quickly disappeared from view.

"This is unbelievable," she said.

Now, I understood Frank's cryptic jibe. I also realised I was in serious trouble. My innocence hinged on proving Dose wasn't the cause of the sickness. But that would be almost impossible now that Rathbury-Holmes had cured the Itch.

"What are you going to do?" Erin asked.

I thought, harder than I ever had. The company couldn't possibly have developed a new compound in such a short time – that could take years – so they must have used the original compound from the disastrous trial. But how had the company gotten it through the approval process? Altering the concentration of the active ingredient would reduce effectiveness. They must have changed the formulation, then; added or removed something. There would be a lot of work around proving an additional substance wasn't harmful, so removing something from the current formulation seemed likelier. And if something had been removed, that might have been what caused the original trial to fail. Perhaps it was the true cause of the Itch.

My first thought was calling Lizzy to ask what she knew about the cure. She answered after only a single ring.

"Right now, I know as much as you," she said. "Frank is keeping everything quiet. He's overseen a lot of the work himself. Most of the team has been reassigned. I haven't seen any of the data. I can't even access the reports."

"How can he do that?" I asked.

"He's restricted access to only a handful of senior staff members. He said that *due to the confidential nature of the cure...* blah blah, lip service, bullshit. You're right, though. He's definitely trying to hide something. If I could see the data, I might be able to-"

"No," I said.

"Not this again. I told you I don't-"

"I know you don't need me to look after you. But if Frank's going to these lengths to hide the truth, think of what he'll do if he finds out you've been snooping around."

"He won't if I'm careful."

"Please, don't. Just concentrate on DEV-45. Have you found anything out about it yet?"

She let out a long slow breath, deliberately close to the phone so that I could hear she was annoyed.

"Not much," she said stiffly. "Frank was telling the truth, though. It was CPT. Finance had some expense records that linked to the project."

"Anything unusual?"

"Not as far as I could tell."

"See what else you can find. And please, please, please don't-"

"I won't, I promise," she said resignedly.

Somehow, I had to find out what Frank had changed in the formulation. If I knew that, I could potentially prove what was making people sick. The question was how I would do it.

"What about Berglund?" Erin asked. "Maybe he could find something."

"I've already told you I'm not going to him for help," I replied, struggling to keep my voice level.

"Why not?"

"Because I'd rather make a deal with the Devil than Klas Berglund."

"This isn't just about curing the Itch anymore. We need to prove that Dose isn't-"

"I said no."

"Are you really so stubborn that you'd go to prison

before asking for his help?"

"Why are you hammering this so much? I mean, what, toe-sucking floats your boat, does it?"

I knew that I was out of line, but I didn't care. Even if it came to a life and death situation, I would really have to consider whether Klas' help was worth the hassle; that was how strongly I distrusted him.

"Jesus, Jack. What's your problem?"

"My problem is that I'm terrified of him," I roared. "Alright? Happy now? Klas Berglund thrives on making people feel as miserable as possible and, trust me, you do not want to let him do that to you. The things that I've done – the things that he's made me do – would disgust and appal you."

Erin was shell-shocked into absolute silence. I'd never admitted that to anyone before. In fact, I wasn't even sure I'd known myself. But now that I'd said it, I couldn't deny it was true. Berglund's power was to manipulate people into doing unspeakable things and, truly, it terrified me. I was clutching my bottlecap necklace so tightly that it was cutting into my palm.

"What did you ask him for?" she asked quietly.

I'd never told anyone about the deals I'd made with Berglund. But if it would convince her of his character, Erin needed to know.

"I was low. Really low. So low, I wasn't sure there was a way back up for me" I explained. I didn't need to give her details. She already knew why I'd been in such a state. "I tried a lot of different remedies. Grief counselling. Support groups. Medication. Nothing worked. After the drugs, I turned to drink. But that only made things worse. Booze just seemed to delay my anger. Suppressed it until I was sober again.

Because I wasn't dealing with it, it mounted. I started getting in trouble at work. More stress, more drink. Then, one night, I just- I went for it. I drank, and I drank, and I drank. I was pretty sure there was only one thing that would have stopped me that night."

"Jesus, Jack. I had no idea" she stammered. "What happened?"

"The first bar cut me off, so I headed to the next. When they did the same, I went to a third, and a fourth, and a fifth. By that point, I was so soused that most places would have turned me away. So, I lowered my standards. Went to the roughest hole I could find. Even they wouldn't serve me, though. The barman asked me to leave. I refused, so he tried to remove me. I don't remember much after that. I woke up the following morning in- well, I wasn't in a good way. I was covered in dried blood. My nose felt like it was broken. Couldn't see through one of my eyes. A couple of teeth were missing. My knuckles were a mess. But do you know what? I felt incredible. For the first time in weeks, I didn't feel angry or sad or desperate or alone. I just felt like I was back to normal."

"Jack, that's- why did you-"

"I know," I said. "I didn't care, though. I'm so ashamed now, but it seemed like the only way at the time. So, I went looking for it. Picked the nastiest dives I could. I'm not a bully. I didn't pick fights to win. I wanted to get beaten. But it's surprisingly difficult to get into a fight at a bar. Most people are quick to anger but avoid action. After a while, I started to dip again. That's when I met Michael. He told me about Klas. I didn't believe him at first but, eventually, I couldn't stand it any longer."

"What did you do?"

"I went to his gallery. The first time, his goons just tossed me out. He said I was *beyond help*. I didn't care what happened to me, so there was no joy in it for him. But I kept coming back. Every night. At first, they just dragged me out. After a while, they got a little rougher. Before long, though, they were beating me senseless. I'd wake up alongside the tracks, barely able to walk. But each night, I went back. Sometimes, I managed to take one or two of them down, but it always ended the same way. I'm not a fighter, so I never stood a chance against them. It didn't matter, though. As long as I got a fight out of it, I kept going."

"What about work? Didn't they say something?"

"If people noticed, they didn't say. I think most were too concerned with the search for a cure to worry about a few bruises."

"Why did you stop?"

"The trial," I said, clutching my necklace. "When I realised Dose might not be making people sick, I knew I had to do something about it. Klas wasn't happy. He's been trying to get me back under his thrall ever since."

"Jack, I- I'm so sorry," she said, a little awkwardly. "We'll find another way."

"What if we can't?" I said.

It surprised me. I'd only told Erin that story to convince her we didn't need his help. And yet, when I thought about it, I wasn't sure there was any other way. Klas Berglund specialised in helping desperate people. At that moment, I was pretty desperate.

"We will," she said.

"No, we won't," I replied. Before she could argue, I held out my hand and asked for her phone.

Michael answered after only a single ring. Although he acted as though he had no idea who was calling, I was almost certain he would have saved Erin's number after the last time I'd called.

"It's me," I said irritably.

"Surprised to hear from you so soon," he said.

"I need to see him," I said.

"Unfortunately, Mr Berglund is a very busy man."

"I'm not playing your games," I said, my voice rising. "When can I see him?"

"Not for a while, I'm afraid."

"When?" I demanded.

"It will be a few weeks, at least. But there might be a way I can persuade him to see you sooner."

I was worried about this. If Klas was seeing me as a favour, it meant that I was on the back foot before I'd walked in the door; not a position I wanted to be in. But with time against me, I had no choice.

"How?" I asked warily.

"Bring your friend," he purred.

I hadn't expected that. Why on Earth did Klas want to see Erin? He was incapable of human feelings, so surely wasn't attracted to her. Did he simply want to see how far he could push her? I imagined he would enjoy testing Erin's resolve.

"Not a chance," I snarled.

"Then, we shall see you when we can," he said.

I thought, long and hard, wondering what game Klas was playing. In the end, though, I realised it didn't matter. If I wanted to see him, Erin would have to come.

"Fine," I said bitterly.

Erin was surprised to hear that I hadn't been planning to take her. I decided not to comment, focussing instead on making sure she knew not to agree to anything he offered without thinking about the consequences. I felt awkward doing it, as if I were lecturing her. But it had to be done.

On the day we were due to meet him, my head was throbbing again, not as severely as it had been recently, but enough that I was struggling to concentrate. I'd asked Erin for some painkillers, but they weren't really helping.

As we drove towards the train station, I wondered how many people had been affected by the Itch. So many had already lost their lives to the sickness, and hundreds of thousands were in a critical condition. How many more were going to die until the truth came out?

Once again, Michael was waiting for us outside the ticket office. But this time, he was flanked by two other gigantic guards. The three of them escorted us to the container in silence. They paid particular attention to Erin's buttocks and chest when they searched her. And then, we headed into Klas's club.

There were fewer people than the last time we'd visited, which felt ominous. It almost seemed like he wanted fewer witnesses. Inside his sanctum, Berglund was draped over a beanbag chair, his head flopping limply on his shoulders. At the sight of us, though, he sat bolt upright. Once his eyes had focussed, they fixed on Erin.

"How nice to see you again," he purred.

pg. 173

"Shame I can't say the same for you," she retorted, locking eyes with him. Although it wasn't a wise move, I felt a begrudging respect for her.

"So hostile," he muttered, before adding something in what I guessed was his mother tongue. The guards around the room cackled with laughter.

"You're not just wasting our time, but your time, too," she replied coolly. Worryingly, his eyes narrowed. I'd only ever known Klas exhibit mild disinterest. His current expression registered as anger. That was the last thing I needed.

"Will you help or not?" I asked, stepping in before Erin could say anything else.

"What do you require?" he said in a low and dangerous voice.

"I need to know what's in the cure."

"Is there an Itch that you cannot scratch?" he replied, prompting more moronic laughter.

"Can you do it?" I said.

"I am insulted that you even need to ask," he replied, pouting.

"What do you want for it?"

At a click of Klas' fingers, a queue of men trooped into the room, each carrying an ornate vase. They arranged the vases in a ring on a circular table. Berglund went to stand beside it, slowly stroking his belly button. He put his free hand inside one of the vases. When he withdrew it, the tips of his fingers were wet. Even a vase full of water was enough to make me shudder. A moment later, another guard stepped forward, carrying a large glass bowl with a fish in it. Its fanlike barbs and colourful stripes were instantly recognisable.

"The lionfish is exceedingly deadly," Berglund purred. "If treated, its venom may not prove to be fatal. But without medical attention... well, I am sure I do not need to spell that out for you. You will be familiar with the premise of this game, but perhaps not the execution. The better-known version is too inelegant for my tastes. There is nothing more disappointing than a bullet to the head; I find it ends things a little prematurely. Instead, you will take turns choosing vases from the table. After each selection, you will reach inside. If you refuse to reach inside, you will forfeit. I am sure I do not need to explain how the winner is decided. Any questions?"

Upon reflection, a gun and a bullet were preferable to poisoning. My brains would be on the wall before I knew I'd lost. This way, I would have to wait for the venom to kill me, knowing all the while that there was nothing that I could do to stop it.

I looked at the table, watching a guard add the lionfish to one of the vases. Another guard reached out and spun the tabletop. Desperately, I tried to track the vase, but it moved too fast. The spinning top slowed, completing a few more turns before stopping. My eyes darted from vase to vase, trying – somehow – to work out how I was going to avoid a grisly death. But it was no use. With no easy end in sight, I stepped forward.

"I don't suppose you'll be playing?" I asked Klas. Of course, he shook his head.

I wanted to broker a better position for myself but had no idea how. Changing the number of vases wouldn't necessarily help. It seemed unlikely that he'd be willing to administer medical treatment.

"Who's first?" I asked, wondering if perhaps I could affect the outcome by the order we chose. He grinned – the oiliest grin I've ever seen. What he said, chilled me to my core.

"You will not be playing."

As if in slow-motion, I spun to look at Erin. Although her expression was unfazed, her fists were balled at her sides. She was already stepping forward when I yelled, "No."

"What are you doing?" she hissed.

"Don't do this," I said.

"What choice do we have?" she replied sharply. "We have to know what they've done to make the cure work."

"You don't understand. It's-"

"I'll be fine," she snarled. But I knew better.

"If you please," Berglund said, gesturing towards the table.

Klas snapped his fingers so loudly it sounded like breaking wood. A guard stepped forward, slid off his jacket and rolled up his sleeve. He plunged his arm into a vase, so quickly that water spilt over the side. When he removed his arm, he sneered at Erin. Before I knew it, Erin was reaching for one of the vases. She must have known there was a strong possibility she would be killed. And yet, she did so without hesitation. First, her hand sank. And then, her wrist. And then, her elbow. Very slowly, she withdrew her hand, grinning smugly.

"Very good," he said. Did I imagine the hint of admiration in his voice?

After the chosen vases were removed, the guard took his next turn. He chose the nearest vase. His face remained passive throughout. He was safe. And with that, Erin's turn came again. This time, she walked a few steps around the table, thinking. But once she'd chosen, she decisively plunged her hand in. She was safe.

Every turn felt like a countdown. Too soon, there were only four vases left. Erin watched her opponent. For the first time, he seemed reluctant. That impression was quickly dispelled, though, when he chose a vase. To my horror, he withdrew his hand, unscathed. Naturally, Erin looked dejected. What she didn't realise, though, was that the game wasn't over.

"The game is not finished," Berglund said smoothly. "You must choose."

"Choose what? Death?" she scoffed.

"A winner must be decided," he explained. "Currently, there are two players. There can be only one winner."

With horror, she realised what Klas was saying. Instantly, she backed away from the table. For the first time since I'd met her, she looked afraid.

"Forfeit. How disappointing," Berglund muttered.

Two guards grabbed her arms. They were much bigger than she was, and I thought they'd have no trouble restraining her. They'd barely touched her when she sprang into action. In less than the time it took to blink, she'd slipped free. Then, she swung a booted foot at one of them. He fell to the ground, clutching his testicles. She was about to attack the other when he produced a pistol.

"Stop," I yelled. Everyone turned to look at me.

"We're a little busy at the moment," Berglund said with a chuckle. "You'll have to wait for your turn."

"Sudden death," I said. "Me versus Michael."

Across the room, Michael growled at me, but I kept my eyes on Klas. He looked at me for a long time, sizing me up. I held my nerve until he started laughing.

"You were right," he said, turning to Michael. "We have found something that Jack Bright cares about. I never thought it would happen."

At first, I wasn't sure what he meant. When I realised, though, my eyes shot to Erin. That was why he'd wanted her to come; he knew that he could use her against me. Even I hadn't realised I felt that way about her until now. But he had a talent for finding people's weaknesses.

I couldn't let him hurt Erin. But I also couldn't let him think that I cared about her. If I did, it would only encourage him to torture her so that he could watch me suffer. Hastily, I considered my options. There was only one thing I could do.

"It's got nothing to do with her," I said, injecting as much disregard into my words as I could. "I need that report. She's not going to get it for me, so I'm making a new deal."

I kept my eyes on Klas so that I couldn't see Erin's face. I'm sure her reaction would have been enough to break my deception.

"Forgive me if I am unconvinced," Klas purred.

"I'll be on my way, then," I said, shrugging. To make myself appear even more nonchalant, I paused before continuing. "Or, you could let me take this into my own hands? I can't imagine how desperate a man gets when he's been poisoned."

Although he didn't say anything for a long time, I

knew it had worked. His finger was tracing the edge of his bellybutton, which was a sure sign he was considering my proposal. When his face split into a wide grin, I wasn't surprised.

"Game on," Berglund trilled.

After Klas clicked his fingers, guards stepped forward and removed all but two of the vases, before one of them spun the tabletop. Once it came to a stop, Michael stepped forward, smiling arrogantly. The guards released Erin. As I stepped towards the table, I couldn't help glancing in her direction. Her eyes were blazing with hatred. I did my best to ignore her.

"Ready?" Michael asked.

"Let's get this over with," I said, sounding more resigned than determined.

Very slowly, I reached out my hand. Michael did the same. We waited until Berglund started counting down. My hand vanished into the vase almost as soon as he reached zero. All the while, I kept my eyes on Michael, praying that I had chosen the right one. And then, I saw something flicker across his face. Slowly, I swirled my hand in the water, realising that there was nothing in there. Meanwhile, Michael's eyes widened. A spasm of fear raced across his face. An almighty howl escaped his mouth as he wrenched his hand from the vase, knocking it off the table. Water spilt across the floor, pooling around my feet, the colourful lionfish flopping limply at the centre of the puddle. With a start, I realised that I had won.

Relief swept over me. Berglund shot Michael a contemptuous look as he thrashed around in the pool of water that had formed between us. Quickly, two other guards picked him up and dragged him out of the room. By that point, he was screaming. I'd never liked Michael, but the mixture of pain and fear in his voice was almost unbearable. When I could no longer hear him, I found myself wondering if he'd moved out of earshot or if something else had happened.

I kept my eye on Berglund as he stood, perfectly still, staring at the spot where Michael had been lying.

"Enjoy your victory," Berglund purred. Once again, I felt as though there was something like respect in his voice. Before I could say anything, two guards grabbed our arms and frogmarched us towards the exit.

It wasn't until they'd escorted us back onto the train track that the guards let us go, at which point the feeling of success finally sank in. Before I knew what was happening, Erin shoved me in the back.

"You miserable little bastard," she snapped.

"Erin, I couldn't-"

"You were really going to leave me there, weren't you?"

"Of course, not."

"What if he'd refused your offer? What then?"

"I couldn't let him know how I feel about you," I yelled, stunning her into silence. "If he'd known that, he'd have tortured you just to get to me."

"What do you mean?"

"I didn't do it because I don't care. I did it because I do."

We glared at one another. Erin opened her mouth to say something, several times, but no words came. I was thinking of something to say when she rushed towards me. And then, she kissed me. At first, I was too stunned to respond. Once my brain caught up, though, I pulled her closer. The kiss was passionate, which confirmed she felt the same as I did. We fell to the tracks, arms tangled around each other. The gravel dug into my back, but I didn't care. My fingers traced up her back, running through her hair, whilst her hands moved down my torso towards my waist. Before long, she reached for my belt buckle. Hastily, I reached for hers.

I woke up in Erin's bed. There was something soothing about the room. It was almost like a temple. Incense was burning. Windchimes were twinkling in the breeze from the open window. From the clock on her bedside table, I gleaned it was just after nine in the morning. Neither of us had slept much, but Erin was already up.

I found Erin practising Tai Chi in the living room. We smiled at one another, which was pleasing. When she asked if I wanted to join, I politely declined. My head was still buzzing angrily, but I told her that I was feeling a little tired.

"Serves you right for keeping me up all night," she said with a smirk.

"Doesn't seem to have done you any harm," I replied, a little smugly.

"Maybe it's an age thing," she said, shrugging.

"What's that, dearie?" I replied, cupping a hand to my ear. She laughed, choking into her glass.

During breakfast, she made numerous jokes about the age gap between us. Although she was only a few years younger than I, she delighted in making it seem like we were from different generations, asking what it was like living in a house before electricity and running water. I made a joke about getting up early to gather firewood and foraging for berries, which made her laugh.

"Why didn't you say anything?" she asked. In response to my confused expression, she nodded towards her bedroom. Inexplicably, I blushed.

"We weren't really on speaking terms, were we?" was all I could think to say in reply.

"Before that, then. No shortage of chances, was there?"

She sounded curious. I felt my cheeks darken. It was a fair point. Whenever I saw Danny, Erin was usually there. The answer, though, was obvious.

"I mean, I didn't exactly make a good first impression, did I?"

As soon as I said it, I wished I hadn't. Erin laughed. I thought she must have been remembering how ridiculous I was. But then, surprisingly, she smiled.

"Don't remember speaking to many other people that night," she said.

Now, when I thought back, I recalled the evening very differently. We'd been inseparable. She'd laughed at my terrible jokes. And even when I'd taken my embarrassment to humiliating new heights, she'd hung around. Perhaps, as was so often the case, I'd overthought my performance. Was it possible she'd felt the same way about me, despite all my geeky quirks and eccentricities?

Something about my expression made Erin laugh. She was still laughing when she went to collect the post. But she looked serious when she returned with an envelope. Eagerly, I tore it open. I wasn't sure what I'd expected, but it certainly wasn't what fell out.

"What's wrong?" she demanded.

Wordlessly, I handed her a small cardboard box, which had been flattened to fit in the envelope. It bore the Rathbury-Holmes logo, along with an exceedingly long and difficult to pronounce chemical name. I knew it was the cure. Carefully, someone had cut a small window from the box, removing the ingredients from the packaging. There was also a handwritten note, as well as a rectangular piece of paper that looked like a ticket.

"*If you want to know, you will have to ask. K,*" it said in Klas' sloping script.

"What does that mean?" she asked as she read the note.

"He's trying to make us go to the launch of the cure," I said, waving the rectangular invitation.

For days, I used Erin's laptop to search for information about the cure. I thought perhaps the company might have posted information about the formulation, maybe even alluded to the changes they'd made after the earlier tragedy. But with the steps that Frank had taken to keep the cure secret, I knew it was a lost cause.

Spending every waking moment staring at a screen was starting to take its toll. I'd been having headaches for a while now, and they'd become so severe I'd had to stop what I was doing and lie down for an hour or two. Despite my discomfort, I persevered. By Friday evening, though, I'd found nothing.

I called Lizzy every other day to ask for updates.

Unfortunately, she hadn't managed to find anything else about DEV-45. She suggested raising the fact that the report and associated data were missing with management – such a breach in data integrity was severe and would warrant a thorough investigation – but I talked her out of it.

"Like I said, Frank's shown that he's willing to hurt people to hide the truth," I said. "Besides, we don't know who else we can trust at the company. He might not be working alone."

Frank was notoriously challenging to work with because of his temper and stubbornness, but he might have had help orchestrating such an elaborate coverup. In the end, she agreed to keep looking for information about DEV-45.

I was looking through Dina's phone, checking for other messages related to DEV-45, when I came across the email, she'd sent to Frank. I was staring at the diagram she'd attached when an idea struck me. Luckily, Erin was home, so I was able to call Lizzy right away.

"Still no update," she said, a little wearily.

"It's not about that. Well, not exactly," I said uncertainly. "Can you send me what you've found about the project so far?"

"I can. Not sure it'll do much good, though."

She sent an email with some attachments. Most were scans of analytical worksheets, along with some charts, tables, and information about chyrolic compounds. Firstly, I read the excerpt. If nothing else, my knowledge of chyrols was lacking, and I suspected I would probably need to study up before checking the raw data.

It was clear from the charts and tables that the results were exhibiting an upward trend, increasing over time. Frustratingly, though, none of it had any headers to indicate what was increasing. I consulted the worksheets to try to figure it out. I wasn't even sure if they were linked but had nothing else to check the tables against. The worksheets were meticulously detailed, which was odd when comparing them to the poorly written tables. Everything that had been used in the analyses was carefully catalogued. None of it seemed significant until I saw the name of the analyst that had performed the analyses. It was Dina.

Hastily, I scanned through the rest of the pages of each attachment until I found a hand-drawn diagram of a series of chemical reactions. I recognised part of it from the email Dina had sent to Frank. Immediately, I knew I'd had a breakthrough.

CHAPTER 14

I called Lizzy right away to explain my discovery. She listened without comment. Once I'd finished, I asked her if she could do some experiments to prove it. Nobody could argue with data; not even someone as devious as Frank.

"Oh, I see how it is," she said jokily. "Before, it was all *danger this* and *peril that*, but now you want somebody to do your grunt work, you can't get me in the lion's den fast enough."

"If I'm right, it won't matter who knows you've been working on it," I said, grinning. If I was right, Frank was in serious trouble.

"Are you going to tell me what's going on?" Erin asked, a little impatiently.

"Dina was working on a project to develop something called CPT," I explained. "It's a preservative that's used in a lot of different products."

To demonstrate, I showed Erin the labels on some products in her kitchen, all of which contained CPT.

"But she found a problem," I continued. "Look at this."

I showed Erin the raw data that Lizzy had sent, which she confessed was nonsense to her. I pointed to the part of the diagram that Dina had sent to Frank, indicating two chemical structures.

"That's a chyrol group," pointing to the first structure. "And that," pointing to the second. "is CPT. Dina was suggesting that chyrols react with CPT."

"What does that mean, then?"

"I think these data tables are charting the formation of a specific CPT by-product. It's increasing over time. Now, it's normal for that to happen but, usually, it takes months, maybe years for by-products to reach harmful levels. In this case, the scale is in days."

"So, you think CPT is degraded by these chyrols?" she asked, to which I nodded. "And it's happening very quickly. What does that have to do with the Itch?"

Next, I showed her a Wikipedia article about Dose. She seemed sceptical at first, but I persevered.

"The chemical name for Dose is L-chyrolic acid," I said triumphantly. "The chyrol groups in Dose's structure are breaking down CPT. That's why the Itch only affects Dose users. CPT is so well-distributed that it's only a matter of time before a Dose user comes into contact with it."

"But why is the CPT by-product making people sick?"

"This here," I said, indicating part of Dina's diagram. "Under the right conditions, it would break down into two smaller chemicals. The first is an alcohol, completely harmless. But the second is a highly reactive acid."

"What about users that don't experience symptoms?" she challenged. It was a fair question.

"Maybe they don't use products containing CPT," I replied hurriedly. "If those products were tested on animals or aren't suitable for vegetarians, some people would naturally avoid them. Hell, it could just be brand loyalty."

"But if Dose isn't the cause, why does the cure

work?"

"The active compound in the cure binds Dose, which prevents it from breaking CPT down," I explained.

"Why didn't the original cure work, then?"

"Because we added CPT to it," I said.

CPT was used in almost all Rathbury-Holmes' products. That explained what happened in the original trial; the Dose in their blood reacted with CPT in the cure. In most cases, subjects will have had too little Dose in their blood to trigger symptoms.

I also remembered something about the seven victims. The flimsy link between them was that they all had underlying health problems. Although I couldn't remember them all, I remembered Kelly, Dylan Keeling's girlfriend, telling me that he'd had cancer. I knew for a fact that some cancer treatments contained CPT.

"But that still sounds like Dose is causing the Itch."

"No, the CPT by-product is the cause," I said. "That's why I've asked for Lizzy's help. CPT is broken down by chyrols. Dose contains chyrols, but so do other products. If Lizzy can prove that other chyrolic compounds break down CPT and that the resulting by-product is acidic, we can prove that Dose isn't the cause of the Itch."

"So, Dose is like a trigger?" she said, to which I nodded.

Any number of products could be triggering the Itch. Chyrol groups were common in a lot of pharmaceutical products. Hormone therapy, steroids, and anti-anxiety medication all contained chyrolic compounds. There was a chance Itch sufferers might have been using a combination of chyrol-containing products to trigger their symptoms.

"But if other products contain chyrols, why don't they trigger the Itch?" Erin asked.

"It could be a lot of different reasons. The concentration of chyrolic compounds might be less than Dose. Dose might be used more often. Dose users would probably take increasing amounts over time. Dose is very stable, too, so it stays in the blood for a long time. Maybe there's a threshold for triggering the Itch."

"But if CPT is so dangerous, how did it get approved for use?"

"Because Dina was the only person who knew about the interaction with chyrolic compounds. I'm guessing her work was never officially published. And then when she told Frank…"

I didn't need to finish that thought. Erin knew what I was going to say. Frank had eliminated Dina. And Wilson, too. He'd also removed all but a few fragments of information relating to the project. After cursing softly under her breath, Erin said the obvious.

"We need to tell people."

"It won't work," I said gravely. "People have been waiting for the cure for so long. How do you think they'll react if we tell them they've been lied to about the cause of the Itch? Plus, CPT is in almost everything. Imagine the panic if we tell the nation that CPT might give them the Itch?"

"What about the police? You could tell them about the emails Frank ignored?"

"It's my word against his," I said. "Plus, I'm still a

wanted criminal."

"What are we going to do then?"

"We need proof. Lizzy's experiments will prove chyrols break down CPT and that the by-product is hazardous."

"This is it," she said, smiling proudly. "You've done it."

I was about to tell her that I couldn't take all the credit when she rushed towards me. When her lips pressed against mine, I was all too willing to take her praise.

We spent most of the day in bed together. That evening, Erin was going to protest the ban. I joked that – in a few days – she probably wouldn't need to do that anymore, but she went anyway.

"That's no reason to get complacent," she chided. "Besides, I think I know why you want me to miss it."

"Can't blame me for trying," I said.

I spent perhaps another hour lounging in Erin's bed before hunger drove me to the kitchen. Once I'd eaten, I did a quick workout and then had a shower. The water felt good. It was as if the icy waves were washing away all the stress and anger of the last few months. I'd not been this happy in a long time. Finally, I was going to get proof that Frank had lied to everyone. Of course, that wasn't the only reason for my good mood.

It was hard to believe that, only a few weeks ago, Erin and I couldn't stand one another. I could admit now, though, that I had judged her much too harshly. What I'd initially perceived as stubbornness were strong principles. Despite everything that we were told about Dose, Erin had refused to believe it. She knew in her heart that it couldn't possibly be true and had stuck by her cause. Part of me wished I'd asked for her help sooner.

In the absence of anything else to use, I washed my hair with Erin's shampoo. It smelled of vanilla, which was deeply satisfying because it reminded me of her. I was using the lather to clean my face when I felt something pinching my cheek. Confused, I scraped the bubbles away, but the sensation persisted. It was almost like the tingling sensation that occurred when moving from a cold to a hot environment. At first, it was confined to my cheek but soon spread to my neck, down my chest and back. And then, it wasn't just a mild irritation but searing pain.

I staggered out of the shower but, half-blind from the suds, I crashed to the tiles. It felt as though someone was pouring boiling water over my skin, the rivulets leaving stinging trails on my flesh. It took seconds to realise what was happening to me. But that didn't make any sense. I hadn't taken anything containing-

Bowker. He and his apes had attacked me in the flat. Even if it was only for a few seconds, I'd taken a drag of Dose. Perhaps that was all it took to trigger a reaction. If I'd been able to check the label of Erin's shampoo, I was sure I'd have seen CPT in the ingredients.

The pain was like nothing I'd ever felt. It came in waves, pulsing from my head to the rest of my body. Now that I had scrubbed the soap from my eyes and could see again, it was a surprise to see that there were no marks on my skin. It felt like I was being sliced to ribbons. Although I'd rubbed most of it off, there was still some foam on my skin. Clumsily, I fell back into the bath, letting the water wash away the last of the shampoo. But after a minute or so, the pain hadn't subsided. There must have been traces of CPT on my body. Perhaps it was trapped within my skin.

It was almost impossible to think. Soaking, I stumbled to the kitchen, collapsing to my knees in front of the cupboard under the sink. I needed something to strip the oils from my skin. The obvious choice was soap, but that would surely contain CPT. Dishwashing liquid posed the same problem. Carelessly, I tore through the cupboard. Bleach might work, but I wasn't entirely sure it was a good idea to pour that over my head. Then, I found a bottle of paint thinner. By now, the pain was so intense that I didn't consider what I was doing. Standing over the sink, I emptied the contents of the bottle over my head, scrubbing the liquid over my face and neck. To my relief, the pain ebbed slightly.

I'm not sure how long I spent there, dripping, and stinking of solvent, but it wasn't until the pain had lessened to nothing more than a dull sting that I went to the bathroom to wash the spirit off. I made sure to rinse all the shampoo suds from the bath before stepping in. Too afraid to use any of Erin's shower products to clean myself, I simply sat under the icy torrent. After almost half an hour, the smell had lessened slightly, so I got out. Even the featherlight touch of Erin's cotton towels was enough to make me wince. Her fabric conditioner probably contained CPT.

Dried and dressed, I went to clean the mess I'd left in the kitchen. So much time had passed that the stench of spirit had spread through the entire flat, so I opened the windows to help air it out. Then, exhausted, I collapsed on one of the beanbags in the living room. Although I was no longer in pain, the skin on my face and neck was tingling. To keep my mind off it, I turned the TV on.

I was still sitting there when Erin got home. Within seconds, she asked me why the flat smelt of solvent. I made up a story about spilling something in the kitchen, which she believed. I knew that I should have told her the truth – if nothing else, it was wise to let her know in case it happened again – but couldn't bring myself to do it. Although she didn't seem like the type to worry, I thought she might make an exception for this. Besides, all she could do to help was call an ambulance if I had another attack. And that would lead to more problems.

The smell of spices from the kitchen was enough to mask the solvent stink. Whilst Erin cooked, I stayed in the living room, hardly moving. Now that my earlier terror had passed, I felt exhausted, to the point that I wasn't sure I could move. Erin asked if I was alright. I told her I was tired.

"Are you sure you're okay?" she asked as I shuffled to the kitchen counter to eat.

"Yeah, I'm fine," I said, forcing a smile.

"Early night tonight, then?" she replied, pouting.

"Well, I mean, I'm not that tired," I said. In all seriousness, though, I was probably too tired for that.

Once we'd eaten, Erin cleared the kitchen, and I returned to the beanbag, hoping to snatch a few minutes rest. Erin's phone rang from the kitchen. Each tone seemed oppressively loud. I recalled the symptoms of the Itch. Mood swings. Lethargy. Headaches.

"Jack," Erin said, a little impatiently. She must have called me more than once. "It's Lizzy."

Groggily, I sat up and made my way to the kitchen. I had no doubts that Lizzy was the best analyst in our team but, even by her standards, I was surprised she'd managed to finish her experiments so quickly.

"Think this might be a new record," I said when I answered. As soon as I heard her voice, though, I knew something wasn't right.

"Jack, listen," she said. "Whatever you do, don't-"

Her voice was cut off. I said her name, once, twice, before shouting it. And then, a voice came over the line that I didn't recognise.

"You shouldn't have involved her," he said calmly.

"Who is this?"

"I think you should be more interested in your friend's wellbeing, rather than my name."

I cursed. I yelled. I fought the urge to throw Erin's phone across the room. After a deep breath, I regained enough composure to speak.

"Look, she doesn't know anything," I said. "Just let her go. You don't have to-"

"It's my job. So, yes, I do."

"What do you want?"

"I'll let you work that out for yourself."

The line went dead before I could say anything else. I cursed, so loudly that my throat ached. After that, I paced back and forth, thinking desperately. Erin was saying something, but her words weren't registering. All my brainpower was dedicated to helping Lizzy. How could I have let this happen to her? Why had I involved her? From the moment of my arrest, I'd known Frank was willing to do whatever was necessary to bury the truth. And now, he'd obviously hired someone to take care of Lizzy. Before I knew it, I was marching towards the front door.

"Wait, Jack, what are you doing?" Erin said, scrambling to stop me.

"I'm going to kill him," I snarled.

"Just think for a second."

"Lizzy doesn't have a second."

"You don't know that."

"So, what? I just wait for them to finish her off. Like Dina. And Wilson. And Kelly."

"I know you're upset."

"I'm not upset. I'm fucking furious."

"Yeah, and I get that," she snapped. "But what the Hell is the point in getting yourself arrested? Or worse? How is that going to help anyone?"

I knew she had a point. And yet, it took a lot for me to admit that. When I finally calmed down, I turned my mind to how I could help Lizzy.

"We need proof that CPT is no longer in the cure," I said.

"How are we going to get it?" she asked. As far as I was concerned, there was only one option.

"The launch."

"What?" she asked, chuckling with disbelief.

"It's the only way."

"You're joking, right? Do you have any idea how risky that is? And anyway, how is that going to help?"

"The packaging. If they've removed CPT, it won't be listed," I said. Klas had given me the idea by taunting me with the doctored packaging.

"That's your plan; to check the ingredients on the label?"

"What's the alternative?" I challenged. "Go to the police without any evidence and hope I'm right? Break-in to Rathbury-Holmes and steal the report for the cure? Or attend an event that I've been invited to?"

"An event hosted by your former employer," she countered. "Somebody is bound to recognise you. Why not just wait for the cure to become available to the public?"

"I have to help her," I snarled. "It's my fault she's in this mess. I can't let anything happen to her. Besides, what about people taking medicines containing chyrolic compounds? What if they start getting sick?"

Without realising, I'd grabbed my necklace. I already thought of my next argument and had it chambered and ready to fire, but I didn't need it.

"No, *I* have to do this," she said.

She pointed out that the police weren't looking for her. All she'd need to do was attend the launch and snatch a box of the cure before she left.

"Erin, this isn't- it's not-"

"I swear, if you tell me it's dangerous, I'll punch you square in your tender parts," she said, raising her fist. "How many times do I need to tell you that I can

pg. 196

look after myself?"

If anything happened to Erin, the two most important people in my life would be in serious trouble. And there would be nothing I could do to help them. After a lot of careful deliberation, though, I had to agree it was the smartest option. And yet, I didn't feel any less anxious about it.

Waiting for the launch was agony for two reasons. On the one hand, I was worried about Lizzy. On the other, my skin was constantly sore. I had to take care whenever using products to avoid anything that might contain CPT, which wasn't easy. More than once, I felt a sting when I washed my hands or brushed against something. Erin noticed, but I simply said I was worried about Lizzy. Whether she was convinced, I wasn't sure.

The last few nights, I'd slept in Erin's bed. I should've been over the moon about that but, unfortunately, the sheets made my skin tingle. Perhaps it was the fabric conditioner she used. Every night, I lay awake, eyes fixed on the ceiling and hands knotted in the duvet to stop myself scratching. One night, she woke up to find me sitting on the edge of the bed. I simply told her I couldn't sleep. She wrapped an arm around my shoulders to reassure me. Her skin felt like a hot iron against mine, but I endured.

On the day of the launch, Erin dressed in formal evening wear. She was wearing a stylish, knee-length dress with black and white stripes.

"What's wrong?" she asked as she finished getting ready.

I was lying on a beanbag, fighting the urge to scratch, and hadn't realised she was standing beside me. As I sat forward, my skin felt as if it was tearing. Hopefully, it didn't show on my face.

"Nothing," I said.

"Then, can you stop digging your nails into my beanbag?" she said, nodding at my hands. Sure enough, I'd sunk my fingertips deep into the material. From the lightness of her tone, I guessed she hadn't worked out the reason why I was doing it.

"I'm just worried," I said hurriedly. Thankfully, she was convinced by my ruse.

"I'm going to be fine," she said, before punching me in the arm.

"What was that for?"

"I told you to stop worrying about me," she said, grinning. "And be thankful it wasn't somewhere more sensitive."

She called a taxi and then headed downstairs to wait for it. I'd offered to drive her, but she'd declined, saying it wasn't worth the risk. It was probably for the best because I wasn't in any state to drive. Once she'd left, I forced myself to the kitchen counter, where I sat with her laptop. I loaded Rathbury-Holmes' website, which was streaming a live feed from the launch.

At seven o'clock, the Health Secretary, Rupert Prophett, appeared on the screen. He was standing next to a podium with a microphone on it. A moment later, he bade everyone welcome. Once the last ripples of conversation had dissipated, he continued speaking.

"I've never been fond of black-tie dinners. For a

man of my shape, a tuxedo is just an expensive penguin costume. My wife assures me I'm mistaken but… well, exhibit A."

As he stepped out from behind the podium, I had to admit he really did look like a penguin. The ripples of laughter that spread through the audience confirmed I wasn't alone in my thinking.

"I should think after 30 years together, you'd know when I'm fibbing," yelled a woman near the front, which triggered another wave of laughter.

"I'll never learn," Prophett mused, chuckling to himself for a moment. "My ridiculous appearance aside, I was more than happy to attend this evening. I'm sure everyone here can agree that the past few years have been some of the most difficult in recent memory. The people of our great nation have endured a terrible and seemingly unending ordeal. But it is because of the determination of those people that we have managed to overcome this adversity. And it is for those people I would like us all to raise a glass. Their unyielding spirit has kept our country going throughout this trying time and, without it, I'm sure we would not have succeeded in creating a cure for the sickness that has ravaged this nation."

"Cheers!" a few people cried as they raised their glasses.

"Well, I feel that I've already taken more than my share of the spotlight, so will hand over to a man more deserving. In a former life, I had the pleasure of calling him my colleague. Even then, I knew he was going to make a significant impact on the pharmaceutical industry. He is – and has been for many years now – my close friend. Ladies and gentlemen, please join me in welcoming Frank Badder to the stage."

I hadn't expected to see him. At the mention of my former boss's name, my temper rose. People had died because he had ignored warnings about CPT. And now, he was going to take credit for curing the Itch.

As soon as Frank got to his feet, he was greeted by tumultuous applause. By the time he'd made it to the stage, the audience was on their feet. A few people hooted and cheered, which was surprising at such a formal event. After shaking Frank's hand, Prophett turned and subtly applied something to his hands. I suspected it was probably a hand sanitiser. It was common knowledge that Prophett was a clean freak. Political cartoonists had exploited that in their works when Prophett had first taken office. Standing beside the podium, Frank beamed pompously, relishing the crowd's enthusiastic welcome.

It was the most prolonged applause I'd ever sat through; easily five minutes, perhaps even 10. Whilst it went on, I decided to make a cup of tea. I was feeling a little groggy and spilt some milk in the process. Remembering what Erin had said about the state of her kitchen, I quickly cleaned it up with a sponge from the sink.

When I sat back down, Frank was finally stepping towards the podium, looking despicably smug.

"Is that all?" he asked, feigning disappointment. The crowd laughed. "I've always envied good speakers. Truth be told, I considered asking Rupert to write my speech for this evening… before I remembered he's terrible at it."

More laughter from the crowd.

"I'm not sure I'd have done you justice," Prophett replied humbly, his voice just detected by the microphone.

"At least it would have been short," Frank jeered. "Well, I hope you're all comfortable because I've got a lot to say. People can sometimes be shy about taking credit. Rest assured; I am not one of those people."

Another ripple of laughter crossed the room. Bizarrely, the sound made me shudder.

"It's taken a lot of effort to get to this point, not just from the people doing the research, but those making the decisions that have led to this breakthrough. There have been a lot of tough decisions to make. But it's those decisions that have led us to where we are now."

As speeches went, Frank's was abysmal. He said decisions so many times that the word started to lose meaning. What annoyed me most, though, was the meaning behind his words. Was he really trying to take credit after what he'd done? How could he stand there and say those things, knowing that he had killed so many people? I was furious. Inconsolable. I was… *burning*.

First, it was just the fingertips of my right hand, but it quickly spread to my palm before scaling my wrist and forearm. Although I knew what was happening, I couldn't think why. I'd been so careful not to use anything that might contain CPT. I hadn't used any soap in the shower and had brushed my teeth for the last few days without toothpaste. Then, my eyes fell on the sponge I'd used to clean up the spilt milk. There must have been some detergent on it. Panic-stricken, I staggered towards the kitchen sink. I'd barely taken my second step before the Itch consumed me.

It was like a thousand hot knives were slicing every inch of me. All I could think about was the pain. I closed my eyes – or perhaps I passed out – but, the next thing I knew, I was flat on the ground. As I lay there, I screamed as loud as my throat would let me. Everything hurt. I thrashed around, scratching my whole body furiously. It didn't help. The floorboards felt like they were covered with broken glass and nails.

I'd scratched my arms raw, blood and bits of skin under my fingernails. I didn't care, though. Suddenly, I found myself in the kitchen. I had no idea how I'd gotten there. The knife in my hand was equally surprising. When I realised what I was about to do with it, I dropped the blade, staggering back into the living room. Many Itch sufferers had died after trying to carve the sickness out of their skin. Although I now knew why they'd resorted to such measures, I wasn't about to fall into the same trap.

Faintly, I could hear someone yelling in the hallway outside the flat. I was screaming so loudly, though, that I couldn't really hear what they were saying. The pain was terrible, but it was nothing compared to the terror. It was impossible to know how long I writhed and shrieked on the living room floor, but, eventually, I stopped moving and slipped into unconsciousness.

CHAPTER 15

My next waking moments were a hazy blur. Flickers of concerned faces. And wailing. As far as I could tell, it was my own. Every time I closed and opened my eyes, the scene changed, different faces swimming in front of me and fresh waves of pain burning part of my body. There were a few occasions when, foolishly, I thought the pain had subsided, but I was never so lucky.

It could have been hours, days, or even weeks before I had my first concrete memory; lying on something soft and warm. My brain was so addled I thought it was a cloud. The only indication of time was the light peeking through the white curtains beside my bed. It took only the slightest movement to bring soreness back to my skin, although it wasn't enough to make me scream.

Everything around me was pale or white. Someone had replaced my clothes with a plain gown. Other than the bed I was lying in, the only other furniture was a single chair. A tuneless melody was playing. It was faint, but I couldn't be sure if that was because it was far away or quiet. Nothing was familiar.

I was sweating profusely. I tried to wipe my forehead with the back of my hand but found my wrist caught on something. That was when my eyes fell on the handcuffs. The shock clarified my mind. I was lying in a hospital bed. The tuneless melody was the monitoring equipment next to my bed. I was wearing a hospital gown. And as I stirred, anxiously, the reason I was handcuffed became apparent.

"Hello, Jack," said Dunhill.

Her silvery hair and pale grey clothes made her almost invisible against the stark white walls. I opened my mouth – to say what, I didn't know – but when I tried to speak, my voice caught in my throat. I thrashed against my bonds; or at least, I tried to. My limbs were terribly weak, like string worn to barely more than a few fragile threads.

"You have been busy, haven't you?" she said in an icy voice. "Drug dealing. Breaking out of police custody. Breaking and entering. And now look at you. Some might think that this is justice being served."

Despite my lethargy, I thrashed with all my might; to Dunhill, I suspected it looked like nothing more than pitiful squirming. As I flopped against the mattress, she smiled serenely, waiting patiently until I couldn't carry on. Once I'd stopped, her smile vanished.

"I'd try not to move if I were you," she said. "Apparently, the Itch can be triggered by *tactile stimulation*."

Lazily, she dumped herself onto the chair, shuffling closer to maintain eye contact. Once she was satisfied, she reclined, stretching her legs in front of her, her hands braced behind her head.

"They told me you probably won't be able to talk for a while," she said. There was no concern in her voice; she was simply stating a fact. "I'm not especially bothered, because I just need you to listen. There are no two ways about this; you're going to go to prison. And as things stand, you're going to be in there for a *long* time, I can tell you. A really, really,

really long time. I'd be surprised if you see another day as a free man."

I suspected she might be emphasising her point to rattle me but refused to give her the satisfaction. Seething, I glared at her, willing myself to speak; to insist that there had been a mistake. But my voice wouldn't sound.

"However, I'd like to offer you a deal," she said, sitting forward on her seat. "Please understand me; you're still going to go to prison for a long time. But if you're willing to give me information – who's been helping you, who your supplier is, names of any other dealers – who knows, perhaps the courts will knock five years off your sentence. 10, if you're lucky."

Even if I hadn't lost my voice, I'm sure that would have left me speechless. By way of a reply, I tugged against my handcuff again, scowling furiously at her.

"I guess you can't answer right now, so I'll give you some time to mull it over. But I'm only willing to wait for so long," she said, getting to her feet. Casually, she strolled to my bedside, peering down at me imperiously. And then, very gently, she patted her hand on my cheek.

The pain was instantaneous. It felt as if my face was tearing from my mouth to my ear. Reflexively, I clenched my jaw, but that only made it worse. In truth, I hadn't been entirely sure that she was real, wondering if perhaps I was hallucinating. But the pain was too intense to be imagined. Pressing my eyes tightly shut, I waited for the stinging to subside. When it had, I opened my eyes, just as Dunhill was leaving my room.

Two or three days later, a police officer questioned me. As I was still in no fit state to answer questions, she'd been hurried away by the nurses. Over the next few days, more police officers came, only to be shooed away again and again. But the medical staff could only keep the police away for so long. And – as bizarre as it might sound – I was dreading the day when I was finally given a clean bill of health.

It took almost a week before I had the energy to hold myself up on my elbows, and another two or three days before I could speak. At first, all I could manage was unintelligible mumbling. Even when I could form coherent sentences, though, nobody listened, no matter how many times I insisted I hadn't done anything wrong.

I had nurses and doctors visiting my room all hours of the day. A consultant came to review my condition, confirming there was still a small amount of Dose in my blood. That explained my symptoms but wasn't enough to prove my theory. Of course, I told anyone who would listen about CPT and what Frank had done but, given the evidence against me, it wasn't surprising that no one believed me. In everyone else's eyes, I was just a drug user getting my comeuppance.

A nurse told me I was on one of the many Itch wards at the Royal Infirmary in the city. He also told me I'd been receiving daily injections of the cure since I'd arrived, a side effect of which was extreme fatigue. As my symptoms had subsided, my treatments had become less frequent, but I still felt as though I'd run a hundred miles. I also gleaned that there was a police officer stationed outside my room

24-hours a day.

Although the searing pain I'd felt was gone, the memory of it lingered. And despite my efforts to ignore it, the pain brought back memories of my brother and what he must have been through. I couldn't imagine how difficult it must have been for him – not to mention all the other sufferers who'd endured the symptoms without treatment.

My hand went to where my bottlecap necklace usually hung but, to my horror, I wasn't wearing it. In a moment of desperation, I tried to search the table beside me and almost toppled off the bed. Luckily, a nurse came rushing in and pulled me back from the edge. When I asked her about my necklace, I was relieved to hear it was with the rest of my belongings. No matter how much I pleaded, I wasn't allowed to have it back until I was released. But she brought the bag containing my possessions into the room. Even knowing it was close was enough to spur my brain into concocting an escape plan.

If there was any positive to be taken from my lengthy recuperation, it was that I had time to think. Somehow, I had to find a way to escape before the hospital discharged me. If I couldn't, I'd be at the mercy of the police. But with the handcuff still biting into my wrist, as well as the officer standing sentry, a brazen dash for freedom was totally out of the question. And even if I could breach those containments, I wasn't sure I'd have the energy to run far.

Determined, I dedicated every minute I was conscious to thinking of a way to escape. Unfortunately, security increased with my recovery.

By the time I was well enough to eat and drink, there were two officers stationed at my door; as if, in my current condition, I could even get past one of them. And to add to the odds already mounted against me, I was told that it would only be a matter of days before I was released.

I had to think of a way out. Wildly, I considered feigning illness. If they thought I was still sick, they would surely keep me in for longer. Somehow, though, I knew it was wishful thinking. By the time a nurse arrived that evening to take me to the toilet, I'd been unable to think of a better plan. One of the officers released my handcuff from the bed stand, only to reattach it to my other wrist. He kept hold of my arms. In a way, it was lucky he did, because after so many days in bed, my legs were a little shaky and I would have struggled to walk without his support.

The nurse followed my escort and I, but she was called away a moment later, leaving me alone with the officer. It was late, and the hospital was eerily quiet. I couldn't help feeling that the few staff I passed were glaring at me. Some, I was sure, recoiled as if I were a dangerous animal that might strike at any moment.

Thankfully, the officer removed my handcuffs when I got to the toilet. Having spent so long chained to the bed stand, it was nice to be able to move freely – if only around the tiny room. I considered holding in my pee but was much too desperate. Once I'd squeezed every drop of urine out of my bladder, I frantically thought how to escape.

There were no windows and only a single door. Pulling the panic alarm beside the toilet would only draw more attention. The vent above the toilet was much too narrow to fit through; besides, it was bolted shut. A knock at the door disturbed my thoughts. Another knock followed – much louder than the first.

"Mr Bright," barked the officer. "Open the door."

What was I going to do? What *could* I do? How could I get past the police officer and make it out of the building without being seen? A third knock rattled the door on its hinges, followed by more shouting. And as the officer pounded on the door, an idea finally struck me.

Hastily, I twisted the taps, throwing handfuls of water on the floor. Thankfully, the officer was banging so loudly that the splashes were masked entirely. My trap set, I stepped around the puddle, braced myself, and then slid the lock open.

The door burst inwards with surprising force. As expected, the officer rushed in. And as soon as his feet landed on the sodden floor, he slipped. Taking full advantage, I shoved him with all my strength, almost overbalancing myself. He fell, landing hard; he bounced unexpectedly high. And then, he lay completely still, arms and legs splayed out around him.

I stared down at the officer's motionless body. The door was still open, and I could hear people moving outside. My hands shook as I closed the door and twisted the lock. Strangely, I found myself hoping that the officer would move, but he was still lying like a starfish. The consequences of what I'd done were filling my brain. There were so many that I could actually feel the pressure building inside my skull.

Hardly breathing, I crouched beside him. After

schooling my nerves, I reached under his collar, checking his pulse. At the feel of a faint beat, I let out a shaky breath; at least murder wouldn't be added to the charges against me.

I'd already wasted a lot of time so, as quickly as I could, I stripped the officer's uniform and put it on. It was a little big for me but would draw less attention than a hospital gown. To my relief, there were car keys in his trouser pocket; I wasn't sure that I had the energy to make it to safety on foot. After dressing the officer in my gown, I took the handcuffs that I'd been wearing and cuffed him to the sink. In addition, I tore a strip from the hospital gown and wrapped it around his mouth.

For a few seconds, I admired what I'd done. Although I was panicking, I couldn't help feeling a little pride. It wasn't a feeling that I wanted to dwell on, though. Cautiously, I peeked into the corridor outside. Certain there was no one around, I started briskly down the corridor.

Even though there was no one around, I moved quickly, eager not to bump into anyone. Every time someone approached, I dropped my gaze. I wasn't sure if anyone would recognise me but didn't want to risk it.

Back on the ward, the other officer was still standing guard outside my room. It might have been a stupid risk to return, but there was no way I'd leave without my necklace. I thought for a moment, wondering how to distract him. Perhaps, before long, he'd leave his post in search of his colleague. I was too impatient to wait for that. Slipping into an unoccupied room, I pulled the blinds shut, tight enough to hide but wide enough that I could still see out, and then pushed the call button on my radio. I said nothing but simply waited for a response, which came a few seconds later.

"Everything alright, John? Over," came a voice through the radio. Once again, I pushed the call button. This time, though, I rubbed my palm across the mouthpiece. To add to the drama, I made choking noises. And then, quite abruptly, I cut off the radio.

It worked. As the officer rushed past my hiding place, I heard him say something like *officer not responding*. After he'd left the ward, I waited for as long as I dared before stepping out from my hiding place and entering my room. It was a tremendous relief when I found my necklace safely tucked inside one of my shoes. After knotting it around my neck, I gave the caps a tight squeeze, took a deep breath, and then left the room. Ideally, I would have changed into my own clothes – they were much less conspicuous – but wasn't sure how much time I had.

Even after only a few steps, I had to stop because my head was spinning. It took a few more attempts, but I eventually made it to the lift at the end of the corridor. The thought of climbing into a sealed box made me uneasy, so I took the stairs. It was exhausting.

Although I had no idea where I was going, I was much too nervous to ask for directions. Without anything better in mind, I followed signs to the main reception, guessing I'd have the highest chance of finding a police car in the main car park. When I finally arrived at a set of doors marked with my destination, I paused to check my exit was clear. I barely had the chance to look when I heard someone yelling behind me. It was the officer that had been guarding my room.

I didn't think but simply ran. My heels squeaked as I raced across the reception. Everyone was watching me, but I didn't care. I had to getaway. I could hear them muttering, some even yelled after me. I glanced over my shoulder. I knew it was risky – that I might trip and fall – but I had to know how far away the officer was. My wake stretched across the room. Some people were cowering. The officer was worryingly close.

There was no way I could outrun him. He ordered me to stop, but fear overwhelmed me, compelling me to keep running. I probably only had a few more seconds before I was caught, but I wouldn't go without a fight. Calling-up my last reserves of energy, I put on what would surely be my final burst of speed towards the exit. I was still a fair distance away when the doors burst open. And suddenly, a wave of people poured into the room.

I was pushed back towards the wall by the tidal wave of people. The crowd was so loud I didn't really know what was going on. People were yelling. Glass shattered. A trolley was knocked over. Something heavy fell to the floor.

It took only a few seconds to realise that the crowd was far too fixated to pay any attention to me. I caught a glimpse of neon yellow a short distance away. The officer was struggling against the crowd. As I gazed around the room, watching the carnage unfold, I realised why they were there. They wanted the cure.

People were clambering over one another, surging towards a stack of boxes in the corridor. I could see the Rathbury-Holmes logo on the side. Even at a distance, it was clear there wouldn't be enough for everyone in the crowd and, clearly, some people had already worked that out. Once the boxes had been torn open, people started wrestling one another for the contents. It looked like a feeding frenzy, starving animals wrestling for scraps of meat.

It was almost impossible to move without knocking into someone. If I'd been fit and well, it might have been easier to move, but my legs were far from steady. On top of that, I barely had the strength to hold my arms up; let alone fight through a crowd. It was strange that moments before, the hospital was almost deserted. Now, it was as if a procession had gone off course and was marching through.

Through the chaos, I saw a woman clutching her hands to her chest. At first, I thought she was struggling to breathe, but I soon realised she was cradling a small box in a desperate attempt to keep it hidden. Unfortunately, she'd been spotted by others. As they descended on her, pulling her hair, and yanking her clothes, the woman fell to the ground. I tried to see where she'd fallen, but there was no sign of her. Although I knew there was nothing I could do to help her, it didn't make it any easier to leave. Eventually, though, I pulled myself away, heading towards the exit.

Across the car park, I saw the familiar paintwork of a police car. With the keys gripped tightly in my hand, I started running.

CHAPTER 16

After hurtling along Oxford Road, I zigzagged through the maze of side streets in the city centre towards the Northern Quarter. It was a circuitous route, but I was keen to stay away from main roads. Whatever had happened at the hospital was sure to attract police, and one of their cars heading in the opposite direction might look suspicious.

Parking outside Erin's flat would draw attention, so I drove as close as I dared, conscious that every yard away from my destination was one I'd have to cover on foot. Eventually, I turned down a very narrow street, wide enough for only one vehicle, and pulled onto the curb. Then, I made my way to Erin's. Although I had no idea if she was home, it was the only place I could go.

I left the body armour and hat in the car, feeling they were too noticeable. More than once, I had to rest against a wall to catch my breath. Anyone watching might have thought I was drunk. I'm not sure how long it took but, by the time I saw her flat, I was soaked with sweat and panting.

The wait after I'd buzzed her flat from the door to the street was excruciating. What would I do if she wasn't home? Where would I go? Thankfully, it didn't come to that.

"Jesus," she stammered. "You're okay."

"Try not to sound too surprised," I choked, practically collapsing on top of her.

After she repeatedly kissed my forehead and

cheeks, our lips met. It was a long and passionate kiss.

"What happened?" she asked when we pulled apart.

"One second, I was fine, and the next, I felt like my whole body was on fire. I couldn't stop screaming. Then, I woke up in the hospital."

"Is it…?"

"Yeah, it is."

I couldn't lie to her about my sickness anymore. I'd considered whether I should tell her about my first attack, too, but upon consideration, there didn't seem any point. At hearing I had the sickness, Erin put her hand over her mouth in shock.

"Oh my God," she said, pulling me into a tight hug. I tried not to wince. "Are you okay?"

"I'm getting there," I said. Honestly, I couldn't tell if I was cured or not.

"The neighbours heard you screaming. They called an ambulance," she said, before adding "Shit, that reminds me. We can't stay here."

"Why not?" I asked. I was exhausted and didn't think I had the energy to move again.

"They must have realised who you were at the hospital. The police came to search the flat the day after."

"Christ. What happened?"

"They didn't find anything."

When she'd returned from the launch to find the door off its hinges, she'd known something terrible had happened. Fortunately, she knew someone like Bowker. Together, they'd cleaned her flat from top to bottom, removing as much physical evidence as they could; anything that might prove I'd been staying there, like hair, clothes, or my toothbrush. After that, Bowker had taken the information I'd gathered and hidden it before the police could get there. Although Erin had been taken to the station, the police didn't have enough evidence to keep her. When they realised I'd escaped, though, they'd surely come to search Erin's flat.

"Where can we go?" I asked.

"Bowker. I know you two aren't the best of pals, but it's better than the alternative," she said. I didn't argue. Even if I'd been inclined to, I was too tired.

Erin drove as if fleeing a natural disaster. My head was spinning so fast I thought I might vomit. I considered asking her to slow down but, as we were evading the police, thought it was best to endure nausea. Obviously, she was curious to know how I'd escaped. Recounting the details of it wasn't easy. Now that I was sitting again, I could barely keep my eyes open. I glossed over the part of my story where I'd assaulted a police officer as quickly as I could, eager not to dwell on it. When it came to the crowd stampeding through the hospital, I faltered, unsure what to say.

"There've been riots all over the country," she said grimly. "People are desperate for the cure. They don't know how long it'll be before their families get it, so they're trashing pharmacies, GP surgeries, hospitals, even supermarkets."

"Lucky for me," I said, although I wasn't sure I meant it entirely.

If the rioters hadn't arrived, I was sure I wouldn't have escaped. Obviously, I was glad to be free, but what was the cost? During the riot, I'd seen at least one person trampled as she fought for the cure. Given how savage the crowd had appeared, it was a safe bet other people had been injured as well. Suddenly, though, a more pressing concern occurred.

"Have you heard anything about Lizzy?" I asked.

"No," she said, which wasn't as bad as it could have been, but still made me nervous. "She's going to be fine, okay?"

"I know," I said. I couldn't bear to think about what it meant if I was wrong.

We headed east out of the city. It was getting dark, and the streetlamps were coming on, bathing everything in an orange glow. We left the main road and pulled onto an industrial estate. Most of the buildings were dark and empty, but there were floodlights illuminating something up ahead. As we stopped outside a metal gate at the front of the site, I saw a sign that read *Booty's Scrappage & Waste Metal Management*.

As we approached, the gate swung open. Once we were inside, I saw mountains of broken machinery and rusted metal towering above us on all sides. There was a small warehouse building in amongst the rubbish, which looked like it had been built a long time ago. Burned-out cars were stacked like a house of cards in the corner. Amazingly, there was even the shell of a tank in amongst the rubbish, Cyrillic letters printed on its rusted metal shell.

Bowker was heading towards us from the warehouse building. After a few hurried words with Erin, he got in the car and drove away. With Erin's help, I staggered into the warehouse. To my surprise, it looked as though someone was living in there. There was a mattress on the floor, along with a clothes rail. They were clearly Bowker's style. A workbench sat in the middle of the room, cluttered with a mixture of tools and kitchen appliances. Alarmingly, industrial products were stacked alongside food on the shelves at the back of the room. But I was too tired to comment on any of that. For the first time in as long as I could remember, I couldn't fight off approaching sleep.

I was barely aware of what happened next. It was as if my memory of it was a series of photographs, with nothing linking one snapshot to the next. When Erin asked me how I was feeling, it took me a long time to realise it was real and not a memory.

"How long have I been asleep?" I asked, sitting up on the mattress.

"About 24 hours," she said. "You shouldn't move" she added as I tried to get to my feet.

"What am I supposed to do? Lie here until-"

"Easy," she said, her tone darkening. "I just don't want you to hurt yourself, is all."

"I'm fine," I said. As soon as I moved, though, I couldn't help wincing.

"Clearly," she said, unconvinced.

"I'm not a hundred per cent, but I will be. I want to finish this right now. The longer I leave it, the more people will be affected by it," I said as patiently as I could manage.

Erin kept my gaze until I finished, then looked away. A moment later, she handed me a small cardboard box. I recognised the Rathbury-Holmes logo. I didn't need to ask what it was. And there, in plain text was the proof I needed; the cure didn't contain CPT.

"This is it. I can use this to prove there's a problem with CPT," I declared.

There had to be a paper trail; an email, a report, or perhaps a handwritten note that explained why the change had been made. Maybe it would be enough to convince others that Dose wasn't the cause of the Itch. There was a good chance that it would also prove Frank was covering up the true cause of the sickness.

I'd expected Erin to smile, or cheer, or say something – anything. But she didn't react. When I asked her what was wrong, she looked a little uneasy, before finally replying.

"I don't think it's going to be that easy. The police are really cracking down. Disrupting protests, making arrests, and tackling riots. What do you think they'll do if you turn up claiming Dose isn't causing the Itch? And even if you can convince them, how long do you think that's going to take? Frank must be taking steps to make sure no one finds out about this."

"All the more reason to act now."

"I'm not disagreeing. I just think we need to consider our options."

I wanted to argue with her, but it was probably due to restlessness. There was no faulting her logic; Frank would surely be doing all he could to bury the truth. I couldn't waste any time, though. I had to think hard and act quickly.

"Frank won't voluntarily tell us anything," I said grimly. "He's too bloody stubborn. We need to find a way to make him tell us."

"Blackmail?"

"We need leverage; something to make him tell us what we need to know."

I shuddered to think what it would take to force a man like Frank to do something he didn't want to. No matter how much I disliked him, I wasn't sure I could stomach torturing him for information. But perhaps I wouldn't have to do anything to him. All I really needed to do was make him believe I had the intent.

"I think I've got an idea," I said suddenly.

I wasn't proud of my plan. Once I'd told Erin, it was clear she wasn't keen on it, either. She said nothing for a long time after I'd finished explaining it. If there was any other way, I'd have chosen that in a heartbeat. But I knew that this was the only way to make Frank tell us what he knew.

"You're joking?" she said finally.

"It's the only way. Without Lizzy's data, I've got nothing. I have to find proof Frank changed the formulation."

"Yeah, but, look at you. You can barely stand. And even in the last few minutes, you've scratched your wrist raw."

She was right. There was an angry red welt on my skin. I hadn't even realised I was scratching. Faced with that, I had to agree; I couldn't go through another attack of the Itch. In the same breath, though, I couldn't let this opportunity slip by. If there was any chance I could prove the true cause of the Itch, prove Frank had lied to the nation for so long, this was it.

"I have to do this," I said grimly. "So many people have suffered because of the sickness. I can't just ignore that. I need to make him pay for what he's done. But I can't do that without your help."

Once I'd finished, I waited for her to speak. I'd expected her to argue, or – at the very least – to have to persuade her a little more. It was a relief, then, when she nodded.

"What do you need?" she asked.

Despite the warm evening sunlight pouring through the large windows, Frank's house was chilly. Bowker had broken in for me. Even if he hadn't been able to pick the lock on the back door, the frame was so rotten I'm sure he could have forced the door.

Everything was decorated in dark shades, matched with brass fixtures and antique furniture. There were pictures on the walls, mostly of Frank and his dog. My skin was feeling tender so, to prevent another attack, I took one of the small cartridges from my pocket. They were supposed to be administered by injection but, in the absence of needle and trained personnel, I had to crack it open and drink the fluid inside. Hopefully, that would be enough. I was wondering how long I would need to continue taking the cure before my symptoms resolved but was distracted by the sound of keys rattling outside.

As the door swung open, I held my breath, waiting for Frank to enter the dining room. After fumbling for the light switch, he nudged the door closed with his foot and then turned to see me sitting at the large oak table.

"What the Hell do you think you're doing?" he snarled.

"We need to talk," I said, ignoring his rising anger.

"Unbe-fucking-lievable," he muttered. "You break

into my house for a chat. This is unacceptable. I'm giving you three seconds to get the Hell out. And if you're still here after that, I'll make you leave. Believe me when I say that you'll be in a worse state than you were when you got here."

I'd known that it would likely come to this. Threats and yelling. That was when I reached into my pocket and took out the bright red collar.

"Do you know what this is?" I said softly.

"Did you hear what I-" And then, his face paled as he recognised it. "Where is he?"

As soon as I was inside, Bowker had taken Frank's dog back to the scrapyard. He'd left his collar with me for effect. Unlike his owner, the dog was extremely friendly and had been all too happy to go with Bowker. He would keep the dog until I had what I needed.

"He's safe," I said. "So, I'll say again; we need to talk."

"You're blackmailing me?" he snarled.

"Call it what you will," I replied.

He glared at me, aghast. There was so much hatred in his eyes that I wondered if he might attack me. When he finally asked what I wanted, though, his voice was desperately hollow.

"Why have you been covering up the cause of the Itch?"

"What?" he stammered. I repeated myself. "You really have lost it, haven't you?"

Very slowly, I began to tell him my theory. How Dina Mulchandaani had discovered an issue with CPT and, after informing him about it, had inexplicably taken her own life. Wilson Loveday –

one of the people involved in the approval of CPT – had been accused of Dose possession and had since lost his mind. And how, when I'd highlighted that Dose might not be the cause of the Itch to him, I'd been framed.

"This again? When are you going to get it into your thick head? I have no idea what you're talking about," he yammered.

"I might've believed you. Until the cure."

I continued my explanation. After seeing Dina's data, he was the only other person at the company that knew CPT would degrade in the presence of chyrolic compounds. When the Itch first flared, he'd known of the link to chyrols and likely worked with Wilson to officially label Dose as the cause of the sickness. Then, when the original trial of the cure had been unsuccessful, he'd known that CPT was the reason. So, he'd made the decision to remove it. And now, despite the lives he'd knowingly cost, he was a hero.

"Jack, I- please, for God's sake, think about what you're suggesting? You can't possibly believe any of this. What you're saying, is- it's- it's- it's-"

"So, you're not going to admit it, then?"

"Admit what? I haven't done anything," he cried.

"We'll see. Follow me" I said.

I got to my feet and headed to the front door. For a moment, he simply gawked at me. Eventually, though, he followed. Erin was waiting in her car outside on the street lined with leafy trees. As Frank and I approached, she started the engine. Before he got in, I held my hand out, asking for his phone. If anyone was helping him, I wanted to make sure he couldn't get in contact with them.

Although the child locks were on, I sat in the back with Frank. He was visibly shaking. We left Frank's grand redbrick house in Hale and headed towards the city. There was very little traffic at that time, so it took us only half an hour to get to Rathbury-Holmes. When we arrived at the barrier, Erin used Frank's key card and headed into the underground car park.

"Are you sure about this?" she asked as I stepped out of the car. Grimly, I nodded. As I saw it, there was no other way. I had to prove that Frank had made the decision to remove CPT. Surely, there would be some proof in his office.

Frank and I headed up the staircase to reception, where a surprised guard was waiting. He would probably recognise me, but there was nothing I could do about that. Besides, I'd soon have enough evidence to prove what Frank had done. I kept my head down as the guard asked why we were there. Frank fed him some nonsense about a crisis that needed immediate attention. When the guard pressed, Frank got angry and started yelling. The guard didn't ask any more questions after that.

As we rode the lift to the fifth floor, Frank fidgeted anxiously.

"Well?" he asked when we arrived at his office. Although it was a demand, his voice was shaking.

"Where's the final report for the cure?" I said.

His plush armchair creaked as he dumped his weight onto it. He surreptitiously peeked at the underside of his keyboard, checking his password as usual. Even though I'd only seen it once, I still remembered the code. A moment later, a document slid off the printer beside his desk. I took it from him, trying not to notice how much his hand was shaking, and rapidly read the summary section.

It explained about the disastrous outcome of the initial trial in unpleasantly plain terms. They referred to seven deaths as *complications*. It also explained that the formulation had been altered and subsequent results were satisfactory. But as I flicked through the document, I read something that didn't make sense.

"This just says that the initial formulation wasn't suitable," I said.

For a moment, he simply stared at me, uncertainty plastered on his face. I had to repeat myself, each word louder than the previous.

"You know, as well as I do, that it wasn't," he yelled.

"But why did you change the formulation? How did you know it would work when you made the change?"

By now, he was stammering. In all the time I'd known him, I'd never seen Frank as anything except brutish and hard-faced. To see such vulnerability in him took me by surprise. Once again, I did my best to ignore my sympathy for him.

"You removed it from the cure. If it isn't harmful, why did you take it out?"

"What do you want me to say?"

"I want you to admit that you've been lying about the cause of the Itch."

"Me?" he cried.

"You ignored Dina's warning. And mine. Now, suddenly, you've removed CPT from the cure. Do you really expect me to believe that you didn't know

CPT is causing the Itch?"

Frank was stunned into silence, compounding his guilt. But then, as I looked a little closer, I realised he didn't look afraid or anxious – as I'd expected he would – but totally and utterly dumbstruck.

"What do you want from me?" he said finally, his tone loaded with disbelief.

"I want you to pay for all the people you've hurt. For Dina, Wilson, Kelly, and any others."

"Kelly?" he said softly.

"So, you remember her, then?" I snapped. "How did you do it? Where is she now?"

"I've no idea what you're talking about," he said.

"Don't lie. I left the note on your desk from her, and then she mysteriously disappeared. Tell me what you did to her."

"That was you?" he said. "I- I didn't- I thought it was just nonsense. I threw it in the bin. See for yourself."

Keeping an eye on him, I edged towards the bin beside his desk. There were only a few items in there, one of which was clearly an envelope. Nudging the bin onto its side, I pulled the envelope away from Frank's desk with my foot – I didn't want to crouch close to him – and picked it up. It was the letter. But that didn't prove anything.

"What about Lizzy?" I barked.

"Chao?" he replied in utter bewilderment.

"You knew she was working with me to prove what really happened during the trial, so you hired someone to get her out of the picture, didn't you? Just like Kelly. And everyone else that-"

"Christ," Frank exclaimed. "Are you out of your

mind? Why would I do that? What possible reason would I have? And how would-"

"Because you've been lying about the cause of the Itch," I said. "You've known all along that CPT is the real cause. And now, you're trying to keep your dirty little secret."

"Listen to me, Jack," he said. He was begging, which took me aback. "I want to make this absolutely clear. I have no idea what you are talking about. The last time I spoke to Lizzy, she texted to say she wouldn't be in work because she was under the weather."

The sincerity on his voice, not to mention the fear in his eyes, was impossible to ignore. Slowly, I reached into my pocket and removed his phone. It was locked but, given how carelessly he guarded the password for his PC, I typed in the same numbers, which unlocked it.

The most recent message was from Lizzy. *Hi Frank. Touch under the weather. Should be right as rain in a few days. Lizzy.* Whenever she emailed or messaged Frank, she intentionally made it as light and jovial as possible. He hated people getting too chummy with him. It was sent the morning after I'd received the call from her abductor.

"This isn't her," I said finally. "You staged this."

"Do you even hear what you're saying?" Frank cried. "Conspiracy. Kidnapping. What the Hell are you thinking?"

Before I could reply, someone else spoke.

"Am I interrupting?" said DCI Dunhill.

CHAPTER 17

The sound of her voice was as startling as a gunshot. Vaguely, I was aware of people entering the office but simply stared ahead, hardly daring to move. There must have been at least half a dozen police officers.

"Hello again, Jack," Dunhill said. "I have to say, you're a very tricky character to catch. I'd almost say I was impressed."

"You took your time," Frank said. Some of his usual brusqueness had returned. "Well, aren't you going to arrest him?"

"Actually, you're both under arrest," Dunhill replied coolly.

"On what charges?" Frank demanded.

"Possession with intent to supply the banned substance known as Dose," Dunhill said matter-of-factly.

Despite my obvious trepidation, I was pleased to see Frank's eyes widening in surprise. But all too quickly, fresh concerns arose. All my efforts had been focused on him. Now, though, it was clear I'd made a mistake; that someone was trying to remove him from the picture, just like Dina, Wilson, and me.

Naturally, he protested, using words like *preposterous* and *outrageous*. When that didn't work, he even accused Dunhill of unlawful misconduct, claiming she didn't have any grounds to arrest him. Dunhill assured him, though, that the mounds of Dose they'd discovered at his home would be enough to convict. It all seemed very familiar.

"Your turn, Mr Bright," she said after two officers had escorted Frank, shouting and cursing, out of the room.

Whilst Dunhill read me my rights, an officer grabbed my arms. I was moments from being handcuffed when an ear-splitting explosion shook the room. It was so fierce that I suspected the whole building shook. Dunhill staggered, desperately flinging her arms out to keep her balance. So did the officers. I almost toppled onto my knees but managed to brace myself against the wall.

An alarm cut through the fading rumble of the explosion. For a few seconds, the light above us flickered. Dust drifted down from the ceiling, making everything look a little hazy. The police officers were gawking at Dunhill, presumably waiting to be told what to do next. And in those panicked moments, another deafening bang filled the room.

Erin was standing outside the office with her left arm raised, a pistol smoking in her hand. She had fired three shots. Three officers lay on the ground, clutching their stomachs in agony. Dunhill was glaring at Erin, her expression a mixture of anger and concern.

"Sit," Erin snarled, pointing the gun at Dunhill. Initially, she didn't move, but eventually, she lowered herself to the ground. The remaining officers did the same.

"I really wouldn't," Dunhill snarled.

"Phone," Erin demanded, holding her free hand out. Again, Dunhill took her time responding. Once she'd handed her phone over, Erin slotted it into her pocket.

"You've no idea what a mistake you're making."

"Handcuffs," Erin said. As before, Dunhill waited before obliging.

After instructing Dunhill and the other officers to handcuff each other to a pipe beneath a radiator, Erin turned to me.

"We have to go," she said.

I cast my eyes around the room, struggling to take it in. Erin repeated herself, but I couldn't move. In seconds, circumstances had rapidly changed. In addition to the current charges against me, I was now an accomplice to assault with a deadly weapon. By now, she was yelling at me. What choice did I have but to follow her? My body moved, but I wasn't sure I was controlling it.

We headed down the corridor towards the lift but had to take the stairs because of the fire alarm. I wondered if the officers that had arrested Frank had been trapped between the floors by the explosion. After we'd climbed down three floors, I suddenly found my voice.

"What was that?" I yelled.

"We haven't got time for-"

"No, we're making time. You just shot those police."

"Low-velocity rubber bullets," she roared, waving the pistol at me. "One shot each, all of which shouldn't be fatal. They'll have hurt like a hammer but weren't likely to kill. Plus, they have body armour on."

"What about the explosion?" I demanded.

"It was a precaution," she replied. "I wasn't sure whether we could trust Frank. I asked Bowker to put something in the car before he dropped it off."

"Are you out of your mind?"

"It's a good job I did," she retorted.

"*A good*- what if somebody was hurt? What if you'd-"

"What other choice did I have?"

Despite how I felt about it, I was unable to think of an alternative course of action. Whoever was responsible for the Itch was trying to eliminate Frank. I could only assume that – given what had already happened – they must be a powerful individual. Our only chance, then, was to fight our way out.

"Let's go," I said. Visibly, her tension dissolved, her fists and shoulders relaxing.

As we descended the stairs, Erin explained that the security system was linked to the fire alarm, so all the doors would be unlocked. When I asked her about the police, she seemed less sure.

"There'll be a lot of confusion, which we can use. Bowker will be here soon."

But as we reached the first floor, Erin faltered, listening intently. I'd heard it, too. By the time the armed police officers appeared on the staircase, Erin was already firing her pistol. Although it wasn't as startling as before, the gunshots were deafeningly loud, forcing me to cover my ears. The bullet cases were still dancing across the floor as Erin grabbed my arm and started running again, back up the staircase.

Angry voices were already roaring behind us. Seconds later, bullets were thudding against the walls, banister, stairs, and ceiling, showering us in sparks and debris. As the gunfire intensified, Erin steered us through a door onto the third floor.

"Where are we?" she asked.

"Quality Control. Mostly analytical labs."

"Is there another way out?"

"There's a staircase on the other side."

In the laboratory, there was a central aisle, with branches fanning out from it and workbenches on each side of each branch. Over the gentle hum of automated equipment, I could hear people shouting behind us. The room was dark, forcing us to navigate by the pale glow of the green emergency lighting. We were almost halfway when a torch beam swept across the room.

"Down," Erin roared over the resounding *clack-clack-clack* of gunfire. Mirroring Erin's actions, I threw myself under a workbench. When the gunshots stopped, she returned fire.

"We'll never make it," she roared, cowering as bullets destroyed the glassware and apparatus on top of the workbench.

She was right. There was little to no chance we'd make it without cover from the bullets. Desperately, I thought of a way out. Despite Erin's shooting, the gunshots were getting closer every second. She'd already reloaded once, and I didn't want to ask how many magazines she had left. Any second, the police would catch us. An image of them bearing down on where we were hiding flashed before my eyes. My eyes fell on the cupboards opposite. The warning labels on the door sparked an idea.

Whilst I rummaged through the cupboard, Erin continued firing. By the time she'd realised what I was doing, I'd found the chemicals I was looking for. With the police fast approaching, I opened another cupboard and pulled out a large glass beaker, clumsily filling it with the chemicals.

"Cover your mouth," I yelled to Erin as the beaker began to fume.

In no time at all, thick purplish smoke was billowing from the beaker, screening us from the police. Unfortunately, lowered visibility was accompanied by increased gunfire. It wasn't ideal, but it was our only chance. Erin fired another flurry of gunshots, and then we broke for the door. The responding barrage of bullets was ferocious. There were so many shots fired that a near-constant roar echoed throughout the laboratory.

It felt as though I was running through a warzone; or at least, as close to one as I'd ever like to come. Despite the chaos enveloping us, I heard Erin cry out in agony. And with rising dread, I realised what had happened to her.

She stumbled, crashing into the door. After the two of us had tumbled through, I slammed the door. Erin was resting against the wall, clutching her stomach. Blood was already pouring down her side, pooling on the vinyl floor. After only a cursory glance, I knew that there was nothing I could do to help her. She needed to go to a hospital.

"Just go," she wheezed. Her teeth were clenched so tightly I could see the muscles in her jaw.

"Not without you."

"Jack, please- I- I- can't- I can't move," she stammered, sinking to the floor. "You have to- have to go."

"I'll carry you," I offered. Surprisingly, Erin laughed. It was an ugly, choking laugh.

"Then we'll both be caught," she said softly. "You- you have to go."

I knew she was right. She had already lost a lot of blood, and I had no idea where the bullet was. It might even have been riskier to move her. Behind the door, I could hear the rhythmic pounding of boots as the police converged on us. And in that moment, my mind was made up.

"I'm not leaving you," I said.

"You can't-"

"Keep pressure on it," I said as I hoisted Erin to her feet. She breathed in harshly as I pulled her arm around my shoulders to take her weight. I had to crouch so that she could reach. Then, we staggered together down the staircase. It wasn't easy. Several times, we almost tripped. When angry voices started yelling above me, though, I quickened our pace. Erin groaned in pain but kept up.

As we crashed through the fire exit at the bottom and stumbled away from the building, the fire alarm faded. But there was a different siren ringing in my ears; that of approaching police cars. Within seconds, I could hear voices shouting. They were all around us.

"Call Bowker," Erin said, pressing her phone into my hand.

"What?" he demanded petulantly.

"Where are you?" I yelled. People nearby gave me concerned looks, but that might have been because I was carrying a bleeding person.

"What you wanting, Princess?" Bowker sneered.

When I told him what had happened, the phone went quiet for a long time. I repeated myself, more urgently. Finally, he responded.

"Quay Street in two," he said, before hanging up.

"We have to move," I said to Erin. Her head was resting on my shoulder. As soon as we started moving, though, she roused, hissing in pain.

There were already people out for the evening. When they saw us, they asked if everything was alright. The blood on Erin's clothes, though, was enough to scare most away. I was disgusted to see one person recording us on his phone but couldn't afford to be distracted by him.

It was probably only a few seconds before a van skidded to a halt in front of us, but it felt like much longer. I opened the back door and lifted Erin inside. Time pressure meant I wasn't as gentle as I should have been. With uncharacteristic agility, I leapt inside. We were moving before I'd closed the door.

For a mile or so, Bowker drove without caution. He threw the van in and out of traffic. As far as I could tell, he ran every red light we passed. As we skidded sideways around corners, I clutched Erin tightly. She was resting against the wheel arch. Each breath rasped like air escaping from a puncture.

"Slow down," I said.

"Chances," Bowker scoffed.

"She needs a doctor," I said as Erin gasped. "Do you know anyone who can help?"

"Fuck do I look like?" Bowker replied.

"Do you know anyone or not?"

He turned his head rapidly. It was clear from the look in his eyes that there was a lot he wanted to say. In a surprising display of restraint, though, he simply shook his head. Refusing to let hopelessness consume me, I thought hard. A hospital was, of course, out of the question. As soon as they realised who we were, they would call the police. Perhaps I could remove the bullet myself. No. Moronic and dangerous. Besides, where would I get the implements to do it? I couldn't go digging around in Erin's abdomen with kitchen utensils or hand tools.

The answer was lurking in the shadows of my mind, waiting to surface. For as long as I could, I kept it buried. It was only when her eyelids fluttered closed that I realised I had no other choice. Erin's phone was still in my pocket. Like always, my fingers typed the phone number out without really registering the digits. Although Michael had likely perished after my last visit to see Berglund, I was sure that he would have simply promoted one of his other lackeys to the role of broker. Sure enough, I recognised the voice that answered, although I wasn't sure of his name.

"I need to see him," I said. I couldn't keep the desperation from my voice.

"Good evening, Mr Bright," he said. His accent was as difficult to place as Michael's. "I'm afraid the club is currently-"

"I'm not fucking playing," I yelled. "I need to see him, right fucking now."

It was a mistake to raise my voice. If Klas didn't help, we would be forced to take Erin to the hospital. Although it was better than the alternative, it came with its own problems that I didn't want to think about.

"Temper, temper," he replied. Even though he was a stranger, I could tell from his tone that he was grinning. "You know he does not usually conduct such business outside normal working hours. I am, however, aware that Mr Berglund is very keen to see you again."

"Where?" I said, forcing myself to speak calmly.

The phone went quiet. It took everything I had not to start yelling again.

"I am sure you will understand that, after your last meeting, Mr Berglund is reluctant to invite you back to the club. Perhaps you would be good enough to host him this evening."

This wasn't good. At present, my one advantage over Klas was that he didn't know where to find me. Once he knew that, I would truly be at his mercy. If things didn't go his way, he could simply call the police. What was to stop him doing that, anyway? As Erin shuddered beside me, though, I knew I couldn't refuse, and so told him about the scrap yard. Bowker turned as I mentioned it but didn't comment.

"Excellent," Klas' assistant replied. "He shall be with you in the hour."

"That's too-" I began to say, but he'd already hung up.

"Who you get?" Bowker asked.

When I told him, Bowker cursed. It wasn't surprising that a drug dealer would know someone like Berglund.

"Lost your head, man, or what? Ain't never good doing deals with him."

"If you've got a better idea, shout up. Because trust me, he's the last person I want to go to."

Bowker said nothing. Foolishly, I'd let myself believe that he might be hiding something up his sleeve.

CHAPTER 18

When we arrived at the scrapyard, I leapt out of the van. Bowker came to the back to help me lift Erin out. Rather clumsily, the two of us carried her into the small warehouse building. We laid her on the mattress. By now, her breathing was so shallow that I could hardly tell she was still alive.

"Telling then, or what?" Bowker snapped.

It wasn't easy to describe what had happened. I felt as though the image of Erin's face, contorted in agony as the bullet had torn through her, was branded on my brain. I wasn't sure I'd ever forget it. Once I'd finished, I was surprised to see Bowker looked a little concerned. I'd gotten the impression he and Erin were more like colleagues than friends. Clearly, I was mistaken.

"What we doing now, then?" he asked. His voice had lost some of his standoffishness.

"One thing at a time," I said. He began to protest, so I added. "I can't deal with anything else right now. I just need to make sure she's okay."

Meeting Klas had always been hideous but, somehow, waiting for him to arrive was much worse. It was as if I was cowering in a bunker, listening as enemy forces drew ever closer. Occasionally, Erin stirred. Worried she might injure herself further, I kept a hand on her shoulder. Several times, her eyes opened. I hoped I was imagining the dullness in her stare. Meanwhile, Bowker kept watch from the door.

"Do you have a gun?" I asked as an idea struck

me. He looked a little puzzled, so I added "A pistol? A rifle? Anything that could be used as a weapon."

"Yeah. Why?"

"I need you to hide somewhere and keep watch."

"What you on about?"

"Look, Klas and his men aren't coming for a friendly chat," I said, a little angrily. "And I can guarantee they aren't going to be very nice guests. So, when something goes wrong – and, trust me, it will – I'm going to need your help."

When I'd finished speaking, he looked annoyed for a moment, but quickly schooled his expression and went to retrieve a weapon. At that moment, I had a glimpse of the soldier he'd been. He barely had time to make it to a vantage point in amongst the scrap before a car arrived at the gate. I raced into the courtyard to greet a luxurious white limousine. The headlamps were dazzlingly bright. I supposed it wasn't surprising that I had to wait for about a minute for the door to open. Much longer, though, and I might have started banging on the windows.

"Jacky, Jacky, Jack, Jack, Jack," Klas said sluggishly. "I must say, I am a little surprised to see you skulking in such filth."

Klas muttered something that I didn't hear, which prompted a laugh from his goons. There were five of them surrounding him in a semicircle. I guessed the man from the phone was standing at his right side, which was formerly Michael's place.

"Well, are we to stand out in the night or are you going to invite us inside?" Klas said. After glancing towards the warehouse, he added, "Upon consideration, I might prefer to be outside."

Once again, there was a smattering of idiotic laughter. I stepped forward but was quickly intercepted by one of his goons. After searching me from head to toe, he let me move closer. Meanwhile, two more headed to the warehouse. They returned a moment later but said nothing.

"Well, to what do I owe the pleasure?" he asked. His tone was as caustic as bleach.

"My friend needs help," I said. The urgency in my voice, not to mention the tremor, was a terrible way to open this discussion. Klas looked to the guards who'd inspected the warehouse, one of whom nodded.

"Not so long ago, you were willing to leave her to my dogs," Klas replied.

Laughter. If I hadn't been in such dire need, I would have rushed at the nearest goon – a tall man with a heavy brow and underbite – and smashed his bulbous nose with my fist.

"She needs a doctor," I said.

"I suggest a trip to the infirmary."

"Will you help or not?" I demanded.

"What do you offer in return?" he asked, toying with his belly button.

This was unusual. Klas had never asked me to name a price before. Why now, then?

"If you don't want anything, then why are you here?" I snapped.

"Oh, I didn't say that," Klas replied. "On the contrary. I know exactly what I want from you."

"What do you want?"

"But you already know."

"Tell me."

I knew it was risky to plead with him. If he

thought I was too desperate – that I would agree to anything without a second thought for my own wellbeing – he might not be willing to help. Then again, he might want revenge for what happened the last time we met. I was surprised to see him smiling at me. It took me a moment to realise it wasn't a happy expression, but that of a hunter that'd spotted their next hapless victim.

"Nothing that you possess will satisfy my desire. I am not interested in trinkets or oddities. What I desire is intangible. What I want – what I truly desire – is to see you squirm like the pathetic little maggot you are. Then, and only then, will I consider your request."

"You miserable piece of-"

I didn't finish my insult. I was too angry. Instead, I charged at Klas, hands outstretched towards his flabby neck. Of course, I didn't make it more than a few steps before I was intercepted by two of his goons. Klas burst into hysterics. It was excessive and infuriating. He was wiping tears of laugher from his eyes when a series of deafening cracks sounded. By the time Bowker emerged from his vantage, Klas' goons were lying on the ground. Whether they were alive or dead, I couldn't say, but they weren't moving.

"Inside," Bowker hissed, pressing the rifle to Klas' skull. Berglund didn't move.

"I am afraid that a bullet to the head would render me utterly useless," he said in an almost bored voice. "And then… well, your friend would be quite helpless."

"This ain't no playground, Princess," Bowker snarled.

"I can see that," Klas replied, regarding his surroundings with disdain. Bowker stepped closer so that his face was inches from Klas'.

"You got until three."

"Are you sure you can count to three?"

"One," Bowker hissed. "Two."

"I should step out of the splash zone if I were you," Klas purred. Bowker adjusted his grip, aligning the barrel in the middle of Klas' forehead. But Klas was unperturbed. He simply stared back at Bowker. His expression was that of somebody waiting for a train to nowhere important or exciting. Bowker never finished counting. After he lowered the rifle, Klas erupted into laughter again. And as I watched him guffawing like a chimp, my final nerve snapped.

Suddenly, I didn't care about making him talk. I didn't care about his help. I just wanted to make him suffer as he'd made so many people suffer. He was much too fat to drag or carry, so I grabbed a handful of his hair to chivvy him along. Although he protested, his tone was still light. In some sick way, he was enjoying this. But I would soon change that. Once I'd forced him inside, Bowker helped me tie him to a battered office chair in the corner of the room. Although Klas resisted, he continued laughing as he was forced into the chair. Once his wrists and ankles were secured with tape, I scanned the shelves along the back wall, checking the bottles. Towards the top, I spotted exactly what I was looking for.

As I sloshed the clear liquid over his thighs and belly, he smelt the alcohol in it and his face blanched. Feebly, he fought against his restraints, but they were secure. After I'd emptied the bottle, I asked Bowker for a lighter. I took it from him, brandishing the colourful plastic in front of Klas' face.

"If you don't help her, we're going to have a little barbecue," I snarled. "I can't be sure, but I don't think this will kill you. But I am sure that it's going to hurt. A lot. So, I'm only going to say this once more. Help her."

"You wouldn't," he replied, blinking the liquid from his eyes.

By way of a reply, I ignited the lighter and, very slowly, lowered the flame towards him. He struggled, but it was pointless. I ignored him at first, but as he yammered the word *okay*, I extinguished the flame and waited for him to speak.

"Cesar Romero," he said sullenly. "He is a surgeon by trade but is happy to work without asking too many questions."

"How do we contact him?" I snapped.

"Phone," Klas murmured, nodding towards the pocket of his leather trousers.

With difficulty, I managed to wriggle his phone out. As I scrolled through Klas' contacts, I wasn't surprised to see many famous names. After dialling Cesar's number, I pressed the phone to Klas' ear. Mercifully, Cesar answered after only a single ring. The conversation lasted only a few seconds, comprising the address of the scrapyard and a description of Erin's wounds. Then, I hung up the phone.

"He will come," Klas said bitterly. After that, I raced to Erin's side.

Her face was deathly pale, but at least she was still breathing. Clutching her hand in mine, I told her that someone was coming to help. I'm not sure whether I imagined her smile. Gently, I kissed her forehead. It was much cooler than I'd expected it to be. Meanwhile, Bowker dragged Klas – still bound to the chair – into the next room. I agreed that it was better if Cesar didn't know Klas was there. Or what we'd done to him.

Cesar arrived within five minutes. He was dressed in an immaculate suit and smelt strongly of cologne. I guessed he'd been out for the evening when Klas had called. I wondered how he'd come to be in Klas' debt but, as he crouched beside Erin, I pushed those thoughts away. At that moment, I didn't want to think of the problems he might have had in the past. Besides, it was none of my business.

He had a bag with him, which I was relieved to see contained medical supplies. It took almost no time at all for him to administer pain relief, remove the bullet, clean, and stitch the wound. Once he'd finished, he removed his gloves and told us that she was stable. I was briefly relieved, but he continued to say that, if her condition changed, we should strongly consider taking her to a hospital. With a single nod at Bowker and I, he left.

As I stood beside her bed, Bowker came to stand beside me. The two of us watched her for a while before he said something that I hadn't expected.

"You know vodka don't burn, right?"

"Yeah. Luckily, he didn't," I said, grinning.

It was a cheap, non-branded bottle. According to the label, it was 37.5 per cent volume, so I knew that the water content was too high for the liquid to burn. Over time, alcohol vapour would have evaporated, which would catch. But that would have taken a lot of time and heat.

"Savage," he muttered. To my surprise, he patted my shoulder appreciatively.

I sat by Erin for most of the night. Every time she stirred, I flinched. Although the colour had returned to her cheeks, she'd barely moved, and hadn't said anything. At first, I simply watched her dozing, but I couldn't ignore the other things that were going through my mind.

All the energy I'd focussed on Frank had been wasted. During that time, I hadn't once considered an alternative. I found myself recalling some of the things that had happened over the past few weeks. Perhaps, contrary to what I'd thought at the time, the bomb in his office had been more than an attempt to hide information. Then, there were the two cars that had chased Erin and me away from the driving range after I'd spoken to Frank. They must have been watching him, and then followed us because they thought he might have told us something he shouldn't. But who could do something like that? And who was capable of murdering Dina and possibly Kelly, poisoning Wilson, Kidnapping Lizzy, and planting drugs to frame Frank and me?

It had to be someone with a lot of influence; I couldn't imagine it was easy to get Frank to do anything. Surely, they would have a connection to Wilson and Dina, too. Impulsively, I took out Frank's phone and scrolled through his call logs. He had to have contacted Kelly to arrange to speak to her. There were a few threads from unknown numbers, which I checked in turn. Most were automated messages from delivery companies or similar. But then, I found an exchange that stood out from the rest.

"*How long before you start to miss him?*" the final message read. With mounting agitation, I scrolled to the bottom to read the rest of the messages. What I saw disgusted me. It was a picture of an erect penis. *Like what you see, Kelly?*

"*Fuck off perv.*"

"*Don't act like you're not impressed.*"

"*Creep.*"

"*You know you want it…*"

"*Happy without.*"

"*Are you?*"

"*Leave me alone.*"

I wasn't sure whether to be sickened or outraged. I'd always known that Frank was a disgusting person but could never have imagined he'd send such grotesque messages to a grieving woman. Reluctantly, I checked some of the other threads, finding similar messages. Only now, I realised why Frank had reacted so strongly when I'd confronted him about Kelly. He was worried that I knew about his sordid texts.

But what had happened to Kelly? I doubted Frank was responsible for her disappearance. And although I hadn't believed him at the time, it seemed I was wrong about his involvement in Lizzy's kidnapping as well. Had I also been wrong about Dina and Wilson? Frank had signed the reports and ignored the warnings, which meant he was involved in but not necessarily responsible for the coverup. Perhaps he'd done so because he was coerced or manipulated.

I knew from personal experience that it wouldn't be easy to make Frank do something he didn't want to. In fact, I was certain that the only way would be to threaten his dog. The alternative, then, was that someone was manipulating him; using him as a puppet to enact their dastardly will. Based on his stubbornness, I thought it would need to be someone senior at Rathbury-Holmes; surely, I could limit my search to people within the organisation. But who? Someone that Frank trusted. Despite his faults, I couldn't imagine him agreeing to something like this unless he'd been deceived by someone he called a friend.

As I thought, a memory surfaced in my mind. It was incomplete at first but quickly solidified into the first page of the DEV-45 report. Although the detail had been redacted, the names of those involved were still visible. Dina was murdered. Wilson was poisoned. Frank was framed. That left only one other name: Rupert Prophett.

Throughout the sickness, Prophett had been working tirelessly to assure the public that a cure would come soon. No matter how hard I tried, my brain couldn't process what was going through it. It was as if something fundamental, like gravity, was suddenly untrue. Quite frankly, it didn't make sense. And yet, paradoxically, it was the only explanation I could think of.

During the project for CPT, which he had approved, he must have worked closely with Dina and Wilson. I'd recently learnt that he knew Frank personally. After leaving Rathbury-Holmes, he'd gone on to become very influential. Was it possible that Rupert Prophett was trying desperately to undo a mistake he made over a decade ago? How could someone in his position allow something like this to happen? Even if it were true, surely, no one would believe me. Somehow, I had to find proof. And, conveniently, I might already have it.

My hands shook, almost uncontrollably, as I scrolled through the rest of Frank's messages to a thread from Prophett.

"*What happened?*" Prophett had typed a few days before I was arrested.

"*Bloody bombing!*" Frank had replied. "*Can you believe it?!*"

"*Any suspects?*"

"*Thought it might be one of those nutters outside the building... Not sure they've got the brainpower, though.*"

"*A competitor, perhaps? Or a colleague?*"

"*Could be. Thought it might be an analyst in one of the research teams. Suspended for insubordination. Absolute arsehole.*"

"*Why do you say that?*"

"*He thought he'd found an issue and proceeded to broadcast it to anyone that would listen. Almost sank the project. In fact, he's still harping on about it now. Truth be told, I wish he'd mind his own.*"

"*What's his name?*"

"*Jack Bright.*"

My mind was racing, but I reigned it in. At best, all this proved was that Frank had confided in Rupert. I needed more. Frank's phone was an older model, long outdated. But had he had it for nearly a decade?

Speedily, I scrolled back through the messages

he'd exchanged with Prophett. Thankfully, they rarely spoke and, if they did, it was usually only a few brief messages. When I saw Wilson's name, I read the messages that followed.

"*Witless oaf,*" Frank had typed.

"*What happened?*"

"*He's saying we should pull CPT. Suggesting there is a problem and it might not be suitable for the market. Lunatic.*"

"*He was a little scatter-brained. Perhaps he's confused with another project.*"

And then, further down in the messages, I found Dina's name.

"*She's trying to derail the entire project.*"

"*Why?*"

"*Adverse interactions. Haven't had a chance to check the data, but could be serious.*"

"*I shouldn't worry. Problems like that can crop up. I'm sure it will disappear soon.*"

Scatter-brained. Disappear. The words were too much of a coincidence. It took tremendous effort not to throw Frank's phone across the warehouse. With everything that I'd been through over the last few weeks – surviving a bomb, being framed, high-speed car chases and shootouts with the police – I had to solve this. And then, in the more recent messages, I found exactly what I was looking for.

"*Could use some advice on the cure, if you've time?*" Frank had typed.

"*Of course. What's the issue?*" Prophett had replied.

Frank had proceeded to explain the situation. Considering Prophett had been a senior manager at the company, Frank used extremely condescending language. If I'd been spoken to like that, I'd have seriously struggled to give a sincere answer. But Prophett had.

"I'd suggest a formulation change. Something might be impacting the effectiveness of the active. Perhaps easiest to discuss over the phone."

He'd known that CPT was the reason the cure hadn't worked. But rather than admitting that in a text, which could be used against him, he'd told Frank over the phone. There would be no record of their discussion, and so no proof that he'd told Frank to remove CPT. I had to find a way to make Prophett confess. But how? I would have to trick him into admitting something incriminating. Without a solid plan of attack, I pressed the call button.

"How are you, Frank?" Prophett said. Although his words were polite, his voice was wary.

"Frank's been arrested," I replied. "But I suspect you already know that."

"Who is this?" he replied.

"I suspect you probably know that, too."

"I'm calling the police."

"Good," I said hurriedly. "Then you can tell them what's really causing the Itch."

"Excuse me?" he said. His tone had darkened.

"I know the truth. Just like Wilson Loveday. And Dina Mulchandaani."

"What on Earth are you talking about?"

"I also know that you murdered Dina. That you poisoned Wilson. Framed Frank. And me, too. Just to hide the truth about CPT."

There was a long pause. After a while, I worried

that he may have hung up. But eventually, he answered.

"You must be Jack," he said.

"I'm going to make sure you pay for what you've done."

"What might that be?"

"You approved CPT, even though you knew it wasn't safe for use."

"I haven't worked at Rathbury-Holmes for quite some time. You'll have to take up any prospective issues with whoever was notified about them."

It was true. Even if he did know about the issue, he hadn't put his name to anything. He must have manipulated Frank to ignore the issues. In effect, he'd made Frank a scapegoat. Although I'd never liked him, Frank surely didn't deserve this. And I wasn't going to let Prophett get away with it.

"I'm sure the police will still be interested to hear what I've got to say. And if they start digging, you can't be sure they won't find anything."

"There's nothing to find, Jack," he said. There was so much smugness in his voice that I wanted to yell at him.

"Are you sure you want to take that chance?"

"Hasn't this gone on for long enough? Think of your… friends," he said, leaving a telling pause before he said *the word friends*. "I'm sure they've suffered a lot because of what you've been doing. And think of the harm you're causing by letting them help you. Are you sure you want them to suffer any more?"

I knew he was talking about Lizzy, even if he wasn't implicit. I cursed. It was all I could think to say.

"Do the right thing and turn yourself in," he said. "Nobody else needs to get hurt."

"Not a chance," I hissed; although, if I was honest, I had been tempted to do just that.

"What's your goal here?" he asked. "How do you see this ending?"

"With you behind bars."

"But I haven't done anything wrong, Jack," he said. "If you won't go to the police, then, perhaps we could meet."

The suggestion came as a surprise. Clearly, he was plotting something, but what it was I couldn't say. I felt like a lamb, and Prophett was a wolf, tempting me into his lair for an easier kill.

"How do I know I can trust you?" I asked.

"Because I haven't done anything wrong. Come, now, Jack. Let's see if you and I can sort this silly little mess out. I'll be at my apartment this evening," After telling me the address, he added. "If you decide to visit, call me on this number, and I'll let you in."

A barrage of abuses tumbled out of my mouth. Before long, I was simply spouting a string of four-letter words. When I'd finished, Prophett chuckled.

"I'm a politician, Jack. Insults are just white noise to me," he said, before hanging up the phone.

For a long time, I simply stared ahead. And then, I cursed, loudly and angrily, until my throat gave out. After that, I paced back and forth, running my hands roughly through my hair. I was sure that Prophett had deceived the nation and, as a result, hundreds of thousands of people had suffered. He had to be held to account. But I needed proof.

"Telling or what?" Bowker demanded.

From his tone, I guessed he'd been asking for a while, and I'd ignored him. Resignedly, I recounted what Prophett had said. Hearing it again made my blood boil.

"What we doing, then?" he asked.

"I don't know."

"What? You ain't even gonna try?"

"I'm thinking," I snapped, rounding on Bowker.

It should have been a simple choice. I should have called the police and let them deal with Prophett. But, of course, I couldn't do that. Lizzy was my closest friend. She'd helped me find key pieces of information, without which I wouldn't have been able to solve this mystery. Suffice it to say, I owed her a huge debt; too much. I knew that I had to help her, no matter what the cost.

"Can you make sure Erin is okay?" I said.

"Yeah," he said, nodding a little uncertainly. "Where you going?"

I told him Prophett's address. He asked if I wanted any help or support. Whilst that would have been reassuring, I knew it wasn't a good idea. If Prophett knew I'd brought backup, he might hurt Lizzy. When Bowker asked what I was going to do, I stayed silent for a long time.

"I'll think of something," was all I could say.

CHAPTER 19

As I got out of the taxi at Deansgate, I looked up at the glass and steel structure in front of me. It looked like a mountain amongst the surrounding buildings. The last of the sun was still bathing the uppermost floors. That was where I was heading.

When I called Prophett, he gave me the code for the door and told me to take the elevator to his penthouse apartment. With little prompting, I wondered how Lizzy or Erin would have handled this situation. In many ways, the two of them were similar. It took a lot to faze them. Knowing how much trouble they were in, though, I pushed thoughts of them away.

The man who answered the door was gigantic. Truly and utterly enormous. From over his shoulder, Prophett told him to step aside and let me in. There were more men inside, perhaps a dozen. Each wore a plain black polo shirt. They were all massively built. I'd seen hired goons before, but these were a different breed. Klas's men were loutish thugs; these men were soldiers. They stood at their posts, unmoving, arms behind their backs and eyes fixed on me.

As expected, Prophett's apartment was glorious. The floors were tiled and immaculate. There wasn't a fingerprint, scuff mark, or speck of dust on anything. Three of the walls were made of floor-to-ceiling windows, which looked out over the city. I was reminded of my flat, although I could see much further from here.

"Beautiful, isn't it?" Prophett asked, noticing me looking out of the window. "Cost a pretty penny, but it was worth it. There's nothing I love more than looking out over my city."

"Whatever game this is, I'm not playing," I snarled.

"Now, now," he chided. "No reason to get snippy. Why don't you have a seat, and we can talk about this."

I glared at him, too furious to speak. He sat patiently on the luxurious leather sofa, smiling expectantly. Naturally, I was more than a little reluctant. But as I was at his mercy, I eventually moved to take the seat beside him.

"If you wouldn't mind," he said, waving me away with his hand.

A little shocked, I moved to the neighbouring chair, only to have him indicate the chair opposite him, which was also furthest away. Despite his reputation as a germophobe, I wasn't prepared for such an aversion to closeness. Before sitting, I looked at him for confirmation that the distance was acceptable. He nodded contentedly.

"How many times have you washed your hands today?" he asked.

"What the Hell does that have to do with anything?"

"It's a simple question," he said condescendingly. In all honesty, I had no idea, so made up a number.

"People are dirty, Jack," he said. Almost absentmindedly, he applied clear sanitiser gel to his hands, so much of it that I could smell the fumes from across the room. "Microorganisms thrive on our bodies. Some are harmless, and some aren't. We can tackle most, but they are continually evolving. It's only a matter of time before our weapons against them start to become ineffective. And if that happens, we'll be at their mercy. Thankfully, CPT is not only an extremely potent antimicrobial agent, but it's also totally safe for use."

"That's a lie," I yelled. Around the room, his guards fidgeted. Prophett eased them with a wave of his hand.

"In of itself, CPT poses no chemical hazards. The sickness arose because of an interaction between CPT and unregulated narcotics. I can't be held to account if a few reckless individuals decided to dabble in something they didn't understand."

I almost conceded his point. The effects of Dose weren't fully understood when it was first discovered. But that didn't change the fact that millions had suffered.

"Three hundred thousand people is more than a few," I corrected.

"Half a per cent of the total population. I think we can both agree that qualifies as a minority."

"Where's Lizzy?" I asked.

"She's safe," he said.

"You killed Dina, didn't you?" I said. "And poisoned Wilson."

"I was really more of an orchestrator than perpetrator," he smiled, grinning sheepishly.

"And what about Frank?" I snapped. Prophett made a noise of disgust.

"He was insufferable," he sneered. "Awfully fond of flashing his privates at women. Filthy beggar. Still, good to have around. Never questioned signing his name to something, regardless of whether he understood it. Predictable, too, which meant that he was easy to track."

Understanding blossomed. Prophett had sent people to follow Frank. That must have been why the cars had followed Erin and me from the driving range.

"You make me sick," I snarled. Although I'd never liked Frank, he didn't deserve this. And Dina, Wilson, Kelly, and Lizzy certainly didn't, either.

"I wouldn't be so quick to judge," Prophett chided. "Dina and Wilson may have identified the issue, but their motives for highlighting it were far from noble. Dina was trying to use what she'd found to wrangle a promotion. As for Wilson, he made a lot of poor choices; mostly, which horse to waste his money on. He wanted to blackmail funds to feed his gambling habit. You're well acquainted with Frank Badder, so I won't say any more about why I let him take the fall for this. Your friend is unharmed, so I can hardly be blamed for something that hasn't happened."

"Are you honestly trying to justify what you've done? What you've put those people and their families through?"

"It was better than the alternative. CPT is perhaps the most widely used preservative in the country. Frankly, I shudder to think what might have happened if Dina or Wilson had blabbed to the media. Or you and your friend, for that matter. There are few sicknesses, if any, that spread faster than panic. But if CPT were removed from the market, other diseases would quickly catch up with the initial hysteria. All it takes is one infected person. And what then? An endemic? Epidemic? Pandemic? It was in the public's best interests. I know you feel you need to tell everyone what you've found and, whilst that is commendable, please consider what might happen if you tell the truth. I'll concede it was wrong to have lied about the cause but, at this point, what does it really matter? You know the cure works. Isn't it better to let sleeping dogs lie?"

"So, what? I just ignore this?" I hissed.

"I'm simply asking that you think about the consequences before making your decision. All those charges against you and your friend. What's her name? Erin. Oh yes, I know all about her. How she's been keeping you safe over the past few weeks. You're both accused of some serious crimes. I can hardly imagine what the punishment might be. But I can help. I can make all that go away. A phone call or email and you can both this mess behind you. So, what do you think? You keep shtum, and we can forget this whole thing. You and Erin will be free to go about your lives."

I'd fully expected to pander to Prophett's every whim. But hearing how coolly he was able to speak about murder – how comfortable he was in all the terrible things he'd done – I couldn't do it.

"If you really think I'm going to let you get away with this, then you're more delusional than I thought," I snarled. "I'm going to make sure you pay for what you've done. And nothing you say will change my mind."

"You're sure?" he asked, chewing his lip thoughtfully.

Although I was sure of my intention, I had no idea how to accomplish it. In the end, I told him I'd called the police before I arrived.

"They know everything," I said. "You might have found someone to blame but now, people are going to start digging. And I can guarantee they'll find something to link you to this. Maybe an email or a memo you didn't get rid of. I wouldn't be surprised if they've already started building a case against you. It's over, Prophett. You've lost."

Naturally, I'd expected him to panic at this point. As far as he knew, it was over. There was nothing he could do that would absolve him. It was chilling, then, to hear what he said in reply.

"We'll see."

Before I could say another word, two men grabbed my arms and hoisted me to my feet. I hadn't even realised they were standing behind me. With more force than seemed necessary, I was dragged across the room. For a heart-stopping moment, I thought they were going to cast me over the balcony. I was relieved, then, when they led me out of the front door.

A car was waiting in the underground car park. I was shoved into the back of it. My escorts got in either side of me, whilst another sat at the wheel. Prophett took the front passenger seat. The tyres screeched as the car roared ahead.

Even though there were only a few cars around, the driver's recklessness was unnerving. He barely paused at junctions before joining passing traffic and took corners so quickly that – had I not been penned in by Prophett's guards – I'd have been sliding around on the backseat. It didn't help that I could hardly see a thing through the darkened windows. I saw enough, though, to realise we were leaving the city.

"Where are we going?" I demanded.

"Wait and see," Prophett said mischievously. "You don't mind if I put the radio on, do you?"

Without waiting for my reply, he turned it on. As *Summer Holiday* blared through the speakers, he tapped his thigh appreciatively.

"I love this song," he added, before whistling along. If I hadn't already been terrified, this would have been enough to push me over the edge.

After leaving the city, we joined the motorway, heading north. We passed through a few towns, before eventually joining the M6. Desperately, I wondered where we were going and why Prophett was so secretive. As my fear-addled imagination ran rampant, dozens of reasons filled my mind. But there was one reason for taking me so far away from the city that stuck out from the rest. With everything I knew, he would surely want to eliminate me, as he had so many others. Even the thought of it was worse than the most unbearable pain I'd ever experienced, which I suspected was probably my brush with the Itch.

It wasn't until nearly an hour later that we left the motorway. We'd passed Lancaster and – as far as I could tell – were heading towards the coast. Realising this only worsened my sense of foreboding but I kept my mouth shut, trying not to think about what was to come. Staring through the windscreen, I could see tiny lights bobbing offshore a few hundred metres ahead of us.

We followed the coast along a road lined with grassy sand dunes, eventually arriving at a chain-link fence. Although I didn't know where we were, I recognised the Rathbury-Holmes logo on a sign at the entrance.

We followed the road to what I thought was a mound of earth. As we approached, though, I realised it was a building. The roof was carpeted in long, wavy grass, which blended almost perfectly with the surrounding dunes. Cages of rocks were arranged around the perimeter, which helped the illusion. Windows of varying sizes and shapes peppered the wall. There was a car park in front of the mound, sheltered by sandbanks on each side. The other men left the vehicle first, before ushering me out and latching onto my arms. The breeze from the ocean was chilly, and my jacket was too thin to protect against the cold.

"Is that really necessary?" Prophett said to the men holding me. "I'm sure you can be trusted, can't you?"

"Why am I here?" I asked once I was released.

"Welcome to The Springs," Prophett said. With a sweeping wave of his arm, he indicated the mound behind us. "I'm sure you know about this place."

I did. For several years, the Springs had been the principal manufacturing site of Rathbury-Holmes. Most of their products were manufactured there and distributed throughout the UK and beyond.

"I'd like to show you around," Prophett said.

I waited for him to give a reason, but he simply gazed at me, smiling patiently. With no idea what lay inside, I was confident following him wasn't a good idea. In the end, though, I knew I had no other choice. If nothing else, I'd be glad to get away from the frosty night air.

Stone steps led down to the entrance of the Springs, which made it seem like we were entering some sort of underground bunker. Passing through a set of sliding glass doors, we arrived in a domed atrium. The floor had the appearance of polished sand. Whilst he walked, Prophett applied more sanitising gel to his hands.

"The facility was designed by Leighton Coulthard. His work is heavily influenced by the natural world, which is why he was chosen for the project. It was felt that his designs embodied one of the company's core principles: protecting the environment."

He went on to explain that the building was almost entirely carbon neutral. It was powered by offshore wind turbines. The toilets flushed using rainwater collected from the roof. He made a joke about how much money they saved because of how often it rained in the UK. The earth that surrounds the structure acted as natural insulation, which kept the building warm in winter and cool in warmer months. He made a joke about how rarely the weather was warm in the UK. One thing he didn't mention, though, was why I was there. When I asked, he ignored me, continuing to explain that some of the steel used in the building was salvaged from old ships.

After passing through some offices, we arrived at a door. Prophett waited for one of his guards to open it, once again demonstrating his hygiene concerns. The room beyond had large windows that looked over a manufacturing area set a few feet below us. It was a hive of activity. Everyone was working busily to the steady beat of heavy machinery, all of which centred around three large silos. A network of pipes and tubes as extensive as blood vessels fed into each.

At first glance, everything appeared to be running like clockwork. But as I looked closer, I realised that the work was happening at a frenzied pace. Nobody spoke. They didn't even look at one another as they passed. To see such fevered work without social interaction was unsettling. It put me in mind of forced labour.

"This is the largest of our production areas," Prophett said, gesturing the room with open arms. "Some have taken to calling it *The Cavern*. It contains some of the most advanced-"

"Why am I here?" I demanded, interrupting his speech.

The men holding me tightened their grip. Everyone in earshot reacted to my words; except Prophett. He continued smiling serenely as he resumed his explanation.

"They're currently manufacturing a batch of CPT," he said. "Nowadays, you'd be hard-pressed to find a product that doesn't contain it, which is largely due to how safe it is."

"You're insane," I snarled. But my insult fell on deaf ears.

"Now, I believe you're aware of a by-product of CPT. It forms in small quantities during production. It's quite nasty due to low pH when in solution but, fortunately, the production process has been modified to extract the by-product. If you like, I can explain using simpler terminology?"

"I understand," I snarled, peeved by his patronising tone.

"Jolly good," Prophett replied; somehow, he managed to sound even more patronising. "Well, as you can imagine, the by-product has to be removed and disposed of appropriately. By regulating the volume released, the site can pump the waste directly into the ocean without affecting the pH of coastal seawater. It was an easy resolution for getting rid of a potentially nasty problem. In fact, the waste itself has proven quite useful, particularly for getting rid of troublemakers."

The true meaning of his words struck me like a fist. Dina had disappeared. The only trace of her was clothing, which had been washed up on a beach on the Northwest coast. She hadn't drowned; she'd been murdered in a truly gruesome way. Now, I understood why the police had found no trace of her. There was nothing left to find. She'd been *dissolved* in the waste by-product and flushed out to sea.

It was a chilling realisation. I was more unsettled by my next thought; surely, I was about to meet the same end as she had. Before that, though, the guards parted and dragged someone forward. As my eyes met Lizzy's, I was consumed by guilt and terror in equal measure.

CHAPTER 20

She was breathing deeply. Her expression was defiant. There was a small bruise below her eye. It was purple and looked a few days old. Instantly, I started thrashing, but it was useless. Physically, I was no match for the guards holding my arms.

"You're a monster," she snarled. Prophett feigned hurt, before pretending to sob into his hands.

"Let her go," I demanded.

"I think not," he said, chuckling with disbelief.

"She doesn't know anything."

"Once again, I must disagree," he muttered, glancing around the room.

"Jesus, what the Hell is wrong with you?" I roared.

"Is it wrong to want to protect the nation from illness?" he asked thoughtfully.

"By poisoning thousands?" Lizzy countered. "Yeah, I'd say that was pretty terrible."

"Jack and I have already discussed this," Prophett said. "Those affected are merely a fraction of-"

"You can't do this," I yelled, before continuing in a calmer tone. "Right now, it's just Dose that triggers the Itch. But how long before another product comes along that triggers it? What if that's used by more people? Millions, maybe? You have to stop this now. Pull CPT. Get it off the market."

I'm not sure if I'd expected him to listen or not. Whilst he considered my words, though, I'd dared to hope. I should've known it was foolish to do so.

"I'd rather just kill you and have this over with,"

he replied.

Before I knew what was happening, a guard stepped forward and jammed something plastic in Lizzy's mouth. I shouted a nonsensical string of curse words, too angry and afraid to form a coherent sentence. When he backed away, she spat on the floor. The guard shook his head at Prophett.

"Disappointing," Prophett said. "Your turn, Mr Bright."

The guard stepped towards me and prized open my jaws. After shining a torch at the back of my throat, he turned to Prophett and nodded.

"Oh, dear," Prophett said excitedly.

"What- what the Hell are you doing?" I tried to say, choking on the plastic in my mouth.

"The by-product will easily dissolve living tissue but will struggle with anything that isn't biological, such as prosthetic limbs or – unfortunately for you – *dental fillings*."

From one of his pockets, the guard in front of me drew a set of pliers. It probably took less than 10 seconds for him to pull out my three teeth that had fillings, but it seemed to last *much* longer. The plastic separator made it impossible to yell, but I gave it a damn good try. Lizzy was shouting, too. By the time the last tooth came out, blood was pouring from my lips and had already soaked through my shirt. Once the plastic separator was removed, I spat out the blood, and then cursed, loudly.

"I'm simply trying to protect the public," Prophett said, his voice infuriatingly rational. "I'll concede I'm partially at fault. But mistakes aren't always a bad thing. In fact, did you know penicillin was discovered by accident? You must appreciate how important CPT is. Microorganisms are getting harder to kill. Who knows how many antibiotic-resistant strains or hyper infectious viruses are lurking on the horizon? I'm simply doing what is necessary to protect humanity."

As soon as Prophett finished speaking, Lizzy and I were dragged forwards. I tried everything I could think of to disrupt my progress – shouting, yelling, kicking, and dragging my feet. In my desperation, I even considered biting one of the guards but knew it was pointless. Even if I managed to break free, there was no way that we could both escape the building.

One by one, the staff in the Cavern stopped working and watched, silently, as we passed, staring with impassive faces. We were led to a recess in the floor, protected by a fence that ran around the edge. Pipes fed into the floor from overhead. There were several hatches in the middle of the recess. A guard opened one of them to reveal a dark hole. Although I couldn't see anything inside, I could hear a liquid sloshing within.

"I'm so sorry," I said quietly to Lizzy.

"It's fine. Worse ways to go, I guess," she replied. Despite what was about to happen, there was a hint of her usual playfulness in her voice.

People were yelling around the room. I waited for the guards to shove us into the tank. Every second that passed, my breathing quickened. Before long, my lungs were throbbing, filled to the brim with air. And then, inexplicably, the guards holding me dropped to the ground. Free, I staggered backwards. I looked down and saw the red stains blossoming on their bodies. It was at that moment I heard the gunshots.

Instantly, I fell to the ground, scrambling for cover behind a piece of machinery. Lizzy followed. From there, I peeked through a gap to see the guards around the room, pulling pistols and firing wildly. Cautiously, I crept to a better vantage to see people pouring into the room, spraying bullets at everything. There were already several bodies lying still on the floor. As far as I could see, the staff that had been working in there had all scattered.

"This might have escalated beyond our control," Lizzy yelled over the gunfire. How she managed to crack jokes at a time like this, I'd never know.

The surviving guards had taken shelter behind a small piece of equipment that was covered in dials. Most of them were broken now, shattered in the hail of bullets raining down from above. There was another volley of gunshots, forcing everyone to burrow deeper into their hiding places. Once the ricochets had finished, a voice barked an order. No further shots were fired. In the silence that followed, one of the guards peered anxiously from where he was hiding, waiting to see what would happen next.

"Surrender your weapons and kneel in the centre of the room," roared a man. "If you do not do so, we will continue firing. You have 10 seconds to comply," he added, before counting down. All but one of the guards emerged immediately. From where I was hiding, I could see the last guard preparing himself. Just as the man yelled *zero*, the guard scuttled out. Apparently, though, it was too late. He dropped to the ground in a hail of bullets.

"How many are you?" the man asked. None of the

pg. 268

guards spoke. A bullet thudded into the ground in front of them.

"20," said one of the guards. 13 men were kneeling. I couldn't be sure how many had been shot, but it looked like the numbers added up.

"Where are your captives?" the man barked. I froze. Should we announce ourselves? What would they do to us if we did? Would they shoot? Although I wasn't thrilled about the prospect, it seemed better than dissolving in a vat of acid. I started shuffling from our hiding place, but Lizzy caught my arm.

"What are you doing?" she asked.

"They're going to find us either way," I said. She thought about that for a moment, and then, resignedly, nodded.

"Here," I said. "We're coming out. Don't shoot."

Taking the silence that followed as an invitation, I stepped out, walked a few steps, and then lowered to my knees. Lizzy knelt beside me. The nearest guard was just beyond my reach. After a few seconds, the gunmen advanced, weapons aimed at us. Prophett was being dragged along at the back of the group. Some broke off from the procession, fanning out around the room, inspecting the corners and other hiding places.

Once they'd swept the room, the gunman surrounded us, closing ranks, and circling like sharks. Someone stood close to my side. Carelessly or intentionally, they let their weapon drift into my eye-line as if to remind me of the severity of the situation. I wanted to protest – to tell them I hadn't done anything wrong – but couldn't bring myself to speak. I couldn't even look up from the floor. The last thing

I wanted to do was stare down the barrel of a gun. Grimly, it might be the last thing I saw. To focus on something other than their gun, I fixed my eyes on their boots, noting that they were surprisingly small. That was nothing, though, compared to the mind-blowing shock, I felt when she spoke.

"You can get up now," Erin said kindly.

For a long time after she'd spoken, I simply stared at the floor. Part of me wasn't willing to believe it was really her. When I finally looked up, she was smiling down at me.

"You can stay down there if you'd prefer," she added.

"I don't believe it," I stammered.

"I'll bet. You must be Lizzy. I'm Erin. Nice to finally meet you."

"Trust me, the pleasure is entirely mine," Lizzy said, grinning broadly.

"How did you- you were," I stammered.

"Guess someone must be watching over me," she said, smiling.

"How did you know where we were?"

"Bowker," she said, gesturing to one of the men. I turned to see him messing with one of the machines in the room.

She told me that, after I'd left the scrapyard, Bowker had called someone to watch Prophett's apartment. When they saw us leaving, they followed to the Springs and told Bowker where we were. I wasn't surprised to hear that Erin had insisted on joining – despite a bullet wound. It was at that point I looked around at her company of gunmen. Each of them had a predatory look on their face. I found it hard to believe they were simply Dose protestors. Who on Earth were they? And why had Erin brought them here? I began to suspect perhaps she'd withheld something from me. But what?

"What's going on?" I asked.

At that point, two men stepped forward, hauling Prophett between them. His hands were bound behind his back. From the colour of his face, not to mention his lifeless stare, the fear I'd felt was nothing compared to what he was going through. Erin regarded him, almost curiously, her hands resting on her rifle. Prophett tried to speak but was shaking so fiercely his words wouldn't come.

"Honourable; that's what they call you, isn't it? The *Right Honourable* Rupert Prophett. Responsible for the health of the nation. I'm not sure which sickens me more. I couldn't tell you how many times I've thought about killing you."

Understandably, Prophett looked terrified. His eyes were so wide I could see the whole of each iris, punctured by his pinprick pupils. I should have intervened, or at least said something to stop her. But something – perhaps morbid curiosity – urged me not to.

"After a while, it just became part of my subconscious. Brush teeth. Get dressed. How to kill Prophett. Got to work. Eat lunch. How to kill Prophett. I dreamed about it, even. I've considered all the different ways I could hurt you – make you suffer before finally choking that last flicker of life out of you. But then, I realised; that wouldn't be enough. All my rage – the hours I'd spent hating you – would be wasted. I knew it wouldn't be enough to kill you; I had to make you feel the pain I'd felt. And then, I realised how I could do it. Can you imagine how dirty a prison must be? All those inmates locked up together. Crammed inside. The sweat. The saliva. The blood. And an alarming amount of semen, I should imagine, too. No matter how many times you wash and scrub yourself, you'll never be clean again."

At that point, she took a step forward. They were so close that his breath disturbed the loose strands of hair hanging over her face. Very slowly, she pressed her fingers against her lips and kissed them. Then, she pressed her fingers against Prophett's cheek. His reaction was visceral and instantaneous. He gagged. He struggled but was unable to move. When she finally stopped touching him, he turned his head and vomited. I wondered if that was because of his phobia of germs or fear of imprisonment.

"Get him out of here," Erin said, her voice brimming with disgust. I watched the men drag him away. Once he was gone, I turned to Erin.

"What's going on?" I asked, more insistently this time.

"I'm going to tell you why I've been protesting the ban."

I remembered accusing her of drug dealing and suggested that she was only protested to make Dose legal for her own gains. She'd then told me that her family had been torn about by the ban. At the time, I hadn't thought to ask any follow-up questions. Now, though, I had plenty.

"A few years ago, police raided our house. They found Dose. My dad's fingerprints were all over it. He swore he didn't know anything about it. Mum didn't believe him, though. Neither did the police. But I knew the truth. A few days earlier, he'd told me that something was going to happen to him. He said he was in trouble. I asked him, but he wouldn't say. He told me people were going to think he'd done something illegal but that it wasn't true. As soon as they took him, I knew something wasn't right. Somebody wanted him gone. They did this to him. And ever since, I've been trying to prove who was responsible."

At first, I didn't follow. But suddenly, I remembered something I'd heard recently from a man who'd been arrested for possession of Dose. Wilson had chatted about how rarely he received visitors. Although it had been sad to hear, there wasn't much I could say in reply. But, as I stared at Erin, I remembered he'd said even his wife and daughter never came to see him.

"You're Wilson's daughter," I declared.

"Erin Loveday, at your service," she said, smiling sadly.

CHAPTER 21

"I wish you could have met him. Before all this, I mean," Erin said. I'd been so dumbfounded that I hadn't realised she was still speaking. "You remind me of him. He was- he *is* a kind and gentle man. After he was charged, Mum refused to let me see him. We argued about it – a lot. But she never caved. Eventually, I snuck out to see him. It was a mistake. It was like dementia. He had moments of clarity. Snippets where I thought he remembered me. But he didn't. I've never been back. From that day, though, there's one thing I've held on to. It wasn't about how poorly my Dad looked. Or how angry I was that he'd been taken away. He didn't have any scars."

I'd had the same thought when I'd seen him. I'd only met a handful of Dose users, all of whom were badly injured as a result of the Itch. In fact, I had personal experience of how little Dose it took to trigger symptoms.

"If Dose was the cause, why didn't someone who was supposedly taking it have any injuries?" she continued. "I mean, Christ, the way the media painted it, one whiff and people were tearing their flesh from the bones. I was convinced somebody was trying to frame him but had no idea why. I spent a long time trying to prove it but didn't have any luck. Then, you came along."

There should have been a lot of different thoughts going through my mind, but there was only one. It was about my brother on the night before he'd died.

"Jack, please," Danny was sobbing. "Do you really think I'd lie about something like this?"

"Well, it certainly looks that way," I'd spat in reply.

"Christ, how can you say that? I'm your brother. I- I need help. I'm- it hurts. So much."

Looking back, I should have known something was wrong as soon as he arrived. In all the time I'd lived at the flat, he'd only visited a handful of times and, in each case, we'd arranged it beforehand. But on that occasion, there was no phone call or message. When I'd answered the door, he'd rushed inside. It was a hot night, and yet, he couldn't stop shaking. Normally, he enjoyed a drink, but barely touched the beer I gave him.

"I can't believe this" I'd yelled. "How could you be so stupid? I mean, you know how dangerous that stuff is."

"Jack, please, I swear to you, I didn't- I've never-"

"And yet, the evidence points to the contrary."

"Please, Jack. I- I'm- I don't-"

"Go to the hospital," I'd said.

Of course, I was worried about him. The Itch had already claimed so many lives. And yet, I couldn't deny that I was annoyed at him, too. He was stammering. He couldn't speak. Usually, he knew exactly what to say, no matter the situation. I didn't give him a chance to explain.

"Look, I don't know what you want me to say," I'd replied. "There's nothing I can do to help. You need to see a doctor. And after that, you need a lawyer. A bloody good one."

"You- you don't-"

"I'm serious, Danny. You need to leave. Right now."

Ever since then, I'd regretted turning him away. Erin's situation was similar. The difference was that she'd never had any fear or doubt in her mind. As soon as her father was arrested, she'd fought to prove he was innocent. Worse still, there was a chance Danny hadn't even taken Dose. Although the drug triggered the sickness, other chyrolic compounds would have the same effect. Was it possible some other product had given him the sickness?

"Is this why you kept me around?" I asked, desperately trying to purge the terrible thoughts from my mind.

"Initially," she admitted. There was something in her tone that suggested her feelings had changed, which I was glad to hear, despite everything else I was feeling. "I knew it was a chance to finally find out who was responsible. Not just for Danny and my dad, but all the people that have been affected by the sickness. And now, we finally know."

After waving her hand, a portion of the gunmen broke away from the group. They surrounded the tanks containing the waste. One by one, the men deployed a hose into the tanks.

"What's going on?" I asked. "What are they doing?"

"We're putting an end to this," she said.

Although I wasn't sure what she meant, her tone unsettled me. There was something dangerous in her eyes, between longing and fury. Frankly, I didn't need to know what she was planning to realise it wasn't good. And yet, I couldn't help but ask.

"What are you going to do with that stuff?"

"The public needs to see. They did this. They let this happen by believing his lies and deceit. People have suffered; not because of the Itch, but because the public refused to believe Dose wasn't to blame. Now, I'm going to make sure they never forget their mistake."

It didn't matter that she hadn't told me what she was going to use it for; I knew I couldn't let her take the waste. Lizzy had the same thought, too, moving to block the tanks from the gunmen. As far as I could tell, the waste was only good for one thing. And I certainly didn't want any part of any plan that involved chemical waste that could dissolve a human being. But how could I stop her? There was no way I could overpower any of her accomplices – not without a weapon.

I reacted without thinking. With both hands outstretched, I lunged for Erin's rifle. I was within touching distance when she sprung to action. Her boot connected with my stomach, driving the air from my lungs. Lizzy rushed towards me but was tackled by a guard. He was much larger than her and, despite her ferocious struggling, she couldn't break free. As I slammed on the floor, gasping for air, a pair of Erin's goons descended on me. Meanwhile, she stood over me, looking both angry and upset.

"Put him over there," she ordered, gesturing to some nearby pipework. "The girl, too."

"Girl?" Lizzy snapped, outraged.

I was still spluttering as the gunmen dragged me across the room. With practised ease, they bound Lizzy and me with cable ties to a pipe as thick as a tree trunk. They did the same with Prophett's remaining guards to another pipe nearby. Once everyone was bound, Erin came to stand in front of me, her expression impossible to read.

"I have to admit, I kind of expected that," she said.

"Don't," I choked, unable to say anything else.

"For what it's worth, I wish this had gone differently."

"Just stop, then," Lizzy said. Erin ignored her.

"That stuff is only going to bring pain," I managed to say. "Please, for one second, just think about whatever you're going to do. Do you really want things to end like this?"

As her expression saddened, I thought I'd convinced her. She leant forward and kissed me, little more than pressing her lips against mine. Beside us, I thought I heard Lizzy mutter something. When we parted, Erin's eyes looked distant, as if she was thinking hard; or perhaps remembering. When she spoke, though, it was only to say "Yeah, I do. Goodbye, Jack."

As she jogged out of the room, her goons followed. The instant they'd left, my mind surged into overdrive. Desperately, I tugged at my bonds, so hard that they dug into my skin. The guards were doing the same thing, straining against the pipe.

"She seems nice," Lizzy said sarcastically.

"Just help me," I said irritably.

Breaking the pipe was impossible; the rivets were as thick as my thumbs. Thirty seconds tugging at the cable ties confirmed that they were much too strong, too. I followed the pipe around the edge of the room, searching for weak spots but didn't find any. Then,

Lizzy nodded towards the other side of the room. The pipe ended in a small hatch. Lizzy couldn't move because of a bracket fixing the pipe to the wall, but I could make it to the hatch.

The guards looked at me with some confusion as I followed the pipe. It was easy at first, but soon the pipe rose above my head. The cable tie bit into my wrists as I shuffled along. And then, finally, I made it to the terminal. Next, I looked for a way to free my hands. I was sure there would be tools lying around but couldn't see any. Then, I remembered the guard who'd pulled my teeth. He'd been shot during the initial gunfight and was lying a short distance away.

I found the pliers in his pocket. They were sticky with my blood. Angling my fingers so that I could use the pliers to cut the cable ties was almost impossible. I dropped them several times but, eventually, cut myself free. After I'd cut Lizzy free, the guards asked me to free them, but I ignored them.

"What now?" Lizzy asked.

"We have to stop her," I replied. Whatever Erin was planning, I knew it was going to be awful. I couldn't let her do it.

"Yes, I got that," she said exasperatedly. "How?"

Recognising the body of the driver who'd brought me to the Springs, I went through his pockets. Once I found his car keys, my eyes fell on the pistol lying on the floor beside him. Although I'd never used a weapon before, I took it, realising I might need it. I wasn't even sure if it was loaded but knew it was better than nothing. If it came to a standoff, having a weapon – even an empty one – would make me exponentially more intimidating. It was no surprise that Lizzy took the pistol and, as coolly as a secret agent, slipped the magazine in and out and checked the chamber.

"Five in the clip. One in the chamber," she said. Impressed, I told her she should probably keep hold of it.

Wasting no more time, we raced after Erin. It looked as though a hurricane had passed through the building. Every office had been ransacked. Jumbled wreckage was scattered everywhere. Sickeningly, a few bodies were lying in the otherwise deserted corridors. I had to resist the urge to see if they were alright, conscious that Erin had a head start.

As we crossed reception and saw natural light pouring through the glass doors, I put on a final burst of speed, up the staircase that led to the car park. The car I'd arrived in was still there. Sand spewed from the tyres as I floored the accelerator. Although it had only been a few minutes since Erin and the others had left, I had no idea where they were going, so I had to hurry if I wanted to catch them. Truth be told, I had no idea what I was going to do if I managed to catch up to her but would simply have to worry about that later.

"What happened to you?" I asked.

"They caught me outside the gym. I thought they were just muggers," she said in a dismissive voice.

"Are you okay?" I asked.

"I cannot believe it's taken you this long to ask that," she said. Although she sounded annoyed, she said it with a smile.

The road leading away from the site had far more bends than I remembered. More than once, I almost lost control, but I kept my foot down. As I approached the main road, I had to choose a direction. Although I was sure she wouldn't head back to the scrapyard or her flat, I could only assume she'd head back to Manchester. Lizzy agreed.

After less than a mile, I saw a van. I didn't recognise the number plate, but that didn't matter because, as we closed in, the van accelerated. Somehow, I had to stop them. My first thought was the pistol, but I quickly disregarded that idea. There was a strong chance Lizzy would miss the tyres and hit someone inside. Prophett's guards had taken my phone, so I couldn't report the vehicle to the police. The only option, then, was to drive them off the road.

"I've got an idea," I said grimly, pressing the accelerator. "Hang on."

"You're kidding?" Lizzy exclaimed.

"Just hang on."

As we gained on the van, I was a long way from convinced it was the right thing to do. A highspeed collision seemed just as likely to injure one of the passengers as blindly firing at the wheels. But then, I reached up, gripping the bottlecaps around my neck. What had happened to my brother, Erin's father, Kelly, Wilson, and Dina was terrible. And yes, it was Prophett's fault. But that didn't justify hurting millions more people. Whatever Erin was planning with the waste she'd taken, it could only end in pain. So, with both hands firmly gripping the steering wheel, I pushed my foot all the way to the floor.

As far as I could tell, the first knock only pushed the van further ahead. But the second made it swerve from one side of the road to the other. With a final burst of speed, I pulled alongside the rear of the van. And then, with a swift flick of the steering, I clipped the van's offside wheel.

It was barely more than a nudge, but enough to send the vehicle careening out of control. After battling for a few seconds, the driver finally left the road, crashing through a hedge. We were travelling so quickly that we shot past the van, but I could see a recently ploughed field beyond the hedge. It was a few feet lower than the road. As the van sailed through the air, it tilted. When two of the wheels touched the soft ground, the van bounced, flipping in the other direction onto its roof. It rolled twice more, before slipping from view.

By the time I finally stopped the car, we must have been a hundred yards from the crash site. Frantically, I slipped into reverse and sped back towards the gap in the hedge. From there, I saw the van, lying battered on its side like the carcass of a flabby animal. Its spinning wheels reminded me of flailing limbs.

"What are you doing?" I asked as Lizzy opened the door.

"What do you think? I'm going to check the van."

By the time we got to the van, the wheels had stopped turning. Lizzy had the gun. I was glad she'd taken it because, despite what Erin was planning to do, I was convinced I couldn't use it. Cautiously, I crept towards the front of the van, craning my neck to see in through the windscreen. The cabin was empty. I turned to tell Lizzy when a shadow swept over me.

Bowker moved with astonishing speed. In roughly the same time it took me to blink, he'd leapt from the roof of the van and knocked me to the ground. Lizzy rounded on him with the pistol, but he disarmed her with ease. The gun flew from her hand. She raised her fists, ready to fight him, but Erin appeared from behind the van. As Lizzy and Erin circled one another, Bowker bore down on me. His hands gripped my shoulders as he hoisted me up, only to slam me down again. He booted me in the stomach, driving the air from my lungs. After kicking me again, he shoved me onto my back with his boot.

"This ain't no playground, private school," he sneered, circling me. "Bout time you learnt that."

He raised his boot above my head. Just as he brought it down, I rolled out of the way. He used so much force that his foot sank into the soft earth. Taking my chance, I scrambled onto my feet and swung my fist. I caught him on the jaw, knocking him to the ground. But he recovered quickly and was soon back on his feet.

"Full of tricks, aren't you?" he snarled.

Suddenly, he seemed more focused. Whereas before, he'd strutted around confidently, he now moved like a practised fighter. After throwing a few wild punches – none of which came close to him – I quickly realised I was no match for Bowker. I knew I could take a punch, but it was only a matter of time before he knocked me out. And what then? Lizzy may well be able to hold her own against Erin, but there was no way she could hold them both off. It didn't take much to convince me Lizzy and I wouldn't walk away from this. The only way I could beat him was with a weapon. I'd initially thought of a branch or something that I could use as a club. But there was nothing nearby.

Bowker knocked me to the ground several times. I hauled myself up, threw a wild punch that he easily avoided, only to be knocked back down again. By now, I was limping. At some point – I'm not entirely sure when – Bowker must have done something to my leg. It hurt so much that I could hardly stand. But I persevered.

As I circled behind the van, Erin and Lizzy were blocked from my view. I swung for Bowker as he appeared. He easily avoided, which was my intention. As he stepped back, I rushed towards him, shoving him in the chest. Caught off guard, he tripped, landing on his back. Sensing my chance, I descended on him. It was a mistake.

Both of his feet caught me in the stomach. I was propelled through the air, landing on my back a few feet away. Choking, I scrambled onto my elbows, trying to get to my feet.

"Game over, Princess," Bowker snarled.

He was standing over me, blood trickling from his lip. Otherwise, he looked unharmed. I, on the other hand, could barely see through my left eye and was reasonably sure my nose was broken. Pitifully, I crawled away from him. I was so heavily dazed I didn't realise my fingers had brushed against the butt of the gun. I still wasn't sure if I could fire it. When I turned and saw Bowker only a few feet away, though, my mind was made up.

"Don't fucking move," I snarled, blood dripping from my lips.

"Got the pebbles, have you?" he asked, eyeing the gun in my hand.

"Try me and see," I countered breathlessly.

"You ever held metal before? You know how to use it?"

"I'm a fast learner," I said. The last word had barely left my mouth when Bowker rushed me.

The kickback from the pistol was surprisingly fierce for such a small object. Although Bowker kept his feet, the bullet stopped him in his tracks. Stunned, he touched his arm. When his fingers came away, they were wet with blood, the sight of which sent overwhelming guilt surging through my body. It lasted only a second before he came at me once more.

This time, I shot his leg. As the bullet struck him, he dropped to the ground. My hand shook as I lowered the pistol, but I kept a tight hold on it.

"Don't move," I snarled, staggering to move feet.

Unsteadily, I shuffled around the edge of the van. Walking was extremely painful. Limping on the squishy mud wasn't easy, and I almost lost my feet several times. I had to brace myself against the bodywork for a moment. I told myself I needed to catch my breath, but I'm sure there was more to my delay than I was admitting. With one hand on the van for support, I crept around the side of it.

Lizzy was lying in the mud. Erin was gone.

EPILOGUE

I sat on a bench by the water, looking over to Old Trafford. From there, the water almost looked like a road, which didn't really bother me as much as it might if I'd stood at the rail. The last time I'd been at Salford Quays, I'd spoken to Dina's father. His misery had gone on for so long. I could honestly say I had no idea how he'd endured it.

It was an uncomfortable memory, almost as uncomfortable as the ache in my jaw. Since the *dental treatment* I'd received at the hands of Prophett's guard, I'd been struggling to eat. I'd been for a check-up at the dentist. It was going to cost a fortune to replace the teeth he'd pulled out; money I didn't have.

"I wasn't sure you'd come," Dunhill said as she took a seat beside me. I almost hadn't but decided not to say that.

"What did you want to see me about?" I asked.

"I've been a detective for a long time," she said, gazing out over the water. "In all that time, I've never had to admit I was wrong."

"Is that supposed to be an apology?"

"More an admission of error," she said, shrugging.

"Did Prophett confess?" I asked, to which she nodded.

I'd found him in the back of the van, a little battered but still alive. With a great deal of persuasion, mostly using the pistol, I'd managed to get Bowker's phone and called the police. The first car had arrived after only a few minutes.

My theory about the breakdown of CPT had been confirmed by three different laboratories. Despite their best efforts, Rathbury-Holmes was not permitted to take part in the process. Although work was being done to assess whether Dose posed any hazards of its own, the ban was still in effect. It could still trigger the Itch.

Now that the link between chyrols and CPT had been established, I'd asked for an inquest into my brother's death. Although traces of Dose had been detected in his blood, there was also an *atypically high* amount of anti-anxiety medication. It was a chyrolic compound. At the time, the coroner had suggested this was perhaps to deal with the stress of his condition. Now, it looked as though that might have been what killed him.

Rupert Prophett's reputation was in tatters. Since the news of his involvement in the coverup had surfaced, he'd been stripped of his title. In addition, his assets had been seized. A statement released by the police indicated that they would be used to pay reparations to the families of his victims. I wasn't sure that would come close to making up for what he'd done.

"We're having a little more trouble with Frank" she explained. "He's insisting he didn't know anything about it. I guess time will tell."

The details I'd received weren't clear but, as far as I could tell, Frank's involvement in the coverup was still under investigation. He had, however, been charged with indecently exposing himself to numerous women. Despite my feelings towards him, I'd given what I felt was an impartial statement about him when questioned by the police. As far as I was concerned, he probably deserved what was coming.

"What about Erin?" I asked.

"We're still looking."

Police had searched the area near to where I'd driven her van off the road but found no sign of her. Ever since then, there'd been a police car stationed outside my flat; whether it was for protection or supervision, I wasn't sure. But for now, at least, it was proving advantageous. Klas would surely want revenge for what I did to him. I'm not sure what happened to him at the scrapyard, but I'd had a text message a few days later. It was in Swedish, which I'd translated. *As you sow, so shall you reap.* I'd been doing my best not to wonder about what he might be planning.

"Did you recover all the waste?" I asked.

"Derbyshire police found containers on the banks of a reservoir. Similar containers were found at other reservoirs around the North West. The local utility provider confirmed atypically high levels of a CPT-related substance in the water. Clean-up is underway."

I shut my eyes, willing myself not to think about what might have happened if they'd succeeded; how many people might have suffered. No matter how angry I felt about what had happened to my brother or me, I couldn't imagine doing something so callous. But then, the memory of her father surfaced in my mind. Somehow, I imagined it would be harder to watch a loved one go through what he had than to lose them. To have to witness their decline, day after day.

"What's going to happen to her father?" I asked.

"He's been transferred from Fairbank to a psychiatric ward," Dunhill said. "Once again, it seems like somebody went to a lot of trouble to stop him talking. His initial psych evaluation was… well, it looks like he'll never fully recover."

"Do they know what happened to him?"

"Poisoning, most likely. Prophett admitted to framing him, as well as hiring a care assistant for his ongoing care. I'm guessing they weren't hired for their skills as a healer. It's not clear yet, but I suspect that's how most of the damage was done. There are traces of a neurotoxin in his blood. Apparently, it's nasty stuff. Basically, it rots the brain inside the skull. Cognitive function deteriorates until the person exposed becomes nothing more than a shell. Between us, the MOD are extremely anxious to find out where it came from, I can tell you."

"What's being done about CPT?" I asked.

"I know as much as you," she replied.

As yet, the government hadn't made it clear how they intended to handle the crisis. Several suggestions had been made, which ranged from a full-scale recall of anything containing CPT to doing absolutely nothing. Each option was so fraught with issues, though, that nobody could agree on which to pursue; many of the affected products were essential medicines, and so had to be supplied. In the interim, Rathbury-Holmes were being forced to provide the cure free of charge, which was reportedly going to bankrupt the company. I'd taken the last of it about a week ago and hadn't felt any symptoms since.

The families of those killed in the initial trial of the

cure were campaigning now more than ever to take Rathbury-Holmes to court. Dina's father had also joined the cause. Several times, I'd been asked to front their campaign. I'd long since lost my job at the company and, as a former employee, I was apparently the ideal man for the job. Frankly, though, I wasn't sure I had the energy.

"How's Kelly?" I asked.

"Better than most would be," she said.

The police had arrested Prophett's guards at the Springs. Most had refused to speak, but it wasn't long before one of them had made a deal. Kelly was being held in a warehouse on the edge of the city. Although malnourished and extremely shaken, she was otherwise fine.

"What about me?" I asked.

"Suspended sentence, I suspect," she said.

My trial was scheduled in a few days. There had been a small part of me that thought figuring out the true cause of the Itch might clear my name. But I couldn't deny that I'd broken the law. Repeatedly. Frankly, a suspended sentence wasn't as bad as it could have been.

Paramedics had rushed Bowker to a local hospital, where he'd been treated before being taken to the local police station. Thankfully, the injuries he'd inflicted on me were a strong indication that I'd acted in self-defence and, as such, might not be charged with assault with a deadly weapon. At the sight of Lizzy's body, I'd feared the worst. The relief I'd felt when I realised that she was still breathing was overwhelming. The first words out of her mouth were "Ready for round 2, bitch?", which made me smile.

The paramedics had treated her at the scene. Despite what I said, she was holding herself personally responsible for letting Erin getaway. I couldn't have cared less. All the mattered was that Erin hadn't inflicted more serious injuries.

"It might be less, now that you're a hero," she said after a long pause. Despite the sentiment, there was no positivity in her tone.

Every news agency in the country – plus a few from overseas – had tried to interview me. Excluding the statements, which I'd given to the police, I hadn't spoken to anyone about what had happened. I was hoping that they would eventually get the hint and leave me alone; not least because I honestly wasn't sure I deserved any recognition for what I'd done.

"I'm not a hero," I muttered.

"The lives you saved paint a different picture, I can tell you."

"What about the ones I didn't?" I said, reaching for my bottlecap necklace.

For a long time, she didn't reply. It wasn't intended as a cry for absolution. I was simply voicing a thought that had been on my mind since Erin had told me the truth about Danny.

"My son was one of the first cases of the Itch," she said matter-of-factly. "He was only 19."

It was a simple fact that almost everyone had lost someone to the Itch. Most people didn't talk about it. I'm sure everyone had their own reasons; for me, I didn't want my loss to remind others of their own. Such a frank admission, then – especially from the detective – shocked me. Not nearly as much as what she said next, though.

"I thought I'd failed him. I should have done more to protect him. At the very least, I should have known about the drugs. When I found out, I blamed myself."

"Sorry,"

"Don't be," she said, shaking her head stiffly. "Now, I know the truth."

"Why are you telling me this?" I asked. I hadn't meant it to sound impolite but was sure it had. Dunhill didn't seem to mind, though.

"Catharsis," she said. "I can let go and grieve properly; healthily. Hopefully, you can do the same."

When I turned to face her, she was smiling, her eyes on my necklace.

"How did you-"

"Because I'm a detective," she said, shrugging. "Do you remember when I questioned you?"

"I'm not sure I'll ever forget."

"As soon as I showed you his picture, you touched your necklace. And at the hospital, after you escaped, again…" Her voice darkened as she said the word. "…the nurses said you'd been insisting on getting it back. I assumed you might use it to get out of your cuffs."

"I'm impressed," I said.

"It's my job," she said.

She smiled at me. Unsure what else to do, I simply smiled back. It was only fleeting but perhaps felt longer because it was so unusual to see such kindness in her expression. Once she stopped smiling, she got to her feet.

"Well, unless there's anything else, I'll be on my way. In the nicest possible way, I hope I never see you again. So, try to stay out of trouble," she said.

And with that, she strolled away.

ACKNOWLEDGEMENTS

Firstly, I must say a huge thank you to my wonderful wife. Whether helping me cope with rejections from publishers or humouring my delusions of grandeur, she's given me the support and encouragement to see this through. Whilst writing this novel, I've cycled through the entire spectrum of self-belief more times than I can remember. *Yes, I can. No, I can't. Yes, I will, No, I won't.* Without her, I'm sure that I wouldn't have had the confidence to complete the work, and certainly wouldn't have published it.

My family have always believed in me, no matter what I turned my hand to. Having such belief behind me has been so helpful for so much more than my writing. My grandma has read everything I've ever written and was my first fan. She's likely biased, of course, but her praise has been so rewarding.

Tony read my first draft and returned a comprehensive review in just a few days, which proved to be incredibly useful. Heather gave me advice about setting, encouraging me to describe more of the city to make the novel more immersive for the reader. Her brother, Stuart, also proofread the work, correcting spelling and grammatical errors. I'm more than a little embarrassed to admit there were a lot of them.

Whilst this is a work of fiction, I wanted it to be as accurate as possible. So, finally, thank you to Ness and Jayne for their medical know-how and to Mark for advising on the judicial process. Dan provided textbook knowledge of chemistry, and Ross pointed out that there were some inaccuracies regarding locations and infrastructure within the text.

And finally, thank you to everyone who takes the time to read it. I'm eternally grateful.

Printed in Great Britain
by Amazon